BOOKS BY JANE HASELDINE

THE LAST TIME SHE SAW HIM

DUPLICITY

Published by Kensington Publishing Corporation

THE LAST TIME SHE SAW HIM

JANE HASELDINE

PINNACLE BOOKS
Kensington Publishing Corp.
www.kensingtonbooks.com

PINNACLE BOOKS are published by

Kensington Publishing Corp.
119 West 40th Street
New York, NY 10018

All Kensington titles, imprints, and distributed lines are available at special quantity discounts for bulk purchases for sales promotions, premiums, fund-raising, educational, or institutional use. Special book excerpts or customized printings can also be created to fit specific needs. For details, write or phone the office of the Kensington sales manager: Kensington Publishing Corp., 119 West 40th Street, New York, NY 10018, attn: Sales Department; phone 1-800-221-2647.

ISBN-13: 978-0-7860-3877-0
ISBN-10: 0-7860-3877-2

First Kensington hardcover printing: July 2016
First Pinnacle paperback printing: March 2017

10 9 8 7 6 5 4 3 2 1

Printed in the United States of America

First electronic edition: March 2017

ISBN-13: 978-0-7860-3878-7
ISBN-10: 0-7860-3878-0

PROLOGUE

Funland, 1977

All around us, they descended for onc last bril-liant summer hurrah.

The Detroit summer refugees invaded our beaches like the Allies swarming Normandy on D-Day and claimed the best our town of Sparrow had to offer during its shining scason. My older brother, Ben, and I had watched them all summer long from the top step of the bandstand at the end of Grand Haven Avenue or perched along one of the white wooden boardwalk benches if we were lucky enough to nab an empty seat on what was considered prime Lake Huron real estate.

Our parents couldn't afford a TV, let alone the rent most months, so Ben and I depended on the out-of-towners for our entertainment. Ben and I would share a skinny carton of Dolle's caramel corn and look on with rapt curiosity as men in hideous Hawaiian shirts scanned the beach with metal detectors for lost treasure while their wives padded up and down the shore in high-waisted two-piece bathing suits. They occasionally glanced over with detached interest at their sunburned-crisp children, who dug furiously for mole crabs in the damp sand. The teenage crowd always set up camp near the jetty. Maybe it felt more dangerous there. They smoked cigarettes and drank Tab from a can as their boom boxes belted Bob Seger and the Silver Bullet Band's "Night Moves." And the days of summer along the eastern Michigan shore slowly slipped by.

On Labor Day weekend, the final surge of tourists arrived en masse, but Ben and I didn't need them anymore. We were ready to reclaim our town. With twenty whole dollars in our pockets, guilt money Daddy had given us, Ben and I wove through the crowd, which was fifty people deep, our feet slapping against the wooden planks of the boardwalk in the cheap sneakers Mom had bought us at the A&P. I watched Ben's suntanned lean arms and legs fly in front of me as seagulls screeched overhead, the scavengers searching to pluck a stray, plump French fry from a careless hand, and the cloying aroma of suntan lotion clung to the sticky September air. A patina of sweat glistened on my skin and made my thin jumper feel tacky against my reed-thin frame. My long, dark hair, flecked with strands of red from the sun, was caught in a ponytail and thumped against my back as I tried to keep up with Ben.

Even though I had just turned seven the week before, I already wondered whether, if I could will something hard enough, the universe would budge ever so slightly and things would shift in my favor. On that afternoon, I truly believed my desperation did just that.

In that one perfect moment, Sparrow was ours again. We didn't care about the start of another school year come morning or recent memories of last spring, when Ben, our older sister, Sarah, and I were forced to jockey for a comfortable spot to sleep in the backseat of my Dad's rusted-out Chrysler, the one he would simultaneously swear and pray would "son of a bitch, dear God, please catch!"

Ben and I silently ached for something good to finally happen, and there it was, shimmering in the heat just a block away: Funland, the Holy Grail of all that was wonderful in our fragile, young lives. The amusement park was housed in a modest wooden building on the beach block of Great Lakes Avenue. Funland didn't look like much on the outside, but as soon as Ben and I heard its welcoming chorus of tinny carousel music, we knew pure spun magic awaited us inside.

Ben raced into Funland ahead of me and flashed me his trademark crooked grin. He held a string of tickets so long it curled to the cement floor.

"Julia, here are five tickets for the carousel," Ben said as he snapped off five paper tokens.

"You won't come with me?"

"Nah, the carousel is for little kids. You have fun though," Ben answered and began to make his way over to the bumper cars. Ben was nine, and I wasn't yet old or tall enough to reach the marker needed for admittance to the big-kid cool rides.

I watched Ben disappear behind the skee-ball booth and reluctantly climbed onto my favorite brown pony with the white star saddle. I stood up in the stirrups and peered over the crowded heads for Ben. When I couldn't spot him, I could feel the sting of tears begin to start.

As the panic grew inside me, there was my brother, a streak of jet-black hair and his favorite red shirt flashing through the crowd. Right before the ticket taker closed the gate, Ben leapt onto the carousel platform.

"No crying, kid. I'll be on the carousel bench where the grown-ups sit," Ben said. "Don't worry. I won't let you fall off. You'll be fine."

"You promise?"

"You've got to stop being a scared baby all the time."

"I'm not a baby. And I'm not scared when you're around."

Ben leaned toward me and brushed away a tear that had started to slip down my cheek. "I promise I won't ever let anything bad happen to you. Not ever."

"Swear to God?" I asked.

"Cross my heart and hope to die. Now stop crying already. We're supposed to be having fun for once, remember?"

The music of the carousel started, and I eased my steel grip around the pony's neck. I looked out at the crowd as it began to slowly spin around me. The tourists waved madly as their children passed and a line of kids began to snake back toward the spin paint booth for the next ride. As the carousel turned faster, I spotted a blur of a man who popped up from behind the ticket booth. He wore a black baseball cap and pointed his Polaroid camera in my direction. A flash of light blinded me for a second. When the ride circled the crowd again, the man with the Polaroid camera was gone.

I thought of telling Ben about the man with the camera on our walk home from Funland and later, before we went to sleep that night. But I didn't want Ben to think I was a scared baby. My decision would later haunt my every day, leaving me to desperately wonder whether, if I had told Ben about the stranger, it could have saved him.

"911, what is the nature of your call?"

"My brother. He's gone! Someone took him. Please, you've got to come here quick!"

"What is your brother's name?" the female 911 dispatcher asked.

"Ben. Ben Gooden. Please hurry!"

"Okay. It's going to be all right. What's your name?"

"Julia. Julia Gooden. I live on 18 Snug Harbor Road."

"Is your mother or father there? Can you put them on the phone?"

"My dad's not here, and my mom won't get up."

"Is your mother hurt?"

"No. She's just drunk."

"Okay, Julia. Is there anyone else at home with you?"

"My sister, Sarah. She's fourteen. She doesn't believe me. Sarah said I was an idiot baby and told me to get out of her room."

"Did you check the house for your brother?" the dispatcher asked.

"I looked all over. I swear. Ben was in his bed when I fell asleep. I woke up in my mom's room. I don't know how I got there. When I went back to our room, Ben was gone. Please, you need to help me!"

"Does it look like someone broke in?"

"The courtyard door to our bedroom is open. I wanted to make sure it was locked before we went to sleep, but I didn't want Ben to think I was scared."

"Okay. We're sending an officer over right now. Do you think your brother wandered outside?"

"No. I looked in the courtyard and the driveway too. Ben wasn't there. I found his baseball on the sidewalk. It's his favorite New York Yankees ball. Ben sleeps with it every night. He'd never leave it behind."

"Okay. You stay on the phone with me, Julia, until the officer gets there. I'm sure everything is going to be just fine. You'll see."

"You're right. Ben would never leave me. He promised."

CHAPTER 1

I became a reporter because I never found out the ending to my own story. Thirty years after Ben's abduction, the only answers I could find were for others, the victims, or those they left behind. The crime beat is a natural for me. The people I write about are the most fragile, the most broken, and they need the most answers. I piece together the frayed strands of their lives. I have to tell their stories. I feel like I owe the victims at least that.

Five p.m. in the newsroom, and I am in the zone. I stare at my half-written follow-up story on the Boyner boy until a blast of static crackles from the scanner above my desk. "Shots fired on the two-hundred block of Rosa Parks Boulevard," the female 911 dispatcher calls out in a staccato monotone.

I turn back to my story and listen with trained detachment to hear whether there's anything more I need to chase on deadline. More likely, it's a drug deal gone bad or a gang-related drive-by. Just another rush hour in inner-city Detroit.

The scanner goes silent for thirty seconds. Nothing further. No follow-up required, for now anyway. I go back to my article on Donny Boyner when my e-mail chimes and the NEW MESSAGE alert flashes across the right side of my computer screen. It's from Bob Primo, the metro desk editor. Primo has been my middleman boss for the past ten years, and he's been consistent, a certified Grade-A solid prick throughout. Primo thinks I owe him for successfully pitching my story for the front page during the big bosses' three o'clock editorial meeting. But it wasn't Primo's pitch. It was the story that sold it, an eight-year-old boy who disappeared on the way to the bus stop. With no new news on day two of the story, it's my job to make the little boy real to the readers. And Primo and his bosses know I will deliver.

I ignore Primo's interruption and glance down at my reporter's notebook. It's filled with quotes I got two hours prior while sitting in the living room of the tidy row house Donny Boyner shared with his grandma, Laveeta, a seventy-year-old whisper of a woman who stared intently at the velvet picture of a black Jesus that hugged the entirety of her living room wall as she recounted stories about her grandson. When I asked about the last time she saw Donny, Laveeta tore her gaze away from Jesus and cast her eyes downward to the scuffed gold vinyl floor. Ever since he started kindergarten, Laveeta said she walked Donny to the bus stop, just one block away. But yesterday she caught a cold—more than a cold, she said, a flu bug that made her body sweat and burn through the night. By morning, she was worse. Donny wanted to stay home so he could take care of his grandma, but Laveeta insisted he couldn't miss school. His grandma knew school was Donny's only ticket out of the projects. So Donny grabbed his backpack, promised Laveeta he'd take care of her when he got home, and kissed her on the forehead before he headed out on his journey: one short block alone to the bus that would safely deliver him to his third-grade class at Gardner Elementary School.

Just one short block.

I throw my reporter's notebook into the top right drawer of my desk and write from memory. The city editor at my first paper told me the best reporters write from both the head and the heart.

I stare at the third-grade class picture of Donny on his missing-persons flyer. I pinned it to my desk when the Amber Alert first went out after Donny didn't get off the bus at the end of the school day. In the photo, Donny wears a short-sleeved blue and white striped shirt buttoned all the way up to his collar. He peers hesitantly through his thick glasses at the camera as though he is uncomfortable being the center of attention even on school picture day.

My eyes flick to the other photo on my desk. It's a framed picture of my sons, Logan and Will, taken down by the lake last summer. Logan is eight, just like Donny.

I turn my concentration back on the article about the missing boy, but I already know how this story will ultimately end. There will be bad news, the kind that decimates the living. Or no news at all. Not ever. Good news in child abduction cases is a bona fide miracle.

And I stopped believing in miracles when Ben never came home. Miracles are like Santa Claus, just stuff kids believe.

My desk phone rings. I stare at it, debating whether to pick it up on deadline or to retrieve the message after I finish the story. Five o'clock. It's not my husband. David and I have been separated going on six months now. In the early days of our relationship, my once golden boy thought he could save me from the demons of my past. But after nearly ten years of trying to help me recover from the loss of my brother and forgive myself for not being able to remember anything from the night of Ben's disappearance that could have helped the police, David walked. He packed up his suitcase one Friday after getting home from his law firm and dropped the bombshell that he was leaving. David's tone was cold and cutting as he told me he was tired of trying to fix me, tired of never being able to make me completely happy, and he couldn't live with my constant fears over our boys' safety anymore. I tried to explain that no matter what I did, I couldn't make myself into the person David wanted me to be. I watched as David's car pulled out of our driveway and couldn't believe he had given up on me. And our family. But I didn't throw the blame on him entirely. No one can cut in when you're doing a slow waltz with the devil.

I stare back at the ringing phone and realize David would never call on deadline unless it's an emergency about our boys. And he would try to reach me on my cell phone first. That leaves a crackpot pitching me a story about how her husband isn't paying alimony. Or it could be the cops.

I take my chances and pick up the phone.

"Newsroom. This is Julia Gooden," I answer.

"Hey, it's Detective Ray Navarro. This didn't come from me, but you better get down here. A tagger found a body inside a burned-out building on the three-hundred block of Mount Elliott Street. It's a kid and the body matches Donny Boyner's description."

I breathe out and stare back at the picture of the shy little boy with the wire-framed glasses in the missing person's photo.

"Julia, you there?" Navarro asks.

"Did you call Laveeta Boyner yet?"

"Yeah. The coroner just got here, and then we'll take the body down to the morgue to be identified. We're keeping this off the scanner for now. So unless another member of the media is tipped off, you'll be the only reporter at the scene."

"I appreciate the tip. I'll be there. I just need to take care of something first."

I hang up my desk phone and recall my meeting last week with the man in the tweed jacket. Post-traumatic stress with borderline paranoid personality disorder. That was my diagnosis. I finally relented after years of resistance to David's urging and saw a psychiatrist to talk about my brother. I was becoming obsessed with protecting our sons. No Little League for Logan, despite his pleas, since sleazy strangers with nefarious intentions could be watching. No play dates or friends unless I had a sit-down with the parents first, which was more like twenty pointed questions on my end and usually scared them off. There were no babysitters, not even David's father and stepmom, and subsequently no date nights after the children came. The topper was when Logan won a lunch with his principal, Mr. Brandish, during a charity auction at his elementary school to raise money for the PTA. Logan was supposed to ride to the restaurant in Mr. Brandish's car, but I pitched a fit to David, who told me to lighten up for just one time in my entire life and not spoil Logan's afternoon. I pretended to acquiesce, but I secretly went to the school, followed the principal's car to the restaurant, and sat in the back of the pizza place trying to blend in with the lunch crowd as I kept my eyes glued on my son. But Logan saw me, which he inadvertently shared with the family during dinner that night. David blew up.

The counseling was part of the agreement if we were going to reconcile, so I tried. I stared at the psychiatrist's advanced degrees, which were hung prominently on his wall, as he told me I became a crime reporter so I could repeat my childhood trauma every day. It was my way of punishing myself, he said. After one session, I decided to never go back. I could handle it on my own. I always have. And I know what I have to do now.

I close out of my story, wind my unruly, dark curls into a makeshift bun, and walk across the newsroom to Primo's office. I pass the thinned-out bank of metro reporters and the ghost town where the recently laid-off feature writers once sat. Primo's office is command central, smack in the center of the newsroom, where he can keep an eye on his dwindling empire. I pause in the doorway. Primo sits ramrod straight in his leather swivel chair, giving hell to someone on the other end of the phone while staring out at rush-hour traffic weaving through my broken-down city.

Primo reminds me of a just-fed spider, spindly arms and legs with a rigid bowling ball of a gut. I tap on the doorframe to get his attention. When Primo doesn't turn around, I enter and smack my knuckles hard against the top of his computer.

Primo jerks his chair toward the unwanted interruption. I've apparently made the cut, and Primo abruptly ends his call.

"Did you turn in the story about the Boyner kid?" he asks without turning around.

"Not yet. I need to talk to you about something."

Primo ignores my request and hunches over his computer. The spider, hungrily trying to snare its next victim, or in this case, its next story.

"Where the hell is it? I'm about to go into the five o'clock editorial meeting. Don't think I won't bury your story inside the local page. I can't guarantee it will even make it on the website if you just recycled the news from yesterday about the kid's abduction."

Primo is just being a bully. He knows this is a front-page story. In fact, it's the story of the day.

"Of course you'll post it. The story got picked up on the national wire. People care about this little boy," I say, calling his bluff.

Primo parts his lips as if he's about to unleash a snarling tirade. Instead, two strings of thick white spit pool in the corners of his mouth. Primo's endless supply of spit always seems to accumulate in mass quantity right around deadline.

I look away in disgust and so does Primo. He grabs his phone and turns his back to me as though I am dismissed.

But I still have a card to play.

"The cops found a body. They think it's Donny Boyner."

Primo swivels his chair toward me with renewed interest and drums his long fingers together as he weighs his options. "When are they going to have an ID? You need to work your sources to get them to confirm it's the Boyner kid. We need to have the story before *The Detroit News* gets it. I will not get beat on this. Understood?"

Primo had long ago crossed the line from ethical journalist with a sense of duty to a full-blown viper.

"I don't know why I expected a humane response," I answer.

"If you care so much, become a social worker. Your job right now is to get the story. You can feel all you want when you're done."

"That's why I'm here. I'm leaving."

"What are you talking about?"

"I'm taking a leave of absence. I need some time."

Primo's rubbery lips contort into a patronizing sneer, and a dribble of built-up spit escapes from one corner of his mouth.

"You don't get time. This is a newspaper. The news doesn't stop, remember? Journalism 101."

"I'll write the story on Donny Boyner, but then I'm gone. I'll contact HR. If you have a job for me when I'm ready to come back, fine. If not, I'll reach out to *The Detroit News*. Either way, it works for me."

"Get an ID on the Boyner kid and get your ass back here. You're a veteran, ten years in at the paper. Don't tell me you're getting soft. The death of another kid in the projects is going to make you give everything up? He's just a throwaway kid who would've wound up selling drugs on the corner in four years anyway. Things are tight right now. We've already shed a hundred jobs, thirty in the newsroom in the past six months alone. You're lucky to still be on the payroll."

I hold Primo's gaze until his hard, dark eyes dart away first. The spider then buries himself back into his beloved computer, where he begins to troll for new stories.

"That's why I need to get out. I don't want to wind up like you."

I launch the insult like a grenade and hustle out of Primo's office before I can give him the satisfaction of being a captive audience to his caustic comeback.

I thread my way back to my corner of the newsroom and ignore the barbs from the guys at the sports desk ribbing me about my New York Yankees' loss to the Detroit Tigers in last night's blowout game. I instead concentrate on Laveeta Boyner and the guilt that will undoubtedly squeeze the life out of what is left of her once she IDs her grandson.

But at least she will know.

At least Laveeta Boyner will have an answer.

I grab my reporter's notebook and tape recorder before I head out to the crime scene. I gather my scant personal effects off my desk. Easier to do it now without explanation than after deadline when someone might notice and ask questions. I hate questions unless I'm the one asking. I stuff the photo of Logan and Will in my duffel bag, reach into my bottom desk drawer, and carefully retrieve an overstuffed red binder.

I make my way through the parking garage, adrenaline flowing, as I chisel down the list of questions I will pose to the police about Donny Boyner. As I slide my key into the ignition, I calculate the fastest route through rush-hour traffic to Mount Elliott Street. Only a mile away, the usual five-minute drive will now take me half an hour in gridlock traffic. There's still time though. There's always time.

I unzip the duffel bag on the passenger seat and gently pull out the red binder, now cracked and faded with age to a muted shade of pink. I open the cover and run my hand over the first yellowed article, safely protected through time by a thin sheet of plastic that holds the newspaper story firmly affixed to the first page.

I know it by heart.

Sept. 6, 1977

Nine-year-old boy disappears in resort town

By Karen Quantico

DETROIT (Associated Press)—A nine-year-old boy remains missing one day after he disappeared from his bedroom in the usually quiet resort town of Sparrow, Michigan.

Ben Gooden, who was to join the rest of his incoming fourth-grade class at Willow Glen Elementary today, was reported missing by his seven-year-old sister, Julia Gooden, who called 911 at approximately 12:30 a.m.

Police would not comment on whether the mother, Marjorie Gooden, is a suspect or will face child endangerment charges, although sources close to the case claim witnesses saw Mrs. Gooden drinking heavily with an unidentified man at a local bar around the time the boy disappeared. Police are trying to locate the missing child's father, Benjamin Gooden Sr., who was reportedly out of town at the time of the boy's disappearance.

"Right now, we're looking at this as a missing persons case, not a criminal investigation. Let me reiterate that Sparrow is a safe town for our visitors and locals alike," said Deputy Michael Leidy of the St. Clair Sheriff's Department. "However, when a little boy suddenly goes missing from his bed in the middle of the night, we want to assure the public that the police will do everything in our power to bring him home safely."

Police confirmed there was no sign of forced entry, but the sliding glass door leading from the outside courtyard into the boy's room was found wide open. Police also found a crushed package of Marlboro Lights cigarettes outside the home in addition to an Indian arrowhead discovered under the boy's bed.

A neighbor, who asked not to be identified, said the Gooden family had just moved to the North Shores neighborhood.

Principal John Derry of Willow Glen Elementary School said the students and staff started the day with a moment of silence for Ben's safe return.

(Photo caption: Julia Gooden, the missing boy's younger sister, sits alone on the front steps of the family home and clutches her brother's baseball against her chest.)

Detective Navarro is true to his word. The early-evening sky is free of any TV news choppers circling overhead, and the Mount Elliott block where the body was found is void of any other media buzzing around like vultures, ready to pick apart any crumb of new news they can find.

I drape my press pass around my neck and head toward the charred shell that was once a building on Mount Elliott Street. I dodge under the yellow tape and make my way up three cement stairs a tagger spray-painted in blue and orange letters, THUNDER13. The officer who is supposed to be playing babysitter to the street must be in the back of the house securing the scene, so I continue on inside. If no one is there to tell you no, they might as well be saying yes. As my eyes adjust inside the dark hallway, the smell hits me, and I instinctively begin to breathe through my mouth. It's not the stench of urine and feces left behind from a rotation of homeless squatters who most likely called this place home. It's the smell of death.

I make my way through what was once most likely a living room and toward a sliver of light shining under a doorway.

"Hey, what's she doing here? No press. Get back outside!"

I've been made known. I turn on my heels to see if I know the officer who spotted me so I can try and talk my way into staying. The door with the light underneath it bangs open and the dark hallway is flooded with blinding white light. I shield the tops of my eyes to try and make out the details of what I assume is the crime scene. Portable high-powered lights are set up in the four corners of the cramped space, which was probably once used as a bedroom. I know I have seconds before I am physically escorted out, so I do a quick scan of the contents of the room. Filthy mattresses stained with plumes of yellow and brown are stacked up against one wall, and the floor of the room is littered with cardboard and discarded fast-food containers. Directly across from me is the room's sole window, affixed with a set of rusted safety bars. Underneath the window, Navarro huddles on the floor near a slight, crumpled shape someone tried to conceal with a frayed rug. I take two steps closer and see a brand-new set of gleaming blue and yellow sneakers poking out from beneath the rug. The adrenaline of getting the story instantly leaves my body, and I freeze in place. The shoes are small. Little boy's shoes. The shoes Laveeta Boyner said she bought Donny as a reward for bringing up his math grade from a C to a B.

A meaty hand wraps around my upper arm and yanks me backward. "I told you, no reporters. What do you think you are doing in here?"

I look up to see Detective Leroy Russell, Navarro's partner and a thoroughbred jackass. His Mr. Clean bald head shines like a lit globe against the backdrop of the heavy lights. Russell is pushing fifty, but is built like an aging linebacker who still has a few good bone-crushing games left in him. Since I'm five-foot-seven and a hundred and fifteen pounds with my shoes on, Russell easily spins my body away from the room and pushes me toward the front door.

I don't try and argue my way into staying. I know technically I shouldn't be there, at least as far as the cops are concerned. But more than that, I don't want to see the body of the little boy once the rug has been pulled back. I tried to train myself long ago to emotionally detach from the people I wrote about. I can get lost in the juice of the moment as I chase the story, but once it's written, once I'm alone, their stories, their faces always come back to me. They never let go. Especially when the victim is a child.

I drop on the broken front step of the house and wait for Navarro as a steady stream of neighborhood gang-bangers drives by, idling curiously until they catch sight of police officers filtering in and out of the crime scene.

"I thought you would put up more of a fight."

Navarro stands in the doorway, his tall and muscular frame almost filling it up. Navarro is hardcore Jersey, even though it's been at least fifteen years since he moved from his hometown of Newark. Navarro runs his fingers through his thick shock of dark hair and gives me a nod.

"Didn't feel much like fighting today. That's Donny Boyner in there, right?" I ask.

"Pending ID from his grandma, yes. Come on. Let's take a walk to your car."

The police know Navarro is my best source, but he at least wants to appear discreet, so I wait to drill him for information until we have some privacy. He opens my driver-side door, and I slide across the front seat of my SUV. I roll down the window and Navarro leans inside.

"What can you tell me?" I ask.

"Off the record or on?"

"Both. Let's start with off for background, and then we'll take it from there. What do you think happened?"

"We found the kid's backpack tossed in a Dumpster two blocks from here. We think whoever took Donny lured him into a car on the way to school. Probably someone he knew. There were no defense wounds or bruising, which means he didn't try to get away. Whoever did this most likely killed him somewhere else and then dumped the body. Pending an autopsy, it looks like he drowned."

"Drowned?"

"Yeah, I know, that's a new one. We're checking every public swimming pool in the city to see if anyone saw Donny, but more likely, he was probably killed in someone's home."

Navarro's gaze moves down to the steering wheel, which I suddenly realize I am holding in a death grip. Embarrassed I've lost my poker face, I quickly drop my hands in my lap. When my hands start to tremble, I shove them under my legs so Navarro won't notice. But my attempt at a last-minute save is too late.

"You all right?" Navarro asks, his rough voice softening to a raspy hum. "Anytime the victim is a kid, it's hard, even on us."

"I'm fine," I answer and try to redirect his attention elsewhere. "You're not going to see me around for a while. I'm taking some time off. I'm going to the lake house for the summer with the boys."

"Your place in Decremer?"

"Yes. There's a story I need to work on too."

"Like a freelance assignment?"

"Something like that."

"If you get in a jam, let me know. Just because you're not officially on the beat doesn't mean you can't call me if you need some help," Navarro says.

Navarro's deep-set hazel eyes fixate on my face for a beat too long.

"Why don't you call me after you file your story? I'll be here for a while, but maybe we could meet up later and grab something to eat. I remember you used to like that hole-in-the-wall diner that was open all night over in Greektown."

"You've got a good memory. I forgot about that place," I answer. "Thanks, but I need to get back home to the kids when I'm done."

"Just a friendly offer."

"I didn't think anything otherwise," I answer.

"Fine then. Just take care of yourself, Gooden," Navarro says. He raps hard on my car's roof with his knuckles and heads back inside the house to the crime scene and the little boy who will never get the chance to grow up.

I decide to file my last story from my home in Rochester Hills. I know Primo will be pissed off, but I don't care. I look off into the distance at the Detroit skyline. Ribbons of pink and orange clouds hang low on the horizon, looking bright and hopeful as they silhouette the Ambassador Bridge. I put the car in drive and hit the gas hard. I want to get out of the city as fast as I can.

CHAPTER 2

Donny Boyner wasn't the tipping point that drove me out of Detroit. Or Ben. Or what the psychiatrist said. It was all of it, but especially Logan and Will. I felt the boys would be safer at the lake house, far removed from the dangers of the city. When I was still on the beat and driving home to the suburbs after a day of writing about murderers, thieves, drug dealers, and pimps, I never felt secure as I watched Detroit disappearing in my rearview mirror. I knew the drill. The bogeyman doesn't just lie in wait behind Dumpsters in alleyways or in shadowy corners of graffiti-infested tenements of the city. He's also lurking with a crowbar in the bushes of your middle-class cul-de-sac next to a NEIGHBORHOOD WATCH sign, just waiting to make his move to your back door after you and your family fall asleep. No place is immune from danger, but I was confident the lake house would provide us a safe haven.

Decremer is a tiny, "don't blink or sneeze or change the radio dial or you'll miss it" kind of town along Lake St. Clair. David and I bought the house in Decremer as our weekend vacation retreat two years ago, right before Will was born.

I pulled the U-Haul into the gravel driveway of the lake house in late May. Three days in, I didn't think I could take it anymore. I missed the buzz of the newsroom and the juice I got from the beat. But after a while, we fell into routines of subdued normalcy and the comfort of simple daily routines. The boys and I spent every day down by the lake. I never took my eyes off them as Logan perfected his rock-skipping technique, and Will stuck to his big brother and mimicked his every move until I thought Logan was going to lose it.

At some point, the constant longing for the newsroom eased as the muggy Michigan afternoons passed without notice and I learned to slow down. And then Labor Day quietly arrived without warning, heralding along with it unwanted responsibilities: my upcoming return to the paper and Logan's first day of third grade.

Six-thirty a.m. The alarm wails like a hateful siren. I slam the off button and roll toward the edge of the bed, instinctively expecting David to pull me back. But those were happier times. I get out of the empty bed and hurry to the bathroom, slide on my jeans, and put on a white button-down, fitted shirt. I use my fingers as a makeshift hairbrush through my thick, dark hair until it is somewhat tamed and curtail any other maintenance besides a dab of lip balm out of the sheer necessity of time. I do a quick inspection of my face for any wrinkles, which I've been able to ward off so far. But at thirty-seven, I know it's just a matter of time.

I leave my vanity behind in the mirror and fixate instead on my morning journey with the boys. I head to the kitchen and begin to load up breakfast on the run,

DVD players, and other necessities to survive the ride to Target, where I'll join other last-minute parents as we paw through the slim available pickings in the dreaded back-to-school aisle.

I fight off a kamikaze deer fly on the front porch, snag the newspaper, and give the front page a thorough look, starting with the dateline: Monday, September 3, 2007. The color piece above the fold is the mandatory Labor Day story. This year it's a parade with workers from the Big Three, Ford, General Motors, and Chrysler, waving flags and offering pointed predictions that the automotive industry could be headed for a major downfall. I give the paper a final, quick scan until I am satisfied it doesn't include the byline of the freshly minted and hungry college grad from Syracuse University who temporarily replaced me on my cop beat.

I pause in the hallway and listen for movement or groans or other little boys' just-waking-up sounds. But Logan and Will are still fast asleep, which is just what I was hoping for. I need to make my annual call before I wake them up.

Like some sort of dark holiday tradition, I've called Detective Michael Leidy every Labor Day for the past thirty years. Leidy was just a few years out of the police academy when he took Ben's missing persons case, and Leidy has since risen to the ranks of director of the unit's cold case division.

I slip into the office, pull down the worn, red album from the bookshelf, and begin to pore through its entirety: a dozen or so yellowed newspaper clippings about Ben's abduction and my scribbled theories on possible motives and suspects. On the album's last page is a story I saved from the *Detroit Free Press* from ten years earlier. It featured the state's then major unsolved crimes. The lead art is Ben's third-grade class picture. In the photo, Ben is wearing his favorite red shirt, which offsets his jet-black hair and olive skin, bronzed and lightly freckled from what we thought would be endless childhood summers at the shore. Ben looks especially proud in the picture, despite the fact that we were dirt-poor back then. He is forever captured looking back at the camera with an air of confidence, like a little boy who knew he was going to be something special one day.

I trace my finger along Ben's strong jawline in the photo and remember our final day together at Funland. After the carousel ride, Mark Brewster cornered us. He was the middle-school bully who could smell the blood of two vulnerable kids from a mile away.

"Hey, Ben, I thought you were too poor to come here," Mark said, sauntering over. *"Why don't you leave so your little sister can go and beg all the neighborhood kids for money so your daddy can buy gas for that beat-up car of his?"*

"Leave Julia alone. She didn't do anything to you."

"What did you say to me? I'm going to kill you, you little bastard," Mark said, puffing out his lardy stomach. *"Hey, loser boy, how's your stringy-haired, alcoholic mother?"*

"Stand back, Julia," Ben warned and shoved me away from the danger of the pending fight and into the crowd that had gathered in hopes of seeing two kids beat the crap out of each other.

Right before Mark could throw his first punch, a lanky security guard in a blue polyester uniform made his way toward Ben and Mark. "What are you kids doing? Break it up, you two!" he yelled.

Ben grabbed my hand, and we raced down Michigan Avenue as fast as we could, away from Mark Brewster and Funland. When we reached the library, breathless and feeling like we were going to die, we turned around to face our tormentor. But we had left the overgrown, tubby bully in the dust.

"He's going to be after us forever now!" I cried. "Mark Brewster's dad is the most powerful man in town, and he's going to sue us."

"He's not going to sue us," Ben answered. "And if he did, what's he going to take? We don't have anything. Do me a favor. Don't ever back down from bullies like Mark Brewster. You've got to stand up to them. It doesn't matter if you're poor. You have nothing to feel bad about."

"I can't fight someone like Mark Brewster."

"Sure you can. Don't give in to the bad guys. Okay? You've got to fight them with all you've got."

I file the red album back on the bookshelf and speed dial the number for the St. Clair Sheriff's Department. Even though it's early and a holiday, I know Leidy will answer. But after the fourth ring, I am about to admit I am wrong when Leidy picks up.

"Detective Leidy here," he answers in his flat Michigan accent.

"Detective, it's Julia Gooden."

"I've been expecting your call," Leidy answers without missing a beat.

I look down at my usual script of questions for our annual go-round.

"Anything new on Ben's case?"

The sound of papers shuffles in the background until Leidy finally resurfaces.

"Nothing new. We had a little girl go missing this summer down in Algonac. A farm kid. Turned out her grandma snatched her up when she found out her son-in-law was cooking up meth instead of harvesting corn."

"We were at Funland the day Ben was taken," I interrupt. "He got into a fight with a boy there, Mark Brewster. His dad was powerful, owned the big cannery outside of town and was the president of the St. Clair County Council."

"Hard to believe a nine-year-old or his daddy would take a kid over a dustup at an amusement park. But we questioned them, along with at least fifty other people including several of your dad's business associates," Leidy answers.

My heart begins to race as I recall the frequent parade of heavy drinking and late-night parties my parents hosted as my dad tried to hook would-be investors to his latest shady business scheme.

"The man who was taking pictures by the carousel. I'm pretty sure he took my photo with one of those old Polaroid cameras. I didn't think much of it at the time, but now I know it was odd for a grown man to take a picture of a child he didn't know. I can't believe no one ever found him."

"It was Labor Day and Funland was packed. The whole town was swarming with tourists, and there must have been at least two hundred people at Funland that afternoon. Finding the guy with the camera would have been like plucking a needle out of an eighty-foot haystack."

I look back at my weathered list of questions. The second one is underlined in red.

"The Indian arrowhead you found under Ben's bed, that had to mean something, like a hunter who made off with his prey."

"Seemed like it at the time. The arrowhead was Chippewa. I interviewed members of their Indian community over in Port Huron, but nothing panned out. Most likely, the person who took your brother bought the arrowhead at a souvenir shop on the boardwalk and it fell out of his pocket during the abduction."

I scramble for a new lead to press Leidy about, but the silence on the phone prompts Leidy to conclude our conversation.

"I promise you, we haven't forgotten about Ben. I still have his missing-person flyer on my desk."

And then Leidy adds a piece of advice I don't acknowledge. "What happened to your brother wasn't your fault. Sometimes people just can't remember. I know dozens of people who witnessed horrific crimes, and they're never able to remember what happened until years later. Sometimes they can't remember anything, ever. If you're still beating yourself up, stop. You were just a kid back then."

"I was in the same room with my brother when we fell asleep that night. I should've been able to remember something. Anything. No matter how hard I try, it's like a black hole of a memory."

A few seconds of silence pass between us before I muster up the courage to ask Leidy what I never could before.

"Do you think Ben is still alive?"

"Julia, I . . ."

I cut Leidy off before he can finish.

"Don't worry about it. I know how these things turn out."

I load Logan and Will in my SUV and feel the burn of mounting frustration and a renewed sense of helplessness over my nonproductive call with Leidy.

"Just share a bite of your donut with your brother. Help Mom out, buddy, okay?" I ask Logan, who is making a mess of his makeshift breakfast in the backseat.

"It's not my fault Will dropped his donut on the floor," Logan answers.

"I know. But you're the big brother. Be the leader here."

Will's little protests begin to escalate into a full-fledged "red-faced, screaming until he stops breathing" temper tantrum.

"Here you go," Logan says as he breaks off a piece of his glazed donut and hands it to his little brother. Will pops the piece of donut in his mouth and smiles, exposing the gap between his two front teeth.

"Good," Will says and gives me a wave with his plump hand.

"Thank you, Logan. You're compassionate beyond your years," I say.

"What does that mean?"

"It means you're especially nice."

"Dad's picking me and Will up later, right?"

"That's the plan."

"Do we have time to go to the library when we're done shopping for my school stuff before Dad comes?" Logan asks. "I want to check out the *Guinness Book of World Records*. A guy from Germany held his breath for fifteen minutes and two seconds. I think if I keep practicing, I can beat him."

"That doesn't sound safe."

"That's the thrill of it. Safe is boring."

"I like boring."

Logan makes a face and busies himself picking the discarded donut sprinkles off his lap. I stare back at my two little boys in the rearview mirror and am amazed at how two children from the same parents can look so different. Will takes after David with his golden blond hair and green eyes, and Logan looks like me with his dark features. But his jet-black hair, handful of freckles that scatter across his high cheekbones, and dark eyes that tilt up just slightly on the ends make him a ringer for my brother. Sometimes when I catch Logan in silhouette, his resemblance to Ben is uncanny.

The boys become temporarily engrossed in their DVDs, and I try and snatch a rare moment to myself. I flip on the radio and turn the dial to 760 WJR-AM to catch a repeat of Mitch Albom's talk show.

My favorite *Detroit Free Press* columnist isn't on though, just a local news call-in show hosted by some announcer with an overly slick broadcaster's voice who launches into his early-morning segment intro: *"This is Ric Roberts, and I'm here at the Macomb Correctional Facility for an exclusive interview with Reverend Casey Cahill and his lawyer, Brett Burns. Detroit's own controversial holy man whom* Rolling Stone *once anointed 'The Rock 'n' Roll Jesus of Motor City' is in*

*the news again and up for parole after his conviction
for tax evasion and sex with minors. Reverend Cahill,
we're live. Are you ready?"*

"Yes, my son."

A cold shiver runs through me as I hear Cahill's familiar smooth baritone.

*"Thanks for joining us. So let's get to it. You're up
for parole after just two years. You've got to be feeling
pretty good about that."*

*"There are many souls to save here, lost lambs that
Satan distracted from God's path to do his wicked bidding. I go wherever God directs me."*

*"My client maintains his innocence and we hope the
parole board will consider this, in addition to his ex-
emplary behavior during his incarceration period,"*
Cahill's lawyer interjects.

*"Reverend Cahill, despite your conviction, you're
saying the charges against you . . . having sex with
three underage girls and stealing two million dollars
from your church . . . are false?"*

"What we're saying is . . ." the lawyer starts.

"I was framed by the press," Cahill interrupts.

"So your incarceration is the media's fault?"

*"That's correct. And because of my absence, many
of the good have fallen by the wayside. The former
pure-of-hearts who heard God's word through my
voice have now scattered, and their faith has blown
away like dry kernels of wheat tumbling through a bar-
ren field,"* Cahill preaches. *"God will only forgive
when He sees true atonement from his true believers.
When God sees sacrifice, when we take what is most
precious, what we covet and adore, and give it all to
him, only then will God see a change in our hearts and*

He will return to us. God's Word tells us in Genesis 22:2: 'Take your son, your only son Isaac, whom you love, and go to the land of Moriah, and offer him there as a burnt offering on one of the mountains of which I shall tell you.' Not all will make it into the gates of heaven, though, despite their sacrifices, the gays, the sexual deviants, the liberal media . . ."

"Asshole," I mumble under my breath.

"What's that, Mom?" Logan asks.

"Nothing," I answer and quickly turn off the radio. "Just something on the news about a man I used to write about."

I brush off my disgust over hearing Cahill's voice and his hateful dribble again, and pull into the crowded parking lot of the big box store. Before I unlock the car doors, I make Logan recite the rules.

"Always stay in your sight. No talking to strangers. If anyone approaches me, I yell and run away as fast as I can," Logan dutifully answers. "Do my friends have to do this with their moms?"

"I have no idea, but they should."

Logan rolls his eyes and we head toward the giant cutout of a pencil that hovers over the back to school aisle.

"Can you pop a wheelie on the cart?" Logan asks.

"No wheelies. You could hurt yourself."

"Could we go over to the toy aisle then?"

"Let's get your supplies first, okay, kid?"

I scour the aisle for any supplies that haven't already been snatched up and spot the last semi-decent backpack wedged far back on the highest shelf. I turn away from Logan and Will and stand on my tiptoes to try and reach it, but it is beyond my grasp. I test the cheap metal divider between the first and second shelves with my foot and take the chance it will support my tall and slender frame. I climb on top of the divider and crane my arm as far as it can reach until I pluck the vinyl backpack down from the shelf and let out a victory yelp as though I've scored the winning Super Bowl touchdown. Even small victories should be celebrated. I look back toward Logan to get his approval over my hard-won prize.

But he is gone.

A wave of panic surges through me. Orange T-shirt and shiny black hair. Those discerning features should set Logan apart in the crowded aisle that is now at least twenty people deep. I jump back up on the shelf divider to try and spot Logan, but he is nowhere in sight. It took me less than a minute to turn around and grab the stupid backpack. And in less than sixty seconds, my son disappeared.

"Logan!" I yell. "Help! Someone took my son!"

The sea of parents and their children parts around me, and I spot a forty-something, heavy-set man wearing faded blue jeans and an Eminem concert T-shirt. He bends down next to a little boy so they are eye-to-eye. Orange T-shirt and shiny black hair. The stranger has Logan.

Three seconds. That's the amount of time I calculate it will take me to check the security strap around Will's waist and slam the shopping cart into the back of the man trying to steal my son.

"Hi, Mom!"

Logan looks up at me, not terrified or desperately trying to ward off his attacker, and gives me a small wave. The man in the Eminem T-shirt ignores me and contin-

ues to race a remote control car between Logan and another little boy who looks somewhat familiar.

"Logan, get over here now."

I lunge, grab Logan's arm, and yank him behind the
protection of my body.

"What the hell do you think you're doing?" I shout.

The middle-aged man in the Eminem shirt drops the
remote control down to his waist and pulls the other little boy in close as though I'm the one who is the threat.

"I'm Jonah's dad," he says in an accusatory tone.
"Our kids go to the same school. I'm not sure what you
think is going on here, but we're leaving."

The reality of my colossal screw-up comes crashing
down.

"I'm sorry. I made a mistake."

I spend the entire painful ride home kicking myself
for humiliating Logan. But even my most earnest mea
culpas can't repair the damage.

"Hey, buddy, will you talk to me, please? I messed
up in the store. I didn't mean to embarrass you. I was
really scared and maybe I overreacted just a bit. I'm
sorry, but you shouldn't have run off like that."

"I didn't run away! I was just playing with a friend
and I could still see you," Logan pouts. "If Jonah tells
anyone at school, I'm dead."

And then Logan serves up the worst kind of punishment, the silent treatment. I finally give up trying to
find clever ways to win Logan's forgiveness, and we
both stew in our misery until the hellish car ride ends.

I pull into the driveway, where David waits for us
on the front porch swing. I don't want to be alone

tonight, but David insisted he would pick up the boys and take them into the city to watch the Labor Day jazz festival along the banks of the Detroit River, a family tradition I used to be a part of.

David rubs his hands together with just an edge of nerves, like he does before he launches into his opening statements of a trial. He spots us and jogs effortlessly over to my SUV, still with the fluid grace of his Harvard lacrosse days.

Logan and Will tear over to David, and he picks both boys up in his arms.

"Hi, Daddy!" Logan says excitedly. "Mom bought me a pair of binoculars. I'm going to take them with us tonight so we can see the stage better. I tested them out at the lake and I think they're going to work. You want to see?"

"Hey, buddy. Why don't you give me just a minute? I need to talk to your mom."

Logan easily acquiesces, peels his orange two-wheeler off the fence, and begins to execute perfect figure eights across the gravel driveway.

I look over at David, whose blond hair curls at his ears. With his end of summer tan, he looks more like a California surfer than a Detroit prosecutor. Ten years together and throw in a separation, David still gives me a thrill every time I see him.

"You look good," I say, trying not to sound too desperate.

"So do you. The break from the paper has treated you well."

Now done with the small talk, David looks away from me, his hallmark move when he has something to say that I probably don't want to hear.

"I'm sorry, but I have to cancel on the boys tonight. Bernie Masten called right before I got here. I have to go into the city. Our case schedule got moved up, and I'm the first chair on this one so I have to be at the meeting. It's the firm's biggest client, and I can't say no. I know you don't want to be alone with the anniversary of Ben's disappearance, so I figured it would be okay."

I grab Will out of the car and breeze past David. I take a seat on the front porch swing, bury my nose into Will's white blond hair, and contemplate taking a page from Logan and giving David the silent treatment. But the direct approach has always worked better for me.

"This isn't about me. You can't do this to Logan again. He misses you. So does Will. They both were really looking forward to spending time with you this weekend."

David stands over me with his arms folded across his chest.

"I'm not trying to let anyone down here, but if I want to make partner, I have to put in the hours. I've worked hard for this. Two mortgages and two college funds keep me up at night. The money has to come from somewhere, and your paycheck can't compare. I don't know why you stay in a high-pressure job that doesn't pay you what you're worth. It would be an easy move over to corporate PR. There's a lot more money in public relations and the hours are better."

"I don't want to be a flack," I answer. "And I'm a damn good reporter."

"The best," David concedes and the crease between his brow softens just a bit.

The compliment is quickly forgotten when David's

phone beeps. I can tell from the look on his face that it's another call from his firm.

"Can't you say no for just this once? It's been a tough day."

David lets the call go to voice mail.

"Okay. What happened?" he asks.

"I made an ass out of myself at the store. I embarrassed Logan in front of a boy who goes to his school and the boy's dad. Logan disappeared for a second and I thought someone took him. I swear, I'm still shaking."

David's jaw stiffens into a tight line. "This is exactly what I'm talking about. You have to stop this. I called the psychiatrist. You only went to see him once. There's no shame in seeing a shrink. You never want to talk about your brother."

"You're checking up on me?"

"You made me a promise," David answers.

"And I kept it. What happened to my brother is my issue, not yours or anyone else's."

"Jesus Christ, Julia. You don't get it. Your past isn't just hurting you anymore. It's a dark cloud hanging over our family and it's starting to make us all miserable. You know what I finally realized? There is absolutely nothing I can do to make you happy."

David's last line shoots me through the heart.

"That's not true. I never meant to make you feel that way."

David pulls out an unexpected trick from his sometimes-difficult-life-with-Julia bag. He sits down next to me on the porch swing and puts his arm around my shoulder.

"We'll keep working on things," he whispers in my ear. "Let's just get you back to see the psychiatrist one more time. Would you do that for me?"

"I'll think about it. I just don't like to talk to strangers about my brother."

"I'm the only person around here who knows anything about Ben or what happened to you when you were a kid. What about the boys? Are you going to tell them one day?"

"I haven't gotten that far yet."

The moment is gone. David gets up quickly from the swing and stares back at me with a look of frustration and a hint of disdain.

I try to tell David I'll change this time, but my well-intentioned promise gets lost somewhere in the back of my throat. I hold Will closer to my chest and wonder why couples whose relationships are about to end can't go back to the time when they first fell in love, before things got messy, and rekindle what brought them together in the first place. An hour into my first date with David, I realized he was charming, stable, and driven. Our first overnight excursion was a weekend in Traverse City. The bill for the hotel and the five-star restaurants David chose was staggering and almost made me broke on my reporter's salary, but I insisted on paying half. David finally relented to my demands and smiled as he told me he admired my fighting spirit. During that weekend, I discovered he came from a well-off family, but he still believed in standing up for the little guy and bucked his dad when David took a job out of college to work as a public defender in addition to doing pro bono work. I thought he was perfect.

David walks to the end of the porch, still with his back to me, and I realize any happy times between us will likely always be in memory.

"I don't understand the secrets. And you need to give the kids room to breathe. Your overprotectiveness is stifling them," David says.

"I'm not overprotective. I just don't trust people."

"You and the boys are safe here."

"You know that's not true. Nowhere is safe. Not here, not Detroit, not the suburbs. There's no magical boundary that keeps the criminals out."

"That's why I bought you a home security alarm for this place. Ten thousand dollars and that's not enough now?"

"Home security systems are a temporary stopgap. Criminals know how to work around them if they have to."

David raps his knuckles down hard on the porch railing and lets out a long exhale.

"I give up. I can't compete with your paranoia anymore."

"I'm not paranoid. I just want to be sure our boys are okay."

Logan senses the tension and props his bike against the garage. "Are you guys fighting again?"

"We aren't fighting. We're just having a discussion," David answers.

"Same thing," Logan responds.

"I'll pick up the boys next weekend. I promise," David says. "I still have an hour before I have to leave. I'll take Logan and Will down to the lake before I go."

David pulls Will from my arms, and he heads over to Logan to deliver the bad news.

"You can join us if you like," David says halfheartedly over his shoulder.

"No, I'm going to stay here. I just want to be alone for a minute," I say and make one more run at forgiveness from my oldest son. "Logan, I'm really sorry about earlier."

"Okay, Mom," Logan grunts as he fixes his attention on his father. I take solace in the fact that Logan took the time to utter three syllables to me.

I watch David from a distance, obviously telling Logan about tonight, and I see my little boy's shoulders sag. My heart breaks for Logan, but I vow to try and make up the disappointment to him later. Logan musters a smile, as David grabs him by the hand, and the three slip out of sight on the way to the lake.

Finally alone, I rest my elbows on my knees and allow a single tear to slip free. I watch it fall to the ground and make a tiny puddle in the dirt. I pick up a stick, mix my tear into the earth, and trace Ben's name.

CHAPTER 3

David leaves for the city, and I call my best friend, Kim, for some much-needed company. Kim was married to Ken, one of the partners in David's firm. Our friendship withstood their divorce, which, although Kim never confirmed this, was probably caused by her inability to have children. Kim got the big country estate near the lake house in the generous divorce deal, and Ken got a new trophy wife, whom he subsequently knocked up on their honeymoon.

Kim is always late, so I gather up the boys to enjoy the last few hours of daylight down by the lake. I dip Will's feet in the shallow end and chase after him as he tears ahead to reach Logan, who is tossing stones with a steady hand across the shimmering lake's surface.

"Sorry about the concert tonight," I say. "I know your daddy is going to try and do something special for you next weekend."

"He already told me. He's going to get box seats for the Tigers game."

The fine art of bribing a child to get your way, I

think to myself. I hold my tongue and give Logan a tight smile instead.

"Lo Lo!" Will cries, trying to get his big brother's attention.

"Check that out," Logan says proudly as his rock skips four times across the lake. "It's all about the smoothness of the rock and the skill of the thrower."

"Again, Lo Lo!" Will begs. He lets out a high-pitched squeal of delight every time Logan tosses another rock across the water. I rest my face against the back of his blond head and breathe deeply, taking in all the wonderful smells that are Will.

The quiet solitude of the lake is interrupted by the snap of gravel under tires as Kim's silver Volvo pulls into the driveway. Kim eases out of the car and gives us a big wave, looking like a 1950s screen siren sporting a pair of large round sunglasses, a matching floral sheaf dress and cardigan, and a scarf tied in a perfect knot around her neck. Kim's impeccable style and grace always reminds me of a modern-day Grace Kelly.

"Hello, young men!" Kim calls out to Logan and Will. "I swear you both have grown an inch since last week."

"What's in the basket?" Logan asks.

"Chocolate éclairs from my very own kitchen," she answers.

"They haven't eaten dinner yet," I say.

"I know the rules. I brought the éclairs especially for Logan. First day of school is Tuesday, right?"

"Don't remind me," Logan answers. He grabs Will by the hand, and the two resume a serious search for the perfect skipping stone.

"God, they are so cute," Kim says as she reaches inside her Coach purse and extracts her cell phone. She walks to the water's edge and points it in the direction of the boys.

"Are you taking pictures?"

"Well, of course. Is that a problem?" Kim answers, her finger still snapping new frames. "I need some new pictures to put up on my page."

"You've been posting pictures of my kids on the Internet?" I ask and snatch the phone out of Kim's hand.

"Why are you acting crazy? This is harmless. I have all the security settings up on my Facebook page. If you were actually on Facebook, you'd know there was nothing to worry about."

A knot of anger builds in my stomach, and I feel like throwing the cell phone in the lake.

"I'll give you back your phone if you promise to take down the pictures of my kids. Predators troll the Internet looking for photos of children."

"They can't copy the pictures. Not on Facebook anyway."

"But they can look at them. And they can find out where a child lives."

"You're going a little overboard, don't you think?"

I give Kim a hard, unflinching stare until her eyes begin to fill up with tears. She looks back at me, unblinking, until she recovers with a forced smile.

"Of course. They're your boys, so whatever you feel is best," Kim answers in a sparrow-shrill tone.

"Look, I didn't mean to hurt your feelings. It's not that I don't trust you," I say and begrudgingly hand Kim her phone back.

"It's just the rest of the world you don't trust," Kim answers, her voice softening slightly. "The boys are growing up so quickly, and if you don't take pictures, you won't have their milestones captured. Before you know it, you'll be sending Will off to kindergarten."

"He's so independent now. It scares me."

"Everything scares you about those boys," Kim says and offers a real smile this time. "You don't want them to grow up being scared of everything. They'll either turn into social misfits, living in your basement until they're thirty, or they'll rebel and wind up in jail before they get out of high school."

"If they're minors, they'd wind up in juvie first. But thanks for the ringing endorsement of my parenting skills. Logan and Will can have as much fun as they like just as long as I'm there to watch them," I answer.

Kim slides the phone back inside her purse, and I can see her mind work as she searches for a less heated topic of conversation. Kim hates confrontation more than anyone I know.

"Did you figure out a plan for when you go back to work? You know, if you stay at the lake house, I could help out sometimes. That way you wouldn't have to worry about leaving Will at a day care with strangers every day."

"Thanks for the offer. I might take you up on that, but you work too."

"Interior decorators have more flexibility than journalists. And I don't have that dreadful daily commute into the city."

"That's true. I'm not sure your clients even know where Detroit is."

Kim rolls her eyes at my attempt at a joke. "Very funny. I just finished a job down in Grosse Pointe, decorating a wing of an estate for a widow whose husband was a CEO at Chrysler. Her dogs were my clients. Imagine twenty-five hundred square feet of fire engines and hydrants. I guess if you have that kind of money, you can spend it any way you want."

"I think if I had my choice, I'd stick to the scumbags I cover on the crime beat," I answer.

"You need to come over before you start back at the paper. The remodel on my guesthouse is almost done. My property is going to be featured in this year's Parade of Homes."

The way she is glowing over the news, I guess the annual local home tour must be Kim's version of a Pulitzer.

"Good for you," I answer.

"You'll come on the tour, won't you?"

"I wouldn't miss it," I answer and silently pray Kim will forget to ask me again.

"What's going on with you and David?" she asks.

"Besides him breaking plans at the last minute with Logan again, not much. We're trying to work on a reconciliation, but it's not been easy. He asked me to see a psychiatrist."

Kim's mouth purses as though she just tasted something rancid.

"A psychiatrist? For what? And what does he have to fix on his end? Nothing?"

"He's supposed to try and spend more time with me and the boys instead of working every weekend."

"Did you see the psychiatrist?"

"Once."

"Is he cutting down on his hours?" Kim asks.

"Not yet."

"He's too controlling. He's always been that way with you."

"I don't want to talk about this right now," I answer.

"You're right. I'm not saying another word because if you and David get back together, you're going to hate me. But you know how I feel."

Kim smoothes the nonexistent wrinkles from her dress and digs inside her cream-colored bag for her keys.

"That's it. You and the boys are coming with me. I have guests, but you're going to join us for dinner."

"Thanks, we're going to just have a quiet night at home," I say. "Is your mom back from Europe?"

"Not for two days. Mother's cousin Alice and her daughter Leslie are staying with me."

"I don't remember you ever talking about them before."

"I haven't seen them in years, at least Alice anyway. The last time I saw her, I was a little younger than Logan. My mother fell out of touch with that side of the family when they moved to California. I know you hate Facebook, but that's how Leslie found me. They're in town looking at boarding schools for Leslie. She's going to be a junior this year."

I look off to the far edge of the lake and the sun beginning to slip beneath it.

"Are you sure you won't come with me?" Kim asks.

"No, enjoy your relatives. I'll call you later."

Kim gives the boys a tight squeeze and slides into her Volvo. Her car disappears down the country road, and I gaze into the distance at the lake house. In the quickly fading light of day, my welcoming sanctuary looks lonely and remote, with only miles of water and woods between it and our nearest neighbor.

"Wow, check out my shadow. It looks like I'm ten feet tall," Logan remarks.

"The long shadows of dusk. Let's get home," I say and hurriedly gather up our belongings before night falls.

The children and I fall into our usual nightly routines. Logan pulls on his Scooby-Doo pajamas and hunkers down in front of his DVD player to watch his favorite old-school Bugs Bunny videos. I collect Will up into the comfort of my arms, and we rock back and forth in the nursery's white wicker chair until his eyes start to flicker.

"Mama loves you," I say as I press my lips against his warm cheek. Will's breathing becomes slow and heavy. I know he is asleep, but out of pure selfishness, I wait for an extra minute and hold him in the rocker before I put him in his crib for the night.

"Good night, beautiful boy," I whisper. I pull Will's door ajar, so I will be sure to hear him if he wakes up.

With one child down, I head to Logan's room, secretly hoping he is too tired to request his usual bedtime story. It's the one Ben told me when I was little, about a magical wizard named Mr. Moto. Even when we were sleeping in the backseat of my dad's old Chrysler, Ben always made sure I got a bedtime story.

I tiptoe into Logan's room, but he is alert and ready for his story.

"Aren't you tired of hearing it?" I ask.

"Never," Logan answers.

I sit down on the bed and pull Logan's Spider-Man blanket up over his shoulders.

"Okay. Once upon a time there was a magical wizard named Mr. Moto. He lived in a castle high above the town where he could watch and protect all the people who lived there."

"What about the dragon?" Logan asks.

"I'm getting to that part, Mr. Impatient. One day a family of mean fire-breathing dragons came to the town and decided they were going to steal all the people's treasures."

"What about the invisible shield?" Logan asks.

"Mr. Moto was watching to be sure the people of the town were safe when he noticed the terrible dragons. Since he was a magical wizard, he pulled out his invisible shield and hid all the people so the fire-breathing dragons couldn't see them."

"So the dragons left, and then Mr. Moto and the people of the town lived happily ever after?" Logan asks.

"Exactly."

"If Daddy doesn't move back in with us, I'll protect you and Will from fire-breathing dragons," Logan vows.

"Don't you worry about that. Time for bed," I respond and gently touch the side of Logan's cheek with my hand and then turn on his nightlight before I leave.

With both boys down, I am anxious to check the deadbolts and activate the security system.

7.9.1977. I punch in the alarm code on the most expensive home security system money could buy. Seven is the age I was when Ben was taken. Ben was nine when he disappeared. 1977 was the year he went missing. My finger pauses over the red activate-alarm button, and Ben's image, so clear, flashes through my memory, as if I could reach my hand back thirty years and be with him just one more time.

"You know, when I get older, I'm going to be a lawyer, and I'll run for mayor of Sparrow. Then I'll kick Mark Brewster and his family out of town for good," Ben said as we walked the stretch home along Beach Drive after Ben's near showdown with Mark Brewster at Funland.

Ben's dreams of the future were suddenly interrupted by a sharp blast of a car horn from behind. The approaching car trying to get our attention was an old lime-green Cadillac with pointy tail fins in the back and a dent in the driver side door. As the Cadillac pulled to a stop alongside of us, the tinted driver-side window slowly cranked down, and Ben and I were greeted by a blast of cheap drug-store aftershave and KC and the Sunshine Band's "I'm Your Boogie Man" thumping from the eight-track player. A man with thick, blond sideburns poked his head out the window and gave us a wide smile.

"Hey, kids, do you want a ride?" the man asked. He pulled out a piece of Juicy Fruit gum from a pack on the dashboard and folded it into his mouth, all the while bopping his head as KC sang he was here to do whatever he can.

"I'm kind of tired," I said and gave my brother my best pleading look. The music coming from the car was loud and hypnotizing. Plus, I saw a few extra sticks of Juicy Fruit gum in the pack, and I bet the man would offer one without me even having to ask.

"No thanks. We're fine," Ben snapped at the driver. *"Our dad is a cop and he's just around the corner waiting for us. He gets mad if we talk to strangers, so I sure wouldn't want to be you right now, mister."*

The man in the Cadillac reached his hand outside the window and gave my forearm a squeeze.

"Hey, let go of my sister!" Ben yelled. The man in the car wasn't impressed. He just stared back at Ben with a shit-eating grin plastered across his face.

Ben stared down the stranger, and my brother's eyes suddenly changed, turning dark and hard, like wet stone. Ben knotted his hands into fists, ready to strike just as a Woodie with a surfboard tucked on top hung a right on Beach Drive and headed right toward us. The man in the Cadillac carefully noted the progress of the approaching vehicle in his rearview mirror and released his grip from my arm.

"Fine. Just trying to help you kids out. No crime in trying to do a good deed. Have a nice day, you two."

As his parting gesture, the man in the Cadillac lifted up his left arm and flashed us a peace sign, exposing a tattoo of Woodstock, Snoopy's yellow bird sidekick, etched on his forearm.

"Get out of here, you jerk," Ben called out to the Cadillac, but it had already shot down Beach Drive.

"Why did you say our dad is a cop? I'm tired, and it's going to be dark soon. It would've been nice to catch a ride the rest of the way."

"If you ever, ever take a ride from a stranger, I will kick your butt, understand me? I'm serious. That guy looked creepy anyway," Ben answered.

We walked the next two miles in silence. By the time we finally got home, the sun was beginning to set, so *we huddled in our room to debrief about our day. Ben and I shared a room since Sarah refused to bunk with an idiot baby like me. That's what she said. But I didn't mind bunking with my brother. Not at all.*

Ben, being the older one, got the luxury hand-me-down bed, while I slept on the squeaky, thin cot next to the sliding glass door that led to the courtyard.

I put on my nightgown and strained to recall the best plays of the last New York Yankees game. While most good children recited their prayers before bed, Ben and I talked baseball, the New York Yankees to be exact. Ben absolutely loved the team and knew every stat of his favorite players: Catfish Hunter, Lou Piniella, Bucky Dent, and the hotshot rookie, Ron Guidry.

"Do you think the Yankees will make it to the World Series?" I asked.

"Are you kidding me? Of course they'll make it, even though they signed that idiot Reggie Jackson," Ben said.

"What's wrong with Reggie Jackson?"

"He thinks he's a big shot coming over from the Baltimore Orioles. It's like he thinks he's too good for the Yankees. And he doesn't show Billy Martin any respect. Remember that Red Sox game? Billy Martin pulled Jackson out in the middle of the inning and he deserved it. Jackson was lazy as heck. You watched the game with me, remember?"

"I think so." Of course I remembered. I just wanted Ben to give me the play-by-play.

"A blooper ball was coming right at Jackson, and Mr. Big Shot couldn't hustle a few feet to catch it. That was a pretty good fight Billy Martin and Jackson almost got into in the clubhouse though. I tell you what,

the only way Reggie Jackson will ever get my respect is if he nails a bunch of home runs in the World Series."

"If the Yankees make it to the World Series, can I watch the games with you?" I asked.

"Sure, I promise. Maybe one day when I'm older, I'll take you to a game."

"Oh, I'd love that."

Ben pulled out his collection of New York Yankees baseball cards he kept in a cigar box our dad gave him, and I tried to get comfortable in my lowly excuse for a bed. The springs of the old cot let out a tired squeak as I turned over on my side and faced the sliding glass door to the courtyard. A feeling, unfamiliar and nagging, wrapped around me and wouldn't let go. Unable to shake it, I got up from the cot to check the door.

"What are you doing?" Ben asked.

"I thought I heard something outside. I just want to be sure the door is locked."

"The sound you heard was probably Mom taking off so she could hit the bars. The door is locked, for crying out loud. You're fine. We've got the first day of school tomorrow. Time to go to bed."

I didn't want Ben to think I was a scared baby. Plus, he was always right. The door had to be locked. That's what Ben said so it had to be true.

I left the door unchecked and climbed back into bed. Ben shut the light off, and I stared up at the ceiling, which was punctuated with a few glow-in-the-dark stars Ben had won for me earlier that summer at Funland.

"Can we leave the light on?" I asked.

"Are you afraid of the dark now?"

"A little bit tonight."

"What do you think is going to happen?" Ben asked.

"The boogeyman is going to get me."

I could hear Ben's deep belly laugh in the darkness.

"I'm not turning the light on. You're fine. There's no such thing as the boogeyman. Besides, I'd never let anything bad happen to you."

"You'll never leave me, right?"

"Why would you ask a weirdo question like that? You're thinking about those scary shows like Dark Shadows *and* Kolchak: The Night Stalker *again, huh? I told you not to watch those with me because I knew you couldn't take it."*

"I could take it," I lied.

"Then why are you scared?" Ben asked.

"Well, maybe I'm thinking about those shows just a little bit. But promise me anyway. Swear you'll never leave. Dad leaves us all the time."

"That's different. I promise, I'll never leave you. Not in a million years. You're my bright spot. We were born into a bad life, but we're going to be okay. You'll see. We're going to come out of this all right."

"I love you, Ben."

And then he said it. He never did anymore.

"I love you too, Julia."

I push back the memory and get back to the business of securing the house. Once the security alarm is activated, my nerves ease slightly, but I still want to double-check the deadbolt on the front door and install the safety bar across the sliding glass door that leads to the backyard in the downstairs playroom. I start upstairs first. I yank the front doorknob as hard as I can until my hands shake from the effort, and the wooden door groans against the metal lock. Satisfied that it is secure, I start downstairs but pause when I see the answering machine's message light blinking a furious red on the kitchen countertop. I hesitate for a minute, and then hit the play button.

First message: *"It's Primo. I know you aren't scheduled to come back to the paper until later in the month, but I need you back in the newsroom first thing tomorrow. Reverend Casey Cahill is up for parole. The parole hearing isn't scheduled for a couple of weeks, but you need to start working on a Sunday centerpiece for the weekend. I'm sure* The Detroit News *is working on the same angle, so we need to beat them to it. Get a face-to-face with Cahill at the Macomb prison. Don't call me back with excuses. I'll see you tomorrow."*

I hit the delete button.

Second message: *"Julia, it's Sarah."*

I stare back at the answering machine as if it's an unwanted old ghost.

"Things ended on a bad note for us. I'm in town. I flew all the way to Michigan to see you. I still have the same number. I just want to make amends for what I did. I hope you'll call. I miss you, Julia."

For a second, the memory of the sister I used to know begins to creep back. My sentimentality quickly gives in to anger and I slam down the delete button.

"Third message," the answering machine's robotic monotone continues.

I wait for a voice, but the only sound on the recording is a loud crackling on the line. *Must be a bad cell phone connection*, I think. I wait for a second to erase the message when a barely audible voice cuts through.

"*Julia . . . get out . . .*"

The voice is almost a whisper.

"*Can't get there in time . . .*"

"Who the hell is this?" I ask.

"*It's coming back . . .*"

My heart starts to pound in my chest.

"*For you this time.*"

The caller ends the message abruptly. A steady whine of dial tone hums through the answering machine for a good thirty seconds until it is replaced by a busy signal.

"*End of third message.*"

My eyes dart across the kitchen countertop and hover for a second on a wooden knife rack, but then move to the house phone. I reach for it and accidentally knock a stack of Logan's library books to the floor. I pull the receiver from the cradle and pound my finger on the keypad to dial 911.

"Come on, come on!" I cry out and jam the phone receiver against my ear.

The phone is dead.

A silent scream begins to build from deep within my core. Paranoid personality disorder. That's what David and the psychiatrist would say. Just a coincidental sequence of two unrelated events.

But the caller said my name.

I force myself to focus. My cell phone is downstairs. I left it in the boys' playroom earlier when we got home from the lake. I slide a six-inch steak knife out of the rack and grasp it firmly in my right hand as I make my way down the staircase to the bottom floor of the house.

The downstairs playroom is completely dark except for a soft reflection of moonlight coming from the sliding glass door that faces the backyard.

I flick the wall switch and fully expect to see someone pressed up against the window, Freddy Krueger style. But no one is there, just pitch-black country night on the other side of the glass.

I exhale, one battle down, and head to the glass door to check the lock.

I take exactly six steps across the playroom when the lights go out. David's voice echoes in my head, telling me everything is fine. Just something faulty in the wiring. All I need to do is check the circuit breaker. *Easy as pie, Julia.*

Bullshit.

I sprint through the dark room in the direction of the stairs when my hip catches hard against the pool table. On impact, the knife flies out of my hand and I struggle to regain my balance.

I fumble on hands and knees to find the knife when a piercing crash echoes from the kitchen and the now-broken object scatters its remains across the upstairs floor.

"Logan?" I call out, trying to quell any trace of fear in my voice. Logan is afraid of the dark. "It's okay. The power is out. Just stay where you are."

Logan doesn't respond.

I scramble like a crab across the floor until my hand grazes the first step of the stairwell. I grab the bannister to steady myself as footsteps, hard and fast, run directly above me. I try to scream but fear chokes off my voice as I finally accept my worst nightmare is no longer just playing in an endless loop in my mind. This time it's real. Someone is inside.

I hear a voice screaming and realize it's my own.

"Logan, run to Will's room and lock the door!"

My desperate plea is muffled by a second set of heavy footsteps that thump down the upstairs hallway toward the boys' rooms.

"Get out of my house!" I cry as my foot hits the landing.

The main floor of the house is dark, except for a faint sliver of light coming through the now open door to the garage. I start toward the garage but instinctively change my route and run to the boys' rooms instead.

"The safe is downstairs. It's unlocked," I cry. We don't have a safe. If the intruders just go downstairs, I can grab the boys and we can get out of the house.

"The police are on their way, and I'm armed," I lie again as I run for Logan and Will.

Logan's bedroom is the first room on the left. His door is wide open. I feel my heart beating up into my throat as I enter the room. In the contours of the darkness, I can make out a small lump huddled in the corner of the bed. I lunge forward to grab Logan, but quickly realize the shape is only his Spider-Man blanket bunched up by his pillow.

"Logan!" I scream as something latches around my ankle.

"Mommy, it's me," Logan whimpers.

I slide down on my stomach and face my oldest son, who is cowering under his bed.

"You need to stay in the room, baby. Follow Mommy to the door and then lock it. Do not unlock the door unless I tell you."

"I want to go with you, Mommy. Please!" Logan sobs.

"No. Stay here. Understand?"

"Okay, Mommy," Logan whispers.

Logan has a flashlight on top of his nightstand. I grab the flashlight and wait until I hear Logan lock the door behind me.

The fresh scent of body odor and cigarettes clings in the hallway.

Will's door is closed tight. I left it open a few inches when I put him to sleep just twenty minutes earlier. I flash the thin beam of the light in front of the closed door. The light catches the Winnie the Pooh and Piglet stencil I put on Will's bedroom door this summer.

The door is locked. I rear my leg back and slam my foot against the thin wooden door, which snaps open after three tries. I strengthen my grip around the flashlight, ready to use it as a weapon. Back and forth, up and down, I point the flashlight in all directions. I have to see the intruders before they see me.

But the light only catches the mundane objects of a toddler's room: Will's brown stuffed dog with the white eye patch, his changing table with clothes I already laid out for morning, and a framed vintage picture of the Sparrow boardwalk I hung for luck. Ben promised he would always be there to protect me, and I wanted to believe he would do the same for Logan and Will.

I let the flashlight fall down by my feet and dive my arms inside the crib. I instinctively expect to feel Will's soft sleeping body against my touch, but instead my hands feel only his crib sheet, still warm, underneath my fingers.

"Will!" I scream.

I flail my hands against the floor until I feel the metal cylinder of the flashlight, which shut off after I dropped it. I have to find Will before the intruders escape with him outside. I picture the open door to the garage. I should have gone in that direction first, and if I am too late, there are no second chances.

I tear down the hallway toward the garage. Inside, I notice the door to the driveway is open and an icy slice of moon casts its pale light onto Will's yellow and white baby blanket, crumpled in a heap on the ground next to his Snoopy doll and a discarded package of Marlboro Lights cigarettes.

"I'm going to kill you!" I scream as I race into the warm carly September night air. "Give me back my son!"

"Stupid girl," a voice hisses behind me. Before I can turn around, something connects with the back of my head.

And then there is only darkness.

CHAPTER 4

Twenty-four. I can see the number floating in neon blue out in the darkness like a single star lost in the night.

"Twenty-four." I feel my lips move as they whisper the number.

"She's regaining consciousness," a woman's voice says above me. "That's it, Julia. Come back to us."

I start to open my eyes when a searing pain shoots across the back of my skull.

"Take it easy there." The voice belongs to a female paramedic kneeling over me. Next to her is a baby-faced police officer I don't recognize. "What's twenty-four, Julia?"

"Twenty-four hours. The amount of time we have to find Will." I say the words before I realize what they mean.

The first twenty-four hours in a missing person's case are the most critical, especially when the missing person in question is a child. Within this narrow time frame, all stops have to be pulled out in order to find the child alive or to find the child at all. Sheer panic whispers in my ear and beckons me away from my paper-thin veneer of sanity.

"Someone kidnapped my son. I have to find him."

"Hold on, I have to check you first. That's a nasty bump you got on the back of your head. We need to take you to the hospital."

"No way. Where's Logan?"

"That's a brave little boy you have there," the paramedic answers and points the beam of a narrow flashlight in front of my eyes to check for a concussion. "And resourceful. He found your cell phone and called 911. He's inside the house talking to the police."

"The police shouldn't be talking to Logan without David or me there."

I sit up quickly and feel a wave of nausea and dizziness wash through me, but I fight through it and force myself up on wobbly legs.

"You really shouldn't . . ." the paramedic starts.

I regain my balance and keep walking through the darkness to the front door with the steadiness of a well-imbibed patron after last call.

I know what to expect based on the driveway. I pass by an unmarked Crown Victoria and a patrol car and enter my home, now a crime scene, and begin to search for Logan.

"Mom!" Logan cries out from the living room and runs as fast as he can away from the circle of officers surrounding him and lands in my arms.

I press my face against his shiny black hair and whisper that everything is going to be fine. It has to be.

"Are you all right, Julia?" Detective Russell asks. Russell holds a sealed plastic evidence bag in his left hand that contains Will's favorite yellow and white baby blanket inside. I stare intently at the blanket, which looks both beautiful and obscene in its current state.

"Have you found Will?"

"Not yet. We're still collecting evidence."

"That's not enough."

"We were just questioning Logan. We'll need you both to come down to the station later to answer some questions."

"I can tell you what you need to know right now. Two people broke into my house. I heard two distinct sets of footsteps, so you have at least two suspects involved. They kidnapped Will and when I ran outside to find him, I got hit on the back of the head. Someone called me 'stupid girl' right before I went down. And there was a phone message. A warning. The connection was bad and the caller didn't leave a name."

"Did you see the people who broke into your house?"

"No, I didn't see anyone. But I smelled cigarette smoke," I answer.

"We checked your home security alarm. Someone disabled it."

"That's impossible. I set the alarm right after I put Logan and Will to sleep," I say and then kick into full reporter mode. "We don't have many neighbors way out here in the country, but you need to canvass the neighborhood to locate any witnesses. Maybe someone saw a suspicious person or vehicle in the area. And registered sex offenders. You need to start knocking on doors right now."

"We've got it covered already."

"There's a gas station about five miles from here. They've got to have a surveillance tape," I continue.

"And shoe prints. We had a bad storm a few days ago, so there could've been mud on the suspects' shoes. I didn't hear a car engine, but you need to check for tire tracks outside. We have a long gravel driveway. Go out there and look now if you haven't done it already."

Russell turns away from me and says something quietly into his two-way radio.

"Just got word the police chief is on his way over. He wants to talk to you," Russell says and retreats back toward the garage.

I reach my hand to the back of my pulsing head. I ignore the pain and refocus my attention on Logan, who is still glued to my side. I squat down and squeeze Logan as hard as I can.

"I'm sorry, Mom. It's all my fault. I hid under my bed like a scared baby."

"Don't you say that for a minute. Nothing is your fault. You're the brave one in all of this. You called the police and saved me."

"Someone bad took Will," Logan says.

I can't let my worst thoughts go there. If I do, I will lose it and never come back.

"Did you see the people who broke into our house?" I ask.

"No. The police asked me that already."

"We'll get Will back, I promise. But it's really important we both tell the police everything we remember."

"Okay, I'll try," Logan responds in a small voice.

The reflection of a massive silhouette passes by the front window, and I instinctively draw Logan closer. The stranger enters the doorway, and I immediately recognize the red hair and perfectly manicured beard of Police

Chief John Linderman. When Linderman and I first had disagreements over stories, I branded him the "Red Devil," which quickly caught fire around the newsroom. But through the years, we developed a mutual respect, or at the very least, a mutual tolerance for each other.

"Logan, I hear that you were a very brave young man," Linderman says.

"Thank you, sir," Logan answers.

"How are you holding up, Julia?" Linderman asks and beckons Logan and me over to the sofa. "I heard you got pretty banged up out there."

"Tell me what you have on my son's case."

Linderman reaches out his mammoth hand and envelops mine for a second. The simple act of compassion catches me off guard, and the stinging pain of tears begins to start. I blink hard and look intently at a plastic cup filled with water on the coffee table until I steady myself.

"I called the FBI, and an Amber Alert went out right after Logan called 911. Critical Reach is distributing the alert to other law enforcement authorities and the media. Our K-9 unit is here, and we're tapping your phones to trace any calls if this is a ransom situation. We're also canvassing the neighborhood and scouring for registered sex offenders. Were you and David on anyone's shit list recently?"

"What do you mean?"

"You being a crime reporter has its perks of pissing people off. David used to work in the public defender's office, right?"

"For five years before he went into private practice."

"He may have racked up some enemies too. Maybe

a case he lost and the guy is looking for revenge. I need you both to think about anyone who might have it out for you and let us know."

Linderman is good. I nod in approval.

"David had a case a while back when he was a public defender. The guy, his name was Joe Matthews, went away for ten years for killing his girlfriend in a domestic. Killed the woman right in front of their three-year-old. I covered the trial. Matthews went wild when the judge gave the sentence. He attacked David, knocked him on the ground, and the bailiff had to break it up. Matthews sent David a couple of letters from jail, blaming him for losing the case, and he threatened he'd get David when he got out."

"We'll check him and anyone else David comes up with."

"I already told Russell this, but there's a gas station about five miles from here. They may have a surveillance tape."

"You were always a thorough reporter. We already sent an officer down to the gas station to get the tape. I put Detective Navarro in charge of the investigation. Navarro just got here. He's getting briefed by the detectives out front."

"David. I need to call him."

"We did already. Your husband was just leaving his law firm. He's on the way here now," Linderman says and stands back up to his impressive six-foot-five frame. "Logan, hang in there, young man. I'll tell Detective Navarro you're ready to talk to him."

As Linderman leaves, I look around at our once-perfect house. The meat loaf I made for last night's dinner is still sitting on the kitchen counter and one of

Will's green pacifiers pokes out from beneath the love seat.

A strong hand grips my shoulder and I turn with a start.

"I let myself in through the garage. Didn't mean to scare you there," Navarro says. He sits down on the other end of the sofa and stares back at me with both grave concern and controlled rage. "Julia . . ."

"You don't need to say it. I don't want anyone else to tell me they're sorry right now, not even you. Just ask Logan and me what you need to. Let's just do this, okay?"

Navarro nods and fixes his attention on Logan.

"Is it all right if I talk to you first? Your mom is going to be right here."

Logan looks up at me and I respond with a reassuring nod.

"I know you've been through a lot tonight, son, and I'm sorry. I need you to tell me whatever you remember, even the small stuff you think might not be important. Tell you what, are you hungry? I am. I usually don't get up in the middle of the night like this, so I need a little sugar to keep me going."

Navarro pulls a package of six small powdered sugar donuts out of his coat pocket. He opens the packet and pops one in his mouth and then pushes the donut packet across the coffee table toward Logan. Logan carefully reaches his hand across the table and picks up a donut.

Donuts and cops, I think to myself. *How damn cliché, Navarro.*

"I understand that some people broke into your house and took your little brother. That must have been very scary," Navarro says, stuffing another donut in his mouth. "I know I would've been scared if someone came into my house, especially if I was sleeping."

Logan looks at Navarro and nods in agreement.

"I need your help. Do you think you can help me?"

"Yes, sir," Logan says.

"Call me Ray," Navarro says. "Now, can you tell me what you remember?"

"Well, sir, I mean, Ray, sir," Logan starts. "My mom told me a bedtime story and I went right to sleep."

Logan looks over toward me, and I gesture for him to continue.

"I was having a bad dream and woke up. I heard a sound down the hall and called out to my mom, but she didn't answer. My nightlight went out and the hall light, too. Mom always leaves the hall light on for me. I got scared and hid under my bed."

Logan begins to fidget, and I put my arm around his shoulder and hold him as tightly as I can.

"It's okay, Logan. Everyone is afraid of something. I'll tell you a secret," Navarro says and leans in toward Logan. "I'm scared to death of bats."

"Bats aren't that bad," Logan says as he tries to suppress a slight smile.

"You're braver than I am," Navarro says. "So let's keep going here. After the lights went out, what happened?"

"I felt like a little baby hiding under my bed, and I was going to come out, but then someone ran into my room. I thought it was my mom. But the person dropped their flashlight on the floor, and I saw their boots. My mom doesn't have boots like that, and we aren't allowed to wear shoes in the house anyway because of Will and all the germs and stuff."

"That's good, Logan, real good. Can you tell me what the boots looked like?" Navarro asks.

"They were brown. And they stunk, kind of like when you're driving by a farm and you can hardly take it because it smells so bad."

"Like manure?" Navarro asks.

"Yes, sir, I mean, Ray, sir," Logan says.

"Were the boots big, like a man was wearing them? Or were they smaller, like women's shoes?"

"It was dark. I couldn't really tell."

"Okay. So this person is standing over your bed. Did they say anything?" Navarro asks.

"Well, they did, but it wasn't nice. Mom and Dad won't let me say those kinds of words."

"It's fine this time. Your mom and dad aren't going to mind," Navarro replies. "Right, Julia?"

"Absolutely. Tell him what you heard," I say.

Logan clears his throat nervously. "They said something really bad. It was something like, 'Selfish is as selfish does. Dirty, selfish little girl. Dirty, selfish little whore.'"

A tear slips down Logan's cheek, and he wipes it away with his pajama top.

"Hang in there," Navarro says. "Logan, buddy, can you tell me if the voice was a man's voice or a woman's?"

"I'm not really sure. They just sounded really angry. It was definitely an adult's voice though," Logan says. "Then they started humming."

"Humming? Like humming a song? Do you know what song it was?" Navarro asks.

"No, I'm sorry I don't," Logan says. "I think I might have heard it when Dad used to take me to church, but that was a long time ago, and I'm just not sure. I'll let you know if I remember."

"Great, a crazed, angry, religious hummer," Navarro mumbles under his breath and then turns his attention back to Logan. "You're doing real good. What happened after the person in your room started humming?"

"I was sure they were going to look under the bed and find me. I closed my eyes for a second. Like if I opened them, they'd be staring right at me."

"But they didn't find you."

"No. The person left. I heard them run out of my room real quick, and they never came back. I stayed under the bed until my mom came in. She told me to lock the door when she went to go look for my brother. Then a few minutes later, I heard my mom scream for Will outside. That's all I can remember."

"That's okay. You did great. Do me a favor. If you think of anything else, you tell your mom or dad right away. All right?"

"I will," Logan promises. "Is Daddy going to be here soon?"

"He's on his way," I answer.

"Can I go in my room?"

"Just be careful what you touch. I'm going to talk to Detective Navarro out here for a minute. Let me know if you need anything," I say and trail Logan's retreat until he is safely out of earshot.

"Please tell me you have something," I implore Navarro. Before I can pump him for information, Russell turns the corner from Will's room holding another plastic evidence bag.

"We just found something under the little boy's crib," Russell says. "It looks like an Indian arrowhead."

Russell holds the plastic bag up for Navarro and me to inspect from afar.

"I didn't know what it was at first, but one of our patrol guys is half-Indian and he confirmed it. Does this belong to you, Julia?" Russell asks.

("I promise, I'll never leave you. Not in a million years. You're my bright spot. We were born into a bad life, but we're going to be okay. You'll see. We're going to come out of this all right.")

Ben's last words swirl in my head like a mammoth black funnel cloud roaring in my ears. I no longer see the evidence bag, or Navarro or the cops canvassing every inch of my house for clues. I'm back in Sparrow in our room on the night Ben disappeared. The Indian arrowhead under Ben's bed was one of the few pieces of evidence the police found in his abduction.

"Jesus, this can't be happening again. There was a call, a warning on my answering machine right before the break-in. The caller said someone was coming back for me this time. It's all connected somehow."

"Julia, what's going on?" Navarro asks.

"It's Labor Day, the anniversary," I cry out.

"Take it easy," Navarro answers and grabs my arm to try and calm me down.

"You don't understand. There's a thirty-year-old case of another missing boy that's directly related to my son's disappearance."

"Who's the kid?" Navarro asks.

"It's my brother, Ben. Whoever took him just kidnapped Will."

CHAPTER 5

The first fingers of daylight slowly break through the darkness of the previous night and cast a fuzzy glow behind two weeping willow trees that stand like bookends on either side of the front yard. David and I planted each tree right after the births of Logan and Will. Just two days ago, Will and I sat underneath his tree and I watched as my baby swatted at the high branches, and Will laughed in delight when he managed to catch one in his hand.

Navarro and I greet dawn in his unmarked police car, where I recounted the story about my brother and the day he was kidnapped. Navarro immediately briefed his team and left a message with Detective Leidy at the St. Clair Sheriff's Department to gather information on Ben's cold case and possibly pinpoint any threads that could connect to Will.

"Did the cops think the Indian arrowhead under your brother's bed had some kind of meaning?" Navarro asks.

"No. They were never able to determine whether it was a symbol or just something accidentally dropped by the person who took Ben. I always thought it did though."

"What about the guy in the green Caddy?" Navarro asks. "Was he ever found?"

"No. It was a dead end. Leidy figured the guy was an out-of-towner visiting Sparrow for the Labor Day weekend."

"How about your dad?"

"What do you mean?"

"Gloves are off, Julia. Your dad had a record. He'd be a suspect even without one. Family always is. You know that."

"My dad had an alibi that checked out. That's what Leidy said. My dad got a temporary job installing flooring in a factory in Fort Wayne, Indiana. It was night work. The foreman vouched for him. I never saw my dad after that night, but I always wondered if he was trying to change. My dad could con the best of them, but he was doing honest work for once. I'd like to think he stayed that way."

"If a man doesn't come back for his own kid, I doubt he changed much."

I ignore Navarro's comment and instead stare at the dashboard clock. Six a.m., exactly eight hours since Will was snatched from his bed. I push down the unimaginable that could have happened in the past few hours and instead visualize my little boy as though I am seeing him for the first time. Will, with his white blond hair glistening like pure spun gold against the sun as he chases Logan up and down the banks of the lake. Will, my hundred-percent all-American boy, his arms overloaded with Matchbox cars as he climbs up the steps to bed, refusing to part with his precious bounty. Will, who already knows how to expertly work me as I easily cave to his whims and read *The Very Hungry Caterpillar* for the umpteenth time to him before bed. And Will, with a child's unspoiled trust, who believed I would chase the monsters away and always protect him from harm.

Jesus. Will, where are you?

Guilt and self-loathing course through me as I realize it's my fault, all of it, my fault again. My heart begins to beat so hard in my chest, I am surprised Navarro can't hear it.

Instead, Navarro picks up a paper cup from his dashboard and spits something inside.

"Sunflower seed casings," he says. "I quit smoking two weeks ago, so I've got to put something in my mouth. I tried gum, but it's like chewing on a piece of disgusting rubber you can't spit out. I quit drinking after you left. So the cigarettes were my final vice."

"I'm glad you finally quit them both. The booze especially."

"Ten years too late though, right?" Navarro answers and tosses the remains of his chew out the driver-side window. "Your brother's abduction must have been a heavy thing to carry around for such a long time. And for a kid who could've been a potential witness not to remember anything, that's got to make you feel a world of guilt."

"Am I a suspect? You think I snapped and did something to my own child?"

"I didn't say that."

"Yes, you did. Family members are always the first people you look at. Remember who you're talking to here."

"That's true. But it wasn't what I meant."

"I didn't hurt my son."

Navarro is quiet for a moment as if he's weighing whether to ask me the next question.

"All the time we were together, you never mentioned your brother or what happened to him. Not once. You never told me anything about your family either, just your Aunt Carol. Why is that?"

I try to avoid Navarro's question and recall the two years we spent living above a taqueria in a one-bedroom tiny apartment in Mexicantown on the southwestern side of Detroit. Navarro was always the protector, and I never had any doubt that he loved me more than anything during our relationship. But at the age of twenty-five, I had a laser focus on my career and felt too young to accept his marriage proposal. And Navarro couldn't accept me saying no. He dealt with the rejection by getting a barbed-wire tattoo that wrapped around his bicep and hitting the vodka bottle hard. He wouldn't go back to how things were between us without a firmer commitment, and his drinking was becoming a problem. As much as I loved Navarro at the time, I had to leave.

"Earth to Julia," Navarro says and raps his fist lightly against the console between the seats. "Why didn't you ever tell me about Ben?"

"It just never came up."

"That's bullshit, Julia."

"I don't like to talk about it. That's all."

"Did David know the story about your brother?"

"He did. It wasn't a good story to know."

"You could've told me anything when we were together. I didn't think we kept secrets."

"It was a bad story with a monster at the end. It wasn't anything I wanted to share at the time."

"I'm sorry about what happened to you and your brother. If you didn't want to tell me back then, that's one thing. But now you need to come clean about every detail of your past and what happened to your brother if you haven't already," Navarro answers. "Coincidences in crime are rare. Your kid being taken on the anniversary of your brother's abduction and the Indian arrowhead found at both scenes make it pretty damn certain the cases are linked."

"I told you everything there is to tell about Ben's case."

"All right then," Navarro answers, temporarily satisfied with my response. "The one thing that doesn't connect is the amount of time that passed. Thirty years is a long time to wait for payback. If the person who took your brother was worried about you IDing them, they would've come looking for you a lot sooner. But I've got the guys searching for every sex offender in a three-hundred-mile radius and for anyone who might fit the abductor's profile."

Navarro looks over at the snaking line of sheriff department and police vehicles parked along my driveway to the street and starts again. "You're a prominent crime reporter in the city. Who would have it out for you?"

"Fifteen years covering crime in Detroit? Plenty."

"What about one of those freaks who followed Reverend Casey Cahill after he went nuts? You broke the story, and those fanatical religious guys are always the worst. Corrupts their minds more than money or drugs, if you ask me. You won some awards for uncovering what a psycho fanatic that guy turned into, right?"

"Yes, something like that," I answer as I recall my exposé on Cahill and his free fall from grace.

Five years ago, Cahill was one of the biggest players on the national megachurch circuit. While other nationally syndicated pastors were mostly middle-aged white guys who preached damnation from an angry God's judging hand, Cahill had a shiny hardcore shell of cool that oozed rock and roll. Cahill was a tattooed preacher who drove a Harley-Davidson around the city with an easily recognizable helmet that read GOD'S SOLDIER on the back. With his hip vibe yet conservative values on the pulpit, Cahill had achieved something most religious icons could only dream of attaining: massive crossover appeal. His popularity exploded with a national television show and standing room only during multiple weekly services at his megachurch, which glittered like a Las Vegas five-star hotel along I-75. But Cahill's glory days were about to end. On the way to a Sunday service, Cahill's motorcycle skidded across a sheet of ice along the highway and he crashed headfirst into a guardrail. He survived after coming out of a two-week coma, but rumors began to circulate that his increasing paranoid behavior and sharp turn to the fanatical right were a result of a dependency on pain pills and a head injury from the crash.

Despite his gutted popularity, Cahill thought he still had God, power, and all-encompassing celebrity on his side. And he blamed me for taking it all away. Based on an anonymous tip from a UAW employee's girlfriend who worked part-time as a church secretary, I discovered

Cahill had skimmed millions from his church and was having sex with several underage girls in his congregation. Cahill told his hundred or so "true believers" that they were handpicked to become part of his true Christian family. Cahill's youngest conquest was nine, a tiny strawberry-blond child whose high-pitched voice quavered and broke during testimony after the prosecution played an audiotape taken from a video they discovered in Cahill's safe that had shown the girl dressed in nothing but a cross necklace, screaming for her mother as Cahill raped her. I covered every detail of Cahill's explosive trial, and his congregation hated me for it. After the guilty verdict was read, Cahill was stoic for a moment and then slowly turned his head toward the back of the courtroom, the tendons in his neck sticking out like angry cords. As soon as he saw me, Cahill leapt to his feet, raised his handcuffed wrists in my direction, and screamed, "Satan is among us!" before his defense attorney and the court bailiff wrestled the madman down.

Cahill was ultimately charged with tax evasion and sexual assault of three underage girls. And memories of the Rock 'n' Roll Jesus of Motor City quickly disappeared when Cahill began his ten-year sentence.

Navarro checks the rearview mirror and inspects his teeth for any stray sunflower seeds. "There were a bunch of zealots in that church. Did you ever have runins with any of them? I'd go looking at Cahill as a suspect if he weren't locked up already. Cahill and his lawyer said it was your fault he didn't get a fair trial."

"Members of Cahill's congregation picketed the courthouse and swarmed me after the trial like a pack of jackals and condemned me to hell. But there were no more threats after Cahill went to prison," I answer.

"Do me a favor. Come up with a list of anyone who may have thought you burned them with your coverage."

"Linderman asked me about that too, but they have no connection to Ben and most of the people who really hate me are still serving time. But I gave him a few names to check. There's Alejandro Rojas. He's a local hood who I wrote an expose on that vindicated Salvatore Gallo. Gallo is the uncle of Nick Rossi, the big Detroit criminal I know you've been trying to bust for years. Rojas was trying to frame Rossi for a killing over a territory dispute, but the cops saw it differently and liked Gallo for the murder, since Rojas planted the body inside a car in front of Gallo's house. My stories pinned Rojas for the murder. He got convicted, but I think he got out early. The only other person I can think of is that woman who killed her kids over in Elmwood Park. Kate Bramwood was her name. Her sister gave her up, but Bramwood got off on a technicality. She was a nut and swore she'd come after me. Please check them out, but there's no way anyone I wrote about would've been able to find me here. I'm too careful."

Being a female crime reporter, I always take precautions. In addition to my reporter's notebook and tape recorder, I also keep pepper spray and a six-inch folding knife in my purse. After a local female TV anchor was raped and murdered, I made it a point to protect myself, and my family, from the dark side I often encountered on my job, including keeping my maiden name, Gooden, as my byline.

"Do you know who that is?" Navarro asks as Kim's silver Volvo pulls into the driveway.

"It's my best friend. David must have called her. Are we done?"

"Yeah, for now. Go take care of your business."

Kim somehow still looks flawless at the crack of dawn in a pair of pressed khakis and a soft pink linen shirt. She gives me a big bear hug that lasts for a good thirty seconds until I finally pull away.

"Oh, Julia, I've just been sick since David called. I told Alice and Leslie what happened, and they are just devastated. We've all been praying nonstop for Will's safe return," Kim rambles as she twists her hands together in nervous knots. "Do the police have any leads yet? Please tell me they do."

"Nothing solid. The suspects left behind a package of cigarettes, and the police found a hair in Will's crib. It looks like they got a good latent print on Will's bedroom door."

"Well, that's something," Kim says.

"It's not enough. The chief is trying to expedite the hair sample. We don't have the luxury of time right now."

"Did they leave a ransom note? If you need money, just tell me."

"No ransom note."

"What does that mean?"

"They don't want money. Whoever took Will has no plan to return him."

"Oh, Julia," Kim cries. Her usually pretty face contorts into a pained, twisted expression as though she is about to break down, but I don't have the reserve to comfort anyone else but my own family right now.

"Kim, I need you to keep it together."

"I'm so sorry."

"Come on, let's go inside."

Kim rallies and puts a protective arm around my shoulder, and we walk into my house, whose every surface is now coated with black fingerprint dust. I search for familiarity amidst the chaos and spot David and Logan, who are huddled together on the living room couch. David, all six feet and hundred and eighty pounds of him, somehow looks small and deflated as he stares with rapt intensity at an invisible point on the wall. I start toward my family when the screen door bangs open.

"Reverend Casey Cahill's lawyer just called. Cahill insists he has to talk to you, Julia," Navarro says. "You need to go down to the state penitentiary right now. Alone. Cahill will only talk to you."

"Cahill?" His name slips out of my mouth like a snake rearing up unexpectedly across my path. "What's this all about?"

"Cahill says he knows who took your son."

"Relationship to inmate."

I stare at the blank line on the prison pass and try to manipulate the unconnecting piece so it fits. But Cahill's almost immediate knowledge of Will's kidnapping makes no sense. Unless someone tipped him off from the inside.

I scribble down the word *source* on the prison pass, remove the wedding ring that I still wear despite my status with David and the silver heart-shaped locket engraved with the boys' monograms, and place my jewelry on the conveyer belt. I hurry through the metal detector, and the prison guard stamps the back of my hand with ultra-violet ink.

"Have a nice day, sweetheart," he says as I enter into the prison. I turn around and catch the guard staring at my ass.

"Some things haven't changed," I mutter under my breath.

The first time I came to the prison was to interview a serial killer who had murdered six nurses after they got off their swing shift at a string of hospitals across Detroit. That was twelve years ago. I was terrified to do the interview and painfully green. I tried to camouflage my nerves, but the prison guards caught on right away. They forced me to go through the metal detector twice and then claimed they had to search me. I could refuse, of course, but then I wouldn't be able to go inside.

"I need to do this interview. I promised my editor. Could you please just let me go through?" I begged.

Then I heard a stranger's voice from behind. "How's your story coming along on corruption in the prisons? I think that's going to be one hell of an article."

I turned to see a handsome, dark-haired, brooding-looking man in a leather jacket. I looked at the stranger quizzically, but before I could respond, the guards let me through. Later, in the visiting room, the stranger approached me.

"Never let them see your fear. By the way, I'm Detective Ray Navarro."

Something dark and broken drew me to Navarro back then, a stark vulnerability I detected beneath the swagger. One night, after finishing off a pitcher of margaritas that we brought upstairs from the taco place below our apartment, Navarro told me how he witnessed his father strangling his mother to death in the family's kitchen. Navarro was eleven when it happened. I held Navarro as he wept and recounted how his father kept screaming that he shouldn't have to come home to a goddamn cold dinner every night, yelling maniacally even after Navarro's mother became limp and lifeless. I always figured Navarro became a cop to atone for not being able to protect his mother from what I discovered were years of abuse. I asked Navarro that night if he ever forgave himself for not being able to save the person I know was most precious to him. He said he never could. I never told Navarro, but I knew exactly how he felt.

I pace back and forth across the prison's visiting room while I wait for Cahill. Since he is in a segregated part of the prison, we normally would be limited to a non-contact visit with a glass partition between us, and quite frankly, I would have preferred that scenario. But per Cahill's demands, Chief Linderman pulled some strings with the head of the Department of Corrections to allow this face-to-face meeting.

At seven-thirty in the morning, the visiting room is empty except for a handful of cheap metal tables and chairs, several Bibles, and a copy of the Koran. I pick up a Bible and contemplate opening it. After Ben was taken, I prayed each night with every ounce of my being that my brother would come home. But when Ben didn't, I stopped praying. And if God didn't listen to me then, I'm convinced he wouldn't hear me now.

The heavy door to the visiting room swings open and Cahill strides in, still charismatic and preening, despite the constraints of his handcuffs and blue-prison jumpsuit.

Cahill is tall, but more muscular now than I remembered, and his well-cropped brown hair has shoots of grey at the temples. Cahill's left forearm still has the tattoo I first saw when I met him. The tattoo is a big black crow, its wings spread wide as a dozen or so smaller crows scatter in the air above their master.

A stocky prison guard stands at the door with his arms folded across his chest and watches Cahill's every move as he approaches, but the supervision doesn't seem to faze the former reverend at all. He looks pleased to have someone in his presence so he can preach again, even though it's only to a potentially adversarial audience of one. I somehow temper my revulsion and the overwhelming urge to throw Cahill against the wall and start beating him until he tells me where my son is.

"Miss Gooden. I see that you are turning to God at this important time," Cahill says, looking at the Bible still in my hands. "You do believe in God?"

I let the Bible slip through my fingers, and it lands with a tired thud on the table.

"At one time, I thought I did. But he never responded."

"God only speaks to His chosen few."

"Let's be clear before we start. Everything I reported about your crimes and trial were facts. I wrote the truth. If this is going to be a debate or a one-sided lecture, I'm not playing."

Cahill glares at me, and his blue eyes, flecked with

hints of gold, don't blink as he stares back at me with clear disdain.

"Those were lies you wrote, and you know it. You destroyed more souls than you can ever imagine."

"What lies are you referring to? That you brain-washed hundreds of people and raped little girls?"

Cahill's full lips pucker up into a displeased pout.

"I did no such thing. They were spiritual unions, ordained by God. You don't understand. You live in the sins of the outside world. I live in the supernatural."

"You're right. I didn't drink your Kool-Aid. What do you know about my son?"

Cahill's mouth relaxes slightly, and he gestures me to a chair next to him. I choose a seat across the table instead and pull out my tape recorder.

"Oh, we don't need that. No, no, no. We're just going to have a conversation. No one likes to have conversations anymore. Everyone is glued to their computers and cell phones these days. Technology can be a blessing, but it can also lead us astray. There are many things of the devil in this world. Television and computers let the devil slip in, and he will snatch up our souls if we turn our faces from God for even a second."

I take my recorder, shove it back in my pocket, and hit the record button. As a journalist, I am not supposed to tape sources without their knowledge or consent. But screw the formality. I'm not a reporter right now.

"Well, that's better. Can you leave us alone for a while?" Cahill asks the guard, who ignores him. "We have some catching up to do."

"You've got ten minutes," I answer.

And then the inevitable preaching begins.

"I'm so worried about the world. Just look around. All the signs are there—the end is near. There are wars and rumors of wars, earthquakes, tsunamis, and tornadoes of Biblical proportion," Cahill says, punctuating each new calamity with dramatic emphasis. "Are you ready for His return?"

"You told the police you have information about my son. What do you know?"

Cahill disregards my question and continues with his twisted sermon.

"It's quite simple, Miss Gooden. God is not happy because people continue to turn their backs on Him. And when we turn away from the Creator, then the people will suffer. The homosexuals will suffer for their dirty sex. The women who rip babies from their wombs will suffer for snuffing out a life God breathed into those tiny souls. And the homeless and drug addicts will suffer for their weakness. And now you suffer, too. Do you know why?"

"I'm sure you're going to tell me."

"Because you have turned your heart from God," Cahill warns. "You were born with sin, tainted with the original sin of Adam and Eve, and that is why He punished you as a child."

Cahill catches me off guard.

"I've been praying for you and the safe return of your son. So horrible for this to happen to you again," Cahill says.

"What do you mean by that?"

"One of my pen pals knows you. They wrote to me about your brother," Cahill whispers and looks over his shoulder as though he is telling me a secret. "I've been praying all morning that your brother wasn't raped and tortured for days on end. There's so much evil in the world."

I grab on to the chair so I won't reach across the table and strangle Cahill.

"Who told you about my brother?"

"No need to be so angry. Just like journalists must protect their sources, I must protect those who come to me for guidance. As for your brother, I pray he didn't suffer too long or call out your name in his last dying breath, just hoping to see his little sister one more time. Because his little sister never came. That must torment you to no end. The mind can go to very dark places sometimes. I can help you through the darkness if you'd like."

The inside of my body feels like it turned into a block of black ice.

"Shut up about my brother. Understood?"

The prison guard glances over as my voice begins to escalate.

"Now, about your son. Will is his name?" Cahill asks.

"Yes," I answer through gritted teeth.

"Poor little boy. I saw your son's picture on the TV news. He doesn't look like you. Such pretty white-blond hair for a boy. He must look like that lawyer husband of yours. Your husband used to work for the public defender's office, didn't he? I used to see him around here when I was still preaching at the Church of the True Believer, but it's been a while."

"What my husband does is none of your business."

"I understand that type of work, defending such people who have committed unspeakable acts, was probably just too hard for your husband. It takes a soul touched by God to work with sinners, especially those of the caliber around these parts. God told me He brought me here for a reason, to help these sinners, just like so many prophets before me. I trust in His will and you should, too."

"You've got exactly one minute, or I'm walking out of here and going straight to the police station. I'll tell Linderman you're withholding evidence in a kidnapping, and don't think you won't be charged with additional crimes."

"I realize you're under a great deal of pressure, but I don't care to be blackmailed. You've done enough to me already. Innocent until proven guilty, isn't that what they say? Not when you've already been convicted in the press."

"You're involved in this. That's how you know who took my son. Is this payback?"

Cahill tilts his head to the side and gives me a toothy, made-for-television smile and the old Rock 'n' Roll Jesus of Motor City flickers back to life for an instant.

"I forgave you long ago for those stories. And to answer your question, of course I'm not involved in your son's kidnapping. I'm a man of the cloth and would never break the law."

I realized Cahill was going to try and play me. He wants a captive audience, and if I take that away, he will be forced to give me what I want. I stand up and begin to head toward the door. But just as I expected, before I can take two full steps, Cahill's voice beckons me back.

"The letters started coming last month," he says. "It was wonderful to get letters again, such glowing letters about how I brought God into their life. Members of my congregation used to write to me religiously when I first got in here, but then most of them stopped writing. They will pay for their discourteous behavior."

"I don't care about your lack of fan mail. What did these letters say about my son? Were they from one of your parishioners?"

"Tens of thousands of my parishioners came faithfully to hear the word of God every Wednesday night, Saturday afternoon, and for all three of my Sunday sermons. What my daddy started as a tent revival bloomed into a worldwide ministry. If people couldn't be there in person, I brought God to them through television. They could be saved right there in the comfort of their own living room. My ministry touched countless believers on every continent through my syndicated show."

"That's until the majority of your parishioners realized you stole their money and had sex with little girls. How old was the youngest, Cahill? Nine? You handpicked them from the video footage from your Sunday school, right? That's pretty convenient. Those children will never be the same."

"You know, I used to watch you in the courtroom, sitting there so pretty with your tape recorder and notebook, looking so serious," Cahill says. "I prayed for you then that you would close your legs to men, but then I found out you had a husband. Are you a faithful wife? I'm so worried hell is waiting for you. I wake up at night and worry about you sometimes."

"Don't bother. So you're telling me you don't know who wrote the letters?" I ask.

"I would love to know every member of my congregation, I truly would, but when God has called a man to do an important job and deliver His message to the masses, a reverend just can't know every member of his flock intimately."

Cahill begins to drum his long fingers on the table for a moment as though he is calculating his next move in a game of chess.

"You need to make me a promise. I'll give you what you want if you give me what I want," Cahill says. "I have an important appointment coming up and I could use your support."

"Your parole hearing? Let me guess. You help the police out with information on a child abduction case and this looks favorable with the parole commission."

"I just like to help when I can, especially when it pertains to the welfare of a child," Cahill answers. "Jesus said, 'Suffer the little children to come unto me.' And I will always be there to help a child who is suffering."

"Don't talk about my child suffering."

"I'm going to help you find your child, but I need you to tell the parole commission how helpful I was to you during this most difficult time and that I provided you the spiritual strength you needed to carry on. I know you're close to the chief of police and that detective who arrested me. You need to make them write letters on my behalf as well."

"I'll see what I can do," I lie. "Now give me what I want."

"You're only as good as your word, so God will hold you to that," Cahill says. "Now that we have an agreement, to the matters of your interest. The letters came to me on blue stationery, unsigned and unaddressed. The handwriting was so lovely, just like my mother's own beautiful script."

"Stop wasting my time. Tell me about the letters."

"Your manner is most defiant," Cahill says. "But I have to deal with you, so I will do just that. About a month ago, I started to get letters from a stranger. The letters said you were a sinner who crucified me with your stories. They filled me in on your tragic past about your poor brother and they said you deserved what happened to him."

Cahill stops suddenly and looks up at the ceiling. "Would you like to pray with me?"

"Cut the shit or I'm leaving," I answer. "What did the letters say about Will?"

"The letters said you were selfish. They said you were a dirty, selfish little girl. 'Julia Gooden is a dirty, selfish little whore. Selfish is as selfish does.' That's what the letters said."

Gooseflesh begins to creep up my arms. Logan said one of the kidnappers used those same exact words as they stood over his bed last night.

"What did the letters say about my brother? He was taken thirty years ago. Nothing has been in the news about him for a long time."

Cahill turns his head to the side and looks at me as though he is humoring a silly child.

"Time is an illusion, Miss Julia, but you think it's real. Time is your personal prison. What you think you see if you look backward may seem far behind, but it has come full circle again. The clock keeps ticking on the wall, but nothing has changed. That is because God is karma, He is all, and you will never stop suffering. You've got darkness on the edges of your soul and the stain will never leave you, no matter how much time passes or how far you try to run."

"Tell me what the letters said."

"That you needed to be punished for what you did, that it is your turn to suffer again, just like when you were a little girl."

"If you're screwing with me, I'll come back for you personally. The police will be here to collect those letters into evidence. Expect to be questioned, too. If you withhold any information, forget about your parole hearing."

"The letters are with my attorney, of course."

I dismiss Cahill and hurry to the visiting room's exit to call Navarro. I am almost to the door when Cahill jumps up from his chair and walks briskly to my side. He leans in quickly before I can move out of the way, buries his face into the back of my hair, and inhales deeply.

"It's so nice to smell something sweet and clean again. I'll see you next week," Cahill says pleasantly, as though we've just enjoyed a cup of sweet tea together on his front porch.

I hold back as hard as I can so I don't punch Cahill in the face.

"You're disgusting. Don't ever touch me again."

"I was just being friendly," Cahill answers. He leans against the visiting room wall casually, steeples his fingers together, and looks as though he is studying me with amusement. "You appear to be so tough. But it's all an act, isn't it? Deep inside, you're a scared little girl who is afraid of everything. I can see through your wall. It's a thin façade. This concept of time that you believe in so fervently froze you thirty years ago. You're still that little girl, left all alone and haunted.

The darkness is following you, child, and you can't escape."

I hold Cahill's gaze so he won't notice the goose-flesh on my arms.

"If you get another letter, you call me personally, understand?"

I hurry out of the visiting room, feeling shaken and like I need a shower to cleanse myself from Cahill and make my way through the confines of the prison's sterile concrete hallways.

I hurry to my car and snatch my cell from the glove compartment. One new message. I steel my nerves and press the play button.

"Hey, Julia, it's Navarro. We're all set for the press conference at eleven o'clock. The FBI is also working the case now. Sometimes they're a pain in the ass, but we've got to push hard, so as long as they don't get underfoot, I'll welcome their help. I'm also bringing in Anita Burton to see if she can hit on anything. Anita is usually a last resort, but she's flying out of town this afternoon, and we need to pull out all the stops to find your boy. We'll be at your house when you get through with Cahill. Let's hope he wasn't trying to sell you a line of crap to get back in the spotlight again and actually had a legitimate lead."

I smack my cell phone against the steering wheel in frustration. Navarro's got nothing, and now he's wasting precious time bringing in a psychic.

CHAPTER 6

I used to love the drive to the lake house. When I returned to what was then a weekend-only retreat after an intense Friday at the paper, the stressors of the day gradually dissipated as red-and-white striped barns and slow-moving tractors replaced Detroit's crippled highrises and the aggressive commuters leaning on their horns as they snaked their way through the buckled freeways, which were torn up from too many Michigan winters and not enough money to fix them. In recent days, the boys and I took leisurely drives past the single-room brick schoolhouse with its cast-iron bell and then over to the wooden Shaw Mill covered bridge by the south side of the lake and watched the fly fisherman in their rubber waders try and reel in a walleye or big mouth bass.

But since Navarro and his psychic friend are about to descend on my house without invitation, I tear through the country roads to get home before their arrival. I punch the gas hard as I check the speedometer, clocking in at ninety-five miles per hour. I glance back up for a fleeting second and spot something large and green spilling over the yellow dotted line in the lane in front of me. I slam on the brakes just in time and narrowly miss rear-ending a slow moving John Deere tractor lumbering painfully along at ten miles an hour, tops.

"Come on," I yell. "Get off the road."

I veer into the left lane to pass, and spot a pickup truck speeding right for me. I instinctively jerk the wheel hard to the right and just miss a front-end collision with the oncoming vehicle.

"Damn it," I yell and pound the car horn with my fist. The farmer operating the John Deere gradually pulls into the adjacent cornfield and gestures me to go around him.

I suppress a strong urge to give the farmer the finger and hit the gas hard as I pass him. My speedometer races back up, and the tractor quickly becomes a tiny green dot in my rearview mirror.

"Please let me make it home before them," I pray as I bank the turn into my driveway. No psychic, but David is perched on the top front porch step with his head buried in his hands.

I push my pulsing anger toward Navarro and the psychic aside and surface back up into the horror of my reality. I race toward David with a sense of foreboding panic. As I approach, David raises his head. His green eyes are moist and bloodshot.

"Jesus, what the hell happened?"

"There's nothing new. I just feel so helpless," David answers. "I'm usually the alpha dog, the one who's always in control. But I'm completely powerless right now. I keep seeing this image of Will crying out to me, but I can't save him. I've never thought of killing anyone before, but I swear, when the police find out who took our boy, I'm going to slit their throat. I don't care if I go to jail. They're going to pay for what they've done to our baby."

I feel the ache of relief move through me, realizing there is no immediate bad news that elicited David's emotional response.

"Keep it together," I say softly. "We have to keep fighting and believe Will is all right and he's coming home soon. Make that your focus. Thoughts of revenge are like an opiate. They'll consume you if you let them."

David breathes out hard as if exorcizing a demon.

"I guess you should know that more than anyone," David answers and rubs his hands across his eyes like he is erasing the dark image of Will from his mind and regains his composure. "Okay. We have the eleven a.m. press conference. That's going to help get the word out about Will."

"And a useless psychic before that. Navarro is about to show up here with some big-haired floozy he worked with on a couple of cases. This is a colossal waste of time."

David does his typical lawyer reaction and lets the news sink in for a second before he weighs in on his official opinion.

"I don't think paranormal investigators are necessarily a bad idea," David finally answers. "The officers are looking at every angle to find a suspect and this couldn't hurt. The psychic isn't that Burton woman who is always featured on TV, is she?"

"That's exactly who it is. Anita Burton, the charlatan psychic who always has a camera-ready smile for any member of the media. I was surprised Navarro bothered with Burton until I met her a few times at the police station and saw her flirting with every officer that crossed her path."

"What's her story? Has she ever been accurate?" David asks.

"Burton gained notoriety when a young mother of three went missing. She claimed it was her tips that led the cops to discover the remains of the missing mother deep in the woods, buried a few miles away from her ex-husband's home. Navarro swore Burton's input was dead-on, but then again, I'm pretty sure he and Burton were sleeping together at the time."

"That can skew a man's judgment," David concedes.

I stare down the driveway to search for Navarro's car and feel the prickly annoyance of Burton's pending arrival. Personally, I never gave Burton an ounce of credibility or coverage. Burton called once, asking if I would write a story about her, but I never returned her call. I never trusted psychics. And with good reason. Desperate to find Ben, I foolishly sought the help of a psychic when I was sixteen. She had a tiny storefront along the boardwalk that was dark on the inside except for some suffocated light that somehow made its way through thick purple drapes that hung across the shoebox of the room's only window. In one hand, the psychic asked me to show her the hundred-dollar bill I'd brought along as payment for our session. She told me to close my other hand into a fist and make a wish. I didn't make her guess. I was naïve and blurted out my only heart's desire: to see my brother again. That was all the bait she needed. The psychic swore my reunion with Ben was imminent. In the end, I was out an ill-afforded hundred dollars and I learned never to believe in anything I couldn't back up with facts.

"You're back. How did things go at the prison?" Kim asks as she opens the screen door of the house. Her hands are covered with flour, and she wipes them across the apron I never wear.

"It was fine. I've been to the prison plenty of times. Where's Logan?"

"He's resting in front of the TV. I made him some sugar cookies. I tried to coax him into icing them with me, but he just wasn't interested. Logan is just fine though, I promise. I found some clothes of David's in the closet. I ironed a white shirt and a pair of his blue dress pants for the press conference. I laid them out on your bed and picked out a matching tie. And Aunt Alice just got here to help."

"You don't need to iron for us."

"I put some fresh cut flowers on the kitchen table," Kim continues. "They're beautiful apple blossoms from the tree in your backyard. I thought they might make you feel better. I know these are probably absurd gestures at a time like this, but I want to help, and I don't know how."

"I appreciate everything you're doing," I answer. "Do me a favor though. If Detective Navarro shows up with some big-haired, big-busted woman, don't let them in until I talk to Navarro privately, okay?"

"You're the one who said we had to pull out all the stops to find Will, so let's go through the process at least," David urges me.

"Oh, a psychic. How fascinating," Kim responds with keen interest. "I've read about psychics who've been able to help break cases the police couldn't."

I roll my eyes and head to my bedroom to change out of the same pair of jeans and shirt I've been wearing since yesterday. En route, I pass by Logan and Kim's cousin, Aunt Alice, who are parked on the living room couch. Logan is transfixed by an episode of *SpongeBob SquarePants* playing on the TV, while Alice clicks her knitting needles with precision as she works on something that looks like the makings of a rainbow scarf.

I try and pass by unnoticed, but Alice sees me and jumps up from the couch. Kim said Alice was from Berkeley, California, and she wears the look of a still attractive, aging hippy. Alice is probably mid-fifties, with long grey-blond hair parted in the middle that hangs down to her waist. Alice's Rubenesque figure is almost camouflaged under a shapeless lavender caftan. She approaches me with an uncertain, tight smile and an outstretched hand, and a waft of patchouli oil reaches me before she does.

"I've heard so much about you from Kimmy. I'm sorry about your baby, I hope my being here isn't an intrusion," Alice says in a nervous rush.

"It's fine," I lie and shoot Kim a look.

"Please let me know if there's anything I can do to help. My daughter, Leslie, should be here soon. It takes her forever to get dressed. You know how teenagers are, but once she gets here, Leslie will do whatever you need. Now please tell me the police have a suspect in custody already."

"Thank you and no. The police haven't arrested anyone," I answer.

"Do they have any idea who would want to take your child?" Alice continues. "I've read about these kinds of things happening, but it's just so unbelievable to meet someone who is living such an unthinkable tragedy. I called my women's group at my Methodist church back home, and we have you and your family on a prayer chain."

"That's nice. If you'll excuse me . . ."

"Let me make you a sandwich, dear. I bet you haven't eaten anything since your little boy was taken," Alice says, oblivious to the fact I am trying to escape.

Alice heads toward the kitchen, her plump backside swishing back and forth behind her.

"Aunt Alice, don't you worry. I know you're trying to help, but let's just let Julia get changed. We'll give her a little space," Kim suggests.

"Oh dear. I'm being a nuisance instead of a help, aren't I? Tell you what, I'll just make you that sandwich and I'll leave it on the counter if you want it later," Alice answers and begins to scour my pantry for bread.

"David said a psychic from television is coming here to help find Will," Kim says.

"When I was a girl, a psychic came to town with the carnival," Alice answers while slathering two pieces of wheat bread with mayonnaise. "We lived outside of Grand Rapids then. Kimmy's mother was visiting for a week that summer. We snitched a dollar from my mom's pocketbook to sneak out to the carnival and have the psychic read our palms. My mother caught wind of my thievery and what I'd done with her hard-earned money, and she took a belt to my backside, she did. To this day, I never forgot what she said."

Logan unglues his gaze from the television and looks back at Alice curiously.

"What did your mother say to you?" Logan asks in a small voice tinged with intrigue and just a hint of fear.

"She said psychics were things of the devil, trying to connect the dead back to the living and that I'd opened a door to let the devil slip on in. She scared me so much, I couldn't go to sleep at night without the light on for years after that," Alice recalls.

"Aunt Alice!" Kim responds and motions her head toward Logan.

"Sorry. I'm just a bugger today messing up, aren't I? Leslie is older now and I don't have to watch what I say around her so much anymore. Sorry, Logan."

Logan looks to me for reassurance, his eyes round and worried.

"Why don't you come and visit with me for a minute," I say and grab Logan's hand in mine as we retreat into his bedroom.

Once the door is closed, I sit down on the side of Logan's bed and pat the space next to me.

"How are you doing, buddy?"

Logan casts his eyes to the floor, and I brush a tuft of his dark hair behind his ear.

"Is the devil real?" Logan asks.

"No. Well, I mean, I don't know for sure. I do know there are bad people on this earth, and I'll do my best to protect you from them, but when I'm not around, you need to be very, very careful, especially around strangers."

"Will is dead isn't he?" Logan whispers and looks back at me with eyes that look much older than they did just the day before. "That's why the police are bringing a psychic here."

I grit my teeth and silently vow to throttle Navarro when I see him.

"No. That's not why. Look, I don't really believe in psychics, but I trust Detective Navarro and if he thinks this person can help us find Will, then I guess we better give it a shot. Is that okay by you?"

"You don't think people can talk to the dead?"

"No, I don't."

Logan nods, seeming satisfied with my answer and pops something into his mouth. In his right hand is a bright yellow wrapper with a red stripe down the center and an old-fashioned picture of a little girl wearing a short dress and a bonnet in the corner.

I snatch the wrapper from his hand. The wax paper still smells like peanut butter and molasses taffy, and a once familiar and pleasant memory comes flooding back. The wrapper is from a Mary Jane candy. Ben and I used to buy Mary Janes for a penny at the Lewes Dairy when we were kids. They were my favorite, but after Ben was taken, I never ate one again.

"Where did you get this?"

Logan holds up his index finger to let me know he is still chewing. Finally, he swallows.

"I found it. It was in my treasure box underneath my eagle feather and my magnifying glass. I've never tasted one before. It's really good," Logan says, licking his lips. "I thought Daddy put the candy in the treasure box. He always brings me home surprises when he comes to see me on the weekend."

"Whoever took Will could have planted it. Jesus, let me see your treasure box," I shout.

Logan rushes over to his bookshelf, where he purposely stashes his treasures, high away from Will's curious grasp. I dump the box on his bed and carefully analyze its contents: an eagle feather, a smooth skipping stone, a silver dollar, and what appears to be a dried-up ladybug.

"Do you feel sick?" I ask, satisfied that I didn't find anything else suspect and that Logan is still breathing.

"No. Geez. You scared me," Logan answers.

My paranoid episode is interrupted by a polite knock.

"Sorry to disturb you, but someone named Sarah is on the phone," Kim calls out from the other side of the door. "She says she's your sister? She heard about Will's kidnapping and says she needs to talk to you right away. You never told me you had a sister, Julia."

"Take a message," I answer curtly.

"That doesn't seem very nice."

"Just do it," I answer, already knowing my sharp tone not intended for my friend will hurt her feelings anyway.

I pause a beat and wait for Kim's footsteps to retreat down the wooden hallway floor and pray Logan will have somehow not picked up on Kim's mention of an aunt he's never heard of before. But he's way too smart for that.

"Who's Sarah? Logan asks.

"Someone I used to know a long time ago."

"Aunty Kim said she's your sister."

"This is important. I need to tell you something before you hear it from someone else first."

Logan drops his silver dollar he is studying intently with his magnifying glass and a look of worry settles on his face.

"I was going to tell you about this when you got a

little older, but sometimes things don't happen like you plan. So here goes. When I was little, I had an older brother. His name was Ben."

"You told me you didn't have any family besides Aunt Carol. Did you lie to me?"

My heart starts to break a little and I try again.

"It wasn't that I was trying to keep anything from you. I love you. I was just waiting for the right time to tell you."

"You're scaring me again," Logan says.

"You don't need to be scared. Give me your hand, sweetheart," I say and Logan timidly reaches out and slips his small hand into mine. "Here's the story. I moved in with my Aunt Carol when I was seven, just a little younger than you are now. When I was growing up, my family was different than ours. My parents didn't do the right thing most of the time, and I had a choice to either move in with Aunt Carol or go live with strangers who I didn't think would care for me. I had an older sister. . . ."

"Sarah?"

"Yes, Sarah is her name, but we were never close. When we got older, Sarah got involved in some bad things, and I needed to distance myself from her for my own protection and later for yours and Will's."

"Is Sarah a bad person?"

"You ask tough questions. I haven't seen her in a long time, so I don't know. But the one good thing I had growing up was my brother, Ben, and I loved him more than anything in the whole world when I was a little girl."

"Ben is my middle name. Did you name me after him?"

"Yes. I know he would've loved you very much. You look a lot like him, you know."

"What happened to your brother? Did he die?"

I am not sure how to answer his question. So I simply tell him the truth:

"I don't know what happened to my brother. Sometimes you just have mysteries you have to solve."

"Have you been trying to solve your brother's mystery for a long time?"

"Yes, I have."

Logan pats my hand like a parent trying to comfort a hurt child. I wrap my arms around his thin frame and hug him as hard as I can.

"I'm going to help you find your brother, right after I help you find Will though. Okay?"

"That's a deal."

"Do you think your brother put the candy in my treasure box for me?" Logan asks and retrieves the yellow and red striped wrapper so he can inspect it with his magnifying glass.

"That's a really nice thought, but I'm afraid that's not possible."

"You don't believe in magic?"

"No, I don't. If you can't prove something with facts, then it's not real."

Our conversation on magic's existence ends as Kim begins to rap on the door again, but she doesn't need to tell me what she wants. I can already smell Anita Burton's perfume wafting down the hallway like a pungent calling card. I kiss Logan on the head and hurry down the hall to fend her off, but Burton is already standing in my kitchen, wearing a skirt about two sizes too small and chatting up David in a very friendly tone.

"Where's Navarro? I surely didn't agree to this."

"Hi, Julia. I'm Anita Burton. Ray asked me to help out in your son's missing persons case," Burton answers, extending her hand. "I'm so sorry about what happened to your boy. I'm not sure if Ray told you about me. I've worked with him on numerous high-profile cases. I'm a paranormal investigator."

Paranormal investigator my ass, I think as I consider strong-arming Burton out of my house.

"I know exactly who you are," I answer instead and move past Burton's extended hand to the front door, which I bang open wide for her exit. "I do not need, nor do I want, your help. It's a waste of time, and time is one thing I don't have right now. So if you'll do me a favor . . ."

"Thanks for holding the door for me," Navarro says as he breezes inside the house. I detect just a hint of newly applied cologne as he passes by.

"I need to talk to you. In private," I tell Navarro. I grab his arm and drag him outside in the direction of the backyard patio, where I know we will be out of earshot.

"Julia . . ." Navarro starts, but I cut him off.

"Are you kidding me? You bring your tarty little girlfriend over here right now? This is the laziest example of policing I've ever seen. If I weren't preoccupied with trying to find my missing son, I'd write a story about how the police turned to a psychic less than a day after a child goes missing because they weren't capable of solving the crime themselves."

"Hold on."

"My son was kidnapped last night and this is all

you've got? I expected way better from you, but men always lead with their dicks, don't they?"

Navarro shakes a few fallen leaves from Will's red baby swing, and his jaw settles in a tight line.

"Are you done?" he asks.

"Not even close."

"You're such a pain in my ass sometimes," Navarro grumbles and gives the swing a push. "Before you crucify me, I got your phone message about Cahill's letters. We've already picked them up from the prison, and a forensic scientist is doing a handwriting analysis as we speak. Not to mention the fact that my guys have been busting their asses all morning, talking to every registered sex offender within three hundred miles of your place. We also checked out the list of defendants David gave us who might have been seeking payback from him. Everyone checked out. Three of them are living out of state and have alibis for their whereabouts last night, and the Matthews guy who killed his girlfriend is still serving time over in Carson City."

"What about the people I mentioned from my crime beat?"

"Rojas was murdered a year ago, right after he got out. We're still trying to track down Kate Bramwood, but I got a pretty good lead that she's living in a trailer down on Delmar Street. Russell is going to pay her a visit this morning."

"What about the connection to my brother's case? Did you speak with Detective Leidy?"

"I've bugged the hell out of the detective who investigated your brother's disappearance with fifteen calls back and forth already this morning. And the FBI is now involved. For the first time in my career, I actually asked for their help. We've got at least three days before we get the DNA results on the evidence we found in your house last night, and that's pushing it. Anita Burton may be unorthodox, but I need to use every resource to find your boy in the shortest time possible."

I hold Navarro's stare for a minute and then finally look away.

"What do you have against Burton anyway?" Navarro asks.

"Despite the fact that she slept with a good portion of the police department and a few firemen, I don't trust her. Journalists base their stories on facts, not fictional accounts from beyond. Burton is a publicity hound who capitalizes on desperate people searching for loved ones, longing for reassurance a dead relative is indeed in a better place. She takes advantage of people and makes a buck from their misery."

"Could you just trust me on this one?"

"I don't put my faith in paranormal hacks. Or sluts either."

Navarro takes a step back and cocks his head to the side as though something has finally clicked.

"Holy shit. You're jealous. That's really what this is all about. It's not that Anita Burton is a psychic. You're pissed because we went on a couple of dates."

"You're totally off base here. I'm not jealous and I could care less who you date, so go check your ego. Someone stole my son and we have zero time to piss away and Anita Burton is a colossal waste of time."

Navarro stuffs his hands in his pockets and tries to suppress a smile that begins to curl around his lips. "Remember, Gooden, you were the one who called it off, not me. You wanted the normal life with the nice guy who didn't drink. That's what you wanted, right? No more cops, no more drama."

When Navarro and I first got together, I thought it would be easy to date a police officer. I knew the dangers from my beat. But after Navarro nearly died in a shootout during a drug sting in an abandoned building on Gratiot Avenue, the reality of his work came crashing down on me and a steady ache of worry stayed with me constantly when he was on the job. With David, everything was safe and routine, especially when he moved into private practice. David's white-collar clients didn't come packing to trial or wait in the parking garage with their guns drawn, ready to cap David if he lost their case.

"Right. That's exactly what I have now. A normal life. My son is missing. So, if you'll shut up, I'll go inside and talk to your little psychic friend. But she's got fifteen minutes. That's it."

I brush past Navarro and I feel his hand graze my elbow as he tries to pull me back, but I keep on going to the house without turning around.

"Wait a second. I wasn't trying to piss you off," he calls out from behind.

I ignore Navarro and make a beeline inside the house without offering him another word. David stands in the living room with Burton and breaks away from her as he notices my expression.

"Is everything all right?" David asks as he walks over to my side.

Before I can respond, Navarro puts out his hand for David to shake.

"Haven't seen you in the courthouse for a while.

I'm sorry about your son, but my guys are working hard to bring him home safely."

David disregards Navarro's attempt at a greeting and handshake. Instead, David puts his arm around my shoulder and pulls me close. "If Julia isn't comfortable with this, then we aren't going through with it. I'm willing to keep all options open, but this seems like a long shot and I don't want my wife to be any more upset than she already is."

I look back at David and feel startled over his comment. I realize we are putting up a united front for Will, but David's protective reaction is a surprise and something he hasn't done in years.

"Julia is tough. I already talked to her. She agreed to go through with this," Navarro answers. "And for the record, no one is trying to make her upset, especially me."

I glance between David and Navarro. On the surface, the two men couldn't be more different. David is an Ivy League–trained lawyer whose dad, a retired heart surgeon, lives in a multimillion-dollar home, where David grew up. And Navarro is the only child of immigrant parents whose father is now serving a life sentence in Marquette Branch Prison for first-degree murder. To me, David was the solid-all-around-boy with the most stable future, something I desperately wanted to attain but never thought I could. Navarro was the handsome, passionate guy from the bad part of town whose grandma told him growing up to be proud and ignore the whispers he heard when he walked by. Navarro overcame his childhood to become a good man, although deep down, I believe it's still a struggle for him to accept that. A person's self-imposed sins from the past never really go away. They hang on like an indelible, dirty stain.

A flash of red begins to spike up David's neck, so I intervene before he can open his mouth again and begin to wonder whether his act is genuine or he's merely puffing out his chest over the perceived competition from his wife's former flame.

"It's fine. I agreed to go through with this. I want to keep Logan away though. Can you take him outside to play until Anita Burton is done?" I ask David.

"No. Kim and her aunt can watch Logan. If a psychic is going through my house with the police, I plan to be here."

"Logan is uncomfortable and scared right now and needs one of us with him. I was here last night when the intruders broke in and took Will, and I may be able to offer something. Please, do this for me."

David nods reluctantly and then gives Navarro a thinly veiled glare of hostility.

"Thanks," I tell David and then turn my sights on Navarro. "Fifteen minutes. That's all she's got."

I wait for David and Logan to get outside and away from the upcoming show. When they are out of sight, Navarro begins to lead his psychic friend on a tour, and I tail them just steps behind.

Navarro traces the route he thinks the suspects may have followed, starting with the garage and then down the upstairs hallway to the boys' bedrooms.

"Whoever took Will most likely had been here before," Navarro says. "They knew the layout of the house and the home security code. The suspects disabled the alarm and then pried the garage door window open."

"So, there are two suspects?" Burton asks as her rear end swishes back and forth like a slow-moving pendulum.

"Aren't you supposed to tell us that?" I ask.

"Yes, Julia heard two distinct sets of footsteps running down the hallway toward her kids' rooms," Navarro answers. "The kidnappers went into Logan's room first, but he was hiding under the bed. We aren't sure at this point if they were looking to take both boys or just one. Either way, when they didn't see Logan, whoever was in his room left quickly and headed straight to the baby's room."

"Ray, can you lead me to Will's room?" Burton asks.

I haven't been able to venture back in there since last night. Navarro and Burton disappear inside Will's bedroom ahead of me, but I pause at the door, wondering for a second if I have the courage to actually enter.

"Come on in," Navarro instructs and beckons me with his fingers.

The three steps it would take to walk inside the room feel impossible, but I force myself forward. My natural reporter's instinct fortunately kicks in, and I scan the scene of the crime. The clothes I laid out for Will to wear today are still sitting on the changing table. The outfit is a yellow T-shirt that says BEST LITTLE BROTHER IN THE WORLD, and a pair of blue cotton shorts.

Burton runs her freshly manicured, red fingernails across Will's bookcase and then sits down in the white wicker chair where I read to Will each night before he goes to sleep. I feel a hard lump begin to form in my chest as I recall how we would rock back and forth, Will's green eyes fighting to stay open, until they finally shut tight for the night.

"Your baby's name is Will, correct? That's such a

sweet name. Do you have anything of his that I can touch?" Burton asks me.

I hesitate for a moment, not wanting her to handle anything that belongs to my child. Navarro gives me a stern nod, and I know I have to comply. I pull one of Will's favorite stuffed animals from the bookcase. It's a plush brown puppy with a white spot over its right eye. I reluctantly hand it over to Burton, and she gently squeezes the toy between her fingers.

Burton rises suddenly from the rocking chair, closes the blue gingham curtain across the window with a quick snap, and turns off the Winnie the Pooh lamp on Will's dresser. Now in near darkness, she walks back to the rocker and closes her eyes. Burton sways back and forth and hums in a soothing monotone. I struggle to stay silent through a good five minutes of her nonsense and am about to break when Burton finally snaps out of her internal séance.

"Your son is alive," Burton utters in a voice now tinged with an uncharacteristic rasp.

"Of course he is," I answer.

"Will is nearby, not too far from your house. I see a farm setting with woods that surround the lot and a cherry orchard."

"The entire state of Michigan is cherry country," I answer, clearly annoyed. "That's all you've got?"

Burton disregards my heckling and stays rapt in her self-induced hypnotic state.

"The woods are thick around the property. Will's not in the main house. There's another building. It's older, smaller, and far off in the woods. There's a red star on the roof and a lake running across the back of the property. The person who took Will knows you. There's a deeply disturbed and violent anger that brews inside of them. They did this as payback."

I feel goose bumps spread like tiny pinpricks down my arms.

"Someone else is coming through now. It's a little boy. The child is not your son. This boy is older. Does the letter B mean anything to you?"

"Did you tell her about Ben?" I whisper in Navarro's ear.

Navarro keeps his eyes on Burton and shakes his head no.

"The boy keeps talking about game six of the 1977 World Series. The boy is very agitated. He says he has something very important to tell you. He keeps calling you 'kid.' 'You need to listen to me, kid.' What is it you want to tell Julia?" Burton asks.

I get an overwhelming sensation to run out of the room as fast as I can, but my legs are frozen in place. Just like in a bad dream when a runaway truck is heading straight for me, I am cemented in place, staring at the truck's oncoming, screaming headlights.

Burton lets out a loud gasp, and I feel my hand rush up to my throat as Will's stuffed dog slips through Burton's fingers and lands on the floor.

"There's a darkness coming. It's coming back for you again, Julia," Burton cries out. "You're in grave danger, you and both your children."

CHAPTER 7

This time, I'm not the one who is chasing the story. It's the story that's chasing me.

Press conferences usually are familiar territory. I know how to drill through the canned nonsense from the talking heads on the podium and hammer away at the question until I get a real answer. My sources might not have always agreed with me or appreciated my doggedness, but I earned their respect by always being accurate and fair. So I was the one they called on amidst a sea of raised hands to ask the first coveted question. But this press conference is going to be much different. My professional reputation doesn't mean shit.

As David and I drive to Will's media event in downtown Detroit, I gnaw anxiously on my fingernails, a habit I kicked ten years ago for David, until they are ripped raw and bitten down to the quick. My hands throb over the self-inflicted assault, but Anita Burton's words sting worse. I shove my wounded hands under my legs so David won't see, but he doesn't notice. His eyes are fixed on the straight shot of I-75 that will take us to the police station and the 11 AM press conference where we will be the big show.

David drums his index fingers along the steering wheel in a nervous beat. The repetitive rhythm begins to get under my skin, and I start to feel like a caged animal desperately needing to find an escape hatch.

"What happened with Anita Burton?" David asks, finally breaking the ice between us. "You looked as white as paper when you came out of Will's room."

I swallow my stubborn pride, ready to admit I was wrong about the charlatan psychic, when a digital billboard flashes a giant picture of Will, gap toothed and smiling, across its screen.

"Jesus. It's Will's Amber Alert," I cry out.

Will's face flashes by and I spin around in the seat and stare in longing and shock at the empty wooden back of the billboard frame. All my hard-fought reserve finally gives, and I begin to cry, softly at first, until the scream I had forced to silence finally erupts, and I slam my fist against the passenger side door.

"Hold on. Everything is going to be okay. You told me that, remember?" David says. "The Amber Alert is going to help us. Someone saw Will. Someone out there knows something about his disappearance, and this will remind them and tip their conscience."

I press my cheek against the cool side of the window and force myself back to the other side of sanity.

"That's our little boy up there. Will's face shouldn't be frozen on a highway billboard. He's supposed to be safe and home with us."

"Are you going to be okay?" David asks and reaches his hand across the seat to rub my shoulder.

"I have to be. I've been trying so hard to keep it to-gether. I feel like if I give in too far, even for a second, I'm going to lose it completely and never come back."

"Do you want to talk about what happened with Anita Burton? We can wait if you're not ready."

"No, I do want to talk about it. I have to admit, I made a mistake. I went in to her visit thinking Burton was a major bullshit artist. I witnessed the fine art of the con from my dad and I was so sure Burton was from the same ilk, but she said some things I couldn't explain away."

"Like what?"

"Burton claimed Will is alive. But I know that already in my heart. She also said the boys and I are in grave danger."

I feel the car gradually decelerate as David eases his foot off the gas pedal.

"Why didn't you tell me this until now?"

"Because we haven't had a second alone since Burton left. Plus, I can handle myself, and I won't let any-thing happen to Logan."

"We'll both look out for Logan. But you need to protect yourself, too. Whatever is going on, you're at the core of it. Cahill's letters said you needed to be punished."

"I'm not worried about me," I answer.

"You should be."

"Anita Burton also said some things about my brother."

A silence fills the car for a good ten seconds as David analyzes this new bit of information.

"If Navarro didn't brief her already, Burton could've found old news stories about Ben," David rationalizes.

"I have no doubt Burton researched me and manufactured some highly probable guesses. But there is one thing she couldn't have known. She said a little boy came through and was talking about game six of the 1977 World Series. On the night Ben went missing, he and I talked about whether the Yankees would make it to the World Series that year. Reggie Jackson was a new hotshot on the team, and Ben didn't like him. Not one bit. Ben said the only way Jackson would win his respect was if he nailed a bunch of home runs in the Series."

"Mr. October."

"That's right. The month after Ben disappeared, the Yankees played the L.A. Dodgers in the World Series. Reggie Jackson nailed three consecutive home runs in just three swings during game six, and his unbelievable performance cinched the Series. There's no way Anita Burton could have known about my conversation with Ben from a newspaper article. That was one of the last things Ben and I talked about that night. We're the only two people who know that story, and my brother's been gone for a long time."

"That's hard to explain based just on facts."

"For the past thirty years, I wanted more than anything for Ben to let me know he was okay. Dead, alive, or somewhere in between, I begged him to give me a sign. But he never did. If it was somehow possible, I know Ben would've reached out to me. He loved me more than anything."

"Do you believe what Burton said about Ben?"

"I'd like to, but I can't. I always thought people who believed in that kind of stuff were suckers. But it's funny. I keep getting reminders of my brother all of a sudden.

Right before Anita Burton showed up, Logan found a Mary Jane candy in his treasure box. Did you put it there?"

"It wasn't me," David answers.

"Ben and I loved Mary Jane candies. They were our favorites. After he disappeared, I could never eat one again. I guess I'm the one who's the sucker this time. A little part of me wanted to believe the candy Logan found meant something, that it wasn't random."

"Kim is always sneaking the boys surprises. I bet it was her. But your feelings are understandable. If you look at it from a psychological standpoint, all these sudden reminders of your brother and your childhood could be a string of coincidences linked together that may hold a bigger meaning. Like synchronicity. Carl Jung came up with the concept."

"Enlighten me."

"Jung theorized synchronicity is a significant coincidence of physical and psychological phenomena that are acausal connected," David explains. "Essentially, Jung said synchronicity is the coming together of inner and outer events in a way that can't be explained by cause and effect and is meaningful to the observer."

"That's a lofty explanation."

"Okay. Do you think the coincidences you're experiencing are random or have a greater meaning?"

"Like some sort of cryptic hint from the universe? You know I don't believe in that stuff."

"A lot of people do and there's nothing wrong with that, like Jung did. He believed synchronicity is more likely to occur when a person is in a highly charged state of emotional and mental awareness."

"I'm definitely in a highly charged state right now.

But it makes sense. Anita Burton's reading and the Mary Jane candy are just coincidences. I want to believe they have a greater meaning when they really don't."

As we pass the exit sign for Midtown Detroit, I push away my thoughts about Burton and throw David a curveball.

"I need to make a pit stop before we go to the press conference. Take the next exit."

"What are you doing, Julia?"

"I need to stop by my old newspaper. Don't park in front. I don't want anyone to see me. You can park in the back by Bill's office."

"Bill Gilroy? Your city editor from the paper you worked at when I first met you? Does Navarro know about this?"

"I need to make sure the story about Will's abduction gets as much coverage as possible. So just trust me on this one."

David takes a quick right onto River Street.

"Why Bill?" he asks.

"Because he's the only newsman I can trust right now. I won't be long, I promise."

"You've got ten minutes. I don't want to be late. I hope you know what you're doing here."

"Believe me, I do."

David parks the car in the back of the building, and I consider my carefully calculated decision to leak to Bill the background story on Ben before the press conference. My former city editor will quote me as an unnamed source close to the family so I won't get in hot water with Navarro, who is dead set against publicizing the story about my brother's abduction, at least for the moment anyway. But I know the angle about the possible tie-in with both abductions will generate more interest and emotion in the story. And the bigger the story, the more coverage and the more people who will know about Will's kidnapping. That's what I have to guarantee.

I hustle along the rear of the newspaper so no one will see me until I reach the sole window in the back of the solid concrete building. I look through and see Bill on the phone, red-faced and giving hell to someone on the other end. Bill is a high-strung, aggressive news-man, but underneath his brash exterior, he is a decent soul with a good heart and unlike the way I feel about most people, I trust him.

I rap hard on the window to get his attention. Bill glowers in the direction of the interruption, and his dogged look softens when he recognizes me. He quickly ends his phone call and jumps up from his desk. The back door to the newspaper swings open, and there's Bill looking exactly as I remembered, bald, skinny, and still smelling like an overfilled, dirty ashtray.

"Julia, gosh come on in. To say I'm sorry about what happened to your son would be stupid, so I'm just going to say, I'm sorry. I mean . . ."

Bill is impossibly awkward when it comes to human interaction unless it is a heated debate with an angry source. So I put him out of his quickly growing misery.

"It's okay. You don't have to say anything. I know you feel badly. We'll just concentrate on getting the story out."

"Sounds good. Let's head down to the back office, where no one is going to see you or bother us," Bill says in his usual rapid-fire delivery and takes off down the corridor ahead of me.

As I follow Bill, I peer over the partition into the newsroom. For a second, I am surprised at the longing I feel tugging at me as I look at my old desk. Bill's latest crime reporter is now its current occupant. I stare at the back of the twenty-something young man's head as he huddles over his computer. I feel a pang of righteous indignation as I judge him for camping out in the newsroom instead of hustling out on the street, especially with a breaking story that could go national. But he's most likely a rookie, fresh out of journalism school. Knowing how newspapers are downsizing and compensating with cheap labor these days, the kid is probably making barely enough to pay off his student loans and buy groceries. And the higher-paid newsroom veterans were the first casualties in the series of newspaper lay-offs, so there are very few experienced reporters left to teach him the ropes.

"Jason's a nice kid," Bill says without turning around. I always thought true newspaper people harbored a sixth sense—either that or they are brilliant at making smart deductions based on the human psyche, ego and all. "I'd move him over to the business desk in a heartbeat if I could convince you to come back here."

I let Bill's offer go unanswered. He ushers me into a vacant room that used to belong to the former copy desk chief, Andy Whittington.

"Andy and twenty other poor bastards got axed when corporate decided we had to downsize again because of declining revenues," Bill says and pulls out a cigarette from his back pocket and tucks it behind his ear. "Newspapers are dying and no one cares enough to save them. You took a sabbatical at the right time. Consider yourself lucky."

Bill instantly realizes his faux pas and smacks the top of his bald head with an open palm.

"I didn't mean you're lucky. Your son is missing. Ah, geez."

"Don't sweat it. You got your tape recorder?"

Bill pulls out his old-school notebook and pencil from his shirt pocket instead. I begin to feed him the story about Ben's abduction, and Bill scribbles furiously until each page of his notebook is full.

"Remember, I'm an unnamed source close to the family, right?" I remind Bill.

"Got it. The cops are being tight-lipped with details again, huh?"

"Yes, call it Navarro's filter from hell," I say.

Navarro insisted the cops will control the message at the press conference and answer all questions about the case, but I need to be sure there is full transparency, as long as it doesn't jeopardize Will or the investigation. I know the fine line I need to straddle. I can't let the cops mess this up with the press. My gut tells me Navarro is going to try and spoon feed the media a bunch of useless non-information spun to the point that it means nothing at all. When that happens, the press will find a way around it and write their own story.

I need to be sure I write this one.

I climb back inside the car, and I can already feel the tension from David, who is heated and flip-flops between gunning the engine and slamming on the brakes as he bobs and weaves through city traffic.

"You said you'd be ten minutes, and you were in

there talking to your old boss for almost half an hour," David snaps. "We can't be late to the press conference. How would that look?"

"Like we didn't give a damn about our own kid," I answer. "We won't be late. We'll get there right on time. I just needed to share something with Bill. You need to trust me. I know what I'm doing."

"You can't keep me in the dark about things."

"I told Bill about my brother. I knew if I leaked the possible connection, it would make the story bigger. The bigger the story, the more people who know about Will."

David sighs, and his level of being pissed off at me seems to ease down by a few notches.

"You've got good instincts with the media. I trust you on that."

I stare at the scene outside the car window and realize my dad inadvertently taught me the fine art of the con. Three blocks away from the police station, the streets are starting to line up with media vans. It's becoming a full house, including reporters from CNN, the *Detroit Free Press*, Fox News, *The Detroit News,* and TV crews from other major networks. My gamble paid off. A missing child's story is big. But the news of Ben's abduction that Bill posted on his paper's website just twenty minutes earlier elicited an immediate frenzy and added even more drama and interest to the news hook, leaving the other members of the press scrambling to cover the story.

"Thank God Kim is at home watching Logan," I say.

With a big story, most reporters would do anything

for an exclusive with a member of the grieving family, including cornering a scared eight-year-old if need be.

Detective Russell spots David and me and waves us toward the podium, where a dozen or so television, print, and radio reporters are jockeying to set up their microphones and digital recorders. The TV cameramen and photographers line up like an army of diligent ants on either side of the stage and fight for a position to nab their best shot.

"Remember, don't answer any questions, Julia," Detective Russell says. "Any member of the press asks you a question, you defer to Navarro or the chief. Got it?"

Now that his marching orders to us are delivered, Russell barrels toward the stage, and David and I fall behind.

"That's Julia Gooden. She's the mom, and the man in front of her must be the missing kid's father. See if you can get the shot of them walking in before anyone else gets it," a local anchor from Channel 3 calls out to his cameraman.

David grabs my arm and starts to steer me away. I turn my face from the news camera and move quickly toward the podium. I reach the stairs of the police precinct when a familiar voice from the crowd makes me pause.

"Julia, wait!" I turn my head toward the voice, which rings distinctive against the din of the crowd, and spot a woman who is elbowing her way in my direction.

"Come on," David calls out. "This place is a madhouse."

I ignore David's directive and do a quick study of the female trying to get my attention. From a distance, she is very pretty, but as she approaches, I can see she is aged a bit beyond her years, probably from too much hard living, a telltale look I know all too well from the drunks and addicts I encounter routinely on the police beat. I start to turn back to the podium but freeze in place when I finally recognize the stranger.

"Please, Julia. Wait! It's me, Sarah."

I stare back at my sister, my feet feeling like lead weights, as she nears. It's been eight years since I last saw Sarah. And I vowed at the time I would never see her again.

"Thank God. I've been trying to reach you, but you won't return my calls," Sarah says as she pushes her way to me and tries to lean in for a hug. "I'm so sorry about your baby. Will is his name, right? I've just been sick to my stomach over what you're going through. Is there anything I can do to help?"

My body stiffens against Sarah's attempted embrace.

"No. If you've come to ask for money, I'm not going to give you any this time."

"That's not why I came," Sarah protests. "I wanted the chance to apologize for what I did. And then I found out about your boy. My trip here obviously happened for a reason. Everything happens for a reason, don't you think? Let me help you. I'll do whatever you need."

"I don't think everything happens for a reason. Things are either random or carefully calculated, and I'm betting, with you, it's the latter. I don't need your help and I don't know why you're here. But this is not the time or the place for your dysfunctional reunion."

"You can't say that. I'm your family."

"I have my own family now, and they won't hurt me."

"Please. You just need to give me a chance. I'm different now."

"I remember what you did. Get out of here, Sarah, and don't come near my family or me again. That's the last warning I'll give you."

Sarah continues to stare back at me as her fingers clasp a gold cross necklace that plunges deep into her scant cleavage. I break our uncomfortable tableau, turn my back on my sister, and climb up the precinct stairs.

"Over here," David calls and beckons me to the center of the stage.

I follow in his direction and notice the talking heads are starting to gather at the podium, including Navarro. We lock eyes, and he barrels past the police press secretary in my direction.

"How're you doing?" Navarro asks.

Navarro has changed into a dark suit and tie instead of his usual attire of jeans, motorcycle boots, and well-fitting, long-sleeved T-shirts pushed up to his elbows.

"I'm fine. We've got a good crowd here. Let's do this."

Chief Linderman strides through the front door of the police station wearing a blue pinstripe suit and a pair of aviator sunglasses. Linderman pulls the sunglasses down the bridge of his nose and squints at the almost noon-day sun.

"I always say not to hold a press conference at this time of day because the damn sun gets in my eyes. But we can't have the sun to our backs because it will mess up the lighting for the photographers and TV camera crews, right, Julia?" Linderman asks.

"Something like that, Chief."

"I hope you and David and Logan are all right."

"Yes, sir, we are just focusing on getting our boy back," David answers.

"Well then, let's get started. Here's how this is going to go down. I'll debrief the press and then Navarro and I will take any questions. Being a reporter, I know your instinct is going to tell you to talk to the press, Julia, but let us handle it. We don't want to do anything to jeopardize the investigation. If we put out too much information, it could backfire, and I know you wouldn't want that to happen."

Once Linderman lays out the foundation, he takes his place of authority directly behind the podium. David and I move to the far right of the makeshift stage, and Navarro flanks Linderman on his left.

"Good morning, everyone. As most of you know, last night at approximately ten p.m., a two-year-old boy was abducted from his home. The boy's name is Will Tanner," Linderman starts.

A picture of Will, blond and smiling with the prominent gap showing between his two front teeth, pops up on a screen behind us. It's the same picture from the Amber Alert. The photo tears through my heart, but I look away so I won't break down. David grabs my hand, and I close my eyes tightly for ten seconds and then force myself to open them.

"Will Tanner has blond hair, weighs approximately thirty pounds, and is thirty-two inches tall. He has a birthmark that looks like a strawberry on the back of his head," Linderman continues. "He was last seen wearing a pair of yellow pajamas with a giraffe on the lapel. The police department is working hard to bring Will back to his family, and we're asking anyone to come forward with any information they may have regarding this child's disappearance."

As anticipated, a few reporters look my way, and I can hear the rapid snap of cameras clicking, the photographers behind the lens hoping to capture the shot of the grief-stricken mother breaking down.

"We're offering a reward," I blurt out, the announcement unexpected even to myself.

Linderman turns around and raises one "what the hell are you doing?" eyebrow at me. Navarro and I hadn't discussed anything about a reward, and I know I am breaking protocol, but I don't care. I need to up the ante.

"My husband and I are offering a fifty-thousand-dollar reward to anyone who can give us information that leads to Will's safe return," I say.

Linderman clears his throat loudly and starts again. "As I was saying, we're asking people who know anything about this child's disappearance to come forward. We have a tip line for anonymous callers who don't want to be identified. Now, are there any questions?"

An audience full of hands flies up.

"I'll ask the officer in charge of this case, Detective Raymond Navarro, to join me for your questions," Linderman says.

"Chief, was this a home invasion?" the reporter from *The Detroit News* asks.

"We can't comment on that right now," Linderman answers.

I open my mouth to say something, but David squeezes my hand and I reluctantly stay quiet.

"Julia Gooden, you're a reporter, correct?" a CNN reporter asks me directly.

"Yes, that's right," I answer.

"A local media outlet is citing an unknown source who confirms your brother was also abducted when he was a child. Your son's abduction last night marks the thirtieth anniversary of your brother's kidnapping, according to the source. Are there any leads that indicate these two cases are related?"

Navarro shoots me a sideways glance of death that I don't acknowledge.

"We can't comment as this is an ongoing investigation," Navarro says.

"Do you have any suspects you're locking in on? How about family members?" the reporter from *USA Today* asks.

"As we've said, we can't comment on that right now as this is an ongoing investigation," Navarro answers.

Navarro's bullshit no-response makes it sound like David and I are involved. The cops always look at family members first, and now so will the media. I gaze out at the crowd of press and notice they seem to stare at David and me with greater intensity.

The *Detroit Free Press* reporter goes next. "Julia, I understand you paid a visit to Reverend Casey Cahill in prison today. Can you verify this and tell me what your meeting was about?"

Navarro looks back at me again, and I hold his stare. I didn't leak this. It must have been the prison guards, but the more the press knows, the more information will go out about Will's abduction. So as far as I'm concerned, Navarro can screw it.

"As Detective Navarro and I have mentioned, any interviews or specific activity relating to this case cannot be commented on since it's an ongoing investigation," Linderman replies.

I inch in closer to Linderman until I am sure the media can hear my voice loud and clear.

"Thank you for coming out today. My name is Julia Gooden. My married name is Tanner, and I am Will Tanner's mother. Last night, at approximately 10 p.m., at least two people broke into my home and took my son. I was downstairs at the time and Will was asleep in his bed. By the time I got upstairs, the intruders were gone. They took my child."

"Julia," Navarro barks and begins to move toward me. But I won't be censored.

"Whoever broke into my home left evidence at the scene, including a hard-pack box of Marlboro Lights cigarettes. The police are conducting a DNA analysis on a hair found at the scene and analyzing other personal effects of Will's that may have been handled by the intruders. To answer your other questions, yes, my brother Ben, Ben Gooden, was abducted in 1977. He was nine years old at the time. We lived in Sparrow, Michigan. His case remains unsolved, and the police are looking into whether there is any kind of connection between the disappearance of my brother and son. One significant link is an Indian arrowhead. Police discovered an arrowhead under my brother's bed thirty years ago and an Indian arrowhead was also retrieved under my son's crib last night."

Navarro has a hold of my arm now, but I keep going.

"To answer the *Detroit Free Press* reporter's question, yes, I did pay a visit to Casey Cahill today. The former reverend contacted the authorities claiming he had information about my son's abduction. The police are determining whether or not these claims are valid. Cahill says he received letters from an anonymous person who could've been a member of his congregation. These alleged letters name me specifically, and it sounds like the author has a vendetta against me."

Navarro is now digging his fingers deeply into my arm, and it hurts like hell.

"We don't know if these letters are even legitimate yet," Navarro interrupts.

I ignore him and keep on going.

"I am asking, as a mother of a beautiful little boy who was snatched from his home and his family, that if anyone has information regarding this case, they will come forward," I say and then stare straight directly into the TV cameras. "And if the person who took my son is watching, know this. I will find you."

The crowd of reporters begins to bark questions in unison as Navarro locks his arm around my waist and steers me away from the podium and toward the police station entrance. Linderman is close behind, saying choice words intermingled with my name under his breath, and the police press secretary is left at the podium to play clean up.

We arrive just outside the doors of the police department lobby and then Navarro erupts.

"What in the hell are you doing? You can't give the press too much because it's going to blow the case," Navarro yells. "Jesus Christ."

"What am I doing? What are you doing? What was the point of your press conference if you had no news to share? That was the lamest thing I've ever seen."

"I should've known you'd pull something like that," Navarro answers. He opens the right side of his suit coat and extracts his cell phone from his hip as it begins to buzz.

"I'm not through with you," Navarro growls and puts the phone to his ear.

Navarro keeps a firm grip on my arm as he listens to the caller on the other end of his phone. His grasp eases slightly as he seems to possibly get an answer he wants.

"He's on the way down to the station? Good work. I'll get the search warrant for his property. But if you detect any signs of the kid, just move, understand?" Navarro tells the caller before hanging up.

"What just happened?" I ask.

"We picked up a sex offender. The guy lives in South Lakeport, just a couple towns over from your lake house. Turns out he lived in Sparrow when your brother went missing. I had a feeling the cases were connected, and I'm betting we just found the guy who took your brother and son."

CHAPTER 8

I hasten my pace to keep up with Navarro's fast-moving trail through the police station reception area, which is filled with a few defense-attorney-looking types who wait impatiently to get buzzed inside to buffer their clients.

"Hold on," I call out, but Navarro just keeps moving. "Let me be there when you talk to the suspect. I could be an invaluable resource. If this guy did take Will and my brother, no one is going to know the backstory, or if he is lying, better than me. Why waste the time?"

"Not a chance," Navarro answers. His back is still to me as he moves toward the glass security door that will lead him into the heart of the police station, where I need to be.

"You're making a critical mistake. You try and sweat the guy for what, an hour or two, and you get nothing. I don't have to be in the interview room with you. I can be on the other side of the glass, confirming what you need to know. You need my help."

Navarro finally slows down and wipes away a few beads of sweat that are beginning to glisten on his forehead. He tosses his jacket on a chair, and begins to hunt through his coat pocket for his security badge.

"What an idiot I am to wear a black suit coat in the noonday sun," Navarro says, and fishes his plastic ID out of his breast coat pocket.

"Will's been missing for fourteen hours now. We're running out of time. Come on. You can't shut me out."

"Do you think I'm stupid? I trusted you, and you sold me out. You made me look like an ass in front of my boss, not to mention the fact you may have leaked critical information about the case," Navarro growls.

"The more information the press has, the better. They need to know the details. You work the press to your advantage."

"You don't get it, do you? Journalists are all about transparency, but you need to get your head out of your ass and realize we don't tell you things for a reason. I hope you don't find this out the hard way."

"It wasn't about transparency. And I'm not a journalist right now."

"Yes, you are. Once a journalist, always a journalist. You're lucky we have a suspect in for questioning, or you would be in deep shit."

"I'd tell you I'm sorry, but I'm not. I'm desperate, and I don't know what other stops I can pull out here."

I realize I'm playing the sympathy card, but I don't care about being manipulative in this situation. And my move seems to be working. The crease between Navarro's brow gives, and his expression softens just enough for me to know I may have found my way in.

"Okay. Just don't pull any more crap like that again,"

Navarro says. "But let me be clear. No watching the interview. There's no way I'd let you do that."

"What's the suspect's name?"

"You're going to continue to be a pain in my ass, aren't you? You get nothing more from me unless I have something concrete to tell you or I need you to verify something this guy says."

"What about . . ." I start.

"Nothing," Navarro replies. He turns his back to me and waves his security badge in front of the thick glass door leading into the precinct's inner sanctum, where the suspect waits.

"Navarro," I plead, but my voice gets muffled as the security door automatically closes behind him.

I pull out my phone to text David to let him know I may be a while. Before I can hit the send button, Pamela Murphy, the records clerk, walks into the lobby fresh from her lunch break. Pamela is a good-natured woman in her mid-fifties with an outdated Farrah Fawcett hairdo shellacked in place by superior hold hairspray and a grating voice like Betty Boop's. For someone who works in a police department, she is surprisingly trusting, of me at least. Pamela inadvertently leaked to me information on numerous stories in the past, and I surely didn't stop her. I watch Navarro through the glass partition as he disappears around the hallway corner to the interview room and realize if I ever needed to work Pamela, now is the time. As she approaches, I stand directly in front of the door so she can't help but notice me.

Pamela stops in her tracks when she sees me and leans in close as she gives me an unsolicited and equally uncomfortable hug.

"Julia, honey. Oh my goodness, I've been so worried about you," Pamela says in her whiny soprano, as she thankfully pulls away. "You and your family have been in my prayers. If there's anything I can do, you just let me know."

"Thank you. I appreciate it. I've been waiting on Navarro for almost half an hour. He was supposed to get me the suspect's file in my son's case. I'm afraid he got caught up in the interrogation and forgot."

"Everyone is busy trying to find your little boy."

"Right, but Navarro said it was important I look at the file to see if I can recall anything about the suspect. My older son, Logan, is at home, and he's just beside himself without me there so I need to take care of this as quickly as possible. Is there anything you can do to help me? I won't take long. I promise."

"Well, if Navarro was going to get you those files, then it should be just fine, sweetheart. Tell you what, you can sit at my desk and look at the file on my computer."

I hold my breath, waiting for someone to call my bluff until we pass through the security door and head down the first hallway to Pamela's office. I search for Navarro but feel reassured I should be able to slip in unnoticed since he's already in the interview room drilling the suspect.

"Now you just sit right down here and rest your weary bones," Pamela says and pats the seat of her office chair.

I finally exhale and sit down at Pamela's desk, which is cluttered with framed photographs of a bedraggled-looking schnauzer wearing a set of antlers and a red holiday sweater.

"That's my Bernie. Isn't he cute? Let me just log in,

honey. They made us change our password recently," Pamela says as she clicks the keyboard with her acrylic, French-manicured fingernails. "There you go. Take your time. I'm just going to go down to the break room and get myself some coffee. How about I bring you back a cup?"

"No thanks. This is a huge help, and I'm sure Navarro is going to appreciate it."

"Glad to help. I don't have kids myself, but I can only imagine what you're going through."

"Can you do me one more favor and shut the door behind you? This may be emotional and I'd like some privacy."

"Of course. You just tell Pamela here if you need anything else," Pamela answers and closes the door behind her.

I swing the chair around toward Pamela's computer and realize my palms are sweating in anticipation. I rub my hands across my pants and try to steady them as I click on the suspect's file.

"Who are you, you bastard?" I ask as a mug shot of Archie J. Parker pops up on the screen.

Just from the photo, I can tell Parker is the type of guy who would make a mother go on high alert if she saw him anywhere near her child. Parker is a seedy-looking man on the other side of middle age with a greasy, dirty-blond comb-over and pitted skin, probably from a combination of acne and years of chronic smoking or addiction. I try and scrutinize every detail and nuance of his picture, from his small, close-set, brown eyes to a jagged scar that zigzags across his chin. But no matter how hard I study Parker, I can't place him from my past or my present.

The only thing I do recognize is Parker's current address. South Lakeport is just a ten-minute drive away from my house. My breathing begins to quicken as I search through Parker's file, mining for any clues or connections that could link him to Will and my brother.

I hunt through the basic information first. Parker is fifty-eight years old, five-foot-ten, and a hundred and eighty pounds. He goes by the alias A.J.

"What are your priors?" I ask Parker's mug shot and then flip to the next tab in the file, which shows Parker worked up quite a sizable record, starting out with nickel-and-dime drug charges and then graduating to the hard stuff and crimes against minors. In 1972, Parker was arrested in Port Huron for possession of drug paraphernalia. By 1974, he'd served time for drug possession and indecent exposure. In 1975, he racked up more drug charges for methamphetamine and heroin possession and lewd and lascivious acts with a child under fourteen. Parker completed parole in 1976, the year before Ben was taken.

I sift through the remaining files and notice a big gap following his '76 parole. From there, Parker was under the radar for sixteen years, doing God knows what. His next arrest wasn't until 1992 for drunken driving, drug possession, and four counts of improper photography or video recording of a minor. The victim, a boy, was nine, the same age as Ben when he went missing.

I stare back at Parker's mug shot with unbridled rage. "I swear to God, if you did anything to my son, I'll kill you."

My threats halt as a pair of high heels clicks down the hallway in my direction.

"She's right in my office," Pamela says from just outside her office door.

I realize she's got to be talking to Navarro and he's going to throw me out of the police station if he doesn't kill me first. I fumble to grab the computer mouse, but in my haste, I accidentally knock it to the floor and the computer screen simultaneously freezes with Parker's mug shot plastered across it. The office door swings open, and Navarro storms in with his hands on his hips like some old-time western where the sheriff is about to pull a gun on the bad guy, and this time, the bad guy is me.

"I was just . . ." I stammer, having no idea what I'm going to say next.

Navarro glowers at the frozen computer screen and Parker's mug shot, and shakes his head. I brace for impact, but Navarro throws me a surprise curveball instead.

"Come with me. I need your help," he says.

Navarro leads me to an empty office across from the interview room and gestures me to sit. He holds a manila envelope under his arm.

"I see you've already familiarized yourself with the suspect," Navarro says.

"Archie Parker."

"That's right. He goes by A.J. Real dirt bag. He's been out of trouble for a while until now," Navarro explains. "It's too much of a coincidence—this guy comes from Sparrow like you did and now he lives just a couple towns away from your house and your boy going missing."

"If this A.J. did take Ben and Will, what's the connection besides me? Like you said, why would he come back now after all these years?"

"Good question. We searched Parker's house. There's no sign of Will, but Parker could've stashed him somewhere else as a precaution. We did find some kiddie porn and a bunch of photographs of kids hidden in Parker's closet."

"Jesus."

"Don't worry. We didn't find any photos of Will. The pictures are old Polaroids. From the condition of the pictures and the outfits the kids were wearing, I'd say the shots were taken sometime during the 1970s."

Navarro extracts the manila envelope from under his arm and places it on the desk in front of me. "I need you to take a good look at these pictures and tell me if you recognize anyone or anything. Are you up for this? These are pictures of kids."

"I understand."

"I've been a cop for almost fifteen years, but I still have a thin skin when it comes to crimes against children," Navarro says and pushes the envelope across the table in my direction.

I stare at the yellow rectangle and grapple with a reporter's fascination and a mother's dread of what awaits inside. I pull back the edge of the envelope slowly and remove each photo, one by one. I place them face down on the table in front of me until all eight are lined up in a row like playing cards in a game of solitaire.

I breathe out hard, drag the first Polaroid across the table, and turn it over. The first Polaroid is a color photo of a little girl posing on the beach next to a sandcastle. The girl is smiling. She has red curly hair and is probably around seven years old. The redheaded girl is missing her two front teeth and she wears a turquoise and white polka-dot two-piece bathing suit.

I look up at Navarro and shake my head as a sense of relief washes over me. I steady myself, feeling a bit more confident, and turn over the second picture. But my instincts are wrong and my hands tremble as I clutch the image before me. The second photo is a picture of the same little redheaded girl, but this time she's naked and holding a Raggedy Ann doll, which she uses to try and cover up her genitals. The redheaded girl stands frozen against the backdrop of a mirrored closet, her eyes are wide, and she bites her lip as if she is trying to keep herself from crying. In the mirror, I notice a reflection of a man who is holding a camera in one hand and his erect penis in the other.

"Do you know her?" Navarro asks.

"God. No."

"Keep going."

"I hate this, Navarro."

"I know."

I force myself to turn over the next picture. Polaroid number three is a photo of a little boy who is maybe ten. The child's hair is white blond against his summer-tanned, freckled skin. The little boy rides atop a white carousel horse with a bright blue and yellow saddle. The child waves to the camera with a shy, reluctant smile.

"You recognize that boy?" Navarro asks.

I shake my head.

"Okay. Five more photos," Navarro says. "Let's go."

I feel for a second like I'm playing some kind of perverted Russian Roulette, not knowing if the next image is going to be a blank or a bullet. I feel a sickness grow in my stomach as I slowly turn over the next Polaroid.

Picture number four is a bullet. It's the same blond, lanky boy. His skinny bare limbs look fragile and posed as he lays naked on a thin, dirty mattress that sits across what looks like a concrete basement floor. The blond child looks away from the camera this time, probably praying to God that his parents will arrive any minute to rescue him from Parker's hell. The Raggedy Ann doll is back in this picture and the toy rests against the bottom of the boy's stomach. The Raggedy Ann has been turned upside down and its stringy red hair splays across the child's penis. I let the photo slip from my fingers and look away toward the door.

"Do you know the boy in the picture?" Navarro asks.

"No," I answer and begin to stand up. "I don't want to do this anymore."

Navarro rests his hand on my shoulder and gently pushes me back down.

"Take your time. I need you to do this. And you know you need to do this, too."

Polaroid number five. I softly run my fingers across the back of the instant-still image. I count to ten and turn the Polaroid over, and my breath leaves my body. Captured forever inside the tiny square, a boy and girl walk in the distance along a boardwalk. The two children stand at the entrance of a large building with a giant picture of a white-faced clown with a tiny hat sitting cockeyed on top of its bald head. The boy in the picture is tan and lean. He has jet-black hair and wears a bright red short-sleeved shirt. The boy is holding the hand of the younger girl, who is wearing a thin pink and white striped jumper.

"Who are these kids?" Navarro asks.

"God. It's Ben and me. We were at Funland. I don't have a picture of the two of us. My mom and dad either lost any old photos or threw everything away when they left," I respond in a barely audible whisper.

Navarro realizes I am veering toward the razor-thin edge of a breakdown. He leans down behind me, and I can feel his face brush against the back of my neck.

"You can do this, Julia. I know you can."

"Okay."

"Where is Funland? Is that in Sparrow, where you grew up?"

"Yes. When we were kids, Ben and I thought Funland was the greatest place on earth. We never had any money growing up—Ben would pick up odd jobs over the summer. He was such a scrappy kid. He'd go door to door, asking if anyone needed any chores done. If he got any jobs, he'd take all the money he earned and treat me to a day at Funland. That day was the last time I went there."

"How old are you in the photo?"

"Seven. Ben is nine. I remember that day like it was yesterday. It was Labor Day, 1977."

"Are you sure? That was thirty years ago."

"I know that as a fact. That was the day Ben went missing."

"Good, Julia. Real good. Three more photos to go."

"If there are any pictures of Ben naked like those other kids, tell me now. Don't put me through that."

"I'm not trying to do anything to you. Just look at the next picture. Please."

Photo number six. I drag it across the table and turn it over and feel a rush of relief and a pang of bittersweet sentimentality. This Polaroid is a photo of Ben and me playing skee-ball at Funland. Ben has a determined look on his face, like he will be damned if he doesn't get the ball to land in the mouth of the highest scoring hole. I stand at Ben's side, staring at him with rapt admiration.

"That photo is from the same day?" Navarro asks.

I nod in silent affirmation.

Navarro pushes the last two photographs directly in front of me. "Whenever you're ready."

My right hand trembles slightly, and I flex my fingers over the seventh Polaroid until the shaking stops. I flip the picture over quickly and stare at an image of Ben and me standing in front of the library on Michigan Avenue. I shudder as I watch the worst day of my childhood unfold like stills of a movie through Parker's eyes.

"That's from the same day. We stopped in front of the library. We were running away from this bully who tried to pick a fight with Ben at Funland. If these came from Parker's house, he was following us," I realize.

"Excellent. Last picture."

Polaroid number eight. I flip it over and immediately recognize Beach Boulevard. In the photo, our backs are to the camera as we walked along in the distance.

"My brother and I were walking home along Beach Boulevard that afternoon."

"Do you remember anything unusual about that walk home? Did anyone approach you?"

"Yes. I was tired. A man in an old Cadillac pulled up next to us and asked if we needed a ride."

"The man in the green Caddy," Navarro repeats, remembering our conversation from this morning.

And then a thirty-year-old memory finally clicks in place.

"I know who A.J. Parker is. I need to watch the interview."

Navarro leads a path to the other side of the interview room and leaves to retrieve Parker. I realize Parker hasn't been formally charged yet, but I can't muster an ounce of objectivity, especially after seeing the Polaroids of Ben and me and the other children whom he obviously abused. I stare through the two-way mirror at the interview room, and a shiver runs through me as a memory of my time on the other side of the glass comes through.

"You've been drinking, Mrs. Gooden?" a moonfaced, young detective asked my mother, who was slumped next to me as we sat side by side along a cheap plastic table in the St. Clair Sheriff Department's interview room.

"Just a glass of wine with dinner, that's all," my mother slurred. "I'm just so tired. Is it all right if I lay down for a minute?"

"That's fine. Do you give your consent for us to ask Julia some questions?"

"Yeah, sure. Do what you want. But don't come crying to me when you figure out you've been wasting my time and yours. My kid probably took off. He'll be back tomorrow morning. You'll see."

"Ben wouldn't run away. He'd never do that!" I protested.

"Don't you back-talk me, girl," my mother's voice soared. She tried to take a menacing step in my direction but lost her equilibrium and grabbed the side of the interview table in a loose, drunken grip to regain her balance.

The detective motioned to his partner. He spoke in a quiet voice, but I could still hear what he said.

"Take the mother to the drunk tank and let her sober up before we interview her. We should book her for now on child endangerment charges for leaving her kids in the middle of the night so she could hit the bars."

I sat small and alone in a cold metal chair and watched helplessly as one of the officers took my mother's elbow and steered her out of the room.

"She'll be better in a little while. She always is. She'll be plenty worried about my brother then. I know it," I said.

"We'll talk to your mom later after she starts to feel better. My name is Detective Baty. I'm going to ask you some questions about what you remember. Do you think you can do that for me?"

"Yes, sir."

Baty was a short, muscular man with a square jaw and military-style crew cut. His knees cracked as he squatted down so we were at eye level.

"I know you must be scared, but anything you can tell me may help bring your brother back. So, let's start from the beginning and see what you can remember. You and Ben share a room, right?"

"*Yes. My older sister, Sarah, got the room by her-self. Is she here, sir?*"

"*The oldest kids always seem to get their way. Yes, Sarah is here. We'll interview her shortly.*"

"*Can she come in here with me?*"

"*How about you and me just talk right now. I want you to do something for me. I need you to close your eyes. Do you think you can do that?*"

I respectfully obeyed.

"*I need you to concentrate and see a picture in your mind of what happened. What do you remember after you and Ben fell asleep? Can you see it?*"

"*I remember waking up in the closet. I called out for my brother. When he didn't answer, I came out, but he wasn't in his bed. Then I ran into my mom's room.*"

"*Do you sleepwalk?*"

"*No. I don't think so.*"

"*Okay. So you get to your mom's room. What do you remember after that?*"

"*My mom wouldn't wake up. She was lying in bed and she was snoring real loud. She looked kind of weird.*"

"*What do you mean?*"

"*She had her shoes on, and her sweater wasn't buttoned right. She wasn't wearing any pants or under-wear. I've seen her like that before though.*"

"*Your dad wasn't home?*"

"*No. He was away again.*"

"*Do you think anyone had been in the room with your mom? Like a stranger she might have met while she was out?*"

"*I don't know. I didn't see anyone in her room. I re-member . . . wait. There was something I saw on her nightstand. I don't think I'd ever seen it before.*"

"You're doing good, Julia. What did you see?"

"It was like a picture or something. Somebody drew it. It scared me."

"Tell me what it was."

"I didn't like it. It was like a giant bird with wings, but it had legs like a man and red glowing eyes, but the eyes weren't right. They weren't in the bird's head. They were drawn in where a person's chest would be."

The door to the interview room swung open, and Baty's partner handed him a piece of paper. I recognized the picture on it. It was my dad's mug shot.

The officer leaned in toward Baty and spoke in an almost-whispered tone. "The dad has a record. Mostly nickel-and-dime stuff. But he has an outstanding felony warrant for writing bad checks. Also, one of our crime scene guys just lifted one of those Indian arrowheads from underneath the Ben kid's bed."

I resurface as Russell leads Parker into the interview room. I push the thirty-year-old memory out of my mind and focus on the suspect. Parker is a slouched ruin of a man and has the same thick sideburns I remember from thirty years ago. He slumps lazily in the interview chair with his legs sprawled out casually in front of him, as if he doesn't have a care in the world. Parker's clothes are filthy. His putty overalls are covered with brown stains, and clumps of fresh dirt cling to his work boots. Navarro's partner, Russell, sits in the chair across from Parker and tries to stare him down. But Russell's try at an intimidating gaze doesn't seem to faze Parker in the least.

Navarro barges through the interview room door and

places a can of soda in front of Parker, who quickly grabs it and slugs back its contents.

"Hey, go easy there. We've got plenty more in the vending machine," Navarro says.

Parker takes the now-empty can and crushes it with one hand.

Navarro moves in closer to Parker and begins to bat his hand back and forth in front of his nose. "Phew. Catch a whiff of you, farm boy. What's that, manure on your shirt? Don't believe in showers or detergent, huh?"

Parker looks up at Navarro and reciprocates with a nasty sneer. "I was out working in the field when you guys showed up. I didn't have time to get all pretty for you."

"That's a big farm you got up there in the country. Plenty of room to hide a kid," Navarro accuses.

Parker's legs retract from their previously sprawled position, and he snaps to attention until he sits ramrod straight in the metal chair.

"What do you mean by that?" Parker asks in a defensive tone.

"So, is it little boys or little girls you prefer these days? Or don't you care?" Navarro continues. "Just as long as they're young. You don't have an age limit, right? It's the hardcore ones who go after babies and toddlers though."

"I don't know what you're talking about. I didn't take any baby. And I don't touch kids. I served my time. I was rehabilitated. I don't do that stuff anymore."

Parker digs at his greasy head nervously and then pushes up his shirtsleeve, exposing the money shot.

It's the Woodstock tattoo, the bright yellow ink now faded to a tired mustard hue on the wrinkled skin of Parker's forearm. The tattoo is the same one I saw thirty years ago on the Cadillac driver's arm.

"Where were you at ten p.m. last night?" Navarro asks.

"I was with my sponsor. I went to an AA meeting at the Church of the True Believers, and then we had a cup of coffee at the diner up the street. You can ask him. My alibi is solid."

"Write down your sponsor's name and address," Navarro says, and pushes a pen and notepad across the table in Parker's direction.

Parker stares at the paper for a long moment. He grabs the pen between his thick, awkward fingers, scribbles down the information, and hands it to Navarro.

"The Church of the True Believers? Isn't that the former Reverend Casey Cahill's church?"

"I have no idea. I don't know who that is. It's the closest meeting from my house is all," Parker answers.

"Do you smoke?" Navarro asks and pulls out a hard pack of Marlboro Lights cigarettes, the same brand as the one found at my house last night. Navarro leaves the open pack on the table.

"I quit smoking a long time ago," Parker answers.

"You like to hunt?" Navarro asks.

"Yeah, deer. I didn't realize it was a crime."

"Very funny. What nationality are you?"

"You ask a lot of stupid-ass questions. German."

"Your skin is pretty dark for a German."

"My grandfather was Indian. Native American. Not one of those foreigner types."

"Nice mouth on you. So, what brought you to South Lakeport? Were you trying to escape from something you didn't want the cops to find out about?"

"No, not even close," Parker says, defiantly. "I told you. I served my time and was rehabilitated. I found God while I was in prison, and He changed my life."

"You served time in Macomb, right? That's where Casey Cahill is locked up."

"I told you, I don't know anyone by that name."

"You didn't answer my question. How'd you wind up in South Lakeport?"

"My uncle let me live on his farm after my aunt died. Must've been twenty years ago. He couldn't stand living in the place without her. He wanted to make sure someone took care of the property, I guess."

"You used to live in Sparrow. Never been there, but I hear it's nice in the summer. Great place to meet little kids. Have you ever been to Funland? They've got games and rides and cotton candy. Kids love that kind of stuff."

Parker squirms uncomfortably in his chair. "Yeah. I've been there once or twice. I used to take my niece Beverly there."

"Is this her?" Navarro asks and motions to his partner. Russell pushes the picture of the little girl with the red hair in the turquoise and white polka-dot bathing suit in front of Parker.

"Where did you get this? You searched my place?" Parker asks as his voice notches up a good two octaves.

"We had a search warrant, dummy. Is this your niece?"

Parker nods and runs his thick, dirt-stained fingers across the photo.

"Yeah. Beverly's mom, my sister, got messed up in drugs and stuff, and I'd take Beverly for a few weeks every summer. I was just trying to make her life easier, you know."

"I'm sure you did. I bet you were a regular prince of an uncle. Did you invite Beverly's little friends to your house during her summer visits?"

"Yeah. You've got to let kids have fun. Parents these days are too worried about structure. Old-fashioned fun is the best thing for kids. They had lots of fun at my house."

"You know this kid?" Navarro asks and pushes a picture of Ben toward Parker. It's Ben's third-grade picture, which the police used as his missing-person photo.

"Nope. Never seen him," Parker mutters and looks away from the table.

"Okay. Then what are these?" Navarro asks and shoves the Polaroids of Ben and me in front of his face.

Parker gives the Polaroids a quick, passing glance. For a brief instant, a flicker of recognition seems to register in his eyes.

"You know who these kids are, don't you? It's Ben Gooden and his little sister, Julia. You saw them at Funland, and you followed them home. You tailed them slowly all the way to their house, and then you broke in that night and took the little boy. You didn't take the girl though. But now I know why."

"I don't know what you're talking about. You're making all this up."

"The girl got away before you could drag her out, too. She hid in the closet when she heard you coming. But she got a look at your face before you could see her. It's been eating at you all these years, wondering if that little girl was going to remember you and tell the police. You know how many years you'd get for a first-degree murder sentence? That's life in prison easy, if the judge doesn't decide to give you the death penalty first."

"I'm not going back to prison," Parker begs in a whiny, thin treble.

"What happened, Parker? What did you do to that boy? Did you accidentally go further than you ever had before? And then you had no choice but to kill him?"

My heart is racing so quickly, I am afraid it is going to burst out of my chest. I place my forehead against the glass that separates me from Parker and try to focus.

"The one thing I can't figure out is why you would wait this long to come back. Thirty years is a long time, but maybe you're a patient guy, or you get off slowly by stalking your prey," Navarro says. "You saw the little girl in the room with Ben that night, didn't you? You saw her, and you thought she saw you, too. You knew you had to come back to finish her off one of these days. That's why you kept all those stacks of papers in your filthy house with her byline. You were stalking her, just like you did with her brother."

"That's not what happened," Parker says, his eyes darting back and forth across the room as though he's searching for an alibi. "I remember now. Yeah, that's right. Those pictures jogged my memory. I saw those kids at Funland. I like to take pictures, just like an amateur photographer. It was a coincidence is all. I was driving to a friend's house and saw those kids walking all by themselves along the side of the road. I stopped and asked if they needed a ride home. I was just trying to help them out. I didn't want anything bad to happen to them, two kids all alone like that. But I didn't break into their house or take a kid. I left right after they said they didn't want a ride. Now I get screwed for trying to be nice."

"A friend of mine remembers you. She said you were a substitute school bus driver. That must have been pretty convenient for a guy like you. They didn't do background checks in the 1970s for substitute drivers, did they?"

"Yeah, I was a substitute school bus driver, so what? That's not against the law. People have to work and I like kids. I'd joke around with them and make them laugh. And they loved my music. I played rock 'n' roll on the bus ride home. All the kids wanted to sit in the front seat so they could hear my tapes. I made homemade tapes up special just for the bus rides. That was probably the best part of the day for those kids. I could tell a lot of them came from bad homes."

"My friend saw you the day you followed her and her brother home. You knew the girl's name from your bus route, and you searched for her a few years ago, right? You got nervous, thinking she would finally remember you, so you searched for her on the Internet and found her byline in a Detroit paper. Then you find out where she lives so you can finally fix your little problem. But when you got to her house last night, you saw that boy, and you just couldn't help yourself. The loss of innocence gets you off more than anything else, doesn't it?"

"I didn't take any kids. I told you. I've never done anything bad to a kid. I'm not a monster."

"Not according to your record," Navarro answers.

A heavy bead of perspiration begins to slide down Parker's temple.

"I was on drugs back then. Drugs made me act crazy. Bad things happened to me as a kid, and the drugs made it all come back. But I never took a kid. I've been clean and sober now for twelve years. You go call my sponsor. He'll tell you."

"So if you're the upstanding citizen you now claim to be, then I guess you're just holding on to these little photos as keepsakes from the past for your memory book?" Navarro asks and then he goes in hard for the upper cut. "Where's the boy you took last night?"

"Why do you keep asking the same stupid question? I didn't take no boy."

Navarro lunges toward Parker and stops just an inch away from the suspect's face.

"What did you do with him? Where's the boy? You think prison was bad before, you haven't seen anything. The hardcores in maximum security don't take too kindly to pedophiles, kidnappers, and baby killers."

"You're full of shit. I didn't do anything. You're just looking for a guy to pin this on because you've got nothing. I know how you cops operate. You guys are all lazy, so you try and find an ex-con in the system so you don't have to do any work. But guess what? You've got no evidence and those pictures don't prove nothin'."

Navarro pulls out a piece of paper from under his arm.

"I have a court order mandating you give me a DNA sample. You're screwed, so you might as well save me the trouble and tell me where you put the boy you took last night. If you don't get the death penalty, you'll get killed in prison. Help yourself and tell me now. Otherwise, there's no deal and you're a dead man."

"Screw you, asshole. I keep telling you, I didn't take no kid last night. You're not going to make me break and cop to something I didn't do."

"Your choice. If you change your mind, let me know. We're going to be keeping you here for a while."

Navarro and Russell get up and leave Parker in the interview room. Now thinking he is alone and no one can see him, he slumps over the table and buries his head in his hands.

The door to my room swings open, and Navarro gives me a wide grin. "We got our guy. It's just a matter of time before he gives it up and we find your boy."

CHAPTER 9

Still without a confession and no further leads on Will, I glance nervously at my watch. It is just after 1 p.m. My mind flicks back to what Cahill said in jail about time being my prison. The clock still ticks on the wall, but nothing has changed. I grab my phone, which I put on mute after I went into Pamela's office, and see that I have ten missed calls from David, who I realize I left outside on the police station stairs more than an hour ago, promising I'd be right back.

I search for David in the parking lot to apologize and spot him leaning against his car with his blue suit coat draped over one shoulder. He notices my approach, shakes his head back and forth slowly, and lets out a low whistle.

"You're over an hour late. That's got to be some kind of record, even for you," David says.

"I'm so sorry, everything happened really fast. They brought a suspect in for questioning. His name is A.J. Parker, and the police think he took Will and my brother. I had to ID some old photos Parker took, and a few were of Ben and me. Some of the children were being abused in the pictures, and it really jarred me. I should've called. I blew it, okay?"

David nods toward the passenger side door and gestures for me to get in. On the seat is a box half-filled with Will's missing-person flyers.

I try and play it cool, but David slams the driverside door shut and I know all is not yet forgiven.

"I know. I went into the station to try and find you and ran into Linderman. He was still hot over the press conference, but he told me what was going on. Do you think you can do me the courtesy of calling me next time, so I get the news from you instead of someone else? I spent the last hour going door to door, handing out Will's missing persons flyer to anyone who would take it, so at least the last hour I spent waiting around for you wasn't a complete waste of time."

"I'm sorry. I made a mistake. I can only say it so many times."

"Sometimes I think you'd prefer to spend time with Navarro. I see the way he looks at you. He's still in love with you. I'm no fool."

"No, he's not. But even if he was, I can't control what other people do or how they feel. He's been a friend of mine for a long time."

"You're turning to him instead of me right now. Why does he have to work Will's case? I'm not comfortable with him always around. I'm sure he's pretty happy he gets to spend all this extra time with you."

"Do you hear what you're saying? That's ridiculous. Navarro is a pro. He's the best detective on the force. I wouldn't want anyone else looking for our son. You have no reason to feel insecure."

"I'm not insecure. I just don't like him. Navarro's a cocky son of a bitch, and I don't want him in our lives or especially in charge of my son's missing persons case."

"We don't have any choice here. If Navarro was a hack, that would be different. But he's not, and if anyone is going to find Will, it's him."

"Yeah, he's a big, tough guy. A regular John Wayne to the rescue."

"David . . ."

"I'm pissed off. I don't want to talk about it anymore."

I reach for David's hand, but he pulls it away. I contemplate trying to re-engage David and make him understand he has no reason to be jealous. Navarro and I had always remained on the best of terms after our breakup more than a decade ago. I needed him for information on my beat, but more so, Navarro was my friend, and I knew that stuck in David's craw. But the thought of cheating on David or even opening the door for the possibility of hooking up with Navarro or anyone else even in the most difficult patches of our marriage never occurred to me. Not even once.

David studies the road ahead with a moody scowl, and I suddenly feel like the one who should be pissed off over his skewed priorities. I refuse to cradle what I think is nothing more than a bruised ego.

"You need to get over it, David. We've got much bigger things to worry about than this petty stuff that deep down, you know isn't true. We just need to work together and stop picking at each other. Okay?"

David's scowl stays intact, and I finally give up. We drive the rest of the ride home in stone-cold silence as

I watch Detroit's infestation of abandoned buildings slip by. I study their crumbling debris and begin to accept that my marriage is in ill repair, unfixable just like the ruins of the now uninhabitable structures that pass outside my window.

The ride that seems like an eternity finally ends as David pulls into the driveway. We stay put for a moment, just sitting in the car, our seat belts still strapped across our chests, neither one of us making a move. David stares at some invisible spot on the horizon and finally breaks.

"I realize this isn't a good time, but I need to tell you something. I started seeing someone. It's casual. I was going to tell you last night when I came over to see the kids, but then the timing didn't seem to work out right."

"Jesus. You're telling me this now?"

"I felt like if I didn't, something bad would happen."

"Something bad did happen. Christ, David."

"Hold on. I'm going to break it off with her. She's another lawyer. I'm sorry. Like I said, it was nothing serious."

"I went to see that psychiatrist against my better judgment because you asked me to as part of our reconciliation agreement. Was that some kind of power play? You manipulate me and act like everything wrong in our marriage is my fault, but then you go behind my back and start seeing someone else."

"It wasn't like that."

"Are you sleeping with this woman? That's why you were acting jealous about Navarro, because you had something to hide."

"I shouldn't have brought it up. I told you already. I'm going to end it. It was a mistake. I was wrong and I'm sorry. I didn't mean to hurt you."

"Your timing is ridiculous."

I slide out of the car and shove the door closed as hard as I can, feeling outside of my body as another piece of my life gives way.

"Julia, wait," David calls from behind. He grabs my arms and forces me to turn around and face him. "I didn't do anything wrong. We're separated."

"Separation isn't a 'get out of jail for free' card, friend."

I stare back at David and my mind flashes back to a happier time between us, and our first unofficial date at Riverside Park. We leaned against David's convertible and ate coneys and watched the cars snake along the Ambassador Bridge, which connects the Motor City to Canada. David invited me to meet him there, supposedly to talk about a case I was covering, but after only a few minutes, I realized it was a front. David was charismatic and confident, and I was instantly smitten. Six months later, I moved into David's apartment in a high-rise downtown. Two months after that, I was late. I took a pregnancy test and got the surprise of my life. I have to give David credit. I don't know if he planned on asking me to marry him so quickly, but he acted like it was all part of some wonderful plan, the happy news for him about the unexpected baby and his proposal one week after my big reveal.

I had never thought about having kids. It wasn't that I didn't like them. I was terrified by the idea of having a baby, someone tiny and vulnerable that I was afraid I wouldn't be able to protect. But David protected both of us, even before Logan was born. We got married when I was six months pregnant. David's father, Bruce, didn't come. We weren't surprised.

("David tells me your father was a con man?" Bruce asked me during our first meeting as his young wife, Bruce's third, to be exact, smiled in unison with her new husband as she dutifully handed him a drink.)

When David's stepmom and I went into the kitchen, I could hear Bruce lecturing David and accusing me of trapping David into a marriage by purposely getting pregnant. David was furious and we left immediately. Bruce came around after Logan was born and David eventually forgave his father. Not that I cared. A jerk is a jerk, and I needed to concentrate on my new baby.

When I first saw Logan after he was born, I felt an immediate love and an immediate worry that never went away. David was the fun parent who bounced Logan high up on his shoulders in the deepest part of the lake while I looked on at them in the distance and held my breath. When David wasn't around, I wouldn't let Logan take off his shoes so he could put his toes in the sand when we went to the shore, in fear Logan might cut himself on a shell or piece of stray glass. David thought my overprotective idiosyncrasies were funny then. And we were turning into a happy family.

After Logan's first birthday, I was torn by my conflicting desires to return to the paper and take care of my baby. My editor let me start off slowly, two days a week, and I'd spend my lunch hour at Logan's daycare, which was across the street from my office and had top-notch security. Gradually, when I realized Logan was safe and seemed to enjoy interacting with the other children, two days became five at work. I had struck a guilty balance. But as Logan got older and more independent, my protective fears heightened. And when Will came along after David's urging for a second baby so Logan would have a companion and not be an only child like David was, an internal panic alarm seemed to go off inside me. With two children now to protect and Logan about to turn the age my brother was when he disappeared, my worries for my children's safety intensified.

I look back at the lake house that had once been a place of beautiful family memories and wonder how things could have unraveled so horribly and how David could have deceived me.

"Please, Julia. Just hear me out," David says.

"I don't have time to deal with this conversation right now," I answer. My voice sounds brittle in my ears, like my words could get caught up in the wind and snap into a million inconsequential pieces and fly away.

The sound of an approaching car engine temporarily dismisses the contentious moment between David and me, and I squint against the sun to see an older-model navy-blue sedan pull into the driveway. Its single occupant, an attractive young girl with waist-length strawberry-blond hair, gets out of the car. As she approaches, I put her at about sixteen years of age. She wears a pair of white shorts that skim halfway down her thigh and a bright orange tank top that curves along the swell of her breasts, which bounce as she walks toward us.

"Hello. Are you Julia?" the girl asks. As she comes closer, I notice a smattering of almost pink, translucent freckles across her pert nose and cheekbones. Although puberty obviously already struck, her voice and mannerisms are more like a young girl than a teenager.

"Can I help you?" I ask.

"Oh, yeah, sorry. I'm Leslie, Kim's cousin. We're visiting her from California. I, um, I'm sorry to bother you," she continues as she seems to grow increasingly uncomfortable with each word that comes out of her mouth. "Geez, I heard about your kid. I'm real sorry. Is my mom here?"

David, who is sitting on the top step of the front porch, stands up and extends his hand to Leslie. Unable to help himself, David flicks his eyes down to Leslie's gravity-defying cleavage and then back up to her face.

"Hi, I'm David. I'm not sure if your mom is here, but feel free to go on inside and see." David then reaches his hand into his shirt pocket for his buzzing cell phone. "Sorry, that's my law office. I've got to take this. Nice to meet you, Leslie."

David moves into the house, and I try and shelve his unexpected announcement—something that would have taken center stage just a day before—until it rises onto my priority list. I notice a curious Logan standing on the other side of the kitchen window, staring at the pretty young stranger on the porch.

Logan moves away from the window and bursts through the screen door with the wild energy of an eight-year-old. He foregoes the steps and leaps directly from the front porch to the yard. He then grabs a fallen branch from a weeping willow tree and begins to swat it back and forth like a makeshift whip. Logan's easy, playful reaction provides me some relief since I know a heavy weight still rests on his fragile shoulders.

Leslie watches Logan dash across the yard and giggles. She picks up another stick lying on the ground, and the two start to have a mock sword fight with the fallen branches.

"Buddy, cut it," I tell Logan. "Someone could get hurt. This is Kim's cousin, Leslie. She and her mother Alice are visiting from California."

"Oh, I don't mind. We were just having a little fun," Leslie says. "I don't think he'd hurt me."

"Not on purpose. Little boys just like to play. That's an amazing thing with kids. No matter what situation they're facing, kids generally can take a break from reality and play like everything is normal, even when nothing is."

"Do you like TV?" Logan asks Leslie.

"Sure," she answers.

"Your mom is inside, so come on in," I say.

The smell of something wonderful hits as I walk inside my house and notice Alice and Kim are busy in the kitchen making what looks like a giant pot of homemade potato and leek soup on the stove. Leslie follows the aroma and makes her way over to inspect the dish. Alice begins to ladle a spoonful of the soup for her daughter to taste when her eyes drift down to Leslie's formfitting shirt. The spoon falls back into the pot, and Alice grabs the front of the tank top with both hands and tries to yank it up to cover her daughter's exposed cleavage.

"Too low cut and too tight," Alice reprimands. "I know the other girls at school wear shirts like this, but you keep it up and Father will be chasing a line of boys down the street with a shotgun."

Leslie's porcelain face reddens, and she crosses her arms across her chest like she is trying to cover up the perpetrators.

"She got my figure, but now if I can just convince her to wear a bra and some loose-fitting blouses," Alice says.

Now completely humiliated, Leslie moves her hands from her chest and covers her face.

Kim sidles over to her flustered cousin and puts a comforting arm around Leslie's shoulder. "Don't worry. You're such a pretty girl and your mother just wants to keep the wrong types of people away from you. Why don't you leave us boring adults and go watch some television with Logan in the living room?"

"I've got the *Wheel of Fortune* on. I just love that Vanna White, but I don't mind if you change it."

Leslie jumps at her chance to escape. She shoots her mother a dirty look and then hurries out of the kitchen and plops down on the couch next to Logan.

"Is there anything new on the case? Please tell me the police have a suspect," Alice says, and gives the pepper grinder two shakes over the top of the pot.

"Yes, they made an arrest."

Alice claps her hands together. "Thank God. Who is it?"

"I'm not at liberty to say," I answer.

"Come on. You can at least tell us. We won't say anything," Kim promises.

"All right. The police arrested a registered sex offender who lives in a rundown farmhouse about five miles away from here. He may have a connection to me from my childhood."

"Oh my God. Maybe he was stalking you all this time," Kim responds.

"It's possible. The suspect had photographs of me when I was a little girl stashed in his house."

Alice's eyes grow wide with surprise.

"Oh, heavenly father. That's unbelievable. What's this man's name?" Alice asks.

"Archie Parker. But he hasn't been formally charged yet. So let's keep this between us for now. You can't say a word to anybody."

Logan turns on the TV and the theme of *SpongeBob SquarePants* drifts toward the kitchen.

"SpongeBob is going to teach his friend Patrick how to blow a bubble in the shape of a duck. Squidward is going to come out in a minute, and he's going to be really mad because those two make him crazy," Logan tells Leslie. "This is my favorite episode."

"Television is filled with shows that turn a child's mind to mush," Alice says. "I let Leslie watch public television or nothing at all. And *The Wheel*, of course. It's my guilty pleasure."

"Logan, why don't you and Leslie go back outside for a bit instead?" Kim offers. "It's a nice day."

"I'd like to see your tree house," Leslie says.

"How do you know I have a tree house?" Logan asks.

"Lucky guess. Almost all little boys have tree houses," she answers. "I can see it from the living room window, you know."

An uncomfortable knot begins to grow in my stomach. Too many people in my house and too many distractions. I need to be alone to concentrate on the case.

"You must be existing on fumes right now," I say to Kim. "Please go home with your family. I appreciate all you've done, but David and I are here now to take care of Logan. We'll call you later to give you any updates."

"Certainly not, Kimmy," Alice answers for her relative. "We aren't going to leave this poor child all alone at a time like this."

I shoot Kim an exasperated glance, and she responds with a subtle nod of understanding.

"Julia probably just needs some quiet time," Kim answers. "We'll come back later. And you call me right away if you need anything or if you get any news on Will."

Kim gives me a twenty-second hug before she goes. Leslie gives Logan a fist bump, and he looks back at his new friend like she is the coolest thing in the entire world.

A sense of relief washes over me as I watch Kim's Volvo back out of the driveway with her entourage. I collapse on the couch and pull out my reporter's notebook from the coffee table. On a single sheet of paper, I write down Parker's name in capital letters and underneath it, my unanswered questions that I can't let go.

Why would Parker wait so long to come back for me?

If Parker came back to kill me last night, why did he take Will instead?

What is the connection between Ben and Will, except for me?

My concentration is broken as David emerges from the study with his hand cupped over our landline's mouthpiece.

"You have a phone call. I think you want to take this one," David says. "Hey, we'll talk about what happened later on, okay? I want everything to be all right between us, especially right now."

"Is Navarro on the phone?" I ask.

"No, it's a collect call from the state prison. It's Reverend Casey Cahill," David answers.

I drop my notebook, grab the phone from David, and retreat into the office.

"This is a collect call from the Macomb Correctional Facility. The call is from prisoner Casey Cahill. Do you accept the charges?" the voice on the other end asks.

"Yes, I do," I quickly reply.

There's a clicking sound on the other end of the phone and then Cahill's voice catches excitedly.

"Miss Gooden, I've been thinking about your visit this morning and your promise about my upcoming parole hearing," Cahill says.

"Why are you calling? Do you have new information about my son?"

"What a blessed day God has given us. The guards let us go outside for a few minutes of exercise and sunshine, and I just can't help but praise our Father for his beautiful world. You know, you can always find beauty in life even in the darkest of circumstances."

"If you have nothing to say about my son's case, I'm hanging up."

"I had an unexpected visitor," Cahill continues. "It was such a nice surprise to meet one of your family members."

"I know David didn't come to see you."

"It was certainly not your husband. It was another member of your family, and let me just tell you, it warmed my heart to meet someone who has such a strong love of the Lord."

As expected, Cahill is trying to play me again, and I won't go along with his game.

"I'm hanging up now, Cahill."

"She's such a striking girl, but I think several years older than you," he continues, undeterred by my warning. "You two look nothing alike, you with your dark hair and features. If she hadn't told me she was your sister, I would have never guessed."

"My sister, Sarah, came to see you?"

"Well, yes, she did. Such a sad story about that poor girl, but she found redemption. I was delighted to find out she used to watch my service on television every Sunday morning. She said it changed her life. I've heard so many people tell me that exact same thing. Only God knows how many lives I've saved."

"Why did my sister visit you?"

"Sarah said it was God's hand that led her to your son's press conference. She heard one of the reporters ask a question about our meeting this morning, and she came right down to the prison to sit with me. She said you didn't want to see her. Your rejection has caused that poor child to suffer. You continue to tear lives apart, Miss Gooden, just like you did with mine. I'm the good shepherd, and when you sent me to prison, you tore away my flock. And they will stray without my guidance. You hurt more people than you'll ever know." Cahill makes a disapproving clicking sound with his tongue. "But I've forgiven all you've done to me. Why can't you do the same for your own blood?"

"I'm not talking to you about my sister."

"You know, she asked a lot of questions about you. That woman is just grieving for your little lost boy and wants to help in the worst way," Cahill insists.

"I bet she did."

"Your sister told me what happened to the two of

you after your brother Ben was taken. Such a feeling of betrayal and rejection you two must have faced."

"I am ending this call now," I respond and begin to pull the phone away from my ear.

"I got another letter a short while ago. It came in this afternoon's mail. I know you would be very interested in the contents of this letter."

"It's from the same person?"

"Yes, with the same lovely penmanship and pleasurable praise for our Father. The letter mentioned your baby."

"Cut to the chase."

"You really should only speak when spoken to, Miss Gooden. But very well then. The letter said, 'Julia Gooden failed her brother, and now she failed her son. For the unjust, the good will be taken away again and again, until they learn.' The author of the letter claims they put an Indian arrowhead underneath the beds of both your brother and son right before they snatched them."

I feel my heart stop for a minute. I take the receiver away from my mouth and try and steady my breathing so Cahill won't hear.

"When was the letter sent?"

"There was no postmark," Cahill answers.

"So it was hand-delivered," I say. And most likely by Parker's accomplice. "The police will be down to collect that letter into evidence."

I slam the receiver down and reach for my cell phone to call Navarro. As I start to punch in his number, a steady knock beats against the office door.

"Can this wait?" I ask.

"I don't think so," David says from behind the door. "Your sister, Sarah, is here."

CHAPTER 10

No matter how grievous the act, if you loved someone once, there is still an indestructible connection that links you to the person. No matter what they did.

("How long have you children been living here by yourselves? My God, where are your parents? I'm going to have to call Social Services.")

My recent angry memories of Sarah are momentarily silenced as I recall our neighbor's startled expression as she peered back at Sarah and me inside our dark house. The power had been shut off two weeks earlier after our parents took off and never came back. The older woman had knocked on the door with a bag of groceries after we had begged her for food earlier that day. Sarah and I had been alone then going on a month, and we had long finished foraging for any meager remains leftover in my mother's pantry.

I stare vacantly at a framed photograph of Lake Michigan hanging on the wall and recall the Sarah I used to know. She was never protective or kind like

Ben. Sarah was seven years older, a very pretty girl who was more interested in high school boys than hanging out with me. We were never close, even after Ben was taken, but she was still my sister. I close my eyes and remember Sarah, who huddled by Ben and me for warmth as we tried to fall asleep in the backseat of my father's old Chrysler. And I remember Sarah, who smoked pot and let the boys feel her up under the bridge by the high school. And I remember Sarah, as we waited by the pay phone for our mother to call us after she took the Greyhound bus south to see my dad and never came home. It was the winter after Ben was taken, and a thin sheet of ice covered the pay phone that never rang. We waited, shivering in the cold for hours, until we silently accepted the fact that no one was going to call. We never said a word to each other. We didn't have to. Sarah and I realized we were abandoned and our parents were never coming back for us. I was devastated after Ben's abduction and tried to cling to Sarah, but she pushed me away, like it was every man for himself.

"Logan, what do you have there?" David asks, snapping me back to the here and now. Logan stands in the office doorway carrying a white box with a big silver bow.

"Aunt Sarah brought me some saltwater taffy. She says it's from the shore," Logan says excitedly. "Aunt Sarah promised she would take me to the park after she visits with you. Can I go?"

"Go to your room and don't talk to my sister again," I answer.

"Why? Aunt Sarah seems really nice. Maybe she heard about Will and came here to help."

"Don't call her your aunt. I told you to go to your room. Don't come out until I tell you to. Do you understand?" I ask and snatch Sarah's gift out of Logan's hands.

A flash of surprise and hurt moves across Logan's face. He nibbles on his bottom lip, trying not to cry, and then tears down the hallway until he is out of sight and I hear his bedroom door slam.

I follow his path, feeling badly about my harsh tone, and prepare to confront my only link to a past I tried to escape from long ago. Any glimmer of warm nostalgia gives way to anger as I turn the corner and see Sarah. She stands in the living room with her back to me as she browses through framed family photos of Logan and Will on the bookcase.

She looks better than I remember from our fleeting encounter at the press conference. Despite years of substance abuse, she is still a beauty with her thick blond hair, lean build, and suntanned long legs that I'm sure she purposely showcased in a short white skirt and pair of black high heel sandals.

"What are you doing here, and how do you know where I live?" I ask, keeping the length of the living room floor between us.

Sarah spins around and gives me a rehearsed smile, revealing teeth so white they look like chalk.

"Aunt Carol had your address from your last Christmas card," she replies and reaches into her purse.

Sarah pulls out a white box that brings me back for a moment to a bittersweet time.

"I brought you this from the Candy Grove. It's caramel corn from the Sparrow boardwalk. You used to love the Candy Grove. Remember? It was your favorite. I'd always buy you a box of fresh caramel corn after my shift at the Starfish Shack."

That is one memory of Sarah I don't recall. Ben was the only one who tried to make my life better.

"What are you up to, Sarah?"

Sarah places the caramel corn down on the table and gives me a disappointed frown.

"I've been living down in Naples, Florida, for the past few years. It sure beats the Michigan winters we're used to, right? I flew out here yesterday to see you. I called to let you know I was in town, but you didn't return my calls. And then I heard the news about your poor baby. I just had to go to the press conference, because I knew that would be the only way I could see you. But you blew me off, and that really hurt me."

"Why are you really here?"

"I was going to write you a letter, but it seemed like the coward's way out. I originally came here to tell you I'm sorry. Granted, you did me wrong when we were kids, but you were too little to know what would happen because of your actions. Regardless, I'm here to help you."

"Let me be blunt," I answer. "I don't care. I don't care what you did. I don't care if you found God. You have a funny way of always turning everything back to yourself. Even now when my son is missing, the spotlight is still on you, isn't it? About how I hurt you and what happened to you after our parents left is all my fault and none of your own?"

"Stop. I know you're mad, and I'm sorry for the things I've done. I'm different now. I found God, and His peace changed my life." Sarah retrieves the gold cross

I saw earlier from around her neck and holds it out to me as if proof she is indeed rehabilitated.

"I can't tell you how many times the dirt bags on my beat tried to feed me that line, as if it somehow absolved them of their crimes and everything was magically forgiven."

"You've changed. You seem harder," Sarah says. "But I can't imagine the pressure you must be under right now with your boy missing."

"You paid a visit to the state penitentiary right before you came here. How was your meeting with Reverend Cahill?"

I've surprised Sarah. She looks angry for a second, and horizontal frown lines crease her forehead. I can see her mind working quickly as she tries to pull out a palatable explanation that will appease me. When she gets the answer she wants, her expression softens and the fake smile returns.

"It's funny how things work out. I came to Michigan to visit with you, but God had other plans," Sarah says. "I've kept the faith all these years, even though you and countless others turned your backs on me. But not God. He rewarded me with the gift of the good reverend today."

"What are you talking about?"

"I've watched Reverend Cahill every Sunday for years now, and it was Reverend Cahill who got me through my darkest times."

"How did it feel to be back in prison today?" I ask.

"You never give me a chance. You always hold me accountable for my past. I forgave you for yours."

"I was seven and trying to do the right thing. What's

your excuse? Are you going to pretend like what you did to me didn't happen, that you're a good person? You served time for fraud, burglary, and embezzlement, amongst a laundry list of other charges."

"Please stop. Your words hurt me more than you'll ever know."

"You're hurt? The last time I saw you, I got a surprise visit from you and your boyfriend. I had just gotten home from the hospital after Logan was born. Don't you remember? You said you were there to see the baby, and I was so excited you came to visit, but while I was putting Logan to sleep, you and your boyfriend cased my house."

"If I could take it all back, you know I would," Sarah pleads. "Please, we're sisters after all."

"A sister wouldn't steal my personal information, my Social Security number, and my credit cards. A sister wouldn't steal the engagement ring I got from my husband. Do you want me to continue?"

"I'm not going to talk about this," Sarah says and folds her arms across her chest in a defensive motion.

"After you and your boyfriend left, it took me a couple of days to realize what happened, but when I did, I confronted you. Do you remember what you told me?"

"I'm not that person anymore," Sarah says.

"You said if I went to the police, you would come after my family and you would come after my son."

"I'm so sorry," Sarah says, her cheeks beginning to flush. "I was using back then. The drugs, they stole everything from me. I've been through rehab, two years clean and sober. My sponsor said you would most likely reject me, but I had to face you again."

"You and your dirt-bag boyfriend threatened my child eight years ago, and suddenly my other son goes missing. Are you involved in Will's kidnapping, Sarah? Did Parker agree to pay you if you helped him break in and steal Will last night? He was a bus driver when we lived in Sparrow, so I wouldn't be surprised if you knew him from back then."

"I don't know what you're talking about," Sarah says. "This isn't at all how I thought things would turn out. You don't have to forgive me. But please hear me out. It was so hard for me. You got to stay with Aunt Carol when Mom and Dad left us. Remember how we went to the bus station and said good-bye to Mom? She gave you a candy bar and said she would see us soon. But she never came back. Neither did Dad. We were left alone and we were just kids. I wound up being shuffled in and out of foster homes. It didn't matter how many homes I went to. It was all the same. No one wanted me there. They just wanted the paycheck. You have no idea what I had to endure. I was abused by some of the families. But I don't want to talk about it."

"That's life. Some people's lives are harder than others. I don't feel sorry for myself, and I don't feel sorry for you," I answer.

"You don't understand how it was for me. You don't know how hard it was for me when Ben was taken."

"You were never close to Ben. You couldn't stand either of us. We were just idiot brats, remember?"

"It was very hard for me to lose a brother," Sarah says and pulls out a cigarette. "Do you mind if I smoke?"

"Yes, I do," I snap.

"I realize you're very angry with me. All I can say is I'm sorry for what I did in the past. Please give me a chance. Please let me help you."

I look at Sarah, and something buried way down deep inside me does want to believe she changed and that maybe there is still a glimmer of the person left inside of her that I thought I saw when we were kids. The spring before Ben was taken, my mom entered Sarah into a local modeling contest the city of Sparrow was putting on that offered a hundred-dollar cash prize for the winner. Sarah came in second. At the end of the event, the girls got to bring up on stage a family member or friend to be included in one of the photos. Most of the other winners brought up their mothers, best friends, or boyfriends. I was shocked when Sarah beckoned me to join her.

("You're prettier than any of the girls up here," Sarah whispered as she bent down to face me, realizing my discomfort. "I'll hold your hand. Okay? Smile pretty for me, Julia. When you smile, it makes everyone happy.")

I try not to show emotion over the unexpected memory, but Sarah seems to sense my sentimentality and drapes her arm around my shoulder.

"Pastor Curtis Cahill told me all about those letters," Sarah says. "He's such a godly man. Pastor Curtis said he was devastated to see your son's picture on the TV news this morning. He said Will is such a beautiful boy with white blond hair. Do you have a picture of him? You know, I brought him a teddy bear. Maybe you could tell me where his room is, and I could leave it in there for him when he gets back. I know he's coming home."

I get a bitter taste in my mouth as something clicks. Sarah's con was decent but not good enough.

"You've been watching Cahill for years, correct? If that's true, then you wouldn't have botched his name. It's Reverend Casey Cahill, not Pastor Curtis Cahill. You talked to a tabloid reporter at the press conference, right? How much did they offer you for inside information on Will's abduction? That's why you went to see Cahill, and that's why you're here now."

Sarah covers her face with her hands and pretends to break down.

"You say such hurtful things," she says and dabs at her waterless eyes.

"How much are they going to pay you?" I ask again.

Sarah leaps to her feet and moves toward the front door.

"Well, you obviously don't want to accept my apology," Sarah says, her tone suddenly shifting from disconsolate to ice-cold. "That's fine, and by the way, I didn't reach out to the press. They reached out to me. They wanted to hear about Ben's story. And they did ask me questions about Will, but I'm an ethical person. I wouldn't make anything up. I was just trying to help you. I was just trying to give the press information on the case to help bring your baby home."

Sarah continues toward the door. But I stand in front of it and block her path.

"Fool me once," I say.

I grab Sarah's handbag and dump out the contents. Scattered across the kitchen counter are a package of Marlboro Lights cigarettes, a set of keys, a wallet, a tube of red lipstick, and finally, what I expected to find. There, smiling up at me, is a picture of Will. I took it last year when he was nearly toothless and immensely happy with his little fat legs poking out of a red onesie. Sarah snatched it off the living room bookshelf when David went to find me in the office to tell me about her impromptu visit.

"You stole this picture of Will to give to the tabloids. Get the hell out of here," I explode.

The beautiful Sarah is caught, and her true face, the one with the permanent sour and hateful look I remember so well, finally resurfaces.

"I would've shared the money with you. They were going to pay me a lot for the picture, but fine. Have it your way. Too bad you're the one who's suffering now. How does it feel, special girl, to have your perfect little life destroyed? You're selfish and you always have been," Sarah says. "You sit here and judge me still, but you're the one who deserves to be judged. You told Aunt Carol what I did. That's what got me kicked out. Every bad thing that's happened to me is your fault."

I feel a familiar stab of guilt and look away from Sarah's hateful stare-down, knowing she is at least partially correct. Aunt Carol initially took both of us in to live with her, but right away Sarah started acting out. She was escorted in the back of a cruiser to Aunt Carol's house on more than one occasion when the police picked Sarah up for truancy or smoking pot, and Sarah narrowly missed a stint in juvenile hall for stealing a necklace. Shortly after that, I caught Sarah stealing money from our aunt's wallet. I told Sarah what she was doing was wrong and to put the money back, but Sarah swore if I said anything, she'd tell our aunt that I was the one who took the cash. Ben always hammered into me to do the right thing, and I was worried about my sister, so I told Aunt Carol what I'd witnessed. That was enough for my aunt. Sarah went into foster care for stealing a sum total of sixty-three dollars and forty-seven cents. I cried for days and blamed myself for not keeping my mouth shut.

"Why are you doing this, Sarah?" I ask.

"Because you deserve it."

"Get out. If you don't, I'm calling the police."

David, hearing the growing altercation, emerges from the office. He looks first to Sarah and then over to me.

"You need to leave now. You've done enough to my family. Now get out of my house," David says in a strong, no-nonsense voice. He opens the front door and holds it there for her exit.

Sarah stares back at me for a long beat, seething with barely contained rage.

"Screw you, Julia. You get what you give," Sarah says and grabs the box of caramel corn like a petty parting gesture before she storms out the front door.

I watch Sarah's retreat down the gravel walkway until her rental car tears down the street, leaving a dust cloud wake behind her.

"Are you okay?" David asks. "You're trembling. What did Sarah do to you?"

"Nothing. It's just the past, you know? Maybe a tiny part of me hoped things were different. But Sarah didn't change. She only came here to steal a picture of Will to sell to the tabloids. I found it in her purse."

"How did you know?" David asks. He tries to wrap his arm around my shoulder, but I move away at the last second before he can reach me.

"I just did. Some people never change. Life made Sarah angry and bitter, and she never had the reserve to fight her way out."

I can smell Sarah's perfume still lingering in the air and wonder how she might have turned out if she was born into a normal life. I was frantic to know Sarah was okay when she first went into foster care. I wrote her letters every week, but she never responded. When I was in college, my aunt told me she'd heard Sarah was suing one of the foster families she had lived with for sexual abuse. To this day, my dreams are still haunted by whether I cemented Sarah's fate, and if the tables had been turned and it was me who went into foster care instead of Sarah, if I'd be the one who'd be on the hustle now. But I have to believe Ben's influence would have kept me on the right track regardless of my fate.

I feel a paranoid twist in my gut as my nagging belief that Sarah could have taken Will as punishment for what she perceives I did magnifies. My thoughts turn to Logan. Sarah might not have threatened him this time, but she tried to bait him. The fine art of the con used on an eight-year-old. Whether Logan is still mad at me or not, my instincts were dead-on to keep him away from my sister.

"Logan was pretty steamed at me. Can you be sure he's all right? I need to call Navarro."

David goes to check on Logan, and I speed-dial Navarro's cell phone number.

He answers on the second ring, and I skip the formalities.

"Casey Cahill called me from the prison. He got another letter today. More hate mail about me. It mentioned

Ben and Will and said something about the good will be taken from the unjust. The letter was hand-delivered. Parker has an accomplice, which pans out, since I heard two sets of footsteps last night. There's got to be something you missed down at Parker's house. You need to go back there."

"We need another search warrant. I'll have my guys pick up the latest letter from Cahill. If Parker breaks, I'll call you right away."

"One more thing. I need you to run a check on someone for me."

"I'm kind of busy if you haven't noticed," Navarro says.

"This is important. Someone from my past just showed up out of the blue. Her name is Sarah and she's got priors. I'm not sure if she is married now, but her maiden name is Gooden."

"A relative you failed to mention earlier?" Navarro asks.

"Something like that."

I can hear Navarro exhale in frustration on the other end of the phone.

"I told you before about filling me in on the whole story. I'll see what I can do," he answers. "I'll talk to you later."

"Navarro . . ." I say.

But he already hung up.

I grab my car keys and head toward the front door, knowing I can't wait around while Navarro works to get a judge to sign off on a second search warrant.

"Where're you going?" David asks as he emerges from Logan's room.

"For a drive. I need a few minutes alone to think. It feels like there is something right in front of me, but I just can't see it."

"Do what you need to do. Keep your cell phone on," David answers.

"Sure," I promise and head to Parker's house.

CHAPTER 11

I've driven the bucolic route to South Lakeport at least a hundred times since my childhood. Most properties in the rural area are tidily kept and look like they have been plucked out of a Norman Rockwell painting. But I'm guessing Parker's place will be the exception.

I fumble for the piece of paper on the passenger seat with Parker's address and take a quick left down a desolate dirt road. I feel relatively sure Parker's house will be empty since the police have enough to keep him in custody, and it will give me a chance to search the property for any signs of Will the cops might have missed.

A half-mile down, I see the only sign of life, a tired old farmhouse that looks more like an abandoned property left by former residents who either died or hightailed it out of there because they could no longer afford the bank loan.

I pull up across the street from the property and do a quick assessment and security check before I venture inside. Below the threadbare roof are two broken, skinny windows Parker must have carelessly covered up with striped bed sheets, long faded from the sun. The wooden fence that once separated the property from the road lost its battle with decay and curls toward the ground like a spiraling wave. And the tangle of grass and weeds out front is thick with discarded soda cans and other fast-food containers, tossed away carelessly by passing motorists who figured it didn't matter if they added their litter to the growing landfill pile.

A beat-up Chevy truck is parked in the driveway. The bottom half of the vehicle has more rust than chrome and a Confederate flag is draped across the back window. A Rottweiler stands guard, tethered to the bed of the truck.

"Bloody fantastic," I mutter over the unexpected and probably highly dangerous four-legged beast.

The massive animal stares me down, quivers its mouth, and then rises on its haunches on high alert. My only saving grace is that the dog is still on its chain. I throw the dice, the stakes way too high not to, and exit the car. The Rottweiler reacts to my brazen move and growls a vicious warning. The dog then lunges forward in my direction, barking and frothing at the mouth, until there is no more give in its metal chain. The momentum jerks the Rottweiler backward with a hard snap, and the dog skids helplessly toward the rear of the truck until it lands with a hard smack against the Chevy's cab, the animal giving out a painful yelp upon impact. I'd almost feel sorry for the dog if it wasn't trying to eat me alive.

"Nice doggy," I say unconvincingly. I reach into my purse and pull out a package of peanut butter crackers

I picked up for Logan. I open the wrapper of the crackers and fling it toward the bed of the truck. The Rottweiler temporarily ceases its frothing onslaught and begins to devour the treat. I put as much room as I can between the dog and my body and hustle toward the front door. Once safely at my destination, I knock and wait for a minute, all the while looking over my shoulder to see if the Rottweiler is in midair, ready to tear my head off from behind.

As expected, no one answers. I try the door, but it is bolted shut.

I hurry to the rear of the property to search for a way inside. If it's possible, the back of the house is worse than the front. It is a virtual dumping ground for all things unwanted. In the middle of the yard, an orange, wheel-less van with the words KEEP ON TRUCKIN' spray-painted in blue bubble letters on its passenger-side door has found its final resting place atop four cinder blocks. What's left of the van's rusted engine lies on the ground next to it. The rest of the yard is a maze of trash. I avoid an old washing machine that looks like it's from the 1950s, a rusted car fender, and a half-eaten hamburger teeming with squiggling white maggots that feast on the decaying meat. I finally reach the back door and try the knob. As expected, it's also locked.

"Trust me, no one but me would want to break in here," I say aloud.

I drag a plastic chair lying cockeyed on the lawn over to a back window. I climb up and try and look inside the house, but the window is coated with a thick film of grime on both sides, allowing for zero visibility. I push up on the window with the flat of my hands.

The window groans and budges ever so slightly. I push harder and carefully shimmy it up side to side until there is a space wide enough for me to fit through. I put my hand over my nose and mouth to block the stale odor of what smells like a combination of years' worth of filth and not quite empty bottles of discarded booze, and poke my head inside the dark house. There are no immediate signs of life or Parker's accomplice, so I hoist myself up and start to climb through the window.

Ben taught me the fine art of breaking into a house when we were kids. It was Christmastime 1976. All our holiday decorations and the rest of our belongings were still boxed up and captive in the house we had been evicted from the month prior. On Christmas Eve before dawn, Ben and I got up early before anyone could notice and climbed through an unlocked back window of our former residence. It was a successful, if not foolish, mission for two little kids, but in the end, we retrieved our precious ornaments and our treetop silver star. Ben wanted to be sure I had at least a decorated tree on Christmas, since he knew there wouldn't be any presents.

("Don't worry Julia," Ben said. "One day, I'm going to give you the best Christmas ever. I'll have so many presents for you, they won't even fit under the tree.")

I put aside the memory and Ben's unfulfilled promise and run my hand along the wall until I feel a switch. The overhead light flicks on, and a dim yellow cast illuminates Parker's squalor-filled kitchen. In the center of the room is a plastic card table piled high with newspapers. Under careful examination, my byline is circled in red on each front page in the tall stack, going back at least three years.

Next to the pile of papers is a black plastic ashtray jammed full of Marlboro Lights cigarette butts, a discarded bottle of cheap vodka, and an empty six-pack of Pabst Blue Ribbon beer.

"So much for clean and sober, Parker," I say.

I start down a dark hallway covered in garish blue-rose-patterned wallpaper until I reach the entrance of a narrow room. It is sparsely furnished with only a thin, dirty mattress and pile after pile of soiled work clothes dumped carelessly across the room. An ornamental gold cross hangs from a nail on the wall and a dog-eared Bible lies on the floor next to Parker's bed.

The stench of body odor, cigarettes, and manure is so overpowering in the room, I duck into the hallway to catch my breath. I start back inside to search the bedroom when a key slides into the front door.

I race down the hallway to escape, but before I can reach the kitchen, a giant hand grabs me by the shoulder and yanks me back. I turn to face my attacker, but two mammoth hands now grip me from behind, and I'm thrown head first toward the wall. I fold to the ground on impact, and look up to see a giant, heavy-set man in a pair of overalls looming above me with a rifle pointed directly at my head.

"Who are you, and what the hell are you doing in my house?" the big man barks, finger still planted firmly on the trigger. "Answer me. You've got ten seconds or I blow your head off."

As a journalist, I am never supposed to lie or misrepresent myself. But right now I am not a journalist. I'm just trying to stay alive.

"I'm sorry. I didn't realize you lived here, too. A.J. Parker asked me to come over. I'm a Realtor," I say, the lie slipping out of my mouth without any premeditation.

"A Realtor?" the big man asks. His dark curly hair is unruly and spiked with bursts of grey.

"Yes, I reached out to A.J. to see if he would consider selling the place. I'm working with a big residential developer, and we're scouting out some properties. A.J. was supposed to meet me here, but when he didn't show up, I let myself in the back door to take a preview of the place. I hope that was okay."

"We never leave the door unlocked here," the big man says, his eyes narrowing to slits.

"A.J. must have left it open for me," I answer, my mind working on overdrive to come up with anything tangible to get me out alive.

The big man looks down at me and weighs my response, but I can tell he isn't buying my story. But sometimes the bigger the tale, the more believable it sounds.

"On first glance, I think the land alone could fetch a sizable amount of money," I say. "Tell you what. How about you put that gun down now that you know I'm not here to rob the place."

The money mention captures his attention. The big man lowers the gun a few inches so it is at least not pointing at my head.

"A.J. asked you to come here?"

"Yes. He was supposed to meet me here over an hour ago. I have other appointments. I couldn't wait any longer. That's why I let myself in. I wouldn't have come inside if I realized it was going to be such a problem. I've seen a lot of things as a Realtor, but no one has ever pulled a gun on me before."

The big man's rifle slowly falls to his side.

"Yeah, sorry. So, you think A.J. could really get a lot of money for this dump?"

"Absolutely. Developers are hungry for properties in the country. A lot of urban professionals don't want to raise their families in the city anymore. They want safety and charm."

"Don't bullshit me. We got a pig farm here. This place sure isn't charming."

"You need to look at the bigger picture," I back-pedal. "This area is such an ideal location for a big subdivision. It's a pretty big property as I recall. I can't remember what A.J. told me when we first talked. How much land does he have here again? If there are other buildings that need to be torn down, let me know. I saw that old barn out front. That would need to be demolished. Demolition costs money, so that would figure into the offer, of course."

The big man, obviously now fully smitten with my line of bullshit, parks his rifle in the corner of the room. Feeling comfortable, he unloads the contents from his pockets, including a driver's license and a package of Marlboro Lights cigarettes, and dumps them across the card table.

"Sorry about earlier. Sit down. Didn't mean to scare you. Lots of kids come by here and try to break into the place. They think it's abandoned," the big man says.

He walks over to the avocado-colored refrigerator, pulls out a can of Pabst Blue Ribbon, and cracks it open.

"Want one? I've got to drink alone these days because A.J. quit on me. I wish he hadn't done that. Sober people suck."

I shake my head at his offer.

"Thanks, but I have to drive back to the office after this, so I'll pass."

"Your loss," the big man says and swills back another slug of beer. "So tell me, how much are properties going for around here these days? We've got thirty acres. It's a real nice pig farm. Besides the main house and the barn, A.J. has a hunting camp tucked away about three miles back in the deep woods. Great spot to shoot deer. It's on the other side of the lake from the Shaw Mill Bridge."

I force a smile and wonder if the police know about the hunting camp.

"Thirty acres? That's a lot of land. A.J. could probably get millions for this place, easy. That's just an estimate of course. I would have to run some comparables."

"Millions? You're freakin' kiddin' me," the big man says. "It's still early yet, but I guess we have reason to celebrate."

He works his way over to the kitchen and pulls out a bottle of vodka. He quickly unscrews the bottle top, lifts it to his lips, and pours a long stream directly into his mouth, no glass required.

"I don't own the place, mind you, but A.J. and I are relatives," he says while wiping the corner of his mouth with his dirty shirtsleeve. "He's my dad's cousin. It's always good to take care of your own blood. I know it might not seem like it now, but when I was growing up, I was rich. I've been rich and I've been poor, and let me tell you, it sucks being poor. I would do just about anything to be rich again."

Including kidnapping a child, my thoughts scream. I

steady myself and realize I need to pump him for information now before he gets totally smashed.

"I'm sure your cousin would take care of you if he sold the place. Buyers always want a good area to raise a family. A.J. has kids, right? I thought I heard a kid in the background when we were talking on the phone this morning. It sounded like it might have been a little boy, maybe two or so. I'm an expert on that type of thing. I have one of my own."

The big man gives me a puzzled look and cracks open another beer.

"Nah. No kids. A.J.'s never been married either. He must have called you when he was out at the market or somewhere, and you probably just heard some bratty kid mouthing off in the background. I've been here for about a year, and there's never been a kid in this house that I can remember."

"My mistake. I'm Susan by the way," I say, the lies now flowing comfortably.

The big man reaches out his dirty hand for me to shake.

"Mark. My name is Mark. We don't get much company here. Being new in town, I haven't met many people and the pigs don't cut it."

"Where are you from originally?" I ask as I try and figure out my exit strategy.

"I'm from Sparrow, not too far from here. It's about a fifteen-minute drive or so. Sparrow is a nice little shore town. I used to hate it there when I was a kid, and I couldn't wait to leave for the city. Just a bunch of tourists in the summer, and everything closes up when the out-of-towners leave come Labor Day. It was like the locals didn't deserve anything good. But Sparrow is a million times better than this boring shithole. The bars here suck."

"You're from Sparrow?" I ask as a knot begins to tighten in my stomach.

"Yep. I was a different man before I came to this cesspool. Just look at my driver's license picture. I had that taken right before I moved in here with A.J."

The big man grabs his license and shoves it under my nose for a close inspection.

"See? I didn't look half bad then, don't you think? You're married, aren't you? I see that big rock on your finger. That's too bad. You're real pretty."

I scan the driver's license for any pertinent information. The man getting sauced in front of me was born the same year as Ben. He would have been in my brother's class in Sparrow.

I check the name on the license to see if I remember him. Brewster. Mark Wallace Brewster. A sickly panic starts to build in my chest. Thirty years after he tried to beat up my brother at Funland, my childhood bully is standing right in front of me. I feel overpowered for a second, like I am a seven-year-old poor kid again. I look over at Brewster and swear that I can detect the makings of a nasty smile beginning to spread across Brewster's face as he senses my fear. But before I give in to self-doubt and panic, I steady myself and remember Ben's words as we sat outside of the library in Sparrow after we ran away from our bully.

("Don't ever back down from bullies like Mark Brewster. You've got to stand up to them, no matter what.")

I look back at Brewster, the once spoiled rich kid who is now drunk out of his mind and covered in pig shit, and I regain control. I had forgotten about the rumors of Brewster's demise. He became a big druggie in high school after his mother died. He smoked pot under the bridge with the older kids before school and then graduated to meth and later heroin. His father was still president of the county council and remarried a woman who was only four years older than Mark. The dad finally cut Mark off after two unsuccessful stints at a military school and later rehab. If Brewster wound up with Parker, he obviously had nowhere else to go.

"Small world. When I was a kid, my parents took me to Sparrow during the summers. I loved that place. I remember Funland. Sparrow also had a roller skating rink with a bowling alley downstairs as I recall. And there was the boardwalk. Back then, I thought Sparrow was the greatest place on earth."

"You've been to Sparrow?" Brewster asks.

He leaps up from his chair and gives me an uncomfortable hug that is too close and too tight. Brewster smells like a biker bar at closing time. I back away and put the cheap card table between us.

"I remember one summer while we were visiting, there were a lot of stories about a kid who went missing," I say. "My mom got really overprotective and wouldn't let us go to the beach by ourselves after that. I'm trying to remember the kid's name. I think it was a boy."

Brewster goes back to the refrigerator for another beer and then lights a cigarette. He starts hacking after his first puff, coughs up a yellow phlegm ball, and spits it into the ashtray.

"Oh, right. You mean that little bastard Ben," Brewster sneers. "Ben Gooden was his name. Stupid brat.

He was poor as shit and came from nothing. But he acted like he owned the whole damn town. He and his crappy little family weren't even good enough to be white trash. He was a big-mouthed jerk, always getting in people's faces if they said anything about his family or that kid sister of his."

Brewster throws his head back and begins to howl with laughter, opening his mouth so wide I can see he is missing at least four teeth in the back.

"May pop! May pop! Ben is wearing may pops!" Brewster sings with glee. "Ben Gooden was so poor, his mom bought him shoes at the A&P. We called them may pops because we said Ben's toes were going to pop out of those ratty old sneakers at any minute."

I sit on my hands so I won't lunge across the table and slug Brewster.

"Yeah, that kid disappeared. As far as I am concerned, he had it coming," Brewster says and takes another chug of beer. "I remember now. It was right around Labor Day weekend before school started. I don't think the police ever found out what happened to him."

"Your cousin was a bus driver, right? A.J. told me how much he loved kids and he used to drive buses back then. Those guys always know what's going on. Did he ever mention anything to you about Ben?"

Brewster puts his beer down on the table and his brow knits together. Even though Brewster is now beyond drunk, he's still sober enough to suspect I'm up to something.

"You seem awfully interested in this kid Ben. Why's that?"

"I told you. I heard about the kid when we were visiting that one summer. I was just curious. I figured if you were from there, you might know what had happened to the boy. It's just a big coincidence you used to live there."

"People talked is all," Brewster slurs as the influx of booze starts to hit him. "There were a lot of stories out there. I heard the dad probably sold the kid to get money. Other people thought Ben ran away to get the hell away from his family. And who could blame him? Poor kids like that don't amount to anything anyway. Never do. Then the rich people get sucked dry by having to pay extra to be sure those poor bastards get their food stamps and Medicaid and other handouts. Poor people like that deserve to die. It would make things easier for everyone."

I spot Brewster's gun still propped up in the corner of the room and calculate how long it would take me to grab it. My escape plan takes a backseat as Brewster pulls out a necklace from underneath his dirty T-shirt. The necklace is a simple silver chain with a charm in the center, a baseball with red stitching and a red, white, and blue hat. In the center is the word YANKEES. Ben's necklace. He bought it after he worked an entire summer mowing lawns. Ben was so proud of that necklace, he never took it off. I close my eyes for a second, and my brother's image sparks clear in my memory. He was wearing the necklace when he went to bed the night he disappeared.

"Where did you get that?" I demand.

"A.J. gave it to me. What's it to you?"

Everything. I feel a rush of heat creep up my face. I have to force myself not to start pummeling Brewster and snatch my brother's necklace from his fat neck.

That necklace touched my brother's skin. That bastard Parker stole my brother, took his prized possession, and gave it to this sorry asshole. I'll be damned if I don't get it back. I feel the burn of tears begin and a blind fury growing inside me. *Keep it together, Julia*, I tell myself.

"My husband loves the Yankees," I say, softening my voice. "I haven't seen one of those charms in a long time. Tell you what, let me buy it from you."

"It's not for sale," Brewster responds coldly, and shoves the necklace inside his T-shirt.

"How about two hundred dollars."

"Two hundred?"

"Two hundred. I'll go to my car and get the money. I just came from the bank and left all my cash in the glove compartment. I'd really like to give you one of my business cards for A.J. and I left them in my purse. Tell you what, I'll get you another beer before I go. Do we have a deal?"

"Two hundred and fifty bucks and you've got a deal. Just hand me that beer before you go, sweetheart," he says and reaches behind his neck to unclasp the necklace.

My heart feels like it is pumping outside of my chest as Brewster holds my brother's necklace out to me in his grime-stained palm. I take the necklace in one fluid move, forcing myself not to snatch it, and Brewster tries to rise on his wobbly feet. He steadies himself against the thin card table as another wave of liquor kicks in. He stumbles over to the corner of the kitchen by the stove, picks up his rifle, and opens the back screen door. I can hear the quick, staccato rhythm of my heart beating as I watch my childhood bully stagger to the edge of the deck and line up a row of empty beer cans in a drunken, uneven line. I quickly press my brother's necklace to my lips, shove it in my pocket, and hurry to the back door.

"Always good to do a little target practice," Brewster says as the screen slams shut behind me. "You never know when you're going to need it."

Brewster stumbles in my direction and places his index finger under my chin.

"Maybe we can get to know each other a little better when you get back with the money. What do you say?"

"I'll be back in just a minute with the cash. Don't go anywhere. Okay?"

"Don't worry, sweetheart. I'll be waiting for you," Brewster promises and puckers his lips together as if he is blowing me a kiss.

I walk at a relaxed pace through the backyard until I am sure I am out of Brewster's line of vision. As soon as I can't see him anymore, I race past the side of the house just as Brewster starts firing shots at the beer cans. The sound of the gun and my probable panic alert the Rottweiler. The dog begins its vicious, tethered rampage as I sprint past. I don't turn around to face the angry beast and keep moving until I reach my car. Safely inside, I try and temper my breathing. I snap the locks shut, feeling my only sense of security in the last twenty minutes since Brewster pulled the gun on me, and then accidentally drop the car keys on the floorboard. I bend down to pick them up, jam the key into the ignition, and look through the windshield. Rounding the corner from the backyard is Brewster. He is running straight toward me like a wild hillbilly with his gun pointed at my vehicle. He stops abruptly at the Chevy truck and unclasps the Rottweiler's leash.

"Come on, come on," I yell and finally turn the key in the ignition. I jam my foot on the gas pedal just as Brewster opens fire. I instinctively duck down and stay in place as a single bullet pierces the rear passenger door.

"You lying bitch! You took my necklace, and now I'm going to kill you," Brewster howls as I peel off the gravel shoulder and begin to escape down the dirt country road.

I keep my eyes on Brewster, who continues to pump and shoot in a pretty good rhythm for a drunk guy, until he becomes a tiny speck in my rearview mirror.

When Brewster is finally out of sight, I pull the New York Yankees necklace out of my pocket and hold it tightly in my right hand.

"I didn't let him beat me, Ben," I say. "I didn't let him beat me."

CHAPTER 12

I fight a screaming, primal urge to search for the hunting camp myself. But since I have a drunken bully with a gun threatening to kill me, I realize I need to go to the police instead of playing rogue investigative reporter again. I fumble for my phone and punch in Navarro's number, fully expecting to get his voice mail.

"Navarro here."

"Thank God," I say hurriedly. "I need to see you right now. I found a new piece of evidence, and there's another building on Parker's property you need to search. Just tell me where you are and I'll meet you."

"Did you go to Parker's place?" Navarro asks. "Holy shit, you did. You're going to get yourself hurt, or worse, killed if you keep pulling stunts like this."

"It doesn't matter. I'll tell you about it when I see you."

"Christ almighty. All right. I'm in Decremer. Meet me downtown. I'm at the Harvest Café."

"I'll be there in five minutes," I answer and hit the gas hard, forcing the speedometer to leap to the right.

I make it to downtown in three. I bypass the jammed line of parked cars along Main Street and pull up in front of the restaurant loading dock in the rear of the building.

I hustle inside and grab the arm of a young hostess who is trying to ignore the swell of waiting customers crowding around the podium.

"I need to find someone, tall guy, good looking, mid-thirties, with a thick New Jersey accent. He's got a barbed-wire tattoo on his bicep. You need to take me to him right now."

The hostess stares down at my hand, which is latched around her wrist, and leads me wordlessly through the double row of cherry-red booths filled to capacity with the late-lunch crowd.

I spot Navarro before he sees me. He's busy devouring a just-delivered sandwich of boiled meat, sauerkraut, and Swiss cheese with so much passion, it looks like he is savoring his very last meal before he goes to the electric chair.

I slide into the booth across from Navarro, grab his plate, and hand it to a passing waiter.

"The detective is all through," I tell the waiter. "We need to talk."

"You didn't have to take my food, for God's sake. What've you got?"

"Parker has a hunting camp on his property. I've got something else. I'm sure it belonged to my brother," I say and carefully pull Ben's necklace from my pocket.

I place it delicately on the table and arrange the chain so the necklace lies perfectly flat.

"This necklace is extremely important to me, so you have to promise me I'll get it back."

"New York Yankees. Where did you get this?" Navarro asks.

"At Parker's place. I ran into someone I knew from a long time ago. He lives with Parker and says he's a relative. The guy, his name is Mark Brewster, told me about the hunting camp. Brewster said they've got thirty acres there, plenty of land to hide a missing child. He told me the hunting camp is by the old Shaw Mill covered bridge."

Navarro raises his index finger and grabs his cell phone. "Yeah, we need another search warrant for the entire property this time, including a hunting camp that is down by the old covered bridge. We've got another piece of evidence that looks like it belonged to the brother in the '77 abduction."

Navarro ends his call and turns his attention back to me.

"You know better than that. What were you thinking breaking into Parker's house? Not only is it dangerous, it's illegal. You could get five to ten years in jail for a breaking and entering collar. I should arrest you right now and then at least you'd be out of my hair for a while."

"But you won't."

"Do me a favor and don't play daredevil reporter again. You're better alive than dead to your kids," he says.

"What else did you get from Parker?" I ask.

"His story checks out about his uncle letting him live on the farm after the aunt died. The aunt drowned during an outing on Port Huron, but no body was ever found. According to census records, Parker has been living there for twenty years at least."

Like most journalists, math was never my strong point. I grab the pen sticking out of Navarro's shirt pocket and jot down a few numbers on the paper place mat in front of me.

"Something doesn't seem right," I realize.

"What are you talking about? Everything is right. We've got the guy who kidnapped your brother and son in jail already. All we need is for Parker to tell us where he's hidden Will."

"The timeframe isn't right. You think Parker was keeping an eye on me all these years because he was worried one day I'd be able to remember what happened the night Ben was taken and I'd identify him to the cops. If that's the case, your theory can't be right. Parker came to South Lakeport twenty years ago. We bought our lake house three years ago. David and I lived in downtown Detroit and then Rochester Hills before that, and neither of those places are right next door to him."

"So maybe he lived there already, and one day he picked up the paper and saw your byline. He got spooked," Navarro says. "It's too much of a coincidence. He found out about your summer property and thought you were getting too close. Creeping up on him from Detroit to Decremer. You obviously know the cops since that's your beat, and he couldn't take any chances. Did you see that stack of newspapers in the kitchen? Every single one had your name circled in red pen. He was obsessing, tracking you. And when he didn't see your byline anymore after you took your leave of absence from the paper, he got scared and came to find you. Parker knew the walls were closing in on him and he had to take care of you finally. Jesus, Julia, an Indian arrowhead was found under your brother's bed and now your son's. What more do you want?"

"If he was worried about me turning him in, why would he take Will instead of trying to kill me?"

"Because he's a sick guy," Navarro says. "He broke into your house thinking he was going to kill you, Logan's hiding under his bed, but he sees Will and can't help himself. Or maybe he heard something and got scared, grabbed the kid, and ran. Or maybe he wanted to punish you for making him look over his shoulder all these years. It doesn't matter the reason he did it. He's our guy. Not to mention the fact Cahill got that letter today that clearly links Ben and Will."

"It was hand-delivered. It could've been from someone who saw the press conference and was trying to screw with us or throw us off their trail. Parker claims he was with his sponsor last night at the time Will was taken. Did his story pan out?"

"Not exactly. The sponsor said he was with Parker until ten p.m., but the time of the abduction was ten-thirty. That would give Parker plenty of time to drive over to your house."

"What if Parker took Ben but not Will? What if it's someone else, and money is the motive? David and I aren't millionaires by far, but with David's promotion in the firm, we're doing pretty well."

"If it was money the kidnapper wanted, you would've been hit up for ransom by now. No ransom note, no chance the person who took the kid has any plans to give him back. You know that," Navarro explains. "We've got the guy. Now we just need to find out what he did with Will and then we'll link him to your brother. You put him before any jury, chances are he'll get the death penalty, easy."

"I know how you cops work. When you lock in on a suspect, you don't look at anyone else. You can't make a mistake on this. You always said I had good instincts, right?"

"Until lately," Navarro says.

"I'm just not a hundred percent convinced on Parker. One thing I don't get—Parker is a pedophile. We know that. But pedophiles target a specific age group. Ben was nine when he went missing and Will is only two. You used to work sex crimes. The pattern doesn't fit."

"Typically, most pedophiles are attracted to a certain age group or sex of a child. But there are always exceptions. These guys are all different. Some like girls. Some like boys. And the bisexual pedophiles like both. Like I said, there are a lot of reasons why Parker might have taken Will. But if I had to narrow it down to one, I don't think sex is the motive."

"What do you think it is then?" I ask, feeling an odd sense of momentary relief.

"Revenge. Parker wanted to get you back."

My mind fills with black and crimson ribbons of dread as images of Parker torturing Will begin to choke off my sanity.

"Jesus. We need to move faster. Did you get the handwriting analysis results on the letters Cahill got?"

"Not yet. But Parker is obviously a religious guy. He had a Bible next to his bed and a cross hanging on his wall. Plus, he went to AA meetings at Cahill's old church. Seems like a no-brainer to me with or without the handwriting match," Navarro says.

I stare down at the number 1977 I wrote on the place mat.

"Did you get anything on the person I asked you to check out? Sarah Gooden?"

Navarro pulls a pair of square-shaped glasses and a skinny notebook from his jacket pocket. He rests the glasses on the bridge of his nose as his eyes check off the multiple offenses on my sister's rap sheet.

"You said this Sarah is a relative of yours?" he asks.

"Yes, my sister."

"Holy shit, Julia. Do you have any more surprises you're waiting to pull out? I told you before, you have to be honest with me about your past. It's crucial that I know everything. If you keep holding back, it could make the difference for whether your boy is coming home or not."

"I understand. I wasn't trying to cover anything up. Sarah was older, a teenager when Ben disappeared. We were never close. She acted like she couldn't stand Ben and me when we were kids. When my parents took off, Sarah started to get into trouble and my aunt couldn't handle her anymore, so Sarah wound up in foster care. I don't think there is any way she was involved in Ben's kidnapping though. Sarah was too young and that just wouldn't make any sense."

"Well, you have suspicions about her now, otherwise you wouldn't have called me. Do you think Sarah is tangled up in this somehow? She definitely has a record."

"I don't know. She showed up out of the blue, had a

sit-down with Cahill at the state penitentiary right after the press conference, and then tried to steal a picture of Will to sell to the tabloids."

"She's a grifter. Was and most likely still is," Navarro says and settles the glasses back in position so he can read his notes. "You may know a lot of this already. It looks like she started early. She ran away from foster homes, caught a couple of shoplifting arrests trying to steal food and jewelry, and wound up in juvenile hall. After she turned eighteen, she got popped for drug possession and burglary. Things got quiet for a while after the courts required her to go to rehab as part of her probation requirement. But then it looks like she fell off the wagon pretty quick. Your sister got arrested for possession of meth and intent to sell. A judge gave her a second chance, and she only got ninety days in prison and then another hundred-and-eighty-day mandatory stay in rehab."

"There's credit card theft too," I say.

"I was getting to that. After rehab, she and a dirt-bag guy . . ."

"Steven Beckerus," I interrupt.

"Yeah, that's right, Beckerus. It looks like they had a credit card scam going on. Your sister . . ."

"Just refer to her as Sarah, all right?"

"Fine by me. Beckerus and Sarah had a pretty good sting. She'd target rich guys in bars and make them think they had an easy lay. Once they got to the guy's place, Beckerus would bust in, pretending to be the jealous boyfriend, and beat the shit out of the guy. Then Sarah swept the house for valuables and credit cards."

"Sounds about right. Where is Beckerus these days?"

Navarro looks back at his notes.

"He did a stint at the Carson City Correctional Facility."

"Carson City, Michigan?" I ask.

"The one and only."

"So he's here. That's why Sarah showed up. She said she was living in Florida, but I'm betting she's been here the whole time."

"Beckerus has been clean for a while, had a steady gig with Sherman Security for over a decade," Navarro says.

"That's a pretty big security guard firm, right? I've got a source there."

"Yeah, the owner is one of those ultra-religious types. He was a former convict himself, found God in prison, and started Sherman Security when he got out. He's known for hiring ex-cons, trying to give them a second chance. I know a retired cop who did some work there. He said it made his skin crawl when he had to do a job alongside of a guy he collared for drugs five years earlier."

"I interviewed someone from Sherman Security when I was writing about Cahill. Sherman Security had a contract with Cahill's church. If my sister's boyfriend was working for the company, there's a strong chance he could've done work for Cahill. He could be involved in Will's kidnapping."

"Bottom line, Parker did it. We're not going to spin our wheels and waste time looking somewhere else. He's got a hell of a motive and pictures of you and your brother he's been hiding away for the past thirty years."

I look down at Ben's necklace, and my biggest fear wraps around me and won't let go.

"I just need to be sure. I'm going to ask you something now, and you need to be honest with me."

"Shoot," he says.

"Do you think Will is still alive?"

"Don't give up, okay? It hasn't even been twenty-four hours yet," Navarro answers.

"You didn't answer my question."

"I think we still have time. I'll call you right after we search Parker's property."

I swing back into reporter mode and try and figure a way to outmaneuver Navarro.

"I gave you something with the hunting camp and the necklace. Now you need to give me something. I want to go with you when you search Parker's property. I can be a huge help and can identify anything that might belong to Will."

"I don't know what we're going to find out there, and there's always a chance it's not going to be good."

"I'll be all right. And as a heads-up, the guy who lives with Parker is drunker than hell and he's armed. He fired a couple of shots as I was leaving and threatened to kill me. And you better bring Animal Control along. There's a pissed-off Rottweiler on the property ready to eat someone alive."

Navarro lets out a long whistle.

"You were always a ballsy reporter, but I've got to say, the way you've been since your kid was taken is either downright stupid or braver than hell. You're not scared of anything, are you?"

"If you only knew."

"What's that supposed to mean?"

"I'm scared of plenty. After Ben was taken, I never felt the same. I've been terrified all these years that whatever took Ben was going to come back. I thought I was being paranoid, but deep down, I must have known somehow."

"Maybe it was instinct," Navarro answers.

"Whatever it was, I didn't do enough. I failed Ben thirty years ago, and now I failed Will. Mothers are supposed to protect their children."

"What are you talking about?" Navarro asks. "You're a good mother. I admire you for that. I always figured you had your life figured out better than anyone."

"I'm not so sure."

"As for your brother, cut yourself some slack. I've interviewed hundreds of kids who witnessed their mothers being hacked to death by their drug-addled boyfriends or worse. Most of the time, kids bury what they saw so deep, the gruesome details never resurface. Did you ever think you might not have witnessed what happened to Ben?"

"I was in the same room when he was taken. There's no way I didn't see anything."

"Memories come when they're ready," he answers.

I look up at Navarro and try to smile. But I can't.

"Tell you what, wait here and I'll pull the car around," Navarro says and slides out of the booth.

"Does that mean you're going to let me go with you to search Parker's property?"

"Against my better judgment. But you've got rules. You listen to my direction and if I tell you to walk away, you walk away, got it?"

The smile finally comes as I follow Navarro out of the restaurant.

"I got it," I answer.

Navarro slips the key into the ignition, and Kid Rock's "Cowboy" blasts out of the speakers.

"Sorry about that," he says and shuts the stereo off.

"I've got to call David to fill him in. He'll want to be part of the search, too."

Navarro rubs his index finger across his temple as though I'm giving him a colossal headache.

"Fine. You two follow the rules. Understand?"

"We will."

"You and David trying to patch things up?"

"I'm not exactly sure anymore."

Navarro and I pull up to Parker's property in his unmarked patrol car. Animal Control is already there. Kim, the ever-devoted friend, easily agreed to watch Logan at my house again, so David and I could be part of the search. I catch David's eye as Detective Russell escorts a handcuffed Mark Brewster out the front door.

"There's that lying bitch. She stole my necklace, the whore over there. You should be arresting her," Brewster yells. "Cheap tramp. I never wanted to sleep with you anyway. I was just offering to do you a favor."

David shoots me a "what the hell?" look, and I shake my head over the allegation. Brewster starts on another rant against me, but Russell cuts him off. He places his hand on the back of Brewster's neck and is about to shove him into the police car, when Brewster lets out a violent shudder. His complexion turns a waxy yellow, just like the dead bodies I encounter on the crime beat. And then with one mighty wretch, Brewster the bully projectile vomits the boozy con-

tents from his stomach, landing a few splatters of beer-
and vodka-laced puke on Russell's shoes.

"Son of a bitch," Russell yells.

"Nice. At least it didn't happen in the back of the
car," Navarro remarks. "That's going to be one hell of
a hangover when you wake up in the drunk tank, pal."

A group of plainclothes police officers and sheriff
deputies stand in front of the farmhouse. Navarro approaches Sergeant John Salinas of the K-9 unit and
hands him Will's blue baby blanket, which I retrieved
from the side of his crib. Salinas bends down and puts
the blanket in front of Roger, the unit's bloodhound,
who picks up the scent. About a year ago, I wrote a
feature story about Roger the police dog. The animal is
an experienced tracker who successfully located a
missing child. The story didn't have a happy ending. A
three-year-old girl disappeared from her parents' camp-
site late one night. Roger tracked the little girl's scent
to the banks of the lake, where he found the child's
lifeless body. The little girl had played in the lake earlier that day with her older brother. She had wandered
off in the middle of the night to return to the place that
had brought her so much joy and adventure, only to
fall in the water with no one there to save her this time.
I interviewed the girl's parents and their eyes were
dead and distant. I left the interview wondering how
they could ever find a shred of normalcy, let alone hap-
piness, again.

David links his arm around my waist, and I let him
leave it there as I bow my head and silently beg Will to
hold on.

David's voice cuts through my desperate prayer.

"What if they find him?" he asks.

There's no hope in David's question, and I roughly slap away its intended meaning.

"Will isn't dead. Don't say that ever again," I snap.

"But, Julia . . ."

"I said never. Now let's go find our son."

David retracts his arm from my waist, obviously annoyed with my pointed tone, and moves toward the other side of the growing circle of law enforcement personnel who have started to gather around Navarro. I steal a quick look toward the thicket of woods behind Parker's property, and my body gives in to a deep shudder.

"Hey, guys. How are you doing?" Navarro addresses the group. "I know a lot of you are working overtime or have volunteered to be here today. Also, a big thanks goes out to our inter-agency help from the sheriff's department, the FBI, and the K-9 unit. Now, let's get to it. As you know, a two-year-old boy was taken from his home last night. We believe he may be hidden somewhere on this property. There's approximately thirty acres of woods that need to be covered. There's supposedly a hunting camp on the property that is located near the Shaw Mill covered bridge. We'll be spreading out into five groups, so we have six miles each to canvass. My team will handle searching the radius that includes the hunting camp. Just a reminder, the property you will be covering is very dense woods so take your time and keep your eyes open. If you find anything, you call me on the two-way radio. Any questions?"

Navarro pauses for a beat, waiting, but is greeted by silence.

"Okay. Let's go."

The officers quickly assemble into their respective groups. David and I agreed to separate so we can cover more ground collectively in our search for Will. David pairs up with the sheriff's team. I follow Navarro and ten other officers as we begin to head to the thick, untamed woods located behind the rear of the house.

"Hold on a second, guys," Navarro says and looks toward me. "You know the rules, Julia. You stay behind. And if I need you to walk away, you walk away. Got it?"

"I got it," I respond.

As we start out, I realize our geographic search area is harder to navigate than I originally thought. Parker has obviously never bothered to clear any of his property. There are no manmade paths to follow, just thick underbrush that teems with wood ticks, angry deer flies, and rabid mosquitoes. We cut deeper through the woods, and the late-afternoon sun dims as it is eclipsed behind an intricate canopy of red pines, white oaks, sugar maples, and spruce trees.

"Son of a bitch. Ragweed," Navarro says and lets out a loud sneeze.

We continue on in silence for about a quarter of a mile when I hear a soft trample of leaves and a low-lying branch rustle to the right of our makeshift path. I quickly turn my head in the direction of the sound and see a young doe timidly peering out from behind a dead stump of a huge oak. Nearly hidden behind the doe are two white-spotted fawns. The doe thumps her hoof onto the ground in front of her as if she is warning us not to come any closer to her babies.

"I won't hurt you," I whisper.

The doe looks directly at me for a second and then sprints away with her fawns close behind.

"Two more months until hunting season," Navarro says.

"Hunting is a cruel sport," I answer.

"It thins out the population. Last November, I almost hit a buck right in the middle of I-96," he replies. "Hold on. I think that's the hunting camp just ahead."

Navarro silently motions to the officers in our group and then bolts in the direction of the hunting camp with his weapon drawn, moving almost silently for a man of his stature. He and the other officers quickly circle the crude structure, which looks like it was cobbled together in a hurry with only scrap wood, rusty nails, ripped tarp, and putty.

I do a quick inventory of the outside of the building. Two windows mark either side of the one-room cabin and look like they were recently boarded up with newer wood. Navarro stands by the sole door of the structure and signals the officers who flank him on either side. Navarro counts to ten silently and then plows into the thin wooden front door, which snaps easily under his muscle.

"Police, put your hands up!" Navarro yells as he rushes inside.

A high-pitched scream wails from the cabin and echoes through the quiet woods like a gunshot.

"Will!" I cry out.

Instinctively, I charge toward the hunting camp. Before I can reach the door, a terrified raccoon dashes out of the cabin and tears into the underbrush.

I bend forward, grab my knees, and try to breathe.

"The sound you heard was just a scared wild animal," a voice says from behind.

I turn to see Salinas, who has sidled up next to me with his dog, Roger, who is still on alert. "Sometimes not finding someone is a good thing," he says.

I look at the animal for a minute, and as if on cue, Roger's stocky body suddenly stiffens, and he begins to bark in an incessant, warning baritone. He springs away from Salinas and makes a beeline to the cabin. The dog dodges around officers' legs and darts inside with Salinas and me following close behind.

I know my orders are to stay back, but I don't care. I make it to the doorway and search the interior of the cabin. A set of ten-point deer antlers is mounted on the wall, and a threadbare Green Bay Packers rug covers the dirt floor. On top of the rug sits a rusty kerosene lantern, a cooler, and a stained putty-colored easy chair pockmarked with cigarette burns. The police dog begins to whimper and then anxiously paces back and forth until it positions itself in the center of the rug. Roger's expert nose picks up the scent again, and he begins to dig furiously against the worn fabric.

"There's something under the rug," Salinas yells and jerks Roger's collar away from the hot spot.

Navarro hustles toward the rug and puts his gun back in his holster. Before he pulls the rug away, he catches my profile in the doorway.

"Get out of here, Julia. Get her out of here now," he yells. "Bannaro, move!"

A young officer, obviously Bannaro, snatches my arm in a tight grip and forces me outside to the back of the camp, where I am shielded from the unfolding scene.

"I need to be in there," I scream. "Please."

"That's no place for you right now. You just wait here with me," says Bannaro, who still has a hold of me so I can't break and return to the cabin.

A feeling starts to churn in my stomach, one that I have tried so hard to keep at bay. It grows larger and darker until it demands I finally acknowledge it. My son is never coming home. Dread and desperation pulsate through my veins like poison. I am about to surrender completely when Navarro turns the corner.

"We found something," Navarro says. "There's a trunk wedged into a makeshift crawl space under the cabin. There are human remains buried in it, but they don't belong to Will. The coroner is going to have to confirm, but it looks like the bones are from an adult."

CHAPTER 13

The adult's remains wedged under the hunting camp were the lone discovery during the search of Parker's property. Thirty acres of land were thoroughly combed by a seasoned team of FBI agents, police, and members of the sheriff's department, and they couldn't find a single trace of Will. The grisly finding felt like both a blessing that my boy may still be alive, and an agonizing disappointment that the investigation was no further ahead. As Cahill said, the clock still ticks on the wall, but nothing has changed.

Navarro ordered Bannaro to drive me home. Kim left an hour ago when I got back. As late afternoon settles in, I anxiously wait by Logan's bedside, keeping vigil. Logan is asleep, his body spent after being up all night the previous evening. I pull Logan's Spider-Man blanket over his shoulders and head to the office to search for a ten-year-old phone number.

Buried underneath a cardboard box of old hard-copy newspaper clips, I unearth a blue address book. I search under the letter S for Sherman Security. I scroll down the page until I find the name I remember. Tony Gowan. He had been a solid source when I first investigated the Cahill story. Gowan ran the security team that handled Cahill's standing-room-only crowd during his once-popular weekly services and was then his personal bodyguard after the reverend took a sharp dive into the deep end of crazy.

Ten years is a long time. I dial the number, fully expecting the receptionist to say Gowan no longer works there. Instead the receptionist tells me to hold as she transfers the call.

"Gowan here," a gruff voice answers on the other end of the phone.

"Tony, it's Julia Gooden. I don't know if you remember me. I'm a reporter. You helped me out with information ten years ago on Reverend Casey Cahill."

A good thirty-second pause goes by as Gowan weighs whether or not he should talk to me again.

"I remember you. You cost the company a million-dollar-a-year contract."

"You did the right thing though. Cahill was raping little girls. And I was true to my word. I never gave you up, even when I got subpoenaed to testify."

"Yeah, I was the unnamed source."

"I could have gone to prison for not releasing your name."

"But you didn't," Gowan answers. "I heard about your kid on the TV news. I'm real sorry to hear about that. I hope you get your boy home soon."

"That's why I'm calling. I think someone you work with may be involved in my son's kidnapping."

"How come you're looking for the guy then instead of the police?" Gowan asks.

"They've got their eyes locked in on another suspect. The police may be right, but I just need to make sure. I have no room for error on this. So how about the same agreement we had before? You give me information, and I won't give your name to anyone."

This time, Gowan only waits ten seconds to answer.

"Okay. I'll help you. I have kids of my own. I can't imagine what I'd do if something happened to one of my girls. Let me see what I can find out. What's the guy's name?"

"Steven Beckerus."

I can hear Gowan exhale loudly. "The guy's a real hothead. What do you need to know?"

"If he was working last night, what time he clocked in, and when he got off duty. The window of time I'm really looking for is between nine p.m. and midnight."

"Beckerus isn't on my team, but it shouldn't be hard to find that out. One thing I can tell you for sure, he's got a good-looking girlfriend. She's a hot blonde. He brought her to the company's Fourth of July party. I see her out in the parking lot sometimes waiting to pick up Beckerus after his shift."

Fourth of July. Sarah has been in Michigan then for at least two months, but probably longer than that, if she ever left here in the first place. She didn't just fly into town to see me like she claimed. Two months is plenty of time to plan a kidnapping.

"Thanks, Tony. I appreciate your help."

I hang up the phone and go back to check on Logan and find him still sound asleep. I turn to leave when someone raps hard on the front door. After the search, David went into the city to hand the rest of his caseload off to the partners in the firm, so Logan and I are alone in the house. A strong pang of paranoia hits me. I grab a pair of Logan's scissors from his easel and then shut his bedroom door behind me. I clutch the scissors tightly in my right hand and watch the shadow of a large man looming on the other side of the front door.

"Who's there?" I call out.

"It's me, Julia. Chief Linderman."

A flush of warm embarrassment reddens my cheeks, and I quickly stash the scissors in a kitchen drawer so Linderman won't see before I let him inside.

"Chief, what are you doing here?"

And then my heart sinks.

"You came here personally. You have bad news."

Linderman removes his hat and reaches for my hand. "I didn't mean to scare you. I was just leaving the scene at Parker's hunting camp and thought I would stop by and tell you this in person. We found something that may belong to Will."

"On Parker's property? I was told nothing of Will's was found by the search teams."

"No, not at the farmhouse. We got a call from a fisherman about an hour ago. He saw a news report about your son's abduction. Earlier this morning, he was fly-fishing down at the lake by the Shaw Mill covered bridge. The fisherman said he cast his first fly into the lake when he noticed a pair of toddler's pajamas on the ground by the water's edge. We think the pajamas belong to Will. They match the description of the ones you said Will was wearing last night."

I know what my next question should be, but I am not sure if I have the courage to ask it. "Was there blood on the pajamas?"

"No blood," Linderman answers. "Don't jump too far ahead. We think whoever took Will to the lake didn't intend to do him any harm."

"Then why did they bring my son there?"

"To baptize him," Linderman answers. "It was actually Navarro who put this together. The fisherman also found a wicker basket dumped behind a tree. Inside the basket were items used in a baptism. He found a candle, a child's white gown, a jar of oil, and a pitcher to pour the water. There was a Bible in there, too, and a worn daily devotional from the ministry of the former Reverend Casey Cahill."

"Jesus. When do you think this happened? Parker has been in custody now for over six hours."

"We think sometime last night, probably right after Will's kidnapping. We got a call on the tip line from a man who was out walking his dogs around eleven p.m last night. He got to the Shaw Mill covered bridge, near where your son's pajamas were found, when something spooked his animals. The caller said his dogs started barking like crazy and wouldn't let up."

"Did the man see anyone?"

"Two people in the distance. He said they were running away from the lake, probably trying to leave in a hurry after they heard the dogs. The caller said the two people jumped into a car and sped away."

"What about Will? Did the caller see a little boy?"

"It was dark. The caller claims it looked like one of the people was carrying something. But he said the person was too far away, and it was too dark to know for sure if it was a child," Linderman says.

"What about a make or model of the car or the license plate? Tell me you got something."

"The suspects took off in a dark-looking vehicle, maybe black or blue. The plates were Michigan, the classic blue and white version, but the caller couldn't make out any of the numbers."

"If it was Parker, then who was the second person?"

"We're looking at Mark Brewster as his accomplice," Linderman answers.

"Brewster is surely not a religious man. So his role in the baptism makes no sense unless Parker was going to pay him. Something isn't right, Chief. We're missing something. I told Navarro about other suspects you need to bring in—my sister, Sarah Gooden, and her boyfriend, Steven Beckerus. He may be tied to Cahill. He used to do security at his church. And with the Cahill devotional found by the lake, it seems like they are likely tied up with the reverend somehow."

"We're confident we have the right people in custody," Linderman answers.

"You need to be sure. If you're spinning your wheels right now looking at the wrong suspects, whoever has my son is still out there. And if you're not going to keep looking, then I will."

"Be careful what you do, young lady. You're going to find yourself in a bad situation you may not be able to get yourself out of," Linderman answers. "You need to trust us. We have Parker and Brewster in custody already."

"If you have Will's kidnappers locked up, then where is my son?"

"I know this is hard for you, but you need to let us do our jobs. There is something I need you to do for us though. I need you to come down to the station and ID the pajamas. Can you come with me now?"

"David had to go to his law firm. I need to find someone to watch Logan. I don't want him at the police station unless it's absolutely necessary."

"Just get downtown as soon as you can," Linderman says. "We need to push Parker hard so he'll flip and tell us where he has your son."

I watch Linderman leave in his Crown Victoria and debate whether I should take Logan with me to the police station. The only person I trust other than David and Navarro is Kim. I hate to keep burdening her, but I have no other choice and dial her number.

"Did the police find Will?" she asks without saying hello.

"No. Chief Linderman just left. A fisherman found a pair of pajamas by the Shaw Mill bridge that could be Will's. I need to go down to the station to identify the evidence. Can you come back here and watch Logan? I know you just got home a little while ago, but I wouldn't ask if I didn't need your help."

"Absolutely, but I can't leave for about half an hour. Aunt Alice is coming down with something. Alice told me she spent most of the afternoon in the guesthouse napping. Leslie went down to the store to pick up some soup and cough drops for her. I just need to wait until Leslie gets back before I can leave."

"Why don't I just take Logan to your house? It's on the way to the station."

"That's perfect. I'll set up the croquet set on the lawn for Logan. We'd love to have him here. Leslie had fun playing with him earlier."

"Thanks, Kim. I really appreciate it. We'll be there in a little while."

I end the call with Kim and head to Logan's room,

fully expecting to see my oldest son still sleeping. But instead he is wide awake and sitting on the side of his bed, kicking his feet against the wooden footboard.

"What's up, buddy? I thought you were still sleeping. I'm glad you took a rest," I say and take a seat next to him on the bed.

"You're never going to die, right?" he asks.

"Why would you ask me something like that?"

"If anyone ever tries to hurt you, I'll protect you."

"Mom is tough. Don't worry about me. And it's my job to protect you, not the other way around. Listen, I have to go down to the police station. I need you to stay with Auntie Kim for a little while until I'm done."

"When is she going to get here?" Logan asks.

"She's not. We're going to her house."

Logan slams the footboard of his bed with two hard kicks.

"I don't want to go there. Everything is so clean, I'm afraid to sit down. Auntie Kim is kind of prissy sometimes. And that Alice lady is kind of weird."

"Don't you say that. Aunt Kim is wonderful to you. And it's not nice to talk about her aunt. Alice was very nice to us when she was here earlier, so I want you to be polite. We're going to Kim's house. End of discussion."

The drive to Kim's country estate winds us through miles of rolling hills and Michigan's finest cherry orchards. It's normally a beautiful ride, but even some of Michigan's most picturesque scenery is not enough to make Logan budge out of his dark storm cloud of a mood.

"If you could get into the *Guinness Book of World Records*, what record would you want to break?" I ask, pulling into my bag of sometimes-helpful mother tricks to somehow bring Logan out of his sullen state.

Mission almost accomplished. Logan turns his face toward me and reveals just a tiny glimmer of interest.

"That's a good question. If you let me, I would try and break the world record for holding my breath the longest. That guy I told you about from Germany held his breath for more than fifteen minutes. I'll never beat him unless you let me practice."

"Aren't there any records you can break where you don't risk your life?"

Logan taps his index finger against the side of his cheek, as if deep in thought.

"Nah, I can't come up with any. But it wouldn't be half as fun if it wasn't risky."

Logan reaches into his backpack and pulls out his *Looney Tunes* DVD, a set of marbles, and what he was searching for, the prized compass necklace I bought him for his eighth birthday. Logan points it toward the furthermost part of the windshield as if searching for a direction on an invisible map and then carefully fastens the necklace around his neck.

"This will help us find Will," Logan says.

"I like the way you think," I answer and put my free hand on top of his.

"Is Daddy going to move back in with us?"

"We're working on it."

Logan turns his head toward the window, but I can detect the makings of the first smile I've seen on his face since yesterday.

We finally arrive at the private road that winds two

miles up into the deep country to Kim's expansive estate. I drive halfway around the circular driveway and stop the car by the front door of the main house, where Kim is kneeling on her perfectly manicured lawn, setting up a game of croquet.

"Mom, please. I don't want to go in there," Logan begs. "Can't I just come with you? I don't want to play croquet."

"I don't have a choice. You love Aunt Kim."

"I know, but her house is boring. I promise I won't bother you at the police station. I brought my backpack, and I have my marbles and books. I won't cause any trouble, I swear."

My cell phone buzzes in my pocket. It's Navarro. I go to answer the call, but it has already gone to voice mail.

"Damn it. Logan, I'm sorry. You need to stay with Aunt Kim. No more questions."

"You don't care how I feel," Logan says.

"Can we talk about this later? I'll be back before you know it."

Kim unknowingly breaks the tension and walks toward the car with a big smile for Logan. "I'm just setting up a game of croquet for us to play, and Leslie is making us a wonderful early evening picnic dinner. Do me a favor, Logan. Can you please go into the house and get us two sugar cookies?"

Logan looks back at me and concedes with a small smile. He gets out of the car, pauses on the top of Kim's front step, and gives me a wave as if all is forgiven and heads inside the house.

"Thanks for watching Logan again on such short notice," I say.

Kim leans in close and rests her elbows on the open driver-side window.

"Your sister, Sarah, was just here."

"Sarah?" I ask, as my mind goes into emergency alert. "How did she find you?"

"Please don't be mad at me. When she called your house and you wouldn't talk to her, I just felt terrible. We talked for a minute on the phone, and Sarah told me she just got into town and didn't know anybody here. I gave her my address and phone number and told her to let me know if she needed anything. It seemed like the right thing to do."

Kim's Emily Post crap went way too far this time.

"You don't know what you're doing. Sarah's a con artist. She's working you. Stay away from her and don't let her anywhere near Logan. I'm not positive, but I'm looking into whether she was involved in Will's kidnapping."

The blood drains from Kim's already pale face.

"Holy mother of God."

"Maybe this wasn't the best idea. I'm just going to take Logan down to the station with me."

"No, Julia . . ." Kim begins to protest.

I look down at my cell phone as it begins to ring again. I need to make a split decision. "Okay. Logan will stay here. But don't answer Sarah's calls. Don't open the door if she rings the bell. And if she tries to contact you again, let me know right away and I'll have the police come by."

"I don't think that's necessary."

"You don't know my sister. She tried to hurt me a long time ago. Sarah and her boyfriend threatened to hurt Logan if I went to the police," I say.

"Your sister did that to you?"

"Not all family is nice."

Kim's thick oak front door swings open, and Logan emerges on the front step with Leslie. He holds two cookies in his hands, including one that is already halfway devoured.

"Hello, Julia," Leslie calls out. "Thanks for bringing Logan over."

"Hello, Leslie," I answer and then look back at Kim. "Do we have an understanding?"

"You're scaring me," Kim says quietly.

"You should be scared. Watch your back."

"I won't let anything happen to Logan. And I'll call you right away if your sister shows up again. I'm not sure if this is important—when your sister came by earlier, I saw a man sitting in the driver seat of her car."

"Olive complexion and dark hair?" I ask.

"They were parked at the edge of the driveway so it was a bit hard to see, but yes, I think that's him."

"That was probably Sarah's boyfriend. He served time as well."

"Oh, God."

"I may be wrong about my sister's involvement, but you need to have this on your radar. Most likely, Sarah stopped by here as a way in so she could get to me. She tried to con me earlier so she could score money from the tabloids and cash in on Will's disappearance."

Logan approaches so the conversation stops.

Kim pulls away from the car, looking somewhat shell-shocked, and grabs Logan's hand. "Why don't we head inside, sweetheart?"

"You don't want to play croquet?" Logan asks, sounding somewhat relieved.

"Not now. Let's go inside to have some treats."

My cell phone flashes a message across the screen from Navarro. I quickly fit the key into the ignition and watch Logan, Kim, and Leslie disappear into the house and I head toward the city as fast as I can.

CHAPTER 14

Inside the evidence bag is a pair of yellow pajamas with a giraffe on the lapel. I put Will in them last night before he went to sleep. I already identified the evidence over thirty minutes ago and now am forced to wait in Navarro's office until he finishes interrogating Brewster to see if he will flip.

Navarro's desk is covered with a mass of clutter and sports memorabilia that fill every square inch of the horizontal space. Some things never change. When Navarro and I were together, dust bunnies the size of small zoo animals and piles of dirty clothes stuck around for weeks at a time until I couldn't take it anymore and cleaned his place up. I take my index finger and dust off a framed photo of a very young Navarro, maybe twenty years old or so, in a blue patrol uniform. Navarro is sporting a well-manicured beard that makes him look like the character "Serpico" from the classic Al Pacino movie. The photo must have been taken when Navarro first started out in the Newark, New Jersey, police department fifteen years earlier. I drum my fingers on top of the desk and lock eyes with a New York Mets Jose Reyes bobblehead doll with a permanent toothy smile. I smack the bobblehead on top of its helmet and set the oversized noggin into full tilt.

"This is no time to smile, Reyes," I tell the jiggling figurine.

I stare up at the clock for the twentieth time in the last minute. It's already 6:30 PM.

I'd search Navarro's computer, but he locked it, realizing I would probably try and pilfer through his files. I just want one more chance to sift through Parker's information to hunt down any clues I might have missed. I gamble on the fact Navarro has Parker's paper file somewhere since I know he would want it readily available for review. I switch into investigative reporter mode and open Navarro's top desk drawer. Inside the drawer, he has squirreled away a pack of legal pads and pencils. The second drawer is filled with police training manuals. I sift through them in case Parker's file is tucked somewhere inside. At the very bottom of the drawer is a photograph. In the picture, I am sitting on Navarro's lap, waving at the camera. It was taken at the police Christmas party, more than ten years earlier and pre-David.

I start to second-guess my hunch about the paper files. But in the last drawer, I find pay dirt. The drawer is filled with case files Navarro worked on through the years, including active ones. Parker's file is on top, with Cahill's file directly underneath it. I bend down even lower in the chair and leave the file in the drawer in case someone walks in and sees me doing something I probably shouldn't be doing. I thumb through the file quickly and hunt for anything new or that might have eluded me the first time around. But it's all territory I have already covered: Parker's rap sheet, time served, arrest reports, copies of the Polaroid photos, and his probation record. I start to close the file when I notice a piece of yellow legal paper stuck in the back. Scribbled across the paper is a sloppy handwritten note with someone's name and phone number scrawled unevenly in childlike block letters. On the right-hand top of the paper is a notation from Navarro, *Parker's sponsor*. The almost illegible handwriting is Parker's from the first interrogation session, when Navarro told him to write down the name and number of his sponsor to confirm his alibi.

"We're taking a break, trying to sweat him," I hear Navarro tell someone from the other side of the closed door to his office. I stuff all the pieces of paper back into the file and slam the desk drawer shut. I bounce back up in the seat, but Navarro is already inside his office.

"I dropped something on the floor," I explain and try to redirect his attention elsewhere. "How did it go with Brewster?"

Navarro bites off a stray cuticle and spits it on the floor.

"Snooping again, huh, Julia? Let me know if you find anything good," Navarro responds. "That childhood friend of yours is a real winner."

"Brewster was never my friend. He was the school bully and terrorized everyone, including Ben and me. We were poor kids, so we were always an easy target for guys like him."

"Yeah, karma is a bitch, right? Look at that loser

now. That was a monster headache he was nursing when I pulled him out of the drunk tank."

"What did he say about Will?"

"Brewster said he passed out last night at about seven p.m. and didn't wake up until this morning. He swears on his dead mother's soul he knows nothing about Will's kidnapping and that he didn't hear anything unusual in the house last night. No kids crying, nothing like that."

"But if Brewster was passed out drunk, chances are he wouldn't have woken up even if a child was screaming in his house. Did he give you anything at all?"

"No. I need you to do something if you're up for it," Navarro says.

"I can watch the interview?"

"Not exactly. Do you have anything official with your name on it?"

I dig through my circus of a purse and pull out my driver's license and passport.

"You have your passport in your purse? What are you planning to do? Jet off to Paris after we're through here?"

"I just like to keep things on hand in case I ever need them," I answer.

Navarro looks carefully at both forms of my identification and tosses them back down on his desk. "These won't work. Do you have anything with your byline? You use your maiden name, Gooden, for your press credentials, right?"

I paw down deep in my bag and pull out my press passes.

"I told you I keep everything."

Navarro looks at my ID and nods his approval.

"Follow me," he says.

I expect Navarro to steer me toward the other side of the two-way mirror again, but much to my surprise, Navarro leads me directly into the interview room instead.

Inside the room is Parker, a much-changed man since the last time I saw him just hours before, when he was cocky and confident and sure he would beat the charge. Now Parker is a melting mess of perspiration and fear. I wonder how many children he made feel that exact same way.

Parker taps his foot against the cement floor in rapid succession like a nervous jackrabbit in front of a pack of hungry dogs. He abruptly stops his anxious tic when he notices the new arrivals. His eyes dart nervously from Navarro to me, the stranger in the room.

"Who's this? Is she from the D.A.'s office?" Parker asks.

Navarro pulls a chair out for me but remains standing.

"Even without the DNA evidence back yet, the D.A.'s office has enough to charge you with two counts of kidnapping and one count of murder, not to mention about a half a dozen more add on charges. You know how that goes," Navarro bluffs and looks in my direction.

Parker stares at me like a nervous child about to discover his punishment from the principal.

"You like the water?" Navarro asks.

"What do you mean?" Parker asks.

"You went down to the lake last night to baptize the

little boy you kidnapped. You planned on baptizing him for some sick religious ritual, but you got spooked when you heard someone coming. We know you did it. We found the little calling card you left behind."

Parker drags his fingers through his sweaty comb over and shakes his head. A few drops of perspiration fall from his forehead onto the plastic interview table.

"I wasn't down by the lake, and I didn't take no baby. I was with my sponsor last night. I told you that already."

"The longer you play this game and the longer you don't tell us what you did with that child, the longer your jail sentence is going to be, if you don't get the death penalty first," Navarro says and glances in my direction again. "A serial kidnapper and child murderer doesn't get many chances. Tell us where the little boy is, and we'll see if we can work out a deal."

Navarro pulls out the manila envelope from inside his leather jacket and places it down on the table. He reaches inside, pulls out a Polaroid, and flips it over so it is right side up and then pushes it across the table until it is directly in front of Parker. The picture is one of the photos of Ben and me. My brother holds my hand in the picture as we stand just outside the entrance of Funland.

"You know these kids?" Navarro asks.

Parker shakes his head.

"Real easy to prey on kids with no money, isn't it?" Navarro asks. "You spotted these kids when you drove the bus, and you knew they lived in the poor part of town so you targeted the boy, right?"

"I don't remember these kids. That was thirty years

ago. I may have fiddled with kids. I admit I got a problem with that, but I never kidnapped no boy and I never killed anyone in my life. I swear."

"Then why are you hanging on to their pictures? Pedophiles can never part with their treasures, huh?"

"I like taking pictures is all," Parker says.

"I bet you do. So on Labor Day, 1977, you see these kids on the boardwalk, and you remember the boy, Ben Gooden. He caught your eye, didn't he? You got your bus route for the new school year, and you see his name on there again with a new address. So you follow the kids home, but they don't take a ride from you because they're too smart. But you know where they live already, so you come back to get the boy that night after you've shot up. That gave you the courage you needed, right?"

"I don't take drugs no more," Parker says adamantly.

"But there was one thing that went wrong with your little plan. You didn't know someone else would be in the room when you came for the boy. You've been looking over your shoulder all these years wondering if that girl was going to come back and identify you."

"You got nothing on me. It's all circumstantial evidence."

"And the bones under your hunting camp came from where?" Navarro asks. "You've got the remains of a dead adult body on your property that someone took the time to bury. Who's the body belong to, Parker?"

"How am I supposed to know? I'm not the only person who lived on that property. My aunt and uncle lived there before me. Why don't you ask Mark Brewster? For all I know, he might've offed somebody and stuck them down there."

"Well, tell you what, I won't waste your time then. Let me just ask you one more question though. You sure you've never seen her before?" Navarro asks, pointing to the picture of the girl in the photo.

"Never."

"That's Julia Gooden. Ben Gooden's little sister. She's sitting across the table from you right now," Navarro says and shoves my press pass in front of his face.

Parker stares at the picture and then twists his head in my direction, looking like a crazed, feral animal as a cage door closes behind him.

"My friend here can identify you as the one who took her brother, Ben, thirty years ago. She saw you, Parker. She can identify you, and that's what you've been scared of all along, right?"

"You said she was from the D.A.'s office. You lied!" Parker yells. "You didn't tell me she was the girl from the room. That's entrapment right there. I've seen this kind of crap on TV. It'll never hold up in court. I told you, I wasn't in that kid's house. You're setting me up."

"Hey, genius, I never said my friend was from the D.A.'s office. You came to that conclusion on your own. Now you've got bigger problems to worry about."

Navarro stands up and puts his hand on my shoulder and begins to steer me to the door when Parker gives.

"Jesus Christ! All right. I took pictures of those kids. That's all. I saw them at Funland, and I liked the looks of the boy. I saw his name on my bus route and trailed the kids to Funland and then back home. But I didn't kidnap the boy. I told you, all I did was take pictures of kids and play with them a little. But I never broke into someone's home and snuck a kid out."

"Then how do you explain how you wound up with his necklace? You're screwed, Parker. Now give up where you have Will Tanner and I'll see if I can work any kind of deal for you if there's still time."

Parker snatches strands of his greasy hair between his nicotine-stained fingers and looks back at Navarro with savage fear as he searches for the truth tangled up in a dense thirty-year thicket of lies.

"I followed those kids home, but they wouldn't take a ride. I wanted to bring the boy back to my house to take some photos, you know? That's it. Just some pictures. I wasn't going to touch him or anything. Or maybe I would have, depending on how things went with him. The boy, the Ben kid, copped an attitude with me when I offered them a ride, though, so I took off."

"That's not all of the story," Navarro says and slams the leg of Parker's chair with his motorcycle boot.

"I didn't say I was done. I drove back to the kid's house that night. I wasn't going to break in. That's not my style."

"What were you going to do then? Jerk off in front of the kid's house while he was sleeping?"

A steam of red shoots up Parker's face as if Navarro nailed his motive.

"I was just driving the neighborhood. I was about five blocks away from the boy's house, and I see a car driving toward me. Something struck me strange about it. The car's lights were off, and it was late, man. Then a backdoor of the car . . . wait, it was a van . . . pops open and something falls out and kind of skitters across the ground. I stop my car and see the thing that hit the ground start running. Then I recognize him. It's the kid, the Ben boy. He's bleeding from his mouth and he's only got one shoe on, but this kid is running for all he's worth in my direction, waving both his hands at me, like he wants me to help him."

"What did you do?" Navarro asks.

"I was frozen, like I couldn't believe what was happening. I had been thinking about the kid, but I wasn't expecting anything like that. So the kid is halfway to my car, and then the van starts moving fast and stops right next to the boy. A big guy jumps out from the back of the van. It was dark, but I could see a little bit because the guy was right underneath a street light."

"If you're lying, I swear I'll kill you," Navarro says and squats down so he's looking Parker dead in the eye. "What did the man look like?"

"Dark-skinned. Not black. Maybe Hispanic or Indian. I don't know. It was a long time ago. The only thing I remember, this guy had a big old nasty scar that was sliced down the side of his face. Kind of in the shape of a crescent moon from his cheek to his jaw. The guy was as big as a mountain. He picks up the Ben kid with one hand and throws him in the back of the van, and then it takes off down the street."

"Nice story. But how'd you get the necklace?" Navarro asks.

"I saw it on the ground. It was shining under the streetlight. I got out of the car and put it in my pocket after the van took off."

"You're a lying sack of shit. And if you are telling the truth, you're a worthless excuse for a life for not calling the police to help save that boy."

"I didn't want to get involved," Parker answers and cowers in his chair, as if Navarro is going to punch him in the face for his response. "You have to understand. I had a record even back then and police would've been suspicious if I reported it. I never wanted to hurt the kid. I just wanted to play with him a little bit. I got an alibi if you're still thinking I did it and it's air-tight."

"Air-tight after thirty years, huh? That's convenient. Memories get pretty fuzzy."

"You call Joe Brighton down at Lou Ion's bar. The place is still there and he's still the owner. I went to Ion's right after I saw the guy throw the kid in the van. I remember the exact time because I was a little freaked out about what I saw. I mean I ain't no saint or nothin' with kids, but I could tell something pretty bad was going down. The time was twelve-fifteen a.m. I got a drink for last call and then I stayed and talked to Joe until about two a.m. He'll remember. I helped him break up a fight between his son and some loser redneck. The son broke the guy's nose and the cops came. That'll spark his memory."

Navarro studies Ben's case file and taps the tip of his pen down on the line where the police report lists the time I called 911 after I woke up and discovered Ben was missing: 12:30 AM.

"We'll call your alleged alibi. But your story stinks. What are you hiding, Parker? And what about those bones we found underneath your hunting camp? Save us some time and come clean. You're not getting out of this one."

Parker taps his teeth together as he considers his options. He then folds his hands across his chest, his decision made.

"This doesn't come back to me, all right?"

"No guarantees," Navarro answers.

"My aunt and uncle lived on the farm for years before my uncle let me live there. My aunt was real sick with cancer. She was suffering bad, terminal, and my uncle couldn't watch her like that anymore. He begged her doctor to do something, but the doctor wouldn't. So my uncle got his shotgun, slipped her a big old dose of morphine, and shot her through the heart. It was a mercy killing. He buried her under the hunting camp so it wouldn't come back on him. You ask my uncle. He'll tell you the truth."

The interview room door pops open, and Navarro's partner, Russell, enters.

"Your job is done here, Julia. You can go now," Navarro says.

I rise slowly to my feet and stare at Parker, sweaty and oozing with desperation. I open my mouth, ready to explode, but Navarro stops me before I can get a word out.

"Keep going."

I start toward the door and then pivot in the opposite direction. I lean into Parker and whisper in his ear, "I could kill you for what you did," and then shove my knee into his balls as hard as I can.

Parker lets out a howl and collapses in a fetal position on the floor, cupping his genitals.

I rear my leg back, unable to control myself now, and am about to launch a kick into Parker's ribs when Navarro yanks me back.

"God damn it. Get out of here!" Navarro yells.

Navarro's hand stays locked around my waist. He throws the interview room door open with his free hand, gives me a hard shove, and slams the door behind me. I run down the hallway as fast as I can, angry and raw and just needing to find an escape from the scene Parker painted in my mind. I clip around the corner quickly and collide into Pamela, the records clerk, and her files scatter across the floor.

"Sorry, Julia! I should've watched where I was going. I was just in a hurry to get back to the office after meeting with Reverend Casey Cahill's attorney."

I force myself to focus, get back on my feet, and help Pamela pick up the files. After my breathing steadies, I play what could be my last card.

"Navarro told me about your meeting," I lie. "What did you find out about my son?"

"Cahill's lawyer turned over the entire list of parishioners and anyone who ever made a donation to the church. There was a lot to go through. He had more than twenty thousand attendees at each service before he got all weird."

"Did you find anything?"

"It was inconclusive. It's not like people signed in at each service, and Parker could've watched the reverend on TV or on one of the church's podcasts. Anyway, it doesn't matter. We've already got Parker and his accomplice in custody."

"Can I see a copy of the letters that were sent to Cahill, the ones about me and my son?"

Pamela digs through the reassembled files and hands me a piece of heavy stationery. The handwriting is fluid and perfect. Parker's handwriting was that of a barely functioning illiterate. There's no way he could have written the letters to Cahill.

"Thanks for your help. I need to talk to Navarro."

I hightail it back down the hall to the interview room. I'm almost to the door when my cell phone begins to buzz in my pocket, but I ignore it. I bang my fist against the interview room door for a good minute and continue to pound until Navarro gives and the door finally flies open. Navarro greets me, red-faced and furious.

"What the hell are you doing? Russell and I were going to get him to tell the truth and then you attack him. He's going to press charges against you. His story was bullshit. I'm trying to get a confession here. He gives up your brother, then he gives up where he has Will."

"Parker didn't take Will. I should've listened to my gut and pushed you harder, but I didn't. My sister Sarah and her boyfriend are involved. You need to find them."

"I don't have time for this," Navarro shouts.

"Remember the letters Cahill got, the ones that said I had more than enough and it was my turn to pay? I saw those letters. The handwriting was beautiful and it was pretty, flowery writing, like a woman wrote it. I saw the piece of paper Parker wrote his sponsor's name and number on. His handwriting is like a five-year-old's. Parker didn't write those letters to Cahill. You've got the wrong guy. He didn't take Will."

"You interrupt my interrogation for this? We don't even know if those letters are legitimate yet. And if they are, maybe Brewster wrote them. Stop screwing around and let me do my job. You're pissing me off."

"Please, we are running out of time. If this bastard killed my brother, believe me, no one wants him caught more than me. But my brother has been gone for thirty years, and as much as I'd like to believe Ben is coming back, he isn't. You said it yourself. We still have time to save Will. But not much. Please, I beg you. You're looking at the wrong guy."

"Get out of here. I'm warning you. Go home and don't come back."

"I'm not going anywhere."

"If you don't leave, I'm going to arrest you for attempting to block an investigation. I'm not playing. Understood?"

Navarro spins me around and gives me a hard shove toward the precinct's front door.

"You're making a mistake," I call back to him.

But he's already gone back inside the interview room with Parker.

I realize I'm in this alone now. I rush back to my car with one focus in mind. I need to find Sarah's phone number. I start to search through my contacts on my cell phone when I notice three new voice mail messages flash across the screen and hit the play button.

"Julia, it's Tony Gowan. I have news on Steven Beckerus. He was scheduled to work backup security at Tiger Stadium last night. He clocked out at eight-thirty p.m. The job was supposed to go through midnight. Apparently, Beckerus left early because he was sick."

I save the message and am about to disconnect when the second message begins to play.

"Jesus, Julia! It's Kim. Call me back as soon as you get this. My mother just called from the airport. She

said her cousin Alice is vacationing in Europe too. Mother met up with her and they had lunch yesterday in Rome. I was so little when I met Alice, I couldn't really remember what she looked like. I'm going down to the guesthouse. I don't know who those people really are. I'm not sure if I should call the police first. I don't know what to do. Just call me right away."

"Shit," I say aloud. Kim shouldn't confront them without the police or me there.

The third and final voice mail message then begins to play.

"Mommy, help me! Please, Mommy! Auntie Kim is . . ."

The rest of Logan's desperate message is suddenly cut off.

CHAPTER 15

I speed-dial Kim's home number for the twentieth time as I fly down the highway, but the line is still busy. *Okay, Julia, keep calm*, I try and tell myself. Kim doesn't have call waiting. She thinks it's impolite. Kim is probably calling the police. I ignore the gnawing ache growing in my chest and try Kim's cell again.

"Come on, come on, answer the phone," I yell and pound my fist against the dashboard.

"You've reached Kim, please leave your name and number and I'll return your call. Have a nice day."

My call goes straight to Kim's cheery voice mail recording.

"Damn it," I yell as a swarm of red brake lights flashes ahead and traffic begins to crawl into a single lane for road construction.

I slam on the brakes and replay Logan's frantic voice message to try and decipher anything I might have missed the first time.

"Mommy, help me!" Logan begs.

My cell phone beeps in my ear mid-message.

"Kim, thank God!"

But the beeping sound continues. Kim isn't trying to call. The incessant beeping is just a reminder my phone charge has dwindled down to less than one percent. I never charged my phone last night and it's about to die. If I hurry, I may have time to make one more call. I make a split-second decision and dial Navarro's cell phone.

"You've reached Detective Ray Navarro. I can't take your call right now. If this is an emergency, please hang up and dial 911."

I made a critical mistake. Navarro is still interrogating Parker, so my only option is to leave a message.

"Navarro, damn it. It's Julia. I just got a message from Kim and Logan. They're in danger. I think my sister Sarah is involved. She and her boyfriend stopped by my friend Kim's house earlier. They know where she lives and Logan is there. I dropped him off at Kim's house so I could meet you at the police station. Two other people are staying with Kim who may be suspects. Their names are Alice and Leslie. I don't know their last names. They posed as long lost relatives, but Kim just found out they are not who they claimed to be. She left me a message about half an hour ago saying she was going down to the guesthouse to confront them. You need to send officers down there right away. Kim's address is . . ."

My phone makes one last, long beep and then dies. I didn't have time to leave Kim's last name, and now Navarro can't track her address. I can't afford any more mistakes.

I veer into the shoulder and pass the traffic, which has stalled to a standstill. I pray a police officer will pull me over for my illegal move, but of course there is none in sight. I shoot off the exit ramp and merge onto the lonely country back roads that lead to Kim's country estate. Kim's expansive property is a good ten miles away from her nearest neighbor, so Logan won't be able to find help unless he flags down a car, if he is able to escape.

At the ten-mile mark to Kim's house, I spot a convenience store in the distance. It's a one-pump gas station, "The Do Drop In." The store has to have a phone inside. I jerk the car to a stop and park next to a sign that reads, COLD BEER, LIVE BAIT, BEEF JERKY, AND DEER PROCESSING IN THE BACK. A tall, elderly man wearing a worn red cardigan sweater and a pair of plaid suspenders is stooped behind the counter. I rush to the front door and give it a strong push, but the glass door doesn't budge against my weight. A sign taped on the door that has a yellow clock with a smiley face posts the closing time as 6:30 PM. According to my watch, it's only 6:25 PM.

"Come on, open up," I yell and bang on the door with my fists.

The older gentleman continues to count out his cash drawer, oblivious to my crazed presence on the other side of the glass.

"Hey, out here! I need to use your phone. It's an emergency."

Despite my persistence, the old storekeeper doesn't look up.

But I won't be ignored. I run back to my car and slam my fist on the horn, which delivers a good twenty-second blast. Finally, the elderly man raises his head up slowly from the cash drawer. The shopkeeper pulls out a pair of wire-framed eyeglasses from his cardigan pocket with a shaky hand and peers in my direction. The old gentleman then leans on his cane and hobbles over to the front door in a pained, arthritic gait.

"I'm getting ready to close, dear," the elderly shopkeeper says. "I was just counting out the cash drawer. Sorry to keep you waiting. I'm hard of hearing, you know. My wife, Bess, keeps saying I need a new hearing aid, but the old one screeches like all get-out sometimes, so I don't put it in when she's not around."

"Please, it's an emergency. I need to use your phone," I plead.

The old man opens the door. As I rush inside, I smell a rank combination of deep fried fish and industrial cleaner.

"What's that, dear? We usually stay open on Labor Day until eight p.m., but we decided to close at six-thirty tonight. There aren't as many tourists heading to the lakeshore this year, I'm afraid. Everyone's hurting from the economy these days. The whole country is going in the toilet, don't you know."

"Can you hear me?" I yell.

The shopkeeper walks over to the counter and pulls out a pink pickled egg from a dusty mason jar.

"Would you like one, dear?" he asks, and pops the culinary monstrosity into his mouth. "Only twenty-five cents each. Bess makes the best pickled eggs this side of Chicago."

Just when I desperately need someone to hear me, the only person I can find is legally deaf. I reach inside my pocketbook and pull out my reporter's notebook and a pen.

I NEED TO USE YOUR PHONE. IT'S AN EMER-

GENCY, I write in giant letters in case the shop-keeper's vision is as bad as his hearing.

The storekeeper gulps down the egg and wipes his mouth with the back of a leathered hand.

"I'm sorry, dear, but we don't have a pay phone anymore. The wife said we didn't need it since everyone uses those cell phones these days. I never understood how those things worked really. And with business down, I had to get rid of our landline. That extra thirty-five dollars a month really added up. Bess likes to use the savings to play keno at the VFW in town, don't you know."

I hurriedly scribble down another message. *MY SON IS IN DANGER. HE IS AT KIM SCOTT'S HOUSE ABOUT TEN MILES FROM HERE. I AM GOING THERE NOW. YOU NEED TO LEAVE HERE AND CALL THE POLICE. KIM'S ADDRESS IS 45 WILLOW DRIVE.*

"Oh my goodness," the shopkeeper says. "I know Miss Scott. She's good people. She always gives us a loaf of her cheese bread every Christmas. Her cousin Leslie stopped by a little while ago to gas up. Leslie filled up her whole tank, she did. We don't take credit cards here, only cash. Credit cards are too expensive for us. Plus, it's a nice way to visit with folks. Otherwise they pay at the pump, and we don't get a chance to chat. When you're old like me, time goes by slower, don't you know. It was probably an hour ago when Leslie stopped by. What a pretty girl. She said she was sixteen, but she acted more like a younger girl. Very pleasant though. Leslie said she was about to leave on a trip with her mother."

"Take this," I say.

I write down the phone numbers for Navarro and David and tear the sheet of paper out of my notebook and shove it into the old storekeeper's hand. I'm halfway to the door when something makes me pause. I write down one more message, *PLEASE. I NEED YOUR HELP. DON'T FORGET ABOUT ME.*

The older gentleman smiles like a sweet and wise grandpa. "I won't, dear. My name is George by the way. George Tucker."

Tucker reaches out his hand to shake mine, but I ignore his gesture and stare at a glass case lined with three rows of gleaming pocketknives.

"I'll take one of those before I go."

PRIVATE DRIVE. NO TRESPASSING.

I punch the gas pedal until the speedometer hovers shakily over the ninety mark. Despite my speed, the car feels like it is driving in slow motion as I pass by the thickets of dense woods that surround Kim's expansive property.

The longest drive of my life finally ends, and I bank the car hard into the circular driveway. Kim's place looks just as I left it, like an enviable cover shot of *Town and Country* magazine. Kim's silver Volvo is still parked outside the garage, and the game of croquet is left untouched on the front lawn. I don't need to worry about breaking in. The front door of the house is wide open.

"Logan, where are you? Just call out to me and I'll find you," I plead as I tear through the open door and begin to hunt for my son.

Logan doesn't answer. The house is deathly silent

except for the steady ticking of a grandfather clock coming from somewhere deep inside the house.

I quickly assess the scene. I fully expected the house would be ransacked. But on first glance, everything seems undisturbed and picture perfect, just as Kim likes. The long entryway is lined with carefully hung black-and-white photographs of the mammoth Silver Lake Dunes, and Kim's purse and keys lie on a table near the open front door. Kim would never go anywhere without her purse.

The sound of a child's voice, soft and pleading, billows up from the downstairs finished basement.

"Sarah, let Logan go," I scream and bound down the stairs two at a time.

As my foot hits the landing, I snatch for my pocketknife and flip open the blade.

"That's all, folks!"

Porky Pig. I stand with a knife clutched in my hand ready to attack a cartoon character, as Porky Pig looms large on Kim's big-screen TV to an empty audience. Logan's *Looney Tunes* video case lies on the floor next to Logan's backpack. Its canvas has been sliced apart, as if someone was searching for something hidden inside.

I turn quickly to continue my search upstairs and slam into an old-fashioned writing desk. The antique shudders against my weight and its roll top recoils with a dull snap like a worn out rubber band. I start to run when something in the center of the desk catches my eye. It's an envelope addressed to Reverend Casey Cahill at the state penitentiary.

I stare at the envelope, trying to understand why Kim would have it in her possession, when a rhythmic, steady thump hums over my head, followed by a scraping sound, like someone is clawing for their life against the wooden floor as they are being dragged across it against their will. The stairs are a blur as I sprint toward the sound. Just as I reach the first floor, a slight and dark shape of a woman moves quickly away from the second-story landing. I race across the room to the other staircase. Lying on its first step is Logan's compass necklace.

"Let my boy go. I swear, I'll kill you!"

One more set of stairs. I scuttle to the top and catch the last second of a silhouette being shoved into a room that Kim uses as a study at the end of the long hallway. The door slams and a steel lock snaps in place. I reach the locked room, ram my shoulder against the heavy door, but quickly realize there's no way I can break it down by myself.

Kim's room is at the end of the hallway. I search for anything I can use as a battering ram and snatch a red leather stool from Kim's dressing table. I look up and catch a glimpse of a reflection in the mirror, my own face choked with panic and desperation staring back at me. I'm about to run when I spot something else in the mirror, a handwritten note on a piece of white stationery lying at the foot of Kim's bed. The paper has a smudged, bloody fingerprint and three simple words, *I'm sorry, Julia.*

Sarah. I knew it was my sister all along. A blinding rage builds up inside of me as I haul the heavy stool toward the locked room.

"Sarah, let Logan go! I don't know what kind of trouble you're in or what you did, but we can work it out. I'll give you money. Just tell me how much you want. I won't go to the police this time. Just let Logan go and everything will be fine. You have to believe me."

"It's too late," a hoarse voice whispers from inside the room. "No one was supposed to find out, and now I must do as I'm told."

The snap of metal crashing against wood peals down the hallway like a piercing scream. I look down at the stool still unused in my hands. The crash came from inside the room.

"Logan, stay with me!"

On the other side of the door, the person in distress lets out three gasps, wet and sticky and struggling for one last precious breath. Then there is a swishing sound of fabric furiously rubbing together like a runner trying to sprint mid-air. The movement stops abruptly and a door bangs shut inside the room.

And then all goes horribly silent.

I smash the metal legs of the stool against the door over and over until it gives. The lock breaks and the door opens slowly with a creak.

I brush past the splinters and run blindly inside, tripping over a ladder that has fallen on its side like a dead horse. I start to pick myself up when something sways back and forth over my head and three drops of something moist and warm land on my arm. I recoil toward the wall and look up at Kim. A stream of blood drips down from her forehead as she swings from a wooden beam. Her lifeless blue eyes bulge from their sockets and stare directly into mine.

CHAPTER 16

I make myself look away from Kim's dangling body and search for Logan, but there is no trace of my son or anyone else in the room. I right the ladder and scramble up until I'm directly in front of Kim and work on severing the thick rope coiled around her neck with my pocketknife. The jerking motion makes Kim bounce back and forth as if she is swaying to the rhythm of a song on the radio.

"Don't die on me," I plead and try to keep my shaking hands steady so I can get Kim down before she suffocates. But from the unnatural way Kim's head is listing to the side, I know it is too late. Kim's neck is broken.

The tears come silently as I work through the last few pieces of the noose. When it finally tears away, Kim's body makes a sudden, sharp drop. Her blond bob poofs up like a parachute on the descent until she lands with a hard smack on the hardwood floor. I loosen the rope from around her neck and then feel for a pulse. Nothing.

An adjoining door that leads to a guest bedroom bangs open, and I prepare for the battle of my life against my sister. But instead of Sarah, the narrow view into the room yields just the back of a small child who is slumped, wearing only a diaper, and sitting on a blanket facing the wall as if he is being punished. White blond hair. *Jesus, it's Will.*

"Mom is here!" I cry.

The sound of my voice snaps Will out of his trance, and he starts running straight toward me, red faced and screaming all the way with his mouth wide open and his arms outstretched. I race to pick up my little boy when a sharp pain slices into my back and explodes a bolt of white-hot electricity through my body as if I've been struck by lightning. The room starts to go from white to black, and I realize I am seconds away from losing consciousness when the excruciating sensation stops. I fold to the floor and land immobilized on my right side.

"Go back in the corner!" a female voice shrieks.

Will ignores the command, his screams now desperate howls, as his bare feet pound against the floor to reach me.

I can't move. I watch in horror with my face frozen against the floor as someone scoops up Will, tosses him roughly back in the corner of the adjacent room, and then slams the door.

Jesus Mother Mary Joseph. I try and come up with any kind of prayer I can remember from when my childhood friends took me to church with them after a Saturday night sleepover. The door to the room where Will is being kept opens again, and the answer to my prayer is a pair of shapely legs in hot-pink Dr. Martens walking straight toward me. My eyes are the only part of my body I can move. I scan up to see the owner of the hot-pink Dr. Martens. Hovering directly above me is Leslie. Her thin hip juts out to the side, and she is posed in a provocative Rambo-like combat stance holding a Taser gun.

I try and reach for my pocketknife, but my arm is dead.

"Hello, Julia," Leslie says in her little-girl voice.

She picks up her electric-pink boot and slams it into my back, right in the spot where the Taser gun hit. A scream of agony starts to build from inside my core but stays trapped inside my useless body.

"Aren't you just a little surprise showing up like this," Leslie says, sounding like a haughty brat who didn't get her way.

She rears her shiny boot back for a second time and connects another blow against my back. A wave of nausea washes over me, and I feel like I am going to throw up. I breathe through the pain and concentrate on a single speck of dust on the floor until the feeling stops.

"Let me see my baby," I demand through chattering teeth.

"Shut up," Leslie answers. "The baby is just fine. He wet the bed and made a big mess for me to clean up so he's getting his punishment. You do wrong, you get punished."

"You murdered Kim."

"She stuck her nose in where she shouldn't have. So I had to do as I was told."

Footsteps, angry and determined, stomp down the long hallway in my direction until a pair of black, orthopedic old-lady shoes stands an inch away from my face.

"Horrible, selfish little bitch. Dirty little selfish whore."

I recognize the voice.

"Alice," I say.

"What's she doing here?" Alice asks Leslie.

"I found her in the room right after I killed Kim, like you told me."

One of Alice's black shoes stamps down hard on the floor in front of my face.

"And I beheld when he had opened the sixth seal, and, lo, there was a great earthquake; and the sun became black as sackcloth of hair, and the moon became as blood," Alice bellows, her voice quaking like a Pentecostal preacher at a Sunday morning tent revival meeting.

"Where's Logan? Let my children go. They haven't done anything to you," I beg as Will continues to scream for me in the next room.

"When I snuff you out, I will cover the heavens and darken their stars. I will cover the sun with a cloud, and the moon will not give its light," Alice moans.

"Jesus. Who the hell are you people?"

"The true believers. Cut from the cloth of God the almighty, who will return only when we truly repent and offer him a sacrifice," Alice answers.

"You're with Cahill," I realize.

Alice settles down on her haunches, tilts her head, and looms sideways, taking me in. Her grey eyes glow bright and manic, and she shoots the tip of her pointed tongue out at me like a venomous snake about to bite.

"Hand me my bag," Alice commands.

Leslie scurries to the hallway and returns with Alice's knitting bag.

"Get it out, but be careful."

"I ain't touching that thing," Leslie answers.

"Give it here then, girl."

Leslie pinches the ends of the knitting bag carefully between her thumbs and index fingers and places it at Alice's feet.

"Behold, I give unto you power to tread on serpents and scorpions, and over all the power of the enemy," Alice whispers excitedly. She quickly moves to the closet and extracts a wire hanger that she uncoils but leaves its curved neck intact and dips it inside her bag.

"Come on out now, I declare, you incarnation of the devil!"

Alice eases the hanger from the knitting bag and pulls along with it a thick, brown snake with coral pin stripes spooled in three wide loops around the center of the erect wire.

"Jesus. Tell me who you people really are," I say.

Leslie sidles next to Alice and points the stun gun an inch away from my head.

"Her name is Alice. We didn't lie about that. She's my aunt."

Alice begins to wave the snake around in a fluid figure eight through the air as she chants in gibberish.

"Satanica berufa miorci, Jesus lantico animon."

"She's pissed because you took her pastor away," Leslie explains. "You wouldn't like Auntie when she's pissed."

"Cahill told you to do this?"

The mention of Cahill's name seems to snap Alice to attention. She shoos the snake back inside the bag and squats back down on the floor and studies me for a moment. She stands back up slowly and walks to the window, where she looks out at the evening dusk beginning to settle across Kim's remote property.

"I went to Reverend Cahill's Pentecostal services every Sunday. The morning services were full of praise and devotion, but the night worships were when things really heated up. Reverend Cahill brought the snakes out then, just like he said his daddy did when he did the tent revival meetings," Alice says and her plump body trembles with an orgasmic shudder. "I could never get the reverend's attention. Too many people at the services. They came as far as Indiana to hear his Word, and I could never get close enough. But one time, he looked out at the crowd, his hands raised to the heavens, and I swear he smiled at me. I used to watch his syndicated television show every night, but Reverend Cahill really caught fire when he went high heaven Pentecostal after his accident."

"What do you want with me and my family?"

"I saw you the first time outside of the courthouse when my reverend was on trial. I was picketing with the other brothers and sisters from the congregation, protesting the dirty lies you wrote. But you didn't see me. You looked right over us like we were trash. It's your fault he went to jail. You've got evil around your soul. It lashes at you like flames, and I know you know it too."

"Your problem is with me, not my children. Let them go."

"Let them go," Alice mimics in a singsong voice. "Reverend Cahill spoke to me on the radio. It was his own personal message for his Alice, just like when he

smiled at me that one time in church. Reverend Cahill said sacrifices needed to be made. *'Take your son, your only son Isaac, whom you love, and go to the land of Moriah, and offer him there as a burnt offering on one of the mountains of which I shall tell you.'*"

"That stupid jailhouse radio interview."

Leslie pulls out a pack of pink bubblegum from her back pocket and stuffs two pieces in her mouth.

"We were planning to kill you, but once Alice heard Reverend Cahill on the radio, we had a change of plans. We'd been tracking you for a while now. Auntie told me to get inside, to get you to trust us," Leslie says. "I started researching you on the computer. It was a little hard to get to you at first. Besides your articles, you don't have any personal pages on the Internet, not even Facebook. But your friend Kim did. She had plenty. Kim put tons of personal information on her page, including pictures of you and your sons. We found out where you lived and what your boy Will looked like. Kim had a family tree page and with a little snooping, I found a distant cousin named Alice. Kim wrote a comment next to her cousin's name, saying she hadn't seen her in thirty years. The cousin and my aunt had the same name, so we knew it was a sign. I sent your friend a Facebook message and we started corresponding. We got on real friendly terms pretty quick, and I baited her. I told Kim that Alice and I would be in Michigan looking at boarding schools for me, and she bit. Even invited us to stay with her. She believed everything. Your friend was real nice but real stupid. She should know you should never trust strangers, especially people you meet on social media. I'm a kid and I even know that."

I look over at Kim and try not to scream.

"Kim was a kind and trusting person."

"Like I said, nice but stupid. I made her write the note I left on the bed before I strung her up," Leslie says, sounding pleased with herself.

"Kim had the audacity to threaten me. She and your Logan boy showed up unannounced. I don't like surprise visitors. Kim was going to call the police. So we had to make it look like she committed suicide after she murdered your boy," Alice says.

"You killed Logan!"

"Not yet. He ran off when Kim started screaming. We'll find him though. I'm a very good hunter," Leslie says.

I still have a chance to save my sons. Unless I can regain the ability to move my body, I need to buy time until the police arrive.

"You two kidnapped Will last night."

"Alice found your home security code in Kim's bedroom," Leslie explains. "We knew she had it written down somewhere. Kim said she checked on your house while you were away this summer. She made everything so easy for us, the stupid bitch."

"Watch that dirty mouth of yours!" Alice warns.

Will's cries have ebbed into a jagged whimper. Before Leslie goes to retrieve him, she sticks the Taser gun against my stomach and turns on the juice. My body writhes on the floor like a live wire until she finally lets up.

My heart leaps sporadically in my chest until I am convinced I am going to die next to Kim. But the pain finally stops and I breathe in and out until my heart begins to beat normally again. I command my body to fight, but all I can muster is a slight twitch in my right arm. The tiny movement shoots a surge of searing pain down my side.

Leslie returns from the other room with Will, who is now lying docile in her arms.

"Will, I'm here," I say.

"Mama," Will moans.

I move forward inch by inch and drag my dead weight toward the wall. Although I've barely moved, I feel like I am in the last throes of a triathlon as sweat begins to stick to the back of my shirt and forehead. I finally reach the wall and collapse against it.

In my new vantage point, I get a full panorama of the hell that is standing before me. Alice has changed out of her faded hippy attire and now wears a shapeless and worn grey dress. Her waist-length hair is tied tightly into a braid that coils down her back.

"My mama," Will cries.

Alice jerks around and covers Will's face with a baby blanket.

"Do not speak to the child again," Alice says. "We've lost our way and must come back to God through sacrifice. There is no greater sacrifice than the blood of a child on an altar before the most holy. Reverend Cahill will find out what I did, and then he will know who I am. He'll thank me personally. That's what he'll do."

"I'm going to kill you," I say.

"Leslie, take the baby back to the guesthouse."

"He better not mess himself again or he's really going to get it this time," Leslie says.

Will continues to scream for me under the blanket.

"My mama!" he begs. Will's anguished cries continue until his small voice disappears down the staircase.

"It's going to be all right," I promise him.

"Now shush your mouth," Alice whispers.

"Cahill is in jail for what he did, not because of any article I wrote. He raped little girls in his congregation and stole the church's money."

Alice bends down, grabs a fistful of my hair, and yanks me up so I can see her cold grey eyes.

"Now you listen to me!" Alice yells savagely as spit flies out of the corners of her mouth. "Those girls were treasured by the reverend. I only wish he'd chosen Leslie."

"Jesus Christ. You're either crazy or completely brainwashed by that son of a bitch."

Alice releases my hair and my head smacks against the wooden floor.

"You just shut your mouth or I'll have Leslie carve it out of your face."

Leslie rushes back into the room, her alabaster skin glistening with sweat.

"I took the baby to the guesthouse and put him in the crib just like you wanted," Leslie pants.

"You need to go find the boy Logan and take care of him. Kill him and bring the body back here."

Logan is smart. He will keep running until he finds help.

"I like Logan. I wish we could take him with us," Leslie says.

"Shut up. You follow my direction, girl. Now go on and change back into your regular clothes. You look like a whore dressed like that."

"I like these clothes."

"Those are devil clothes. You get out of them and put on something godly, you hear?"

Leslie lifts up her index finger and thumb, like she is holding a gun, and points it in Alice's direction.

"Boom, boom!" Leslie says.

"You get out of here now, little girl, or I will get a real gun and shoot you dead with one shot," Alice says.

The threat brings Leslie back in line, and she hustles out of the room to do Alice's bidding.

"Something's never been quite right about that girl," Alice mutters as she watches Leslie disappear down the hallway.

"You wrote those letters to Cahill," I say.

Alice nods and begins to run her finger along the windowsill, like a dutiful Stepford wife dusting before her husband comes home after a hard day's work.

"The letters were key, because they would throw the police off track and then I wouldn't be looked at as a suspect."

"How did you know about my brother?"

"Old newspaper stories. Google is a gift from God. You do a quick search, and you can find out anything about a person. I found out about the Indian arrowhead in a *Detroit Free Press* online article and had Leslie plant one under your baby's crib. Ordered it on eBay, I did. The Lord helped me craft a perfect plan. No one was supposed to find out, but then Kim figured it out, and you and your brat Logan showed up here. You'll all be dead soon enough and the Lord will have his offering."

"I heard that radio interview with Cahill. He wasn't

talking about a human sacrifice. Cahill is a deranged pervert, but he's no killer."

"Get behind me, Satan. I will not listen to your trickery. You're nothing but a miniscule ant in God's eyes."

Alice slams her foot against the back of my head, shooting bands of white stars that explode in front of my eyes. I close them tight until the pain in my head reduces to a dull throb.

"I told you to change out of that sinful outfit," Alice says to Leslie, who has returned in her tank top and shorts.

"I didn't have time."

"You will get back into your dress once she's taken care of, understand? Now, tie Julia up. Bring her downstairs and throw her in the trunk of the car. I'm going to gather our belongings and start wiping down the place. Be careful not to touch anything like I told you."

Alice pads heavily down the hallway, and Leslie dutifully begins to coil the rope she used to kill Kim around her arm.

Leslie is a murderer, but still young and stupid. She may be my only way out.

One thing I know how to do is make people talk.

"Don't listen to Alice. You're just a kid. Where are your parents?"

"My mother died when I was ten and my dad took off before I was born. Alice was the only person who'd take me in. I'm not supposed to talk to you."

"You must miss your mom. You can't believe the crazy religious stuff Alice is feeding you."

For a second, Leslie looks like a hurt child instead of a cold-blooded killer.

"I do miss my mom. Alice is nuts, but I got my own room and she paid me five hundred bucks to help her kidnap your kid. I'm going to take the money and move to New York City. I'm going to be a model. Do you think I'm pretty?"

"Alice is manipulating you. Do the right thing and let me go. I'll tell the police you were brainwashed into believing this bullshit and they'll help you."

Leslie nibbles on the underside of her bottom lip and considers my argument.

"Then I won't get the money. Alice is all right. She's crazy religious, but she treats me okay, especially when she takes her medication. She hates you though. She's got a room in the basement back home with pictures of you up on the wall and all the stories you wrote about her reverend are tacked up there too."

"Just let me have the phone so I can call the police. I'll tell them this was a big misunderstanding and none of it was your fault."

"I'm not stupid and I'm not going to jail. I've been to juvie twice already and I know jail is a million times worse. Alice always took me back in with her after I got out, no matter what kind of trouble I got into, so I owe her. She hits me sometimes when she's angry, but it's usually because I deserve it."

"No one deserves to be hit."

"I'm going to be on the cover of *Cosmopolitan* magazine once I get to New York. None of those other models I see have tits as nice as mine."

Her decision obviously made, Leslie begins to bind my hands and feet together with the thick rope. My body is still too weak from the Taser gun assaults to fight back.

"I know how to tie a real good knot," Leslie says and cinches the rope around my hands so tightly it slices through the skin on my wrists.

"Please, just wait, Leslie."

Leslie's hands latch around my ankles, and she pulls me down the hall to the stairs. The back of my skull slams against each of the sixteen ceramic tile steps until we finally reach the main floor.

"I'm tired, Alice," Leslie complains. "I can't carry her anymore."

"Julia hardly weighs a thing," Alice lectures from the kitchen. "Do I need to do this myself? I think not. Go get the wheelbarrow from the garden and use that to haul her out to the car."

Leslie dumps me in the middle of a great room and hurries to the outside patio, but stops dead in her tracks when the doorbell rings.

"Get her in the closet right now," Alice whispers in a deadly hiss. "Why didn't you gag her?"

"You didn't tell me to."

Alice rears back her arm and slaps Leslie across the mouth.

"Don't you sass me, child. Here," Alice says and hands Leslie a black cotton scarf from the coat rack. "Stuff it in her mouth. Now."

I start to gag as Leslie jams the fabric down my throat.

"No talking, Julia," Leslie says quietly. "I'll have to choke you otherwise."

Leslie tugs me across the living room floor to the

hall closet and shoves me inside. In her haste, Leslie leaves the door open a sliver, just enough for me to get a direct view of the front entryway.

"Get out of here!" Alice tells Leslie. "Go out through the screen door and hide in the backyard. Don't come back in the house unless I tell you. I don't need a stupid girl saying stupid things and ruining it all for me."

Leslie darts to the screen door and disappears outside.

Alice takes a deep breath and clasps her hands together as if she is about to pray, when the doorbell chimes a second time. Alice reaches inside her knitting bag on the coffee table and pulls out a pair of silver shears. She carefully tucks them inside a pocket in the front of her dress and opens the front door a crack.

A man's voice greets her from the other side of the door.

"Good evening. Sorry to bother you, but I was on the way home and I wanted to stop by to see if everything was all right. A very worried young lady stopped by my store a little while ago. She said there was some kind of emergency here at this house, and her son was in danger."

The visitor at the door isn't the police as I had so desperately prayed for, but the older shopkeeper, George Tucker. I begged him not to forget about me. And he didn't.

Alice sizes up the old man, throws back her head, and laughs.

"No emergency here. I almost burned the dinner rolls, but I rescued them in time. I don't think that constitutes an emergency, do you?" she asks.

"That's odd. The young lady, Julia was her name, was very agitated. She asked me to call the police when I got home, but I wanted to stop by here first," he says. "I even put my hearing aid in so I could hear the police when I called them. That young lady just seemed so genuine with her concern, and I promised I wouldn't forget her."

Alice's jaw muscles begin to twitch.

"I don't know anyone named Julia. You have the wrong house."

"That's her car there in your driveway, isn't it? I recognize it from the store," Tucker answers. "In my line of work, days go by kind of slow sometimes so I get real interested in the cars that pull up, especially when business is quiet like tonight."

"That's my niece's car," she answers.

"Miss Kim? She's a real nice girl. But doesn't she drive that other one parked in the driveway, the silver Volvo? I've seen her pull up to the store in that nice-looking vehicle," Tucker says. "That's a mighty expensive automobile. I looked up the Kelley Blue Book value on that one, I did. That's a real fine car. My Bess and me, we can only afford my old Ford truck. I bought it in '69, but it still runs real good."

"We have more than one car here," Alice answers. "Now is there something else I can help you with?"

"No. I guess not then. I met Miss Kim's cousin Leslie earlier. Real sweet young girl. Have a nice evening. Sorry to bother you. I see you're already in your nightgown ready for bed."

"Good night," Alice says and begins to shut the door.

"Well, happy Labor Day. I guess it means summer is officially over, don't you know," Tucker answers.

My heart sinks as Tucker leaves and Alice bolts the door after him.

Now that the inconvenient visitor is gone, Alice pulls out her knitting shears from her pocket and heads toward my hiding place in the closet. Her hand grasps the knob of the closet just as the front doorbell rings again. Startled, Alice slides the shears back into her dress pocket and storms back to the front door.

"Sorry to bother you again," Tucker says as he fondles his cardigan buttons nervously between his arthritic fingers. "I made that young lady a promise. She gave me two phone numbers to call. It's a good thirty-minute drive still to my house. Bess is making me boiled dinner tonight and I don't want to be late, but I really should make those calls. Could I use your phone? I need to call that young lady's husband and some policeman, too."

Without invitation, Tucker hobbles into the house like a naïve lamb foolishly heading to the slaughter. Tucker reaches the foyer, his fate already sealed as the screen door to the backyard silently slips open. A glint of silver flashes in the light as Leslie sprints toward Tucker from behind with something raised in her right hand. Leslie is holding an ax.

I raise my bound feet and pound them against the side of the closet to alert Tucker. He turns his head slowly in the direction of the sound but a second too late. The sharp blade makes impact and slices into the center of Tucker's skull and a surprised groan comes out of the old man's dry lips. Somehow, despite the assault, Tucker continues to stand for a moment, just staring wide-eyed with surprise until his well-lived body collapses in a heap on the floor.

"Please. Please. My Bess . . ." Tucker begs.

Leslie doesn't heed Tucker's desperate pleas for his life. She raises the ax up high and lets it fall a second time. It connects and burrows deep into the back of the old shopkeeper's neck.

CHAPTER 17

Leslie tugs the ax out from Tucker's neck with a grunt and rears her arm back, ready to continue the assault. Before Leslie can deliver the third strike, Alice grabs her wrist and squeezes until Leslie lets out a yelp of pain.

"I said to stay outside until I told you it was all right to come in," Alice barks.

A look of hurt stings Leslie's pretty face. "I was just trying to help. Just like I did with Kim. You told me to kill her, so I figured you would want me to kill the old man, too. He was interfering just like she did. What do you want me to do now?"

"Clean up this mess," Alice says, pointing a stubby finger at the pool of blood collecting around Tucker's head. "Go get some towels to sop up the blood. Now!"

"I'm sorry," Leslie answers, as her bottom lip juts out and begs to quiver.

"That's better," Alice says. "Go get a mop and bucket. And get the body out of here."

Leslie lets the hatchet fall to the floor and runs to the

garage to fetch the cleaning supplies like a good dog obeying its master.

Alice pulls a small mirror out of her pocket. She shines it against her ample hip and then places it under Tucker's nose and mouth for a few minutes and then inspects the glass carefully.

"Fogged up. Still breathing, I'm afraid. That's a shame. You're probably praying right now for God's mercy aren't you, silly old man?" Alice asks Tucker, whose chest is slowly managing to heave up and down.

Alice turns away from Tucker's dying body and studies her watch. "Five minutes to seven. It's time for my nightly communion. I'm certainly not going to commune in fellowship with the likes of you two."

Tucker opens his mouth to speak, but the only thing that comes out is a thin wheeze.

"Suffer in silence. There will be no disruptions during church. That's what my mother always told me," Alice says. "None of this is proper or orderly. Everything is supposed to be orderly. When you don't have order, that's when the devil slips in."

Leslie hustles back into the room with a mop and bucket. She begins frantically trying to sop up Tucker's blood by swaying the mop back and forth in hurried strokes. But the mop is bone dry and only smears the red stain further across the floor.

Alice grabs Leslie by the neck and shoves her face just above Tucker's pool of blood, like a master punishing a dog for defecating on the floor. "You don't even know how to mop properly. You need to fill up the bucket with water first and then get the mop wet before you start. See this? Fix it. I'm going upstairs for my nightly communion. This better be cleaned up and the body gone before I get back."

Alice ascends up the staircase and begins to sing in an off-key soprano, "Praise God, From Whom All Blessings Flow," a staple religious hymn I remember Logan learned when David took him to church. A chill runs through my body as I realize that was the song Logan must have heard last night when Alice was standing over his bed.

A door slams shut upstairs as Alice enters her make-shift religious sanctuary, and Leslie's feet paddle toward the kitchen with a bucket in her hand. She turns the corner and I hear a steady hiss as the kitchen sink turns on.

"She's such a mean, ungrateful bitch," Leslie complains from the kitchen. "Someone should teach her a lesson."

Leslie leaves the bucket in the sink with the water still running and bolts over to the closet. She grabs my feet in a vise grip and hauls me out of the closet, toward the front door. We get halfway across the great room when Leslie suddenly freezes.

"The water. I put the plug in the sink and left the water running. Alice will flip again if it spills all over the floor."

Leslie drops me next to Tucker and races back into the kitchen. I now lay face-to-face with the dying old man, whose only mistake was trying to help me. Tucker opens his mouth slightly, exposing a set of dentures that are coated in a thick, sticky film of red. Tucker's lips begin to tremble as though he wants to tell me something, but the only thing that comes out is a moist rattling noise from his throat that sounds as if he is gargling jelly. I am sure he is seconds from death when Tucker's eyes shoot wide open.

"I came back . . . for you," Tucker barely whispers.

Tucker is panting now, his breath shallow and strained. "Tell my Bess I love her."

Tucker lets out a slight cough and a gush of blood spurts from his mouth. His eyes begin to roll back in his head, but somehow, he is still breathing.

Heavy footsteps plod from the kitchen in my direction. "I looked everywhere. I don't know where the towels are in this big, stupid house," Leslie says.

Leslie stands over me with her hands on her hips, and her eyes narrow as they fixate on the black scarf. She yanks it out of my mouth and stuffs it around Tucker's head to try and plug up the blood that continues to seep from his head.

"Leslie . . ." I gasp, my mouth raw and dry from the makeshift gag. "You don't have to take Alice's abuse anymore."

"Shush your mouth, Julia," Leslie scolds. "I don't want to hear your stupid talk. Let's go."

Leslie puts her arms around my waist and drags me with effort out of the house and over to her blue sedan in the driveway.

"One down," Leslie says, panting. "I've got to finish off the old man now."

Leslie throws my bound body against the rear right wheel of the car and runs back inside the house to tend to the next chore on her list.

I try and slip my arms and legs free from the knotted rope, but Leslie tied the restraints too tightly. I lift up my arms and try and sever the rope against the metal edge of the car, when something darts into view. A slight figure peers out from behind an apple tree on the far corner of the property and then cautiously steps out from the hiding place.

It's Logan.

"Run, Logan! Get out of here!" I call out to him quietly.

Logan runs as fast as he can until his thin arms wrap tightly around me. His heart beats wildly against my chest and his face is smudged with dirt and tears.

"They have Will," Logan cries. "I heard Aunt Kim talking to her mom on the phone, and I knew something was wrong. She told me to stay in the main house, but I followed her. She was talking to Alice and Leslie in the guesthouse, and that's when I heard a baby start to cry. Leslie and Alice dragged Aunt Kim inside, and I heard her start to scream. Aunt Kim started yelling that they kidnapped Will. I could see them through the window. Alice had a gun. She said she would kill Will if Aunt Kim called the police. Alice hit Aunt Kim with the gun, right across her face, and she started bleeding. I got scared and ran into the woods. I prayed you would come and find me."

"Listen to me, Logan. You don't have much time. I have a knife in my pocket. Take it. You need to get out of here right now."

Logan fumbles in my pocket and pulls out the knife. He flips it open and begins to cut back and forth against the thick knot around my wrists.

"No. You have to go. There's no time. Run and get help."

Logan ignores my order. He keeps cutting, determined to get me free.

"I'm not going to leave you, Mom," Logan vows.

"You have to. I'll be okay. I promise. Just get out of here. Run as fast as you can until you get to the main road. Then flag down a car and call the police."

"I'm going to go find Aunt Kim. I heard Alice and Leslie say they were going to take her to the house. Aunt Kim will help us."

"No! Don't go in there."

As soon as the warning comes out of my mouth, Tucker lets out one last moan from inside the house.

"Logan, run!"

Logan leaps to his unsteady feet. He turns to go but hesitates for a moment and looks back at me, struggling with the decision of what he should do. I force the tears back so Logan will think I'm strong, and I silently say good-bye to my little boy.

"I'm going to save you and Will," Logan promises. "I won't let Alice or Leslie hurt either of you."

His choice now made, I watch Logan's thin arms and legs race across the yard until he disappears into the woods. I say a silent prayer he will make it to safety.

Alice appears from the house, swishing her ample bottom side to side, with Leslie following behind, as she pushes a wheelbarrow through the front door. A pair of long, thin legs dangles from the wheelbarrow's side. The spindly legs belong to Tucker.

"Throw them both in the trunk," Alice commands.

"The old guy is too heavy," Leslie cries. "You don't do anything. You could help me for once. I want more money when this is over. You owe me for all this extra bullshit."

"Shut up and do it!" Alice screams. She hauls back her arm and slaps Leslie hard across the face.

Leslie begins to cry quietly and goes back to the business at hand. She grunts as she lifts Tucker and drops him in the trunk. A few of his brittle bones snap like toothpicks on impact. Leslie wipes away a drop of sweat from her forehead and comes for me next. She jams her long, slender hands under my armpits. I instinctively turn my head and bite Leslie as hard as I can on her forearm until I feel my teeth sink into her flesh.

"Bitch!" Leslie cries out in surprise and pain.

Alice bends down and shoves one of her fat fingers in the dirt. She then rubs her finger against my forehead.

"You're a dirty girl. You must wear your sin for all to see," Alice chastises and then directs her attention to Leslie. "Get her in the car, now."

Leslie spits in my face as payback and tosses me roughly inside the trunk. I land on top of Tucker, who is soaked in blood and covered with bits of flesh and brain matter.

Before the trunk closes, Leslie throws in a long shovel that smashes against my bent knees. I savor the last few seconds of fresh air and quickly fading sunlight until the trunk slams shut and I am jammed into a pitch-black coffin with a dead body. The odor of blood, urine, and sweat from Tucker quickly fills the car, and I hold my breath so I won't get sick. I fight the panic growing inside of me and make mental notes of the car's movements. I don't hear any other vehicles, so we must still be on the property. We drive for what seems about five miles when the car comes to a sudden stop and the driver-side door opens.

"Here, Alice?" Leslie asks.

"No. Not out here in the wide open. Start digging behind those trees," Alice says.

"How many holes?"

"Two for now. We should leave the boy's body in the house near Kim's, so it will be obvious to the police she killed him. I'll be inside. Don't bother me until you're done. Understand?"

"Yes, Alice," Leslie says.

The trunk opens, and Leslie reaches in for the shovel. I then realize its intent: Leslie plans to bury me alive. I look up toward the melting blues and purples of twilight and beg the universe for help.

"I don't care what happens to me, but please just let my boys be safe," I pray.

The sound of metal striking dirt echoes in the background as Leslie begins to dig. I rock back and forth to see if I can gain momentum and try and swing my feet over the side of the trunk but freeze when heavy footsteps approach the car.

"Why do I have to do this all by myself? Alice never does anything. She's just a big fat pig," Leslie says. "Stupid dried-up bitch. I bet she wants Cahill to screw her, but he'd be a fool to touch her jelly ass."

She walks over to the trunk and stares through me with a vacant, careless gaze. I hold my breath as she reaches in and grabs Tucker. His limbs flop like a marionette's as Leslie tugs at his limp, awkward body and hoists him out of the trunk. I hear his body scrape along the dirt as Leslie drags Tucker over to his grave. Even though it is a muggy early September evening, I begin to shiver uncontrollably as the sound of a shovel hitting the earth repeats until the last scoopful of dirt scatters atop Tucker. There is an eerie stillness for a moment, as though the woods and its creatures are mourning Tucker in a moment of silence. Leslie's quick feet break the quiet as she returns for me.

Leslie is above me now, still panting from the exertion of burying Tucker. Her head is drenched in sweat, which rolls down her face and drips onto mine. She kneels toward the trunk, grabs my feet, and begins to pull me out.

"No, Leslie!" I say, scrambling to come up with anything to buy more time. "You shouldn't do anything Alice says."

Leslie ignores my plea and drags me across the ground until the exposed skin on my arms is rubbed raw. The journey over, she suddenly stops and drops me down in front of a small mound of fresh earth, Tucker's final resting place. Next to Tucker's grave is a second hole, the one she dug for me.

Leslie falls to her haunches, just inches away from my face. Her breath smells like sticky, sweet bubblegum. I refuse to let my last memory be of her. I picture Will, smiling wide with the gap between his two front teeth. And Logan, my brave little boy, skipping rocks across the lake and promising he will always protect his brother and me. Fear leaves my body and I am resolved for what will come, as long as my children will be safe.

Leslie stretches her arm behind her, expecting to grab on to the shovel, and then jerks up to her feet. She logs circles around Tucker's grave like a runner around a track until her hands claw through her strawberry-blond hair in frustration.

"I left it here, I did!" Leslie cries. "Alice, come out here, now!"

A door slams in the distance and Alice's leaden footsteps approach.

"What is it now?"

"The shovel. It's gone," Leslie says, her voice a high-pitched whine. "I left it right here by the tree when I went back to the car to get Julia. I know I did."

My stomach drops. Logan. He must have followed the car and stolen the shovel when Leslie came back for me.

"What do you mean the shovel is gone? How do you lose a shovel?" Alice asks. "Are you actually dumber than I thought? Is that possible?"

Leslie shakes her head back and forth.

"I left it right here after I buried the man. I swear. Someone took it."

"There is no one here to take it, little girl. How dumb can you actually be?"

Leslie's eyes turn to slits and she stares back defiantly at Alice.

"All right. Bring her inside. If you want something done right, you just have to do it yourself," Alice says.

"It wasn't my fault!" Leslie answers.

"Because of another one of your screw-ups, we've got a new plan. Go back to the house and get rid of the suicide note from Kim. Burn it."

Alice bends down and looks at me with lifeless, grey eyes. "I'm going to kill you, but before I do, you're going to write a note. You're going to say you killed your sons and your friend. Kim found out that you killed Will, and when she confronted you, you killed her and then your other son, Logan. You killed the old man, too, because he came to check on Kim after you stopped to see him at his store. You killed them all because you finally snapped after all those years of guilt over not being able to save your brother."

A bloom of fury, burning bright and hateful, explodes inside my chest. I lock eyes with the monster trying to destroy everything that is most precious to me—my brother's memory, Will, and now Logan. I hold her gaze defiantly and silently vow I'll kill her and Leslie before I let either of them hurt my children.

"Screw you, Alice. You've already got two dead bodies. Your plan is unraveling and you know it."

"You want me to kill her?" Leslie asks.

"Not yet, girl. Bring her inside first," Alice says. "If you want something done right, you just have to do it yourself, so I'll take care of Julia. Are you ready? It's time to play *Wheel of Fortune*."

CHAPTER 18

Daylight begins to surrender under the horizon as I scramble to make out where we are on Kim's property, but nothing looks familiar against the quickly darkening sky. A structure lies up ahead. It's a modest wooden building with a red star on its roof. The psychic predicted the red star, but I know Will is not inside. It's not the guesthouse where Alice stashed Will but an old maple sugar shack on the edge of the property the previous owners left behind. The sugar shack is the only building on the estate Kim hasn't remodeled yet. She got rid of most of the maple sugar production equipment and began to transform the space into an art and writing studio.

"Put her in the chair," Alice orders as she storms inside the shack.

The crude structure still smells like a hint of sweet maple syrup mixed with a more powerful musky aroma of dampness and decay. The shack is a single room, with a small sink in one corner, a few leftover pieces of banged-up furniture scattered about the relatively large space, which is narrow and long like a railroad car, and a door in the rear that probably leads to a bathroom. Leslie drops me onto a seat next to a thin wooden table tucked against one of the four long walls. I quickly do a more thorough scan of the contents of the sugar shack to see if there is anything I can use as a weapon if I am able to get free. My eyes catch a large cast-iron maple sugar pot that sits on the floor in the kitchen area. I feel a primal strum go off inside of me as I spot the ax used to kill Tucker lying on the kitchen counter. My mind ticks off a quick estimation: six steps, all I would need to reach the weapon if I can only get myself untied.

My body, although raw from the dragging, has fully recovered from the assaults with the stun gun. I rub my bound hands against the bars of the wooden chair, and for a moment, I convince myself, hope against hope, the knot gives just a little bit.

"I have to go to the bathroom bad," Leslie complains and begins to dance in place.

"Do it and get back out here quick."

Leslie hurries to the bathroom, and I steal a look inside as she opens the door. The bathroom is tiny, but there is a small window above the toilet that I may be able to shimmy my way through.

"The police know I'm here. I called them right before I got to Kim's house. They know Logan is in danger, so it's just a matter of seconds before the cops storm this place," I say.

Alice ignores my idle threat, turns her back to me, and pulls out a pair of cat's-eye reading glasses from the front pocket of her grey dress. She begins to sift through a stack of letters scattered across a small desk in the corner of the room. In the dim yellow cast from the single bulb hanging from the low ceiling, I can see the letters are addressed to Casey Cahill.

"You slaughtered that good man with your nasty little stories," Alice says while stuffing a piece of blue stationery into a matching envelope and sealing it with a quick lick.

Outside of the shack, the early-night breeze rattles the still-ajar front door and edges it open a few more inches, and I clutch onto the new glimmer of possibility it offers for all I'm worth. If I can only get loose, I know I could make it outside and outrun Alice and Leslie both. I contemplate an escape plan when a thin silhouette darts past the open door. The shadow comes closer, and in the contours of the quickly falling night, I can make out Logan.

No, baby, keep running toward the road, I silently beg my son.

The bathroom door opens, and Leslie ventures out with slow, hesitant steps toward Alice.

"Did you wipe?" Alice asks.

Leslie's face blushes with embarrassment. "Don't talk to me that way. I'm not a child."

"It's a test God has given me to take care of such a pagan child. But I do it with love and compassion and an iron fist when I have to," Alice says, still engrossed in her fanatical letters to the imprisoned reverend. "The Bible tells us that sinners must be punished. And when your child does wrong, you can't turn a blind eye."

I sneak a glance toward the outside and spot Logan crouched behind Leslie's car. I watch in horror as Logan begins to creep from behind the vehicle with the pocketknife flipped open in his trembling hand, ready to charge. I can't let Alice see him, and I can't let him venture any further.

"Alice, your niece left the door open," I say. "Thanks, Leslie. The police are going to have an easier time finding me now."

"Shut your selfish piehole," Alice bellows and throws her reading glasses down on the desk. She slams the door shut and waddles over to the kitchen, where she begins to wash the ax, which still has a tuft of Tucker's thick white hair matted to the blade.

"It would be a lot easier to shoot her in the head," Leslie says.

"No. Let's make this fun, shall we? It's time to play *Wheel of Fortune*. You get to pick, Julia. Ear or nose? What should we chop off first?" Alice opens her arms wide as though she is engaging a live and adoring studio audience. "Oh, please, stop your applause. I do quite fancy the idea of cutting off her nose to spite her selfish face, but let's start with her ear first. She never listened to God's word, so now she needs to hear only silence. Go ahead, Leslie. Do it."

"Don't listen to her, Leslie. You're going to get caught and you'll go to jail for the rest of your life if the police don't kill you first."

Leslie looks between Alice and me and then calmly makes her way across the shack floor in my direction with the ax.

In one last, desperate attempt, I tug against the thick knots tied around my hands and feet. The rope around my wrists gives just enough. I rip one hand free and leave it hidden behind the chair. Leslie is just steps away now, her slender hand pressed tightly around the weapon's handle. She begins to rear the hatchet behind her head, but I snatch Leslie's arm with my free hand and yank her arm backward in one fluid movement. Leslie screeches, and the hatchet slips from her fingers and clatters to the floor.

A high-pitched wail sounds like an urgent alarm and fills the room. I look toward the noise and see Alice charging toward me with her shrieking mouth wide open. I snatch the hatchet and swing it sideways toward Leslie. The blade connects and slides deep into her thigh seconds before Alice reaches my side.

"I'm hit!" Leslie cries and grabs at her wounded leg.

Alice barrels into me at full speed like a crazed linebacker until she collides shoulder first against my chest. I crash to the floor, still holding onto the hatchet for dear life. Before I can get to my feet, Alice slams her foot down on my wrist.

"I'm hurt bad. I need a doctor. I could bleed out and die," Leslie says as a deep stain of red seeps down her bare leg.

"I don't care if you bleed to death. Get the weapon," Alice says.

Leslie limps toward me, and she wraps both of her hands around mine in a vise grip.

"I'm done being nice," she moans and squeezes my hand until I feel the bones crunch and then give way.

My cry reverberates through the small room and out into the night. It is answered by a pounding that begins against the back wall of the shack, steady and hard knocks made by little hands.

"Give me that hatchet," Alice orders.

My knuckles and fingers are shattered, but I struggle to keep holding on.

"Selfish girl," Alice says. She stomps down again

on my broken fingers and easily pries the weapon from my ballooning hand.

"They're coming for you, Logan. Get out of here!" I scream.

"Shut up," Alice says. She hauls her fist back and smacks me in the mouth, splitting my top lip open. She then fixes her sights on Leslie, who is crouched in the corner, clutching her bloody leg.

"Get up. We need to find the boy," Alice says. "Take the hatchet and kill the child."

"I need to go to the hospital. I don't want to die."

"You aren't going to the hospital. Now move."

Leslie does as she's told and hobbles outside with Alice close behind. The pair disappear into the thick shadows of the country night as they head to the grove of trees by Tucker's grave to search for Logan.

"Mama?" a small voice calls out from behind the front door.

Logan emerges in the doorway, muddied and clutching the small pocketknife I gave him earlier.

"Get out of here. There's no time to save me."

Logan rushes inside the shack and tries to dab away the blood now flowing freely from my lip.

"What did they do to you? I'm going to get you out of here."

"Run to the road like I told you. Don't come back for me until you find help. Will is in the guesthouse. Tell the police where he is."

"I'm going to cut you free, and we'll get Will together," Logan says and begins to saw at the rope around my feet. "Almost there, Mom."

"Stop! I hear something outside. Go into the bathroom and lock the door. Don't open it, no matter what.

There's a window above the toilet. Lift yourself up and go through."

The front door of the sugar shack bangs open, and Logan bolts toward the bathroom, fastening the lock in place just as Alice's fat hands seal around the door-knob.

Leslie stands motionless in the doorway and watches as Alice lifts a single finger to her lips as a warning to me. Alice then clasps her hands around my throat and presses her thumbs against my windpipe.

"Logan, you poor baby. I'm so sorry," Alice says. "Leslie did this. She took the baby and then tied up your mother. I had to commit Leslie before, but I thought she was all right now. I've already called the police, and they're on their way. Come on out. Your mother is waiting for you."

"I need to ask my mom something first," Logan answers.

"Yes, go ahead, son. Your mom is here, just like I promised," Alice says and digs her fingers deeper into my neck.

"What Alice said . . . if that's true, tell me what Mr. Moto's secret weapon is," Logan asks.

Logan knows from our bedtime story, Mr. Moto's secret weapon is his invisible shield he uses to protect the village from fire-breathing dragons.

"Tell him," Alice grunts as she relaxes her grasp slightly.

"Sure, baby. You know Mr. Moto's secret weapon is his ability to turn his enemies into stone by giving them one withering glance."

"That's right," Alice answers. "Now come on out. I would never hurt anyone."

Alice looks expectantly at the bathroom door, but it doesn't open as Logan easily catches on to my lie.

"That's it," Alice says. "Where's the key?"

"Kim told me all the keys to the property are in the guesthouse," Leslie says.

"God is testing my resolve. Drive me there, Leslie. We'll get the key and my gun and I'll slaughter them both. I'm going to make you watch as I kill your boy," Alice warns me.

Alice charges over to the desk and pulls out a padlock. I hear it snap in place as Alice padlocks the front door shut as she and Leslie leave.

"Don't come out, Logan," I warn. "This could be a trap."

I listen for movement as Leslie's car engine roars to life and then muffles to a distant rumble as they drive away. Feeling safe, Logan unlocks the bathroom door and cautiously peers out from behind it.

"Come here, sweetheart," I say.

Logan hurries over to my side and throws his arms around me. His breath is rapid and warm against the side of my face.

"It's okay, buddy. We can do this. That window in the bathroom, climb through it and get out of here before they get back."

"They're going to kill you. I'm not leaving you behind."

"No matter what happens, just remember I love you always. Understand. Forever and ever, no matter what."

"Please, Mommy," Logan begs.

"It's time for you to go now, baby."

Logan thumps his fist against his heart.

"I'm coming back for you. I won't ever let you go."

"I love you, beautiful boy."

The shack is now shrouded in darkness except for a sliver of moonlight coming through the bathroom window. As Logan turns to make his escape, I take in his jet-black hair and tan, lean legs one last time. For a split second, he looks exactly like Ben.

But then my son is gone as the bathroom door shuts. The old window squeaks as it opens, and I hear Logan's clothes scrape against the window frame as he slides through and out into the sticky night air.

"Run, baby, run," I whisper.

A car engine cuts through the sudden quiet in the sugar shack. The padlock rips open and Alice lumbers inside. She slides the key in the bathroom lock and the door swings open. The crimson curtain that hangs above the open bathroom window dances gently against the breeze.

"He's gone. Enough. Take the gun and shoot him when you find him," Alice tells Leslie. "Now go. I'll take care of her."

Leslie hustles out of the shack with the gun, ready to hunt down Logan. I have to rely on the fact he is fast, and Leslie's leg wound should slow her down.

Alice moves to the kitchen and attaches a hose to the sink. She begins to fill up the giant cast-iron pot with water. Once it is full, she drags it across the room and places it on the floor in front of my chair.

"*Praise God from whom all blessings flow*," Alice sings in a lilting soprano. Her hands lock around the back of my head.

"Wait, stop," I cry.

Alice shoves me forward and plunges my head into the icy-cold water.

Please God. I need to save my children.

Alice yanks me out of the water, and I fight to inhale a single breath.

"*Praise Him, all creatures, here below,*" she sings.

My face slams under the surface of the water for the second time. I thrash my head back and forth to try and knock the cast-iron pot over, but it is too heavy.

("*I want to beat the world's record for holding my breath the longest. A guy from Germany held his breath for fifteen minutes and two seconds. I think if I just keep practicing, I can beat him.*")

I love you Logan.

Alice's thick hands latch around my hair, and she yanks me up. I open my mouth to try and catch a breath.

"*Praise Him above, ye heavenly host.*"

Alice forces my head underwater again.

I love you Will.

Like a cat toying with a mouse before it is killed, Alice pulls me out of the water for a final time.

"*Praise Father, Son, and Holy Ghost.*"

"No, stop," I try and scream, but nothing comes out. I stretch open my mouth to try and fill my lungs up with air.

But it is too late. The song is over.

Alice wraps her hands around my neck and pushes my head under the water for the final time.

I love you Ben. I am sorry. I wish I could have remembered and helped bring you back.

God, please take care of my children.

And with that last conscious thought, everything goes black.

CHAPTER 19

I hear the comfort of familiarity whisper my name like an old friend welcoming me back warmly to a place I wish I had never left.

"Julia, time to get up. Time to get up, sleepy head."

I flick open my eyes and wonder if it is time to get up for the first day of school.

A small black-and-white TV is on in the corner of the room. Its broken antenna is taped together, and a set of rabbit ears points wildly in either direction in a hard-fought attempt to get a signal. A little boy in a red shirt and thin khaki shorts sits on a chair and gazes intently at the shabby TV set. He bends as close as he can to the screen with his elbows pressed firmly against his suntanned, lean legs.

I strain to see what the boy is watching as grainy images flash across the screen.

"Come on!" the boy yells.

I hear the crack of a bat and a collective roar as the stadium crowd goes wild. The boy leaps to his feet. He jumps up and down, exploding with excitement, and pumps his small fist victoriously in the air.

An announcer's nasally Brooklyn accent booms from the TV set. "*OH, WHAT A BLOW! What a way to top it off. Forget about who the most valuable player is in the World Series! How this man has responded to pressure! Oh, what a beam on his face. How can you blame him? He's answered the whole WORLD! After all the furor, after all the hassling, it comes down to this!*"

The little boy spins around and flashes me a big, crooked smile.

"Howard Cosell. That's the name of the announcer guy you're trying to remember, Julia. It's game six of the 1977 World Series. Reggie Jackson just nailed his third consecutive home run on the first pitch, clinching the series against the Los Angeles Dodgers. What a game. I had my doubts about that hotshot from the Baltimore Orioles, but I have to give it to him. Reggie Jackson finally won my respect."

No one loved the New York Yankees more than my brother.

"Oh, Ben," I cry. "I've missed you so much."

I try to run to him, but I am startled by something rhythmically tapping below me. I look toward the sound and see drops of water falling steadily down and forming a sizable puddle around my feet.

"You're okay, Julia," Ben tells me. "Just stay where you are."

I look around to get my bearings. It looks like we are in the living room of our childhood house in Sparrow. The tinny sound of carousel music plays softly in the background, and the distinct aroma of cotton candy wafts lazily through the air.

"Could we go to Funland, Ben?" I beg. "Maybe you could work some odd jobs, and we could get enough money to go to the boardwalk just one more time before school starts tomorrow. All we need is a couple of bucks, and we'll have enough to ride the bumper cars and play a couple games of skee-ball. Hopefully we won't run into Mark Brewster."

Ben kicks the floor with the threadbare toe of his cheap sneakers Mom bought him at the A&P.

"I'd love to. More than anything. But I can't," Ben says. "Besides, you're an adult now, and adults don't like to play or do fun stuff anymore."

"No way. I love to play, and I always will even when I grow up," I promise.

I look toward the black-and-white TV set. Reggie Jackson swings and connects with a thunderous stroke of the bat. Jackson watches the ball sail high into the stadium as he jogs easily around the bases and savors his ultimate moment of victory.

"*He answered the whole WORLD!*" Cosell's voice echoes from the television.

"I'm proud of you," Ben says. "You turned out exactly like I'd hoped you would."

I wipe away a droplet of water that begins to slip down my forehead.

"I just wish we could stay in this house forever. Wouldn't it be wonderful?" I ask. "I don't want to get evicted again. We always get kicked out of places, and I want to stay in one house for a while. One day, when I'm older and I have my very own house, I'm going to draw all over the wall with crayons, because it will be mine and I can. I'll draw orange for you and purple for me, okay?"

"You can't stay here."

"Don't say that to me," I plead. "Don't ever say that. You're never going to leave me. You promised. And you can't make me go."

"I'm sorry. I really am. But you need to listen to me. You need to remember everything you have, and you need to fight for it with all you've got. This isn't real. It's the place of the in-between, the good part. The Yankees won the World Series, but I never came back. But you have to."

"It's cold in here," I say as I begin to shiver. "Mom and Dad didn't pay the heating bill again, did they?"

"You need to fight. Promise me you will," Ben says. "You can't stay here. And you can't go any further. I won't let you."

"I don't want to leave you. I don't want you to ever go away," I cry. "I couldn't live without you. You're my hero, you know."

Ben turns his face away from me and blinks hard. He looks up at me finally, and his dark eyes are intense and filled with resolve.

"You have to. I promise I'll be with you though. I always have been. I promised you I'd be here to protect you, and I never left your side. Love that is pure and true and hopeful never dies. I never stopped loving you, little sister."

Ben walks over to the television and adjusts the antenna.

"Never could afford a good one," Ben says. "I duct-taped those rabbit ears together though so at least we were able to watch the baseball games when the power was on."

A blast of cold hits me like a massive rogue wave, and my teeth begin to chatter.

"You made it though, huh? Just like I thought you would. I tried to make it good for you when you were a kid. You were always my bright spot. You and me, we were born into a bad life, and most people don't know how to fight their way out of it like Daddy and Sarah, who just gave up and became hustlers. But not you. I told you to fight and learn everything you could in school. That was your ticket out of our life. I made you believe life could still be full of possibilities even though deep down, you weren't sure if it really was. I said you had to fight the bullies even if I wasn't around, and you did."

"I would do anything you told me. I always listen to you."

"Then listen to me now. You need to remember all you've got. You've worked hard, and you created a beautiful life for yourself even though you feel like you don't belong in it sometimes. You're good enough. You're better than good enough," Ben says. "I've missed you, kid."

"I feel so cold."

"Concentrate. Think about your family, David, Logan, and Will. Logan is a really special boy. He's going to do something great one day that will save thousands of people if he only gets the chance. He won't if you don't go back for him. You have to go back and save Logan and Will. They need you."

"I'm tired. I want to go to sleep. I'm just going to take a little rest for a while. I promise I won't sleep long."

"Logan loves you with all his heart. He's brave. Will is waiting for you to come back for him. Will aches for you. Logan and Will are going to die if you don't go back."

"I'm sorry. I don't understand."

"Look at me," Ben says in a stern voice.

I stare back at Ben, but instead, I see another little boy with jet-black hair racing ahead of me. The boy runs along a lakeshore and stops at the water's edge, where he picks up a smooth, flat stone and tosses it across the water.

(*"Check that out. That one skipped four times, Mom. It's all about the smoothness of the rock and the skill of the thrower."*)

I then see the same little boy sitting in my lap. His face is crimson and his hair is drenched with sweat from fever as I rock back and forth with him in a white wicker chair until his fever breaks. The boy looks up at me to be sure everything is all right before he closes his eyes.

(*"Mom is here, beautiful boy. Go back to sleep."*)

And I see the same little boy crouching behind a car with a pocketknife, unafraid of the evil that surrounds him as long as he can save me.

(*"I'm coming back for you, Mom. I won't ever let you go."*)

Logan. My son. He ran to the guesthouse to rescue Will, and Leslie is going to kill him.

"My sons are in danger! I need to go back."

"I knew you could do it," Ben answers proudly.

The memory of Alice and Leslie rushes back to me, and I struggle to catch my breath.

"I know what I have to do, but I'm scared. I don't know if I can beat them. I tried, but I wasn't strong enough," I say.

"Don't be scared. You have to fight."

"Sometimes it seems like no matter how hard you fight or pray or hope, you lose anyway. What you love gets taken and the bad wins every time. It took you away and it never brought you back."

"Listen to me," Ben insists. "If you give up, then it will win. Call it what you want, the darkness, the evil, the bad, it's all the same black monster, and it will prevail. Some people belong to the darkness before they are born, like Alice, and others are lured into its spell later, like Leslie, who is attracted to its power. The darkness becomes their master and blows out their light forever."

"You're scaring me."

"I'm just telling you the truth," he says. "The darkness preys on fear and anger and latches on like a parasite to ambivalence, selfishness, and desperation. It grows when people turn their back on what's right and stop fighting for the good. You're part of the good, so you need to fight for it and you can't give up now."

"Please. I'm so tired."

"You have to do this for me."

"I can't beat Alice and Leslie."

"The evil makes them strong, but you're stronger. You have so much goodness in you, but you never realized it because you felt guilty about what happened to me," Ben says.

"I don't see much good in myself. I never did."

"It's in you and all around you," Ben answers. "Don't you see it? You need to fight for it now just like I fought for you. Don't you remember? The night the man came, I couldn't sleep. I kept thinking about how summer was over, and you and I didn't even get to have too many adventures. I decided when I got older, I would take you wherever you wanted to go and we would just pick up and leave whenever we felt like it because we could."

"I know you would have," I say. "I always wondered who you would've turned out to be if you'd just gotten the chance. I know you would've been someone wonderful."

"You were the one who wanted to check to be sure the sliding glass door to the courtyard was locked that night, but I told you not to."

"I didn't want you to think I was a scared baby I wish I hadn't listened to you."

"I could see a shadow by the screen door, and I knew something was wrong," Ben says. "You were still sleeping. I picked you up and hid you in the closet so you would be safe. That's why you never could remember what happened in the room that night. You were sound asleep the whole time. As soon as I shut the closet door, the man came through the screen."

"Parker?"

"No. The man with the scar. He came for both of us," Ben answers.

"Me too?"

"When he didn't see you in your bed, he started to search around and was heading to the closet. My baseball was on the dresser, and I threw it at him. I nailed him right in the head. I couldn't let him find you. The man . . . I swear, he looked like a giant . . . put his hand around my mouth to keep me from screaming, and he dragged me into the courtyard and out into a van. There was another guy in the driver seat."

"What Parker said was true then," I realize.

The puddle of water around my feet continues to rise and I look down to see it lapping above the top of my shoes.

"The man with the scar turned away from me for a second to say something to the driver, and I saw my chance. I reached for the door handle and made a run for it. But the man with the scar was too big and fast. He pulled me back inside the van. Right before he slammed the door shut, I looked out for a second and I could see the stars, bright and hopeful, and I prayed you would be all right. I would do it all over, a million times again, as long as you would be safe."

"Who took you, Ben?"

Ben stuffs his hands in his pockets and stares down at the floor.

"Just worry about yourself right now. There's not much time."

A searing pain shoots through my lungs as though a hundred-pound weight is strapped across my chest.

"What happened to me wasn't your fault. Now you know. It will make you stronger in your battle. You're good. You belong to us and you always have."

Howard Cosell's voice booms from the television set. *"After all the furor, after all the hassling, it comes down to this!"*

Ben walks over to the TV just as Reggie Jackson begins to round home plate.

"I need to know what happened to you. Where are you now? So many times, I begged you to let me know you were okay, but you never answered."

Ben flashes me his trademark crooked smile again.

"You just weren't listening. There'll be something for you on the table. Use it to fight the bullies, Julia. Use it to cut a hole in the darkness."

"What is it?"

"Hit it out of the park for me, Julia," Ben answers. "I love you. I'll always love you, forever and ever."

"I love you, too," I answer. "I promise, I'll fight as hard as I can."

Ben gives me a smile one last time.

"Is this real?" I ask. "I really want to believe it is, but I'm afraid this is just a hallucination."

"It's okay to believe in magic sometimes, kid."

Ben walks out of the room as the grainy TV screen fades and then shuts off with a sharp click.

CHAPTER 20

A high-pitched scream rings in my ears and the pressure in my lungs builds until I am sure every part of my body will imminently explode.

I gasp for precious air and seize upon my first breath as though I am entering the world for the very first time. I flick open my eyes and find myself on the floor, soaked to the bone and lying next to the cast-iron pot still filled with freezing-cold water.

The hopelessness of my situation comes back to me as I hear an angry buzz start up between Alice and Leslie, who are huddled just outside the door of the shack exchanging heated and worried words.

"They're at the house. I saw them," Leslie cries. "I was running after the boy, and I saw the lights of a car. It pulled into the driveway of the main house."

"Are you sure?" Alice asks.

"Yes, I saw the lights. I told you. Someone is at the house!"

"If it's the police, they'll see the gravel tracks of the tires heading back this way. We don't have much time."

Alice pulls out the small mirror from her pocket and shoves it under my nose, just as she did with Tucker.

"I was just finishing with her before you interrupted me. Let me be sure she's dead."

My bruised lungs have to take one more beating, and I hold my breath and force myself to lay perfectly still until Alice is satisfied.

"No fog on the mirror. Praise God. She's dead," Alice says. She tucks the mirror back into her waist pocket and grabs Leslie by the arm. The two hurry outside to search the horizon for the newly arrived vehicle.

When they are completely out of sight, I greedily gulp in air as fast as I can. It sears my throat and lungs as it goes down, but I continue until my breathing stabilizes. My time alone is limited to probably seconds, minutes if I'm lucky. I scan the room for anything I can possibly use as a weapon when my eyes catch on a glint of something shining in the dim light. Teetering on the edge of the table directly above me is one of Alice's silver knitting needles. I lift up my bound feet and thump the base of the table, jarring it just enough so the knitting needle begins to roll. It travels slowly at first until it builds momentum. It skitters across the wooden surface and falls off the table's lip and lands with precision directly in the palm of my uninjured hand.

"Oh my God, what is that?" Alice squeals from the doorway. She waves her hands busily around her head like she is batting away a swarm of pesky bugs.

"It looked like a bird," Leslie answers.

Alice shudders and then shakes her long grey-blond hair loose from its tightly wound braid.

"Disgusting creatures out here in the woods. I can't

wait to get out of here. Now answer me. Why didn't you kill the boy when you had the chance?"

"I'm sorry. I saw the car pull into the main house and I panicked. I ran back here to tell you because I got scared."

"Was the car still parked in the driveway when you ran back to tell me?"

"I think so."

Alice tears her fingers through her thick swarm of hair, leaving it wild and unruly like a crazed Medusa.

"Go back to the guesthouse and shoot them both," Alice says. "There's no time for the ceremony. Kill the baby and the boy."

A cutting shiver runs through me. I feel the knitting needle, cold and smooth in my hand. I curl it around my fingers and make a tight fist.

"I don't want to hurt a baby. Punishment is one thing, but I don't want to kill him. I can't do that," she says softly and looks away from Alice's laser-focused gaze. "I don't want to hurt Logan either. I have morals, you know."

Alice barrels over to Leslie's side and swats her niece hard across the face with a fat, open hand.

"Give me the gun."

Leslie whimpers like a dog that knows it is about to be beaten and hands Alice the weapon.

"Go in the corner and get down on your knees with your head against the wall," Alice commands.

"Please!" Leslie cries out.

"Before I pull the trigger, I want you to remember how I was the only family that would take your white-trash ass in. Are you ready? One . . . two . . ."

"Stop! I'll do it. Give me the gun. I'll kill the kids."

"There. That's better," Alice answers, now content, and drops the gun to the side of her plump hip.

Now back in line, Leslie reaches out her obedient hand for the weapon.

"There are two gas cans in the shed. Bring one to me and take the other one with you to the guesthouse. Once you kill the boy and the baby, put their bodies in the trunk of the car. Douse the guesthouse with the gasoline and set it on fire. We don't have time to wipe the entire place down for our fingerprints now, so light it up. I'll have to write the suicide note myself on the computer at the main house. We'll leave it there, along with Julia's body, before we leave."

"Won't the fire bring more people around? Why don't we just leave the bodies somewhere further back in the woods?" Leslie asks.

"Shut up. I know what I'm doing here."

The plan settled, Leslie hustles to the shed and Alice begins to comb through the room, looking for any items of value to save before she torches the place. She sifts through the desk and retrieves a Bible and a still unfinished letter to Cahill.

"For you, Father, I do this for you," Alice prays.

I struggle to calculate how I can bring down Alice with just a plastic knitting needle as my only defense, when my focus is abruptly interrupted by a whirring sound of something flapping nervously above my head.

Alice finishes collecting her valuables and goes outside to put them in Leslie's car. I quickly open my eyes to pinpoint the sound and realize I am no longer alone in the shack. Hovering in the corner of the ceiling is a bat, small and brown, with long pointy ears, a piglike nose, and tiny eyes that stare back at me with rapt intensity. It must have been the bat that collided with Alice earlier, and it retreated inside the shack to flee from her assault. *A bat out of hell*, I think to myself.

Leslie runs up the porch carrying a large red gas can, which she drops to the floor as soon as she makes it inside. "Alice . . ." she pants.

"Don't you fall apart on me now," Alice says from the doorway. "It's not my fault you can't handle your workload. When I was a girl, I did whatever I was told by my mother and didn't break a sweat. If I didn't, I'd get locked down in the basement for days with nothing to eat and only my Bible. You would've trapped and killed that boy by now if you hadn't slipped up and let Julia steal the ax from you."

"No, just listen. I don't see the car at the main house anymore," Leslie answers. "Whoever was knocking on the door is gone."

"I knew it," Alice says. "God will protect the righteous who honor His name. Now, go back to the guesthouse and take care of the children. Then set it on fire when you're done."

Leslie heads toward the door with the gun, leaving me alone with the monster.

I clutch the knitting needle, now prone and warm in my hand, and wait for Alice to approach.

"Water to fire, fire to water. Praise you, Lord, I am your daughter," Alice chants and opens the top of the gas can.

The noxious smell of the gasoline quickly fills the room and begins to burn my throat.

Alice moves to a desk in the corner. She scatters a stack of papers on the floor and douses them with the gasoline. My feet are still bound so I can't stand up or run, but if Alice just gets close enough, I can reach her.

Alice's backside twitches in her loose dress as she moves from side to side, crisscrossing the floor as she covers it with fuel.

"Praise God, from whom all blessings flow," Alice begins to sing in a quavering voice. *"Praise Him, all creatures, here below."*

She takes two more steps in my direction.

"Praise Him above, ye heavenly host."

I grasp the knitting needle as tightly as I can until my hand shakes.

"Praise Father, Son . . ."

Alice stands over me now, so close I can see the dark, wet fabric under her armpits.

"And Holy Ghost."

"ALICE!" I scream and rear up from the floor.

Alice freezes in surprise and drops the can, spilling the remainder of the gas, which flows across the floor. She stares at me in disbelief as though I've risen from the dead, and her thin lips form a startled O expression.

A howl of fury and vengeance boils up from inside of me and explodes. I rear my arm back and set it flying toward Alice. She tries to scramble backward, but my arm is coming down too fast. I plunge the knitting needle as hard as I can toward Alice's face. The knitting needle connects, slices into the center of Alice's right eye, and makes a wet sucking sound as it plunges in.

"Selfish bitch!" Alice howls as she falls to her knees.

Alice's hands grope at her face as she tries to pluck out the knitting needle.

"You little whore," she cries. Alice's equilibrium shattered, she folds in half and begins to vomit.

Alice lets out one last mighty wretch and then rights herself. She pulls at the knitting needle with both hands and lets out a long, painful moan as she extracts it from her now-ballooning eye, which is streaked with bright stripes of crimson.

"I'm going to get you good this time," Alice screams and tears into the kitchen. She reaches inside her knitting bag and yanks out a hatchet.

I latch my hands on the stubborn knot around my feet, pull the rope loose from my swollen ankles, and limp in a fast, stilted gait toward the door.

Alice's long hair is loose and spills around her face as she looms toward me with the weapon.

"Get ready for hell," she howls. A sick grin spreads across her face as she lifts the hatchet with both hands above her head, and I brace for impact.

A building crescendo of wings flaps together faster and faster and distracts Alice for a split second. I look towards the commotion and see the bat, now highly agitated, its angry eyes glaring directly at Alice as if it wants payback for her earlier beating. The bat lets out an otherworldly high-pitched squeal and swoops down at Alice with breakneck speed and nose-dives into her thick nest of hair. Alice shrieks and tries to swat the bat away with her free hand, but the more she moves, the deeper the bat burrows in.

"You hideous creature of the devil," Alice screams.

She begins to run around in circles to free herself, but the bat holds on tight like it is prepared to scalp its adversary.

"Help!" Alice begs me.

She snatches pieces of her hair out in clumps and

lurches in my direction, waving the hatchet wildly in her right hand.

Halfway across the room, her foot catches on something and she starts to tip backward as if she is slipping on a patch of ice. Alice scrambles to grab the table to steady herself, but her feet kick out from under her before she can reach it and she starts to topple to the floor. The bat releases its grasp finally and ascends back to its safe perch in the corner of the room, its work finally done. Alice falls face first and lands with a hard thud against the wooden floorboards. The object that tripped Alice rolls across the room until it comes to a sudden stop.

I look down at my feet and see Alice's knitting needle, the magic silver bullet that brought down the terrible giant.

The sharp throbbing from my broken hand reawakens my senses and I realize I might have less than ten seconds to run before Alice gets up to finish me off. Ten seconds if I'm lucky. I race blindly across the room until my fingers close around the doorknob to the safe haven of outside and turn to face my attacker. But Alice is motionless, pressed face down against the warped, wooden floor, which is now tattooed with a stain of blood pooling from her torso.

Alice wrestles to her side, the hatchet protruding from the center of her chest. Her long, yellow-silver hair is soaked in red dripping tips that cling to her neck and shoulders. She slowly turns her sweat-laden head toward me and offers one last look of cold, hard evil.

"You selfish girl . . . you ruined everything."

"Go to hell, Alice."

Alice's eyes turn to slits and then she blinks heavily

as she tries to focus. She opens her mouth as if to curse me to damnation one last time, but something passes across her face and the light drains from her eyes.

The momentary quiet of death is interrupted as the shack door bursts open.

"Police! Put down your weapon," Navarro yells from the dim doorway, his gun drawn.

"Navarro, it's me, Julia," I scream.

Navarro pans the room, his gun still pointed in front of him. Once he checks the entire space, he bends over Alice to feel for a pulse.

"She's dead. Who's this woman? What happened, Julia? Jesus Christ, are you all right?"

"Her name is Alice. She's one of Cahill's parishioners. She kidnapped Will. Her niece, Leslie, is heading to the guesthouse. Leslie's got a gun. She's going there to kill Logan and Will."

"Where is the guesthouse? Come on," Navarro says as he grabs my hand and we hurry out of the shack toward his car.

"The guesthouse is on the other side of the hill from here. We'll take this road a half-mile past the cherry orchard and it'll be on our right. I'm coming with you."

"Stay here. Wait for Russell. He should be here in a few minutes."

Navarro ducks into his police car and secures the door locks right before I can try and make my way into the passenger seat.

"You can't do this. You can't leave without me," I cry and pound my fist against the window.

Navarro starts the engine and barrels down the road toward the guesthouse, and I follow in his vehicle's direction.

I feel my calf muscles tighten as I sprint up the steep hill and ignore the searing pain in my ankles, still raw from the friction of the rope. As I reach the top of the hill, the moon breaks free from a passing cloud and casts a soft light on the scene below. I can see the guest-house now. Leslie is stalking the place, going from window to window to try and catch sight of Logan and Will.

"Logan, it's your friend Leslie," I can hear her call from just outside the guesthouse door. "I brought your mother with me, and I called the police. Everything is all right now. Come on out and bring the baby with you."

A small shadow darts quickly across the bank of windows, directly to the front door.

Logan's shadow then scoots away from the door and retreats toward the back of the house.

"Okay then. If you're not coming out, I'm coming in. How about we play or watch TV together for a while?" Leslie asks as she reaches for the door handle.

I hold my breath as I watch the scene unfold below me. I try and push myself to run faster as the tall grass slaps against my legs on my descent.

Leslie stands motionless at the front door, and I realize Logan was smart enough to lock it from the inside. Surprised that she didn't get her way, Leslie begins to stomp her feet on the ground as though she is having a temper tantrum.

"Not fair. Bad boy. You aren't supposed to do that."

Leslie paces back and forth in angry, short steps as if calculating her next move. She abruptly stops her pacing, picks up the gun, and points it toward the locked door.

A deafening blast roars from the guesthouse, and I hear myself screaming as Leslie fires and decimates the lock. Leslie drops the gun for a second and covers her ears, apparently surprised by the magnitude of the gunshot's loud blast. She recovers, snatches up the weapon, and pushes against the battered door until it creaks open a sliver. She kicks the door in, draws the gun in front of her, and starts to head inside.

"Police, put down your weapon," Navarro yells from a crouching position behind his car.

Leslie ignores Navarro's command and continues to walk inside, blind to everything except Alice's final order and the dream of five hundred dollars and New York City.

"Stop where you are," Navarro calls out again and fires a warning shot.

The sound snaps Leslie back to reality and she freezes in the doorway. She pauses a beat and turns toward Navarro with the gun poised between her slender hands.

"Put down your weapon," Navarro yells.

In the distance, sirens begin to blare from approaching police cars as Navarro's partner, Russell, and back-up arrive.

Realizing she is bested, Leslie drops the gun to her side in defeat and sits down heavily on the front step. Her mouth turns down on both ends as though she is about to cry.

"None of this was my fault! I just did as I was told. Alice made me do it."

"Let's talk about it. Just put the gun down on the ground," Navarro says.

"I'm the victim here," Leslie answers.

"I believe you. Put down your weapon and we'll talk."

Leslie looks down at her feet for what seems like a lifetime and finally stares straight ahead with dead eyes.

"There's nothing to talk about. I know what I did. And I'm not going to jail."

Leslie begins to raise her gun until it's pointed at Navarro.

He is about to fire, but Leslie jams the barrel of the gun into her mouth and pulls the trigger.

"Damn it," Navarro yells.

He runs over to Leslie's body and covers up what's left of her face with his leather jacket.

"Logan, are you all right? It's Detective Navarro. Everything is fine now, son."

I finally reach the gravel driveway to the guesthouse, broken, out of breath, but never so happy in my entire life.

"Is my mom here?" Logan calls out from inside.

"I'm here, Logan. It's all right. Come out."

"If it's really safe, then tell me what Mr. Moto's secret weapon is."

"That one is easy, baby," I say as I feel the tears start. "Mr. Moto's secret weapon is his invisible shield. It protects him from fire-breathing dragons."

The front door of the guesthouse swings open. Logan emerges, small but with a heart as brave as a warrior, holding Will tightly against his thin chest.

CHAPTER 21

"**Y**ou going to finish that? I just realized I haven't had anything to eat since that Reuben sandwich you tried to steal from me yesterday," Navarro says while hungrily eyeing the remnants of my bland hospital lunch tray. I push the tray in his direction and pick up the room phone to pester the nurse one last time.

"I'm sorry, but if the doctor doesn't come by to discharge me in the next five minutes, I'm leaving this hospital and going home to my kids."

I hang up and watch Navarro as he digs a spoon into a rubbery-looking cup of cherry Jell-O.

"That looks disgusting."

"Tastes that way, too," Navarro concedes and drops the plastic cup back on the tray "You look good, a whole lot better than you did last night. How's the hand?"

"The cast is making me crazy, but believe me, I'm not complaining."

"That's a relief your boys are okay."

"Physically, Logan and Will are fine. Logan got a

few scrapes. But I'm still worried what happened may pay a toll of them eventually."

"They've got counseling for trauma survivors. Will is still so young, but it might be good for you and Logan."

"I'll talk to Logan and see how he feels. But for me, I think I've got to figure out my own things. No one else can give me answers."

The on-call doctor breezes into the room and assesses my chart through a pair of thick Coke-bottle glasses.

"Three broken fingers, a broken wrist, and four broken knuckles on your left hand. You're right-handed?" the doctor asks.

"Yes."

The doctor pushes his glasses down the bridge of his nose and looks back at me with keen interest, like I'm some sort of curious specimen he's examining under a microscope.

"I heard about what happened to you. You're a lucky woman," he remarks.

"That's the first time anyone's ever said that to me."

The doctor adjusts his glasses back in place and returns to my chart. "I see no traces of acute respiratory distress syndrome from the near drowning. Besides the hand, there's just a cracked rib, some lacerations to your ankles, and three stitches to sew up the gash in your lip. You're fine to be discharged."

I snatch the discharge sheet from the doctor, and he beats a slow retreat out of the room.

"Thanks for coming back to the hospital and for staying with me all night. You didn't have to do that. I didn't want David to bring the kids here."

"No problem. I didn't want you to be alone."

I gather up my scant belongings, which Navarro brought me from home. As we exit the hospital to the parking garage, I push away the memories of last night and instead cherish the thought of seeing my children.

"Your chariot awaits, madam," Navarro says and opens the passenger-side door of his Crown Victoria.

I slide in and impatiently tap my fingers against the dashboard. Before Navarro starts the car, he turns and a look of worry knits across his brow.

"Are you all right? Really?" he asks. "You've been through a lot."

"I'm fine. Honest to God."

"Just take your time and be sure you're really okay. And tell me if you're not."

"I will. What did you track down on Parker?"

"I got some answers, but you're not going to like them," Navarro says and cruises onto the freeway ramp. "Parker's alibi panned out. I talked to the owner of the bar and he vouched for Parker. I also got a copy of the police report that was filed over the dust-up between the bar owner's son and some other guy, and it lists Parker as being at the bar right after Ben got snatched. The bar owner said Parker hung out with him after the fight and stayed there until around two a.m."

"Damn. That's what I was afraid of. What about the van Parker claimed he saw?"

"I checked. The only thing I could trace was a report filed about a van that was torched near a field by the Detroit Metropolitan Airport."

"That could be anything."

"Hold on. At the time, the cops found a little boy's

pajama shirt in the field near the burned-out van. The description of the shirt matches what your brother had on when he was abducted."

"Incredible Hulk. I remember his pajamas. Jesus. That's something. What about plates?"

"Burned to a crisp. So was the VIN on the vehicle. I'm sorry, Julia."

"All these years, I just want to know what happened, and with Parker, this is as close as I ever got."

"It's not a dead end. We've got a partial description from Parker about the guy in the van who came after Ben when he tried to escape."

"The man with the scar like a crescent moon who was as big as a mountain."

"And the Indian arrowhead. Parker said the guy looked like he might have been Indian," Navarro says. "When things settle down for you, I can help you start looking for your brother again. We've got some fresh leads."

"From thirty years ago. Too much time may have passed. When I visited Cahill in jail, he told me something about time being my own personal prison. Maybe he was right."

"The guy's a fruitcake. I wouldn't put too much stock into what that wacko religious nut job thinks."

"Has Parker been released?"

"Yes. We had nothing to hold him on anymore. His uncle confessed to killing his sick wife to put her out of her misery, so that explains the bones we found under his hunting camp. But Parker isn't out of your life yet. He's pressing charges against you for clocking him in the privates."

"He's lucky that's all I did. If he really saw Ben that

night and didn't do anything to help him, Parker's lucky I didn't kill him."

"Easy there," Navarro answers. "I guess I owe you an apology. You were right. You believed all along Parker didn't kidnap Will, but I wouldn't listen. It's funny how two cases that seemed so connected weren't intertwined after all," Navarro says.

"Synchronicity."

"What do you mean?"

"A bunch of high-minded, hoped-for philosophy that doesn't really mean anything. Sometimes life hits us so hard, we want to believe there's a deeper meaning in something when there isn't."

"Just a series of random coincidences," Navarro says.

"But there weren't any coincidences in this case. It was all planned. Alice had Leslie plant that arrowhead under Will's crib so we'd think the two kidnappings were related and she added all the background about Ben's abduction in the letters she sent to Cahill to throw us off."

"What about the phone call? You said someone called with a warning right before Will was abducted. The caller told you to get out and that someone was coming back for you."

"Right," I answer and my mind drifts back to the Mary Jane candy I found in Logan's room. "Alice didn't say anything about that call. But obviously she orchestrated it as part of her plan to make me think Will's kidnapping was linked to Ben."

"Maybe. But you don't know for sure."

"I guess I never will," I say and then pause for a

beat, deciding whether or not to share what happened in the shack with Navarro.

"What's on your mind?" Navarro asks.

Decision made. "Something happened when Alice tried to drown me."

"You going to tell me?"

"It's just . . . I'm not sure if it was real."

"Come on, Gooden. Spill it."

"It was like a dream. I saw my brother, and all these images came together, the past, sights and smells and memories from my childhood. And they intertwined with the present, like the knitting needle on the table I used to take down Alice. Ben told me he'd leave something on the table for me to fight her, to fight the bullies and to cut a hole through the darkness."

"Maybe you saw the knitting needle before Alice tried to kill you and it was in your subconscious already."

"Probably. Ben also told me about the man with the scar."

"Okay. Did he tell you who he was? That would solve everything."

"No. God, I wish I hadn't mentioned this."

"Come on, Julia. I was just kidding. I'm glad you told me. I'm not sure if I believe in the afterlife theory, but I like to keep my options open, just in case, you know? My nana took me to Catholic Mass until I was eighteen, so hopefully I'll earn a pass card if it turns out all this is true."

Navarro reaches across the console and squeezes my hand. His touch feels warm, innocent, and comforting, so I accept his act of affection without a twinge of guilt.

"Before I went to your house last night, I made a pit stop to see your sister at Beckerus's place," Navarro says.

"You did? How did that go?"

"Let's just say she won't be bothering you anymore. I warned Sarah and her boyfriend the cops would be keeping an eye on them, and if they decide to go back to Florida, we've got eyes down there too."

"You didn't have to do that, but thank you."

"Glad to help get her out of your life," he answers.

"That's one person I don't think will ever change."

"Things that happen when you're a kid can stay with you and turn a person bad. I keep remembering that Leslie. She was like some crazed, violent Lolita. I checked her juvenile record. For a seventeen-year-old, she had worked up quite a rap sheet, shoplifting, lighting a neighborhood cat on fire, and drug possession. Her mom had been a prostitute and was killed by one of her johns. Then she wound up with Alice. The kid didn't have much of a chance."

"What about Alice? Did you find anything on her?"

"She'd never been arrested, but she'd been in and out of mental hospitals since she was a kid. She and Leslie's mom were taken away from their mother by Social Services when they were little. Apparently, their mother had some mental problems of her own. She was a religious zealot, peppered in with a whole lot of crazy, and would lock her daughters in the basement for days on end with just their Bible if she thought they had done something wrong. According to the hospital records, a neighbor saw Alice staring up from a basement window one day, naked and crying with a big black eye, so the neighbor called the cops. I'd almost feel sorry for her if she hadn't been trying to kill you and your children."

"My brother told me sometimes the dark chooses us before we're born, and other times, we choose it because of the hand we're dealt in this life. Either way, it's a choice, and it's up to us to make the right one."

"That's some heavy thinking for a little kid."

Navarro blasts his horn as we approach a traffic jam.

"Come on," he yells and then turns on his police siren as he navigates around the bottleneck of cars. "I've got to get you home to your kids."

Navarro flicks on the car radio and sets the dial to a local AM news station.

"We've got the former Reverend Casey Cahill coming up next to reveal how he helped police crack the missing toddler case. Cahill claims it was a revelation that led to his single-handed discovery that a fanatical member of his former congregation was the kidnapper," the announcer says. *"Call in and tell us whether you think the former Rock 'n' Roll Jesus of the Motor City should be released by the parole board in light of his help that brought a little boy home."*

Navarro shuts the radio off with a quick snap of his wrist. "Give me a break. You know, I put my vacation on hold to work this case. I rebooked my ticket for next week."

"Where are you going?" I ask.

"The Jersey Shore. I can cancel if you need me to. I'm not sure what's going on with you and David, but I figured you might need someone around."

"That's a generous offer, but go on your vacation."

"You and the boys could come along. A change of

scene might be good for you all. I could check the hotel where I'm staying to see if they have an extra room. What do you think?"

I stare back at Navarro and wonder what my life would have been like if we'd stayed together. But then there would be no Logan and Will, and no matter the potential outcome of my situation with David, the boys are the best thing that came out of my marriage and the best thing in my life. And whatever choices I make going forward, their interests have to come first.

"I can't," I finally answer.

The dance between Navarro and I ends as we pull into my driveway. I wait a moment before I get out of the car and take in the scene. My house looks absolutely perfect. Logan races his orange bike across the lawn, and David sits on the front porch swing cuddling Will in his arms.

I turn to Navarro one last time to settle things. "Thank you for everything. If you hadn't shown up last night, I don't know what would've happened."

"I'm not sure about that. Something tells me you would've found a way to save Logan and Will even if I hadn't been there."

"No. You saved their lives. I owe you. More than you will ever know. You're a good man and a good friend."

I lean over the console and give Navarro a kiss on the cheek.

"I still care about you, Julia. I always will. But you know that," Navarro says as he looks over to David. "I just want you to be happy, you know. Whatever that is."

"I know. See you around, my friend."

Logan spots me exiting the car and tosses his bike to

the ground. He tears across the yard, his arms and legs flying in every direction as he approaches.

"Mom," he yells and embraces me so hard, I almost fall over.

"Hi, sweet boy," I answer and kiss his head.

David sprints over to us, and I grab Will out of his arms. I bury my nose in my youngest son's hair and breathe in until I feel happily intoxicated.

"Mama," Will cries and rests his head against my chest.

"I've been trying to keep Will up until you got home," David says. "He's exhausted and ready for a nap, but I know how much he's missing his mom."

As if on cue, Will opens up his little mouth and lets out a cavernous yawn.

"He's got another tooth coming in," I say, beaming as though Will just accomplished something extraordinary. "I'll go in and put him to sleep. I'll be right back."

Inside the house are the signs of everyday life, the framed picture of David and the boys at the lake, a stack of dirty dishes left in the sink, and Logan's baseball glove and sneakers lying in a heap by the door. All things so simple and mundane, but right now, they are absolutely wonderful.

Will's eyes begin to flutter, and I sit with him in the white rocking chair in his room. I am unable to let him go, even when his breathing becomes heavy and I know he is asleep.

There's a tiny tap on the door, and Logan peeks his head inside. I place Will in his crib and cover him with a plush white blanket.

I stand at Will's doorway for a moment, and then turn my attention to Logan. I grab his hand, and we retreat into his room, where he has spread all the contents from his treasure box across his bed.

"Taking stock of your loot there, kid?" I ask.

Logan gives me a crooked grin.

"Are you all right, Mom? You're looking at me kind of funny."

"You just reminded me of my brother Ben for a minute."

Logan picks up his magnifying glass and begins to study one of his prized rocks from the lake. I sit down on the bed next to him, amazed at how a child can experience a horror so unimaginable but still be able to retain his wonder and imagination, believing the world is still good despite the evil he now knows really exists.

"How are you doing?" I ask.

Logan grunts in response, still examining his rock.

"This is important. Look at me," I say.

Logan drops the rock and magnifying glass and meets my gaze.

"What happened last night was horrible. It was worse than horrible. You saw and had to endure a situation no child should ever have to experience. I need to know if you're all right. It's okay if you're not. Just tell me. There are people you can talk to, and sometimes that's a really good thing."

"I'm fine. Really," Logan says.

I exhale deeply and run my fingers through his shiny dark hair.

"You're incredibly brave. I'm proud of you. But don't ever risk your life for me again. Got it?"

Logan shakes his head.

"I love you. I promised I would protect you and Will."

Logan walks over to his dresser and begins to load up his new backpack with pencils and a notebook. And then I remember. Tomorrow is the first day of school. With all that happened, I forgot. But somehow Logan didn't.

"Don't worry about starting school tomorrow. It's too soon. You should take some time. I'll call the principal and let him know. He'll understand."

"I want to go to school tomorrow."

"Okay. But if you change your mind, that's all right."

"Is it okay if I go outside to play for a while? I want to hang out in my tree house by myself."

"Of course," I answer and give Logan one last mighty hug.

Logan dashes outside to play, and I look for David. I find him standing guard by the window, keeping careful watch as Logan runs across the yard to his tree house.

"It's hard to keep the kids out of sight for a second now. You too," David says.

"What are you talking about?" I ask.

"Jesus Christ, Julia. You scared the hell out of me," David says. He grabs my face with both his hands and kisses me like it's the last chance he'll ever get.

"I'm fine," I answer, feeling startled by David's unexpected embrace.

The buzz of the house phone interrupts our reunion as the whine of my city editor's voice starts to drone on in the background. I lean over to the answering machine and turn the volume down to zero.

"I figured you wouldn't want to answer that. Primo has been calling all day. He wants you to call him back as soon as possible. He said something about an exclusive on your story. He promised it will go on the front page."

"I'm sure he did. I've been thinking hard about this, and I decided I'm not going back to the paper."

"You shouldn't make any kind of decisions yet. But if you don't want to go back to work right away, we'd be fine on my salary. Maybe it's time for a career change for you. You'd be so good in public relations. I could make some calls."

"Let me rephrase that. I'm not going to work for Primo. I'm going to ask Bill for my old job back. Granted, it's a smaller daily and I may wind up with a pay cut."

"If that's what you want to do, I'd support it. We don't have to talk about everything right now, but with all that's happened, I want you and the kids back in Rochester Hills. I want you to come home. I want us all to be together."

"I know Logan wants that more than anything."

"What about you?"

Two days earlier, my response would have been crystal clear. Now it's not so certain.

"I just need some time to think."

"I understand. I'm not trying to push you," David answers and loops a stray strand of my hair around my ear. "I've got news. I was offered partner."

"Wow. That's great, and well deserved. I know how hard you worked to get that promotion."

"I'll be at the office more, but we can hire a housekeeper. We'll make it work. I just want our old life back. I love you, Julia."

I watch David as he walks to the kitchen, feeling uncertain of my future and wishing somehow the right answer would always be easy to see. David waves his finger at me to follow. I head in his direction and watch as he leans down and rummages through his briefcase. He stands back up with a baseball in his hands and tosses it in the air.

"I thought you'd be interested in this," he says. "I found it while I was downstairs in the utility room looking for an old stack of case files. The ball was right in the middle of the room. I can't believe we never saw it before."

"The utility room is the land of unwanted toys. I'm sure we have all kinds of balls and other kid's stuff strewn all around down there."

"Maybe so. But this isn't a regular baseball. It has a signature on it," David says and cups the ball in the palm of his hand for my inspection.

I take a closer look and then stare in disbelief at the signature.

Reggie Jackson.

"I did some research on the computer right before you got home. This looks like an official Reggie Jackson autographed ball from the 1977 World Series."

"Game six?" I ask as a chill runs down my spine.

"You got it, the game when Jackson nailed three consecutive home runs on the first pitch to seal the Series for the Yankees. Mr. October. Truth be told, it got me spooked for a minute. It's quite a coincidence. But then I remembered. When we first bought the house, the previous owners were from New York. They had a huge New York Yankees poster hung up in the garage when we first looked at the place. Remember? It was a framed picture of Reggie Jackson nailing a home run. You thought it was a good sign. The ball must belong to them and they accidentally left it behind when they moved. The ball has to be worth something. I bet our old Realtor could track them down."

I stare out the window and see Logan playing outside. The sun beams down on him as the Indian summer breeze gently sways the leaves back and forth. I think of the fierce love I have for my children and the enduring love I will always have for my brother.

"No. Don't call," I finally answer. "I'd rather not know for sure."

"Really?" David asks.

"I think, for once, I'd like to believe just maybe there really is some magic in the world."

I leave David and make my way outside into the warm September morning. I find Logan running back and forth across the yard with his arms open wide like a plane expertly navigating through the clouds. I look up into the blue, endless sky, where time is meaningless, and throw the baseball into the air as high as I can.

In Jane Haseldine's new novel of riveting suspense, Detroit newspaper reporter Julia Gooden is up against the city's most devious criminal—and her own painful past.

Julia Gooden knows how to juggle different lives. A successful crime reporter, she covers the grittiest stories in the city while raising her two young boys in the suburbs. But beneath that accomplished façade is another Julia, still consumed by a tragedy that unfolded thirty years ago when her nine-year-old brother disappeared without a trace.

Julia's marriage, too, is a balancing act, as she tries to rekindle her relationship with her husband, Assistant District Attorney David Tanner, while maintaining professional boundaries. David is about to bring Nick Rossi to trial for crimes that include drug trafficking, illegal gambling, and bribery. But the story becomes much more urgent when a courthouse bomb claims several victims—including the prosecution's key witness—and leaves David critically injured.

Though Julia is certain that Rossi orchestrated the attack, the case against him is collapsing, and his power and connections run high and wide. With the help of Detective Raymond Navarro of the Detroit PD, she starts following a trail of blackmail, payback, and political ambition, little imagining where it will lead. Julia has risked her career before, but this time innocent lives—including her children's—hang in the balance, and justice may come too late to save what truly matters . . .

Please turn the page for an exciting sneak peek of Jane Haseldine's

DUPLICITY

Coming soon wherever print and e-books are sold!

CHAPTER 1

Glenlivet, light on the rocks. A cocktail waitress with bright fuchsia lipstick delivers the drink and motions her head to two tables down, in the direction of a group of aged fifty-something women. The recipient of the cocktail turns his head toward the hoots and low whistles from the likely recent divorcées who are ogling him like participants in a lusty spectator sport.

"Want to join us, hon?" the ringleader asks, and adjusts her leopard print halter top to reveal an extra inch of orange, tanned cleavage. In case her intent wasn't clear enough, the woman scoops a sugar cube from her champagne cocktail, places it between her teeth, and starts sucking.

"No, thank you," the businessman answers coolly, and places the unwanted drink back on the cocktail waitress's tray.

He turns his back on the spurned women and locks in on a tall, willowy blonde in a white dress that clings to her slender curves as she moves fluidly in his direction across the casino floor.

She pauses at his table, slides into the empty seat across from him, and carefully tucks a leather briefcase between her legs.

The rowdy commotion from the neighboring table of women abruptly stops as they wordlessly concede that they've been bested by a thoroughbred.

The businessman slips an Italian charcoal gray suit coat over his tall and tightly muscled frame. He tips back the last few sips of the drink he ordered for himself ten minutes earlier and heads toward the lobby, not bothering to look back. He knows the blonde will follow.

In the elevator, the mouth of a camera lens captures its occupants' activities. The pair stand close, but just far enough apart so it doesn't look obvious they are together—just two attractive strangers heading up to their respected rooms. The blond stunner holds the briefcase in her left hand and takes a risk. She lifts her pinky finger up and brushes the back of the businessman's hand for less than a second.

The elevator arrives on the VIP floor, the best the MGM Grand has to offer.

The blonde bends down, slides a keycard out of the front pocket of the briefcase, and opens the hotel room door. Inside, the man stands in front of the floor-to-ceiling windows. He takes a quick pan of downtown Detroit and then snaps the curtains shut. When it is safe, when they are alone, the blonde, now anxious and wanting, drops the briefcase and goes directly for his zipper.

"Wait." He takes the briefcase over to the bed, opens it, and fans the stack of bills across the mattress like a seasoned blackjack dealer some thirty stories below.

"Two million. You don't trust me now?" the woman asks with a contrived pout.

He ignores the question until the cash has been fully accounted for.

"Come here," he commands.

He starts to remove his coat, but she is already there.

"I've missed you," she whispers, and cups her long, delicate fingers around his crotch.

He reciprocates by running his hand across the thin silk of her dress directly over her breast, and then squeezes until the blonde lets out a gasp.

The blonde easily submits when the man pushes her down hard on the bed, letting him believe he still has the upper hand, that he is the aggressor. She stares up at his beautiful face, his breath coming faster now as his body starts to move in a rapid, steady rhythm above her. She doesn't mind when he closes his eyes. He wants her again, reestablishing her position of control, at least for now. That's all that matters.

When they are finished, the businessman turns toward the wall in disgust.

"I knew you weren't through with me yet," she says. "You take all your hostility out on me in bed. You're a rough boy, but I like it."

He ignores her, gets up from the bed, still naked, and heads to the bathroom. The blonde is useless to him now. She knows it but still holds on.

"The birthmark on your ass is so sweet. It looks like a crescent moon with a shooting star underneath," she remarks. "Come back to bed and let me take a closer look."

The man spins around, anger flashing in his eyes as if the blonde's comment violated something personal.

"Shut up," he says.

"No need to talk dirty to me. You know I'll give you what you want, as long as you give me my share of the money."

"When it's over, you'll get it. That's the agreement."

"How do I know you won't screw me?"

"Because I'm not that guy. The money will be in a safe place."

"I want access to it."

"I don't think so."

The door to the bathroom slams shut and she is dismissed. Inside the shower, he scrubs every trace of the woman off his body, hoping she will be gone when he comes out. But the blonde is still in bed. At least she is sleeping.

The businessman climbs back into his suit, grabs the briefcase, and closes the hotel room door quietly behind him. The second elevator in the hallway opens, and he disappears inside just as elevator one chimes its arrival to the VIP floor. Its single occupant emerges—a man, squat and thick but moving swiftly like a gymnast. He wears all black—a bulky Windbreaker, sweatpants, and a baseball cap as if he's just come from the hotel gym. He lets himself into a room with a keycard he extracts from a bulky fanny pack that flanks his waist. Inside, he quickly assesses the scene, pulls a tiny camera out from its hiding place inside a fake antique clock on the dresser, and tucks it into his coat pocket.

He then retrieves a razor blade and scarf from the

pack and heads toward the bed where the blonde is still sleeping.

The man moves silently as he eases his body onto the bed. He inches forward across the mattress and then straddles the blonde, locking her in place until she is prone and pinned to the bed. Without opening her eyes, she smiles, thinking her lover has returned. She flicks her tongue across her lips and then opens her mouth expectantly.

"Shhh," he whispers. "You pay now. We know what you did."

The woman's eyes fly open, and she tries to scream out her assailant's name, but he seals one stubby hand across her mouth before she can utter a word. He lifts the razor from his pocket and gently glides the unsharpened side of the blade down her stomach until it reaches the top of her pubic bone.

"Please!" she begs. "I'll give you what you want."

The razor stops short before it makes its final descent.

His breath is warm and steady against her ear. "How do you know what I want?"

"Money. I'll give it to you."

He pauses as though considering the request and flicks the dull side of the blade back and forth across her skin.

"God, please. You don't want money then. Okay. Just tell me what you want and I'll give it to you."

He shakes his head and teases the sharp edge of the razor blade against her leg.

"Who is it?" he whispers as the razor makes a tiny, precise knick on the inside of her thigh, drawing a single drop of blood that trickles down her ivory skin like a crimson teardrop.

"The name. I'll give you the name!" she pleads. "Sammy Biggs, the Butcher. He's the one. I just found out, I swear. I didn't betray you. He did. Now, please! Let me go."

The hired hand sighs deeply, as if savoring an indulgent pleasure, now finally satisfied. But not quite. Lessons must be learned and never forgotten. The man stuffs the scarf down the woman's mouth to muffle the pain of her penance. It is ingrained in his soul that those who sin must atone. He clasps the razor blade between his thumb and middle finger and cuts off the blonde's left earlobe in one clean slice.

"Hail Mary, full of grace," he prays as he pulls out a locket from underneath his black T-shirt. He kisses a likeness of the face of the blessed Virgin Mary etched into the front of the gold necklace charm and stuffs his newly won keepsake from the blonde into his pocket.

CHAPTER 2

Concrete—gray, cold, and quickly passing—is the only thing Julia sees. The running started the previous summer when she was at the lake house, the place she mistakenly thought would be a sanctuary for her boys after the separation from her husband, David.

The runs started as just one lap around the rocky coastal loop along Lake Huron. But when Julia migrated back to the Detroit suburbs for a second shot at her marriage, her runs progressed; three times a week turned into seven, and the start times became earlier and earlier.

Five a.m. Julia conquers the stretch of her Rochester Hills comfortable suburban neighborhood within five minutes. She expands her perimeter to downtown and then all the way to the Auburn Hills border. Ten miles today. No negotiation.

Julia races through the darkness just starting to break and ignores everything she passes—the funky downtown stores, the tidy homes with daily papers waiting on the icy driveway blacktops, and the Assembly of

God church with its message board warning: "Sin: It Seemed Like A Good Idea At The Time."

None of the scenery matters. The steady rhythm of her sneakers pounding against the concrete pushes Julia forward, getting her closer to some invisible finish line as she races her one constant opponent: herself.

Spring officially arrived in Michigan a week prior, but the depressing mounds of frozen gray snow from another cruel midwestern winter obviously didn't get the memo. Julia pushes herself harder and starts to sprint as she passes the elementary school that her oldest son, Logan, attends—her half-mile mark to home. She breathes in deeply. The cold air stings as it goes down, but it's worth it. Julia is certain she can smell the ground starting its impatient thaw and the bulbs, in a deep slumber since October, beginning to stir. Change is coming, and she is ready for it.

A car drives by slowly, reaches the corner, and then turns back around in her direction. Julia instinctively moves away from the curb and reaches down toward her waist pack. Instead of a water bottle, Julia packs protection: pepper spray, and a folding knife with a three-inch blade. Paranoia always ran hard and deep after what happened to her brother when Julia was a little girl, compounded by twelve years covering the crime beat, not to mention a deranged religious fanatic who kidnapped her youngest son. For Julia, it all adds up to one thing: Trust no one.

The car slows to a crawl as it approaches a second time. A dark sedan, nondescript, probably a Ford model about five years old with tinted windows, Julia calculates, as her hand sweeps inside her pack. She runs her fingers across the flat side of the knife's blade as the car's driver-side window opens.

"Hey, Gooden, I thought that was you. If you're going to jog in the dark, you better wear brighter colors or you're going to get mowed down out here," Detroit Police Detective Leroy Russell says. Julia recalls that Russell lives somewhere in the Rochester Hills community, where his ex-wife is an assistant professor of journalism at Oakland University.

Julia finally exhales, her breath turning into a puff of white that disappears into the frigid March morning. Now knowing she won't have to engage in hand-to-hand combat, Julia fixes her gaze back on Russell, whose trademark Mr. Clean buzz cut looks freshly shaved. She feels the sting of adrenaline coursing through her body as the fear leaves her.

She begins to respond to Russell when the smell hits from the open car window. Julia makes out the distinct aroma of almost metabolized late-night, heavy drinking and Old Spice, the latter applied so liberally, it makes her eyes sting.

"How are you doing, Russell?" Julia asks. "Are you on the early shift?"

Russell reaches toward his glove compartment and extracts a green bottle of Excedrin, which he pops open, and then he crushes four white tablets under his tongue.

"Retirement party last night for Sergeant Walter Shaw," Russell explains. "I'm meeting Navarro for breakfast, so hopefully an order of scrambled eggs and home fries will soak it all up before a hangover hits."

"You and Navarro are meeting up to discuss the

Rossi trial," Julia states, no question necessary. "I caught both your names on the prosecution's witness list."

"That's right."

Julia jogs in place without realizing it and strategizes how she can pump Russell for information for her story. The court part of the crime beat is her least favorite, despite the fact Julia is married to a lawyer. To her, courtrooms feel like tight little boxes where various versions of the truth run fast and loose amidst the big show, and the winner is often selected not by the culmination of the presented facts but by which side puts on a better performance.

"I heard there's going to be a surprise witness the prosecution is going to pull out at the last minute. Do you know anything about that? We can go off the record. You know I won't burn you. I just need a name," Julia pushes.

Russell reaches up and massages his right temple with his index finger.

"I don't know," he says. "Even if there is some last-minute witness, Judge Palmer probably won't allow it if they aren't on the list. Why are you asking anyway? You've got a much better source at home. You and David are back together, right?"

"We're working on it. I can't ask David, though. It would be a conflict of interest. The D.A.'s office doesn't want to get sued for leaking information to the press. Plus, David and I are pros. Neither of us would cross that line."

"Come on. You can't tell me you don't pull some favors in the bedroom to get your husband to talk. Sex is a woman's secret weapon. It always has been since the dawn of time. A sweet, firm ass has toppled many a mighty man. I'm more of a leg man myself, though," Russell says as he gives Julia's well-toned runner's legs a nod of silent approval.

At thirty-seven, Julia has long mastered the fine art of the dodge and weave around unwanted advances. Unless the guy is completely out of line, Julia ignores the come-on as if it never happened. The talent serves her well covering the cop beat, where egos and virility are often intertwined, enormous, and surprisingly fragile.

"Where are you and Navarro having breakfast?" she asks.

"Chanel's in Greektown. You want to join us?"

Julia gives just a hint of a smile. Dodge and weave successful.

"Thanks for the invite. I'll try."

"All right, Gooden. Tell the assistant D.A. we'll see him later. And be careful out here in the dark," Russell answers, and raps a red-chafed hand outside his driver-side window before he disappears behind the tinted glass.

Julia watches Russell's car pull away, and a small shiver runs down her back.

(Don't ever take a ride from a stranger, Julia, or I swear, I'll kick your butt.)

The sudden childhood memory jolts her, and Julia starts to sprint as if she could race fast enough to outrun the passage of time and warn her younger self to lock the door the night her older brother, Ben, was taken.

Julia finally reaches home, nowhere left to run. She drops onto the front step, looks up at the first soft lights of dawn finally penetrating through night's heavy cloak of darkness, and chokes back a sob. She knows how to get through the pain. She always has. Julia pushes her emotions down deep and focuses on what she can control.

Her mind clicks off the pieces of the Rossi story she will have to assemble and file into some kind of compelling piece to run in the paper's online edition before opening arguments. The facts will be the bones of her story: Nick Rossi's illegal Detroit empire is believed to encompass hijacking and shipping stolen goods, mainly computers and electronics, illegal gambling, and drug trafficking. Both the feds and the Detroit PD had been trying to nail him for years. Rossi finally got busted in a city police sting courtesy of hidden cameras placed in the VIP suites of the MGM Grand Hotel. Images on the tapes showed payoffs to the former Detroit mayor and a city councilman, in addition to drug trafficking and cash exchanges for high-stakes gambling bets.

Julia kicks at the frozen ground with the toe of her sneaker and assembles the color elements she will add as sidebars to the main article, the ones that will make the story real to the readers and ultimately make them care: the seventeen-year-old West Bloomfield high school track star who overdosed and died at a party after he graduated that night from ecstasy to heroin for the first and final time, courtesy of Rossi's stash. Then there is the story of Rossi himself, only nine years old when he witnessed the rape and murder of his mother during a home invasion while the young Rossi bore silent witness as he hid inside a closet and watched the horror unfold through a crack in the door. Since Rossi's dad had taken off before his son was born, the young Rossi moved in with his uncle, Salvatore Gallo, who ran a moderately successful dry cleaning business with a small bookie operation on the side. Julia and Salvatore Gallo have history, and Julia makes a mental note to call Gallo before she gets to the courthouse to see if he'll talk.

Julia's cell phone buzzes inside her waist pack. She looks suspiciously at the phone. 6:15 a.m. Even as a reporter, no one calls that early unless it's an emergency, and she knows David is still at the house with their boys, Logan and Will, who are sound asleep. She is about to hit the ignore button but stops at the last second when she recognizes the number. Gavin Boyles, the acting mayor's chief of staff. The other piece of color she needs for the story.

"Gooden here. You're lucky I'm up."

"You told me you ran at dawn, so I figured I'd catch you before you got into the newsroom," Boyles answers. "I checked online a few minutes ago, and I didn't see your story posted yet."

"It'll be up later today. Do you have something for me?"

Boyles, a former TV news anchor before he became a flack, still has the oozing, ultrasmooth voice of a game show host. Julia met him ten years earlier at the scene of a major fire that obliterated a Detroit high-rise and eighteen of its residents who were trapped inside. Boyles showed up late and asked Julia if he could take a look at her notes and she could debrief him on the situation.

"Always working the story, that's why you're so good," Boyles says.

"You're too kind," Julia answers, and plays the pleasantry game while she waits for Boyles to cut through the bullshit.

"Are you including Mayor Anderson in the story?"

"Acting mayor Anderson?" Julia asks.

"Semantics. We'd prefer not to have Mayor Anderson's name mentioned unless it pertains to how he is working tirelessly to turn the city around since former mayor Slidell's indictment for his involvement in the Rossi case. If you write another story about how Slidell took bribes from Rossi to shut him up, you're doing a disservice to the people of the city. Detroit has suffered enough, don't you think? You could turn this into a positive story."

"And how has Anderson turned the city around exactly?"

"Public perception. I want to share something with you. This is off the record for now, all right?"

"Of course," Julia answers, and wonders whether the call might not be a complete waste of her time after all.

"Mayor Anderson will be holding a press conference today announcing a strategic task force dedicated solely to promoting all things positive in Detroit, including a volunteer-driven beautification project to help improve blight. It was my idea. Detroit is trying to make its way back. The residents don't need a rehashing of another corrupt city official story."

"Politics isn't my beat."

"Neither is business, but your articles are hurting the casinos. Detroit got gutted after the auto industry crashed, and God knows we can't afford to take any more hits. There's a responsibility, a fine line, we journalists need to ethically tow."

"I'm still a journalist. Last I checked, you weren't."

On the other end of the phone, Boyles blasts an obnoxious guffaw.

"Always blunt, aren't you? The press conference is scheduled for twelve-thirty on the steps of city hall. I assume you'll be available since the trial will break for lunch. Mayor Anderson specifically asked for you to be there."

"Thank you for the invitation. I'll run this by my managing editor and let her decide who to send. You know how this works. It's not my call."

"Got it. I'll call Margie myself and put in the request. I'm surprised the paper is letting you cover the story when your husband is prosecuting it. Good for you, though. You won't have to work as hard this time."

Julia grits her teeth and forces herself to still play nice. She may need Boyles in the future.

"I always work hard."

"I just meant . . ."

Julia cuts off Boyles before he can finish. "Thanks for the call and the heads up on the press conference."

Julia gives her phone the finger, the sentiment she'd really like to give Boyles directly. Instead, she shuts her phone off and heads into the warmth of her house, which hits her like a blowtorch. She strips off her North Face jacket and then peels off her running pants and nylon shirt, which are sticking to her clammy skin. She frees her curly, dark brown hair from its ponytail and pads softly down the hall as not to wake the boys. Inside the office, she leans over the desk and begins to search for her competitor's coverage of the Rossi trial. She pulls up the *Detroit News* website and feels a tug in her stomach. In addition to a big picture preview story on the case, Julia knows the *Detroit News* reporter is writing a sidebar profile on David as first chair for the prosecution and his likely run for D.A. next year, a promise David made to himself after he gave up a lucrative private practice partnership six months earlier to become a public servant. Still standing, Julia bends down closer to the desk and begins to search whether the *Detroit News* found out about the surprise witness or, worse, if they got the name before she did.

"Nice view."

Julia spins around to see David inside the office doorway. He is half-dressed for trial in a pair of blue slacks and an unbuttoned white shirt that hangs below his waist. Julia stares at his close-cropped blond hair he recently cut short for the case, finally losing his California laid-back surfer look and longer hair he had worn since Julia first met him ten years earlier.

"Do I know you, sir?" Julia asks.

"It's the hair, isn't it?"

"You look like a lawyer now."

"You say that like it's a bad thing."

"You used to have a Matthew McConaughey look going," she says.

"Not *Lincoln Lawyer* I'm guessing?"

"No, more *Magic Mike* or *Surfer, Dude*."

"Never seen either of them," David answers.

"You need to get going before the kids wake up and find you here. But it's still early."

Julia pulls away from the desk, still in just her running bra and panties, and tries to slide inside David's open shirt.

"I like your new look. It's like I'm cheating on my husband with a preppy stockbroker or something. Despite the hair, I bet you still have moves that would make Magic Mike blush."

"Sorry, babe. I have to get to the courthouse early. I don't have time for a second shower either. It's probably not a good idea for me to show up on the first day of the Rossi trial smelling like sex and my wife's sweat."

Julia, feeling suddenly exposed, spots one of David's University of Michigan sweatshirts hanging on the back of the door and pulls it over her head.

"Thanks for making me feel like a leper. Did I do something wrong?"

"I need to stay focused on the case and my A game this morning without a hot reporter distracting me. It would probably help if I could sleep in my own bed without having to run out in the morning before the kids see me. When do you think I can move back in? I know all the employees at the Marriott Residence Inn so well at this point, the front desk manager invited me to her daughter's wedding."

"I just need to be sure. I don't want the kids to get hurt if anything goes wrong again. Moving back to Rochester Hills to be near you is a good first step."

"A typical Julia Gooden safe step, you mean. The kids are going to be happiest if we make it permanent and become a family again. I need to be back here with all of you. I'm not myself otherwise."

"Let's talk about it after the trial is over. I know it would mean a lot to the boys."

"Is that the only reason? You are so damn romantic, Gooden," David says. He pulls Julia close and then turns her around so her back is facing him.

"Are we about to play pin the tail on the donkey or is something kinky about to happen?"

"Neither. I bought you a present. Don't turn around until I tell you."

Julia waits impatiently as David digs inside his briefcase.

"Okay, you can turn around now," David says, and hands Julia a small red box.

She feels a strum go off inside of her as she opens it and discovers a long silver necklace with a blue topaz in the center that glints against a shaft of morning light shining through the office window.

"It's beautiful," Julia says.

"I planned for the light to hit the necklace like that when you opened it, you know."

"Sure, you did. Can you put it on?"

Julia pulls her dark, wavy hair away from her face, and David brushes his lips against the nape of her neck as he clasps the necklace in place. Julia looks at their loving reflection in the mirror, a seeming portrait of domestic bliss but with some deep, hidden fissures that she knows still lie beneath. Julia fights an urge to turn around and tell David that she wants him back for good, but she knows what broke their marriage the first time. After ten years of trying to help Julia get over the loss of her brother and his growing concerns for Julia's hyper-overprotectiveness of their own children, David had walked. He packed up his suitcase one night after getting back from his practice and announced he was sick of trying to fix her. And following David's brief and clandestine fling with another lawyer during their separation, trust needed to be re-earned.

Julia feels stiff under David's embrace and stays firm in her resolve that she has to be certain about David moving back, not just for herself but mainly for Logan and Will. She won't let them suffer the consequences if things don't work this time, leaving them casualties of a failed marriage like those children who are reminded of their doomed status each weekend as their parents bicker bitterly during the ceremonial exchange of kids to ensure the court's visitation rights are met.

"The necklace is beautiful," Julia says.

"But it won't buy me a key back into the house yet. I can deal with baby steps if that's what you need."

"I started to see Dr. Bruegger again. I actually think it's helping."

"The shrink? Aren't you the one who called psychiatrists useless quacks who take advantage of people's emotions and manipulate their thoughts by asking over and over, 'How do you feel?'"

"Dr. Bruegger says if I let go of some of the pain and guilt over what happened to Ben, it doesn't mean that I'm abandoning his memory. He says I can still love Ben without feeling the hurt that goes along with it."

"That's some serious progress. I'm proud of you, Julia."

David pulls Julia into his arms and is about to kiss her when his cell phone sounds on the table. David groans as he looks at the incoming number.

"Sorry. I have to take this. It's Don Brewbaker from the D.A.'s office."

"Get your A game back. It's okay," Julia answers as David retreats to the hallway and away from her curious reporter's earshot.

Julia thinks about her own A game on the Rossi coverage and returns to the computer to see what the

Detroit News has on the story. A trickle of dread moves through her as she worries she'll get beat, the cardinal sin and biggest downfall any reporter can face.

Julia feels a temporary reprieve as she finishes a quick scan of the headlines and doesn't see a new story filed by her competitor. She plugs in a flash drive that contains all the information she's gathered so far on the Rossi case and the bones of the story that she will fill in and file later, after opening arguments.

The dark star of the article is Rossi, the once poor, young boy who witnessed his mother's rape and murder and was later adopted by Gallo. Julia pauses over an article about the mother's funeral, including a photo that shows a grieving and very young Rossi, his shoulders stooped in front of his mother's grave as Gallo's arm is draped protectively around the boy.

Julia clicks through the rest of the material about Rossi. He returned to Detroit four years ago from California to take over the family business after Gallo suffered a series of heart attacks. The police and Feds believe Rossi expanded his uncle's legitimate dry-cleaning business to a vast and powerful illegal empire.

Julia reviews her bulleted list that will run along her main story.

Ten Million: as in dollars, the annual estimated revenue Rossi reaps from his illegal and legitimate businesses each year.

Forty-two: Rossi's age.

Zero: the number of times Rossi had been arrested until now.

Julia quickly scans another folder that contains pictures of Rossi, the handsome criminal caught smiling in thousand-dollar suits.

"I've got to head out and meet Brewbaker before seven," David says as he reenters the office and leans over Julia's shoulder. "Is that your story?"

"So far, but it's got some holes. What's the name? The witness who is going to flip on Rossi?" Julia asks without turning around.

"How do you know about that? Did Navarro tell you?"

"If Navarro told me, I'd know the name as well."

David, still as strong as when he played lacrosse at Harvard, picks up Julia's chair and turns her around to face him. He drops to his knees so their faces are level. His green eyes shine with anger and intensity as he looks into hers.

"Listen to me, Julia. I mean it," David says in a sharp tone he's rarely used with her before. "If the identity of this witness comes out before the trial, he'll be killed. No question. I'm skating a razor-thin line here, and if I have to beg, I will. I've spent weeks trying to gather enough evidence to convict Rossi, and what I've got is circumstantial at best. Rossi is smart and didn't leave a trail that could connect back to him. I gave the witness my word I'd protect him and his family in exchange for his testimony. That includes not leaking anything to the press."

"The *Detroit News* can't get this story before I do."

"This isn't about getting beat on a story. It's about doing the right thing."

"That's the second time I heard that this morning," Julia says. "The witness should be in protective custody, if he's not already. The Feds should be handling this."

"This is my case. The FBI had its chance to nail

Rossi on hijacking and selling stolen goods, but they couldn't. Now, stop digging around about my witness, understood?"

"It's not my responsibility to protect your guy. I have a duty as a journalist to write the truth."

"Bullshit. There's no public good achieved in reporting the name of this witness ahead of his testimony. Whatever mighty responsibility you think you have, take a step back and really think about it."

David puts his hand under Julia's chin and lifts her face toward his so she can't look away this time. "I know you. You're a good person. You would never hurt someone on purpose. Please think about what you're doing here."

"Okay. I understand where you're coming from, and I promise I'll think about it," Julia concedes.

"Maybe when this is all over, we can get away, just you and me. We can ask Helen if she'll watch the boys overnight and we can escape to Mackinac Island. No cars, no kids. No distractions. Just us."

"I'd like that."

"I promise I'll pull out my best Magic Mike moves."

"So you've seen the movie?"

"On a flight once. It's not a good thing for a guy to admit. I looked at it as merely research for my woman."

"So do we need a code of conduct in the courtroom?" Julia asks as she swings back to reporter mode.

"What do you mean?"

"I'm going to approach you in the hallway to ask questions, just as I would if you were any other lawyer."

David takes a moment to consider this as he buttons up his shirt and then begins to fasten a bright blue tie around his neck. "Good luck with that. The only comments anyone will get from me are written statements I'll send to every member of the press and whatever is said if we hold a press conference after the trial. That's it."

"You know how to use the press. You may need to plant something, and I know you've done it before. Just don't discount me. All I'm asking for is a fair playing field. And that blue tie is too monochromatic with your blue suit. You need some color," Julia answers, and hands him a light gold tie with blue stars.

"Lucky I still have all my clothes here. Not too obnoxious?"

"Much better."

"Tell the kids I'll see them tonight."

"Logan has a field trip at the courthouse, remember? You might see him there. I'm going to meet his bus at the courthouse when it arrives."

"How are you going to do that?"

"It's during the lunch hour. I'm the queen of multitasking, baby," Julia says. "I'm not sure if you'll have time this morning, but if you get a few minutes, I think I'll stop at Chanel's over in Greektown before I go into the newsroom. Navarro and Russell are meeting up there."

David shoots Julia a sideways glance and is about to respond when his cell phone vibrates on the desk. He snatches it up, looks at the number, and then shoves the phone into his pants pocket.

"You can take that."

"Not around you. This one can wait. It's nothing urgent. I'll call them back. How's Navarro doing? Still coveting my wife?"

"Now who's insecure?" Julia asks. "You have nothing to worry about. Never have. Navarro is dating some big restaurateur from New York anyway. She opened Chanel's and a couple of other restaurants in the Art Center and Eastern Market."

David stretches into his blue suit jacket and drapes his long wool coat over his arm.

"Wish me luck," he says. "Don't worry so much about what the *Detroit News* puts out. And stop your hunt for my new witness. Understood?"

Julia crosses her arms in a natural defense move. A light tapping on the front door tables any chance of a rekindled argument as David hurries down the hallway with a heavy briefcase in either hand. Julia follows his path and watches as David greets their housekeeper, Helen Jankowski, a painfully thin, older woman with a thick Polish accent and the best pierogi recipe in all of Greater Detroit. She nods at David and gives Julia's bare legs a disapproving glare.

Julia ignores the judgment and gives David a thumbs-up sign. "You're going to be great."

He leans in and whispers in her ear, "We'll take some time after this is over. I promise. Just you and me."

"We'll talk about your moving back in after you get a guilty conviction for Rossi."

"I like the way you think," David says. He walks out the door toward his car and then hesitates, turning back one last time as he takes a long look at Julia, who for a second thinks her husband is going to cry.

"Are you okay?"

"I just missed you guys and I'm glad you all came home. I wasn't myself without you."

* * *

The hot water of the shower runs over Julia's still cold body, which begins to thaw underneath the heat. Julia does her usual ritual, turning the water temperature to the coldest setting, and stands underneath the icy spray until her shivers become uncontrollable and she grants herself a reprieve.

Julia stands soaking and naked in front of the bathroom mirror, and a striking reflection stares back at her—her eyes, the same shade as her con man father's, a bright, startling light blue, contrasting against her olive skin and dark hair. But like most women, all Julia sees are her flaws. Journalism was the lifeline that first pulled her out of her often-crippling insecurity and gave her strength beyond the reserve she had stowed from her brother Ben's love and protection from the ugly life they shared as children. But then David and her boys became her salvation. Julia catches herself smiling in the mirror over her realization that maybe this time, she and David could really make it work.

The sound of little boys' feet tearing down the hallway breaks Julia out of her dark trance, and she hurriedly gets dressed, pulling on a fitted yet tasteful black skirt and a loose cream-colored top. She hustles barefoot toward the kitchen, carefully balancing her heels in one hand and her laptop in the other. She sticks her flash drive with the Rossi file in her purse and turns the corner to see the back of her two sons' heads pressed together over the kitchen counter.

Logan, her eight-year-old, sits on a barstool and is engrossed in his Minecraft game on the family iPad. Will, her two-year-old, teeters on the other stool as close as he can to his brother so he can watch the action on the screen.

Julia rushes over and rights the stool before Will takes a spill.

"Good morning, beautiful boys," Julia says, then kisses Will on the top of his golden-blond hair.

"Play with Lo Lo," Will says, and keeps his eyes riveted on the action on the screen. Julia smiles over the mundane domestic bliss and realizes she's already become second fiddle to Logan in Will's eyes, but takes comfort in the fact that the two boys will always likely have a close bond.

"Sorry to spoil the fun for both of you this morning," Julia says. She places an ABC picture book in front of Will and snags the iPad out of Logan's hands. Julia then gets on her tiptoes so temporarily she can tuck it away from his grasp on the pantry's highest shelf.

"Hey, Mom, why'd you do that?" Logan asks.

"You don't need to play video games first thing in the morning. Let's practice for your spelling test instead," Julia answers, and gives Logan a playful swat on his bottom with his homework folder.

Helen brushes into the kitchen and begins to stir brown sugar and raisins into a pot of steaming steal-cut oatmeal simmering on the back burner of the stove.

"That smells delicious, Helen," Julia says while handing Logan a notebook and pencil. "The first word is 'between.' "

"Between," Logan recites, the tip of his tongue poking out of his mouth as he carefully writes each letter. "Are you going to be there for my field trip today?"

"Absolutely. Next word is 'system.' There's a tricky letter in the word. One that is sometimes a vowel. I'm meeting your bus outside the courthouse at twelve-thirty."

"Don't be late again. The tricky letter is y."

"I'm sorry about that. I got stuck at work just one time, and I swear it will never happen again. I should be at the courthouse all day, so I'll already be there before your bus arrives."

"You don't have to volunteer for everything," Logan answers. "There's like four teachers and a bunch of other parents always at these things."

"Cities are dangerous places. You need to be very careful whether I'm there or not. Besides, I like participating in your school activities. I'm proud of you, you know."

"My friend Sarah wishes Daddy would go instead. She thinks he's hot."

"Good lord. Third graders shouldn't think anyone is hot," Julia says.

"I think you're beautiful, Mom."

Julia smiles and looks back at Logan, with his jet-black hair, dark eyes that turn up on the end, and a sprinkling of freckles that scatter along his high cheekbones. She is always amazed how much her son looks just like her brother, Ben. And Will is a dead ringer for David.

"That was a very kind thing to say. Thank you."

"Things are still good with you and Dad, right?" Logan asks.

"Everything is fine. Why would you ask that?"

"I thought I heard his voice this morning. Were you guys fighting?" Logan asks.

Julia curses herself silently for not being more discreet and for opening the door of possibility for Logan to hope that his parents may be reuniting.

"Daddy came by to pick up some work papers. That's all. Things are fine between your dad and me."

Logan nibbles on the inside of his cheek, a lingering nervous habit he picked up after the incident at the lake house last summer.

"Swear?" Logan asks.

Julia draws an X across her heart with her finger.

"Cross my heart. I'd never lie to you. You know that."

Logan gives Julia a small smile, seemingly satisfied with her promise.

Julia scoots Will's stool up closer to the counter as Helen places a bowl of oatmeal in front of each boy.

"I'll be home by five-thirty tonight. Six tops. Helen, please leave Will's door ajar when he takes a nap. You'll stay with Logan at the curb and not leave until he gets on the bus?"

"Of course," Helen answers. "I always do. I've raised four children of my own and all survived to adulthood."

"It's not that I don't trust you," Julia says, and pats Helen's hand.

"It's just the rest of the world she doesn't trust," Logan answers. "Don't worry, Helen. She does that to everyone. She just wants to keep us all safe."

"Please call me if anything comes up. I'll keep my cell phone on vibrate even in the courtroom," Julia says to Helen. "Something tells me you won't need to call me, though. I get the feeling it's going to be a great day."